"I will never let you die here."

~~∽oʒ℃~~

Kali stood her ground, meeting his determined glance with one of her own. She came up onto her tiptoes; indeed, their bodies were so close, they stood practically nose to nose. She could feel the heat of his breath on her face, the force of his anger on her being as he towered over her. But she refused to be intimidated, and she said, "It's my choice to make."

"Not today it isn't."

And that's when it happened.

He closed the distance between them, his head coming down to hers. And before Kali could utter a word of protest, he had taken her lips with his own, sweeping his arms around her waist and pulling her into his embrace. His tongue unerringly found hers and danced with it until a low groan escaped from his throat.

Or was that her own voice?

Other **AVON ROMANCES**

KAREN KAY

SOARING EAGLE'S EMBRACE

AVON BOOKS
An Imprint of HarperCollinsPublishers

Excerpts from *The Old North Trail: Life, Legends, and Religion of the Blackfeet Indians* by Walter McClintock courtesy of the University of Nebraska Press; *When Indians Became Cowboys* by Peter Iverson courtesy of the University of Oklahoma Press.

This is a work of fiction. Names, characters, places, and incidents are products of the author's imagination or are used fictitiously and are not to be construed as real. Any resemblance to actual events, locales, organizations, or persons, living or dead, is entirely coincidental.

AVON BOOKS
An Imprint of HarperCollins*Publishers*
10 East 53rd Street
New York, New York 10022-5299

First Avon Books paperback printing: July 2003

Avon Trademark Reg. U.S. Pat. Off. and in Other Countries, Marca Registrada, Hecho en U.S.A.
HarperCollins® is a registered trademark of HarperCollins Publishers Inc.

Printed in the U.S.A.

10 9 8 7 6 5 4 3 2 1

This book is dedicated to two special people.
To: Patricia Devereaux Running Crane.

May your dreams become realities.

And to: My mother-in-law, Joyce Bailey,
who has helped in so many ways.

Acknowledgments

I would like to acknowledge the work of
Jeanette MacDonald and Nelson Eddy,
whose music has given me
so much pleasure and inspiration.

And a special acknowledgment
to my husband, Paul,
who continues to help, to plot with me,
and who continues to love me.
I love you, too.

SOARING EAGLE'S EMBRACE

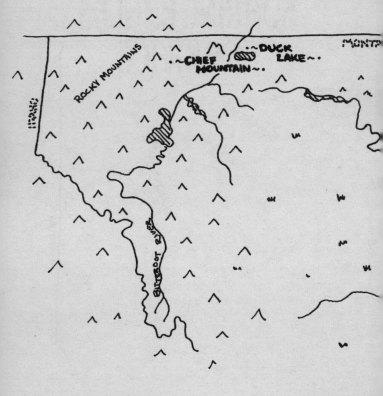

TERRITORY --·
895 --·

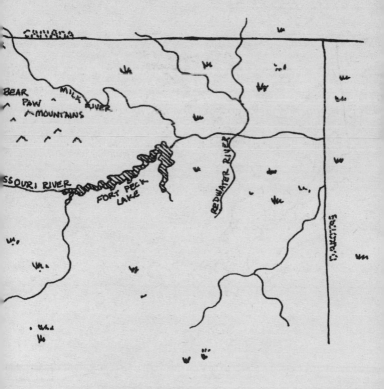

Chapter 1

Somewhere on Chief Mountain, Montana
1895

"It started with a song."

"A song?" asked Kali, straightening her shoulders and flexing the tense muscles in her neck. It had been a grueling hike up to this remote yet beautiful spot atop Chief Mountain—even for Kali who was accustomed to trekking through the untamed wilderness. "What do you mean?"

"You and your father . . . here to learn legend of mountain, is . . . not right?" Kali's guide, Gilda Shadow Runner, gave Kali a glance that could have been construed as calculating, if it weren't for the seriousness in Gilda's demeanor.

Kali, however, inured to the unusual nature of hired guides, ignored the look and said, "No, I'm afraid that

1

my father and I are here for no other reason than to record and capture the beauty and romance of the West on film." Kali bestowed a smile on Gilda, though after a moment, she couldn't resist asking, "What legend?"

"Legend of Star Bride."

"Star Bride?"

Gilda nodded. "It is said that on nights like this, when . . . sky is very clear, one can hear . . . song; song of lovers calling to one another."

"Lovers?" Kali looked askance at Gilda.

"*Aa*, yes," said Gilda.

"How interesting," said Kali, looking toward the sleeping figure of her father. "You know, Gilda, I think my father and I have perhaps missed something by never having used a female guide before now. Tell me, is your legend romantic?"

"*Aa*, yes, it is," confirmed Gilda, "It . . . said that she was . . . star, and him, no more than . . . mortal man who fell in love with her."

Kali smiled, the expression pure indulgence. In her experience, if there was one thing a body could count on amongst the aboriginal tribes, it was their legends and superstitions. However, that didn't mean that Kali wasn't interested. Neither she nor her father would be here today were it not for their curiosity of the native populations, their customs, their beliefs.

"What kind of song was it?" Kali asked after a slight pause. "Have you ever heard it yourself?"

"No, not this one, but I know of many in . . . tribe who tell of it."

"Oh? Really?"

Gilda nodded. "It . . . said that only place on earth where a person can hear song is on what my people call *Nina Istukwi*, Chief Mountain—here. Maybe we . . . be quiet and see if you can hear it. You should close eyes."

"Me? Oh, no, not me. I'm afraid I don't believe in—"

"Try. You might . . . be surprised."

"No, I . . . Do you really think so?"

Gilda nodded.

"All right. Maybe I will," Kali said, and after a moment, she shut her eyes.

Nothing happened. Nothing at all. Kali opened her eyes.

"You must listen with . . . heart," Gilda encouraged, "for only a person pure in purpose can hear it. Try again."

"Well, maybe," said Kali. "But I must warn you that I have never believed in—"

"No need . . . you believe. Now try again."

Kali sighed. "All right. I will." As she closed her eyes, she was quick to observe that her heart beat quickened. *Why?*

Perhaps it was because of the wind, which was howling around the chasms and rocks, sounding to Kali's ears like a ghostly serenade. Perhaps it was this that others had heard, thinking it was a song, thought Kali skeptically.

Still, the entire affair was enchanting, wasn't it? To sit here on a summer's eve, high atop the plains, with nothing but the wide sky above you and the pureness of nature all around you. Even the air up here felt clean and fresh on the lungs.

After a time, a coyote bayed far below them, then came another yelp and another, as though each one were a successive call to the other. Ah, thought Kali. It was wonderful, breathtaking. But alas, Kali heard no song.

So much for legends.

Taking a deep breath, Kali opened her eyes, catching a rather expectant look on Gilda's face, which caused Kali to frown. How odd.

Stranger still was Gilda's reaction when Kali shook her head and said, "I'm sorry. Although I'd like to think that my purpose here is pure, I must admit that I hear nothing . . . nothing but the wind."

Goodness, what had she said that should cause such a reaction with her guide? Gilda looked downright crestfallen, as though the woman might have more at stake in the telling of this legend than simply mentioning a song. It caused Kali to speculate.

Had the woman brought Kali and her father here for some other purpose than shooting a few good pictures? What, after all, did Kali really know about Gilda Shadow Runner? Though Gilda had come highly recommended, Kali couldn't help wondering if the woman might be putting her through some sort of test.

Lost in her own thoughts, Kali was startled when Gilda asked, "Would you like to hear story?"

"Hmmm?" Kali had been in the act of unbuttoning the first few buttons of her blouse—letting the evening breeze cool the bare skin beneath it. But glancing up, she shot a glance at Gilda, and what she saw there caused Kali more concern. Why did Gilda appear anxious, as though she were waiting for something? Kali cleared her throat. "Excuse me. What was that you said?"

"The story of lovers—the legend . . . would you like to hear it?"

"Yes, Gilda," Kali admitted cautiously, "that would be lovely. I believe that my father has bedded down for the night—perhaps I should awaken him that he might hear the story also."

"If you wish."

"But again," said Kali, wondering aloud, "maybe not. I'm afraid the climb up here was rather difficult for him, something we should watch in the future. Although he insisted on making this trip, I'm not sure he's well enough for another hike like this. Perhaps we might try a more gradual path tomorrow?"

Gilda nodded. "I will let white woman decide where we go, and how fast."

"Thank you. That will do just fine, then."

"And story?"

"I would be charmed to hear it, if you would be so kind."

"*Aa*, this is good," said Gilda, turning away to pick up a dry bit of wood. "Come closer," she said as she threw the wood on the fire, "and I will begin my tale."

Kali shrugged. There could be little harm in that. Besides, her curiosity was, by this time, more than a little piqued . . .

"This is the legend of . . . Star Bride. It is said that it happened in dog days, those days before horse was known to my people," narrated Gilda. "Ah, but it was glorious time. It was peaceful time, too; a time when my people lived close to the land, when stars were gods and goddesses who listened to the pleas of my people.

"Now, it happened that at this time there was a young Blackfoot man . . . him handsome and pure in spirit. His name was Strong Arrow, and he was looking for a wife. But his would not be easy task.

"It true that there were many young women who would have gladly taken Strong Arrow as husband, for it was well known that him wise, generous and skilled in hunt. But Strong Arrow have big flaw: him believe himself to be perfect, no faults. Worse, him convinced him could give heart to no one except she, who also be perfect . . ."

"My son," said Strong Arrow's mother. "I fear that you will be disappointed as you go through life, if you cannot find it in your heart to understand the imperfection of those around you."

"I understand them well enough, my mother," said Strong Arrow.

But Strong Arrow's mother was wise and she said, "Heed my words, my son, for in order to be happy, you must learn that in all the world, there is not one single, faultless human being."

"Ah, my mother," responded Strong Arrow. "I know that you speak with concern in your heart. But surely you can see that your words are not true. Look at me. Do I not obey the commands of my tribe? Do I not bring home much food? Do I not give freely to others all that I have? Do I not live an exemplary life? My mother, can you honestly tell me that I am not and have not been a perfect son?"

Strong Arrow's mother, Shining Woman, did not know what to say to this, knowing that to dispute her son would only make his resolve all the stronger. Yet, she feared that if Strong Arrow could not allow for weaknesses in others, he would never come to appreciate the intrinsic beauty that was to be held in another's soul.

And so it was that Strong Arrow became more and more steadfast in his belief of his own perfection, and he resolved that he would only marry one as unblemished as he.

Now, it is said that he was true to his cause. He searched for such a being. He attended every dance, every social gathering given by his tribe.

However, as might be expected, he failed in his quest time and again. In truth, as time passed, he became quite despondent.

Now, Shining Woman, seeing her son's unhappiness, at last begged Strong Arrow to beseech the Evening Star. After all, said she, was it not the Evening Star who was honored for her compassion, her understanding, her love? Perhaps the star might share some of her wisdom with Strong Arrow.

And so it was that one lazy summer evening, Strong Arrow climbed to the top of *Nina Istukwi*, Chief Mountain, and, sitting down, took out his sacred pipe. He smoked, letting the fragrance carry up into the sky so that she, who was the Evening Star, could sniff it and know that he meant to speak with her. He looked up at her, she who shone so brightly in the silvery glow of a half-dark, half-bright sky.

It was then that it happened. Suddenly Strong Arrow's heart began to beat so fast and so furiously, he felt as though he might have been chasing a foe. Yet, he had not moved.

As he gazed up at the beautiful star, he realized that he had, at last, found perfection. Truly, he had fallen in love. But alas, what a love. For he had picked as a soul mate no less than she who was the Evening Star.

Now, as time marched on, many in the tribe, hearing of Strong Arrow's unusual adoration, laughed at him. But Strong Arrow remained true to himself. And each night thereafter, he would return to sit alone upon the plain, there to give his devotion to his star. Many times he would return to Chief Mountain, and when he did, feeling closer to her, he would talk to her, saying, "Oh, Evening Star, how I wish you were made of flesh and blood that I might take you in my arms and show you all the love that is here in my heart. I implore you, Evening Star, do you return my devotion?"

Sometimes one could hear him singing:

"Ooooo, ooooo, how my heart beats for you.
Ooooo, ooooo.
Ooooo, ooooo, how my lips hunger for your touch.
Ooooo, ooooo.
For I love you. You, the Evening Star."

But he waited in vain for an answer.

Now, it so happened that one day Strong Arrow came again to Chief Mountain. As he climbed up a slope, he heard a strange sound, an unusual music. Where was it coming from?

Gaining the crest of the mountain, he scoured the countryside around and below him, his sharp eyes assessing all he could see. But try as he might, he could not locate the source of it. Still, his spirits took flight. Had it been a song? And if it were a song, could it be she, who was the Evening Star?

But as quickly as the music had begun, it stopped and he heard it no more. He waited all day, and the next and the next, climbing up to the mountain's summit each evening, hoping to hear again the strange melody. But alas, it came no more.

Now, Strong Arrow was not a stupid man and it took little effort on his part to devise a plan. The next day came and Strong Arrow hid himself behind some boulders. And there he waited, and he waited. In truth, so long did he pause there that he began to wonder if his tribesmen were right about him. Was he chasing a mere phantom?

However, this day, his patience was rewarded, for soon—before the sun had barely reached its zenith—it happened again. On the wind came an alien, yet beautiful refrain.

Where was the voice coming from? All across the wide mountain range there was nothing but the winds which whispered across barren rock. Nothing to his right, to his left; behind him, in front of him.

Still, the music was becoming louder. Puzzled, he looked up, and there he espied the most uncommon sight he had ever seen. A bird, looking much like a large eagle, coasted down from the heavens. And upon its back was a very beautiful woman.

At the sight, Strong Arrow's heart began to pound, faster and faster. It was then that he knew that it was she, the one who was his true love.

Soon, the maiden began to sing the unusual, eerie song, at first in words he didn't understand, and then in the language of his people.

"Come out, come out, oh, warrior mine.
For I know that you wait for me.
Come out, come out, take me for wife.
For I have heard your plea.
Come out, come out my truest love,
    come out and play with me.
Show yourself, my warrior, true.
For I am the Evening Star."

With these words, Strong Arrow stood up from his hiding place. The maiden turned to look at him, and they gazed upon one another. And so long did they stare, that Strong Arrow feared she might run away.

At last, however, she smiled at him, saying, "Because you are a great hunter, my father, the Sun, has taken pity on you. He has heard your appeal. I, too, desire to marry you, for I have seen you here, night after night, alone upon the face of the Earth. And as you fell in love with me so, too, did I fall in love with you. Consequently, my father gives me to you in marriage, freely, asking only that you take no other for a wife for the rest of your life."

Strong Arrow said nothing to this, though he yearned to speak of much.

She continued, "My father, the Sun, knows that this thing he asks of you transgresses upon the custom of your people, for within your tribe a man of standing might take more than one wife. But you must refrain from doing this. Do you promise?"

Still, so great was Evening Star's beauty, that Strong Arrow could not speak. In faith, it was all he could do to simply nod.

"You must understand further," Evening Star said, "that my father does not give me to you easily. Know that if you ever betray this trust he places in you—if you should ever take another to your sleeping robes, my father would ensure a penalty."

"I understand," voiced Strong Arrow at last. "And what would this punishment be?"

"You would cease to exist upon this, the face of the earth. So it is said by my father, the Sun," she said. "Know, too, that my father, the Sun, is a jealous man, and he might test the courage of your resolve. Do you still agree?"

Strong Arrow took a step toward her, his heart in his throat as he said, "Long have I admired and loved you,

Evening Star. I will take you as my own. I will honor you. *Aa*, yes, I agree to your father's demand."

Evening Star smiled and extended her arms toward him. "Then come, my love," she said. "Take my hand and lead me to your people."

He did as she bid, and they were married that night. Indeed, in years to come, it is said that they embodied the best that is known of love and marriage.

Many years passed. Because Evening Star was a goddess, the regular chores of a wife did not fall to her. Skins were dressed, food was made, wood was gathered without her expending any labor, so great was her magic. Evening Star was also a generous woman and gave freely to the people the things that they desired, and she became the most well-respected woman of the tribe.

However, all was well for so long that the people began to forget that they, too, needed to work, hunt and repair clothing in order to survive. Alas, so easy was it to obtain the goods they needed from Evening Star, the men in the village lost interest in hunting, while the women depended upon the crafts of Evening Star to repair their moccasins and homes. Even the little boys in the village no longer played hunting games, while young girls mimicked the charms of Evening Star.

Truth be told, the people became lazy.

Now, perhaps these things might have had little consequence were it not for the fact Old Man, the Sun, had yet to play out his full hand. Here is what happened:

Strong Arrow was out on the hunt. But on this day, Strong Arrow saw a most unusual sight. Into his path walked a beautiful maiden, one who openly flirted with him; one who begged him take her home. But she pleaded in vain. After all, Strong Arrow believed himself to be perfect; he had given his word to his wife and to her father that he would take no other into their home. He would stand by his word.

And so he passed by the maiden. Looking back, Strong Arrow observed that the girl vanished, and it was then that he knew the time had come for Old Man to test him.

The next day, again while Strong Arrow was out on the hunt, Old Man sent an even more beautiful woman into his path, this maiden also begging Strong Arrow to take her home. But Strong Arrow was as wise as he was virtuous. He passed this one by, too.

Then Old Man smiled. Indeed, his son-in-law was a faithful husband. Still, there would be one more trial.

The next day, Old Man sent again a beautiful maiden into Strong Arrow's path. But this time there was a difference. This woman looked so much like Evening Star that Strong Arrow hesitated, confused.

Seeing this, the woman spoke, saying, "Take pity on me. For you are my own brother-in-law. My name is Bright Shadow. I, too, am a star and, like my sister, I desire a good husband."

"I cannot take you as a wife," Strong Arrow responded.

"And yet it is your right to have me."

"No," said Strong Arrow. "It is not. I gave up that right when I married your sister."

"Yet," said Bright Shadow, "I need your help. Do not ask how, but my own future depends on you. If you take me with you, I could aid you in becoming glorious in war."

Strong Arrow sneered. "You waste your breath, woman," he said. "For if it is my home that you seek, I cannot help you."

"Could you not?" she asked. "Think well, my brother-in-law. If you do me this small favor, I could give you much. I could assist you to become the best hunter in your village."

"I already am the best." And so saying, Strong Arrow began to walk away from the woman.

"Please," came again the maiden's plea.

Strong Arrow glanced over his shoulder. "I do not need or desire glory, or another wife," he called to her. "I love the one that I have."

Bright Shadow stared at Strong Arrow, and her eyes narrowed before she commented, "Then you make a mistake, my brother-in-law, for you will surely bring pain to my sister if you do not take me with you."

This statement gave Strong Arrow reason to pause. Coming to a halt, he looked back at the maiden. "What falsehoods are these that you tell me?"

Bright Shadow took a step toward him. "I do not utter untruths. I am in trouble," she said, her gaze at Strong Arrow full of appeal. "I am with child, and my father, the Sun, says that there is no room in the sky for another star, my baby. Alas, my father has sent me here, upon this earth to bear this child alone. But I am frightened. All I wish to do is to see my sister, that she might care for me."

Strong Arrow hesitated, and turning so that he faced the maiden, he looked deeply into Bright Shadow's eyes. "If this is all you desire, why did you try to seduce me?"

Bright Shadow cast her eyes down. "Because I am afraid to be alone, and I thought this might be the only way to beseech you."

Strong Arrow frowned, and it is said that he puzzled over what to do. Duty to a woman in Bright Shadow's condition would not allow him to walk away from her; however, he could also not bow down to her pleas, for he knew well the consequences of his actions. What was he to do?

He hesitated but a moment before making his decision and then, lifting his face up to the skies, he shouted, "Do you understand this, Old Man? Do you see that I am taking pity on your other daughter, who is with child? Know that I do not take her to my home as a wife. I take her only to be with her sister." And with this said, Strong Arrow grabbed hold of Bright Shadow.

Yes, his intentions were honorable, yet in doing what he did, Strong Arrow sealed his fate, for though he could not have made any other choice—not and remain perfect—with this decision came disaster: He never arrived home.

A thunderstorm came suddenly upon Strong Arrow and Bright Shadow, causing Strong Arrow to seek shelter. And though his intentions were decent toward his wife's sister, a man is, after all, but a man . . .

Meanwhile, it took little enough time for Evening Star to discover her husband's betrayal.

A tribe of visiting Crees, seeing the wealth and laziness of Strong Arrow's people, defeated them in battle, taking Evening Star as their own. And doing so, they fled.

Perhaps it was not Old Man's doing what happened next. Some kind folk say that it was not. Others, however, tell a different story.

By some trick of fate, the victorious Crees, enroute to their own home and bringing Evening Star with them, came upon Strong Arrow and his ward, where the two of them had sought shelter. Strong Arrow had no choice but to fight the enemy and fight he did, well and hard, for unlike the others in his village, Strong Arrow had never failed to take to the hunt each day, and his body was lean and fit. But the outcome was inevitable. There was only one of him against ten Cree warriors.

Seeing this, Evening Star was overcome with grief, as well as with conflict. On one hand, she cried out. For she realized, as she watched the combat, that her husband would die this night.

However, even as her heart broke, Evening Star knew jealousy. For there by Strong Arrow's side lay her sister, plus the evidence of his treachery . . .

Still, as Evening Star beheld the enemy's knife come down to stab into Strong Arrow's heart, she knew she could not watch. She waved her hand, causing the mortals to freeze.

"What am I to do?" she pleaded toward the midnight sky, opening her arms wide. "Oh, father, my husband and I were so happy. Why did you do this to us? For I know this is your work."

But it was night.

"Your father is not here to hear your pleas, my daughter. He is on the other side of the world." It was Old Woman who spoke, she who is Night Light, the Moon.

"Yes, mother," answered Evening Star. "In my grief, I forgot that he is gone. But please, what am I to do?"

Old Woman paused. "It is indeed a bad thing that has come to pass," she said. "I fear that your father forgets that men are but mortals. My daughter, what is it you would like me to do?"

"I . . . I am uncertain."

"Do you love your husband?"

"I . . . yes, I did . . . once . . ."

"Perhaps you should understand that your father tested Strong Arrow to the utmost, and he tempted him greatly. Your sister looked exactly as you do, and your husband was bringing her back to camp, not to take her in marriage, but to bear her to you for help. She told him she is with child."

"With child? Oh, Mother, if she were with child, she should have come to me directly instead of—"

"As I said, this was your father's work. It was also your husband's plan to bring her to you, not to bed her."

Evening Star sighed. "That may be so. However, it is clear that he failed in this, too."

"Yes, he did," said Old Woman. "Perhaps your husband is not as perfect as he would like us to believe."

"You are right, my mother. I was wrong to think he could be as pure as a star. Only we, who are gods and goddesses, are without flaw."

"Are we?"

"Yes, of course we are. But Mother, this talk gets us nowhere. Though I might abhor what my husband has done, I do not wish to see this, the end of his existence. Alas, perhaps I have loved him too well. Is there nothing I can do? You can do?"

"There is nothing," said Old Woman. "Only your father can change what is to take place."

Evening Star sighed. "Then I will lose Strong Arrow forever."

"Yes, although . . ."

"Although?"

"There is one enchantment that is within my power. It would save his life, but it is not without risk."

"Risk means nothing to me."

"Very well, my daughter, but first let me explain.

While the charm would save him, it might doom you."

"Me? I think not, mother. Nothing can harm me. I am a star, and unlike these mortals, I am proof against anything."

"As you say, my daughter. Still, the spell might yet come to be a test."

"A test?" asked Evening Star. Now as we all know, a god or goddess can little resist a challenge, and so she uttered, "Tell me more, my mother."

"The only way I can keep your father's curse from taking its natural course is to have your husband trade places with you."

"With me? I would become mortal?"

"I am afraid so, my daughter."

But Evening Star was barely listening. She had paced toward Strong Arrow, reaching out a hand to touch the powerful line of his jaw. Bending, she whispered to him, "Why—why did you do it? How could you betray me when I have loved you so greatly?"

"My daughter, our time grows short."

Evening Star stepped around the inert and silent figure of her husband and, casting him one last look, lifted her sights into the midnight sky. She asked, "Is it because of my belief in my own perfection that you are able to do this?"

"Yes, my child."

"Then say no more, my mother. I will become mortal, if for no other reason than to prove that I can do it. But how long must I remain this way?"

Old Woman cried. "There is but one place in the sky for the evening star, my daughter, and if I am to save him, your husband must take that place until . . ."

A long pause followed. "Yes?"

". . . Until a future time when you will both return to

the same spot on Chief Mountain—the place where you first met."

"That is simple enough."

"Have a care, my daughter, for it is required that you remain chaste in order to return. However, if you can do it, if you can remain innocent, you and your husband will be given another chance: you to understand him, he to beg forgiveness. If you both can do this, all will be well. If you cannot . . ." There came a drop of rain upon the earth. "Oh, that I could do more than this for you, my daughter."

But Evening Star was unafraid. "Do not fret," she said to her mother. "I will prove how easy this is. Go on, my mother. Go on and do it."

Tears began to fall in earnest from the sky. And in Old Woman's voice was nothing but grief as she said, "Understand, my child, that you will have no memory of this, nor will he."

Evening Star thought for some moments, her mind turning over images of the warmth of her beautiful home; remembering again the love of her mother, her father, her sisters. To never see them again . . .

But upon this thought came another: Did she have so little faith in herself that she could not submit to a dare?

At last she said, "Do it, my mother. Bring him into the sky, but do it quickly."

"There is one last thing I must tell you, my daughter. Look to the land, to the mountains, for your heart's desire. For it is in the mountains that the spirits reside. They will help you."

"I will," said Evening Star.

"Remember, too, your lover's song; for you will know him by it, and he you."

"I understand."

And so it came to pass that Strong Arrow was taken into the evening sky, there to shine brightly upon the earth, while his own true love became doomed to an earthly life.

There are some who say that on a night such as this, when the moon shines so brightly in the sky, that Old Woman searches the mountains, looking for she who is her true daughter, listening for her song. But alas, it is also said that the true Evening Star must have failed the test of chastity, for in all this time, she has not returned.

Still, there are those who hope . . .

Chapter 2

Sun is (their) supreme god of earth and sky . . .

James Willard Schultz, *Blackfeet and Buffalo*

A nighthawk squawked in the distance while closer to hand the crickets kept up a constant serenade. However, their noise did much to accentuate the stillness in the camp.

Kali stared out in front of her, noting that the fire had long since died away, leaving a frost in the air, a crispness which helped to revive her, as though she had been lost in a daze. Shaking herself, she said, "Then Evening Star and Strong Arrow will never be able to be reunited? She failed her test of chastity?"

"No one knows," Gilda replied. "But there . . . some in tribe who say that Old Man, seeing what his mischief brought, and fearing his daughter could not remain untouched, interceded. And so . . . legend goes on to say, someday Evening Star will return to mountain. And when she does, she must listen for his song."

"Hmmm. That is a powerful legend, Gilda, isn't it?

His song . . ." Kali stared off into the night. Suddenly she smiled. "You are a very interesting guide, Gilda Shadow Runner. And I will have to admit that although my father and I were skeptical of hiring a female as our escort, you have certainly proved yourself."

"Thank you."

"So tell me, Gilda, do you spin this story to all the young ladies who come to this mountain?"

"There . . . not many of our gender who would venture to climb mountain."

"No," said Kali, "I suppose not. And now that you mention it, I don't mind telling you that I am well tired out from our hike to get here." Turning, Kali settled down to snuggle deeper into her sleeping blankets, pulling the warmth of the wool over her head. "That's a fascinating story, yet—"

Thud! Crash! Clank!

"What was that?" Throwing off the blanket and sitting up, Kali glanced around her.

"Rocks falling. Wind . . . strong tonight."

"I see. By the way, are you certain we've done everything we need to in order to keep bears away from our camp?"

"You put away cooking gear as I told you?"

Kali nodded. It wasn't that she was afraid of bears—not necessarily. Her concern was generated more from the fact that she wanted to be assured that she had done everything she could do to strategically avoid a bad situation. She said, "I washed them in a stream, wrapped them up in towels and put them in a basket in the wagon."

"That be fine, then," Gilda said as her dark braids fell over her shoulders. "It late in summer, and the bears . . .

not hungry at this time of year—they not out, looking for food." Gilda nodded. "We . . . get sleep now. Have long day ahead, if you and your father wish to get good pictures of mountain." She glanced up briefly at the sky. "It should be beautiful day tomorrow."

Kali stretched out her slender five-foot-five frame upon the ground and pulled up the covers. Looking up, she stared at a sky which appeared to boast millions of stars. "Which star is it, by the way?"

Gilda pointed. "The bright one closest to horizon—does white woman see it?"

"Hmmm, yes. And please, Gilda, you can call me Kali. Do you think the two lovers will ever find one another again?"

"I hope that it . . . be so."

"Really? Why do you hope so?" Kali shifted, turning and coming up onto an elbow, so that she could look into Gilda's midnight black eyes.

As the two women stared at one another, there across the embers of a dying fire, an awkward silence hung between them. "Because," Gilda said carefully, "a person should never live without hope. Besides, it beautiful legend and legends need have happy endings, I think."

Kali sat forward and shook her head, reaching up to remove a hairpin from her coiffure. She set it on the ground, there on top of a few other pins. "Do you think," she asked, "that Evening Star would ever be able to forgive him?"

"No one knows." A brief pause followed, and then, "Would you?"

Kali sighed, bending forward to reach beneath the blanket and unbutton the gaiters which covered her shoes. "I don't know," she said. "It would be a rather difficult thing to do, wouldn't it? After all, how could she ever trust the man again?"

"But why not? After all this time . . . gone by?"

Kali looked up at Gilda. "He *did* betray her."

"Yes. However, Old Man tempt him overmuch, and Strong Arrow be, after all, only a man."

Kali shook out the last of the hairpins, delighting in the feel of her long tresses as they fell down over her shoulders. After a moment she began to brush out her hair, using her fingers as a comb.

"But he was perfect, wasn't he? Or at least he thought so. And being perfect, he should have done something differently . . . he should have walked away from Bright Shadow."

"Even when she pregnant?"

"Was she really with child, or was that a ploy?"

"She truly be pregnant."

"And Old Man cast her out of the sky?"

Gilda nodded.

"What an odd thing for a father to do," said Kali, almost to herself.

"Old Man sometimes mischievous."

"Yes, I would say that must be true. Still I don't quite agree that Evening Star should be duty bound to forgive Strong Arrow," said Kali. "I'm not certain that I could. Oh, I'll admit that there was an age, years ago, when it was the custom for a man to have several mistresses. But that was a very long time ago. Our modern woman wouldn't stand for such a thing. Oh, don't get me wrong," Kali added when she espied Gilda's long face. "It would be horribly romantic if they were to be reunited, wouldn't it? But I dare say, it might also be the height of folly if she were to take him back."

"Folly? Why folly?"

"He *did* betray her," Kali repeated, then gasped as a loud rustling sound came from behind her. She turned over, if only to stare down into the rocky terrain for a moment. "Excuse me, Gilda, but are you really certain I've done everything I should to prevent a bear attack?"

"*Aa*," said Gilda. "That means 'yes' in . . . language of my people. Since before I walk, my family has come here to mountain—every summer. Not bears, not wolves have attacked in all that time, not mountain lions, too. I tell you true that I know no person of my tribe who has been attacked by bear."

"You don't say."

Gilda nodded. "It true. Perhaps it because animals are familiar with the scent of my people. Bears have strong sense of smell. Maybe we have been here for so long that they think we part of land. Perhaps to them, we . . . not enemy."

"But *I* would be, wouldn't I?" Kali grinned. "Do you think if a bear ever came our way, I could point to you and say, 'friend'?"

Gilda laughed. "White woman could try, but I not certain it . . . work. Besides scent, there not much similarity between us. Your hair too red, your eyes too green and your skin too light. Would it help if I tell you what to do if bear . . . attack?"

"Maybe."

"My grandfather once told me that a person, no matter how fast of foot, should never try . . . outrun a bear, for bear can travel swifter than horse. There be one exception, however, and that is if you . . . lucky enough to be able to run downhill. Bear not so surefooted then and cannot run as easily or as swiftly as you."

"But I would think that a person's first impulse would be to run."

"Yet you must not. Best thing you . . . do, said my grandfather, is to roll up in ball and tuck head down. Bear might bat at you and might scratch you, but cannot harm you."

Kali's jaw literally dropped. "You must be joking. Are you truly telling me that I would be expected to roll myself up and let an angry, two to three hundred pound bear paw at me?"

"You would not outrun him. It more certain that you live to tell the tale if you did this simple thing. Besides, bears almost never attack a person unless bear is . . . mother bear and you have come between her and her cub."

"Thank you, Gilda, but I'm not familiar enough with bears to know if they would be male or female. Maybe a person should shoot first and ask questions later."

Gilda smiled. "No shoot. It very hard . . . kill bear—should treat . . . bear with great caution. Did you know that mother bear is only ferocious because . . . male bear will attack and kill her cubs?"

"Really? No, I'm afraid that I didn't."

With these words, silence once more fell between the two women until, with a shrug, Kali asked, "Do you think he would stoop to beg forgiveness?"

"Stoop? He?"

"Well, Strong Arrow . . . you know . . . the legend. He did consider himself flawless, after all, didn't he? And he won't . . . he won't remember all that has gone on before, will he?"

Kali met the look in Gilda's eyes, surprised to detect a faint trace of humor there. But when the other woman spoke, all she said was, "No one knows. But come, let us talk about something else. I am glad that you and your father decided to come here—visit my people—set their image to paper."

"Are you?"

"Yes," said Gilda. "Many . . . old ones are dying. And when we lose one of them, it great loss for my people, since our traditions and history are kept alive by our elders. Perhaps by you and your father photographing them, some of . . . old ways might be remembered and recalled to mind . . . in future."

Kali nodded. "It has been my dream—and my father's, too—to come here and do exactly this. Ever since we saw a delegation of Blackfeet Indians, who were visiting Washington at the same time that we were. My father has been here once before, but not me. But at last here we are."

"Yes," agreed Gilda. "At last." A moment followed then, "You . . . not be disappointed with your work, not with view of . . . scenery at dawn, either."

Kali smiled. "I know you're right, but—oh, no. . . ."

Kali came up onto her knees and grabbed hold of a crate filled with equipment. Immediately she began fishing inside it.

"What is white woman looking for?"

"Extra flash sticks. I think I packed several, but suddenly I'm not so certain."

"My friend," said Gilda, her voice carrying a note of humor. "You should see how you look . . . now."

"Now?"

"*Aa*," she pointed upward. "Moon shining down on hair makes it look glittery and light—as though you . . . be enchanted."

Kali grinned. "Enchanted?" She snorted. She didn't

believe in such things. Legends were interesting, fun and full of the history of a place. But they were, after all, simply legends. She said, "Thank you for the compliment, Gilda. You are too kind. But it's probably the effect of the stars. Perhaps they've never seen someone like me out here before. Maybe they're trying to tell me I don't belong."

"Perhaps. Or . . . maybe they try—tell you that you do."

Kali raised an eyebrow. "Doubtful. I was born and bred very far from here in a small village in New England."

But Gilda simply smiled. "And yet . . ." She didn't finish the statement. "But come, it late and we should try to get some sleep, I think."

"Ah, yes, here they are," said Kali, holding up something in her hand. ". . . A few extra flash sticks."

"Oh, I almost forgot—tell you one important thing," Gilda raised her head. "Do not get up in the middle of night, even if you have call to nature. At least not do it if you fear you might run into . . . bear."

Kali sank back down and pulled the blankets over her head. There it was again: the thought of bears. "Good night, Gilda."

"*Soka'pii*. That means 'good' in Blackfeet language."

"Does it? *Soka'pii*."

Twenty-three-year-old Kali Wallace lay awake, wondering, worrying. But the exact cause of her anxiety escaped her.

Was it the talk of bears? The camping? Certainly it couldn't be the project upon which she and her father were engaged. No, not that. Photography was her life.

So, if not that, what was it that was causing her thoughts to race through her mind?

The legend? Ridiculous. Kali had accompanied her father on enough of these expeditions to realize that there was little evidence to substantiate native myths and legends. Such things were simply the superstitious meanderings of a native people who had yet to learn the laws of the physical universe. There was always a logical explanation for what might appear to be magic, if one cared to look for it.

Yet, she couldn't deny that tonight's story had touched something deep within her. She sighed. She needed sleep, that was all. With a grimace, she turned onto her side.

"Ooooo, ooooo.
Ooooo, ooooo."

Sitting up quickly, Kali stared around her. What was that? It had sounded like singing . . . the baritone strains of a man's voice.

She shook her head. What was wrong with her? It couldn't be singing. Here? On the rocky crest of a mountaintop? In the middle of the night? Surely not.

It was that silly legend influencing her, she thought, causing her mind to create things it might not understand. Why it was probably no more than the wind whistling through the pines below them.

"Ooooo, ooooo.
Ooooo, ooooo."

Or was it? Hmmmm . . .

Kali pulled down the woolen covers and took a moment to glance around their camp. *"Don't arise in the middle of the night,"* Gilda had cautioned . . . as though Kali needed the advice. Anyone who had done as much traveling as Kali had, would know better than to venture a midnight stroll. Yet foolish though it might be, Kali couldn't deny that something was pulling at her, making her yearn to investigate that sound.

"Ooooo, oovoo, iihtawaakomimmotsiiyo'p.
Ooovo, ooooo, iihtawaakomimmotsiiyo'p."

Kali sat up. That hadn't been the wind or some magical incantation. Though she didn't understand the words, there was no denying that this time she had heard singing.

"Oooov, voooo, iihtawaakomimmotsiiyo'p.
Ooovo, ooooo, iihtawaakomimmotsiiyo'p."

There it was again. She moved to her knees, glancing first at Gilda's sleeping figure and then at that of her father, who lay not more than twenty feet away from her. Why didn't the noise awaken either of them?

Kali briefly considered rousing them, but immediately decided against it. For one, her father needed the rest; for another, he would not appreciate the reason for concern, since *he* hadn't heard the legend.

And Gilda? . . . Kali wouldn't awaken her guide—she would feel silly in doing so. It would be as though to show fear. And Kali was nothing, if not analytical.

Well, wasn't this perfect, then? That left only her.

Kali rose onto her feet, trying to be as silent as possible. Luckily, she still had her shoes on—a precaution on these wilderness trips, since one could never be certain of how quickly she might have to move.

She needed a weapon, however. Bending over, Kali picked up the revolver which was never far from reach. Now, which direction should she go?

"Ooooo, ooooo.
Ooooo, ooooo."

To the north. Taking a deep breath for courage, Kali stepped forward. In minutes, she had trod out of their camp and jumped down into a small, rocky gully. The clattering made by small pebbles accompanied her movement, but she tried to ignore the sound, since there was little she could do about it.

Immediately, darkness engulfed her. Looking right and left, she tread forward cautiously, coming up onto the other side of the gully and climbing out of it, careful not to put weight on a foothold until she was certain of its strength. Even still, she made even more noise as a few rocks gave way beneath her feet.

Funny, she thought, how the darkness could make ghostly figures out of the most innocent of things. For instance, in the light of day, that boulder ahead of her would appear as no more than a mere formation of stone. In the darkness, however, it became a spook.

Perhaps, she conjectured, the mind's wanderings were all there was to the belief in the supernatural.

Yes, that was most likely it. It wasn't fear she was feeling at this moment, it was the product of her imagination.

"Ooooo, ooooo. Inihkatsimat.
Ooooo, ooooo. Inihkatsimat."

How lovely. The voice was a low baritone, the sound coming from somewhere directly in front of her. She squinted. What was that? Up ahead of her, she could see . . .

Fear or not. It was always best to be safe. Setting the gun into a ready position, she tread closer and closer to a ledge that overlooked a deep chasm. The moon was casting a glow over the rocky land and Kali was almost certain she could make out a silhouette ahead of her. Either that, or Kali's mind was creating a figure out of something that was no more than stone and shadow.

She took another precarious step forward and almost breathed out a sigh of relief. No apparition, this. She had been right. It was a man.

He was facing away from her, his countenance turned toward the moon. His position treated her to quite a view of his posterior, although his most striking feature, she was quick to note, was his hair, long and dark, which fell to a midpoint on his back . . . a back, she observed, which was wide at the shoulders, and tapered to a narrow, *naked* waist.

Naked. At the sight of all that skin, Victorian-raised Kali shut her eyes, fighting against an odd feeling of weakness. She quickly curbed the response, chalking the emotion up to one of surprise.

Should she speak?

Somehow she didn't think so. She tread forward over the pebbly pitch of the land, placing her footfalls as silently as possible. Luckily he was still singing and didn't appear to hear her.

At last she was no more than five feet away; she stopped. At that very moment, the moon shone brilliantly over the man's figure, illuminating him in a misty, silver light. He looked . . . ephemeral, yet real, all at the same time.

Was he real?

From where had that thought materialized? Of course he was real, wasn't he?

All at once, Kali longed to reach out and touch him, if for no other reason than to satisfy her curiosity. But she refrained, preferring to study him from what she considered a safe distance.

She saw him raise his head to the heavens, heard him utter:

"Ooooo, ooooo. A'painahkimma.
Ooooo, ooooo. A'painahkimma."

She yearned to see more of him. It was a natural curiosity; a feminine one, too, perhaps. Would he be as handsome from the front view as he was from the rear?

Kali crept around to the side of him so that she could satisfy her curiosity, and as she did so, she caught her breath. This man was young, probably in his mid to late twenties. Lean and fit—*he was . . . beautiful.* There was no other word to describe him.

Of course, her judgment could be influenced by the effect of the moonlight. But moonlight or not, there was something about him that made her want to . . .

Moving around him again, so that his posterior was toward her, she stole up behind him, silently, until he was no more than an arms-length away. Slowly, her hand inched toward him. It was as though she *had* to touch him.

Her fingers shook with effort, she noted, though that didn't detract her from her goal. She reached out farther and farther toward him, the light of the moon seeming to encourage her to do so. And then it happened. A mere fraction of an inch away, he moved. She stopped, gasping.

At once he turned his head toward her.

She dropped her arm.

He caught her eye, yet he didn't say a word; he simply stared up at her, at her face, at the length of her hair, the open buttons at the neck of her blouse. Then, his gaze skimmed downward, down the length of her bosom, to each arm, where his scrutiny lingered over the gun which she still held out in front of her.

Slowly, almost laggardly, his stare came back to her eyes. Held her gaze. But there was no animosity that she could see, there in the depths of his eyes. No fear, no dread . . . only curiosity.

Should she speak? Would he understand English? Or should she use the sign language she and her father had learned? She did neither.

Leisurely he turned toward her, towering some seven or eight inches over her. Now it was Kali's turn to stare at him. In the dim light of the moon, he appeared to be the embodiment of masculine beauty, all muscle and sinew. His dark skin shone as though he might, himself, be comprised of a special glow, and it seemed to accentuate all the reasons why she should reach out toward him once again . . . if only to assure herself that he was no more than flesh and blood. Yet, she couldn't do it.

For one, the man wore nothing more than breechcloth and moccasins . . . as well as a little jewelry. To touch a man so scantily dressed, would be the height of immodesty. However, that realization didn't keep her from looking, and she noted that around his neck he wore a necklace that fell in loops over his chest, hiding what she thought might have been a most perfect form. Shell earrings fell from his earlobes, she noted, too, and it was interesting to see that the effect of what was usually considered feminine attire, looked, on this man, the exact opposite.

And his face . . . Two eyes, straight nose, full lips and high cheekbones. Nothing out of the ordinary in an Indian face, yet what should have been commonplace was somehow not. Stately eyes, revealing a keen intelligence, stared back at her. Proud lips remained silent, however, though she felt in the depths of her soul that this man would have liked to speak.

Kali opened her mouth to say something . . . anything, if only to convince herself that she was looking at a real man, not some imaginings based on her own fear. But she had no more than prepared to speak when he reached out to her.

She looked at his hand, seeing for the first time that he held a fan out toward her. One that looked as though it might be made of eagle feathers.

Did he mean for her to take it? Surely, not. Yet no sooner had the thought materialized than, by way of signals, he encouraged her to take the fan from him.

She reached forward. He didn't move. Her fingers grazed the end of one of the feathers.

Ah, it was real . . . completely real. Should she accept it? Was that what he intended, or did he desire something else from her? Something more personal?

That thought, although it came out of nowhere, let loose an avalanche of feeling, which surged through her like a fire gone wild. It seemed a contradiction, for she wanted to hold back, yet touch him all at the same time. Alas, she moved her hand forward one small, slow fraction of an inch, then another.

That's when it happened. All at once, her hand shook with the effort, the tremor spreading to her arm, then to her entire body. She stood there quivering like a newborn babe. Suddenly she sobbed. It was as though the sound was dragged from the depths of her soul.

She couldn't do it; she just couldn't touch the man.

And it wasn't fear that was the source of the problem; nor was it inability. It was as though something within her protested, telling her she must remain separate from him.

Dropping her hand, she did the only thing left for her to do. She spun away from him and fled, little caring that, as she ran, pointed edges in the rocks slashed at the material of her dress, tore through the soles of her shoes, cutting into the delicate skin beneath.

She had to get away, which she did with all possible speed.

And not once, during her long trek back to camp, did she look behind her . . .

Chapter 3

We could look in vain in such camps as that of the North Piegans, nestled among the cottonwoods, to find the depravity, misery and consuming vice, which involve multitudes in the industrial centres of all the large cities of Christendom.

Walter McClintock, *The Old North Trail*

"**M**'dear, I was of the opinion that you might wear that pretty white dress tonight."

"White?"

"Hmmm, yes. The one that you bought last year. You know . . ."

Kali stared at her father as though he might have sprouted an extra head. "Father, although I love you dearly, please leave the fashion sense to me. White is for garden parties or weddings."

She seasoned her words with a smile. Though her father might be a genius when it came to native history, he was notoriously absentminded and not in the least bit fashion conscious. She continued, "This dark green two-piece may look drab to you, but I assure you it is the height of fashion for someone in my position. Besides, though it may appear as if what I'm wearing is no more than a suit, it is sprinkled with black lace at the

36

collar and black embroidery on the skirt to give it a
more feminine appeal."

"True, my dear. True, but in my opinion the white
makes you look more womanly and pretty."

Womanly? Pretty? Was that the sort of image she
wanted to present this evening?

Kali didn't think so. Besides, in her own mind she
wasn't quite the type. Oh, make no mistake, she could
be as feminine as the next one. But if she were to be
truthful, she would admit that her heart belonged to
the out-of-doors, to her work, to the open spaces and
mountains.

The mountains. Unwittingly, her thoughts returned to
her most recent trek—no less than a week ago— to the
summit of Chief Mountain.

Gilda had not lied about its beauty. Under the filter-
ing streams of an early morning sun, mist had formed
over the trees and brooks, the land resisting the light
for as long as possible, although a few pink and silver
beams had managed to glide down to the earth, appearing as though they were illuminating some specially chosen creature.

It had been more than beautiful; it had been awe-
inspiring, looking more like a place of enchantment
than a mere earthly haunt. Funny, she thought. At the
time, images of gods living there, playing there, had
come to mind.

Kali smiled and shook her head. Enchanted? A godly
retreat? Now she was sounding like some romanti-
cized poet.

Her father harrumphed, interrupting her thoughts.
"Do you think he'll be there tonight?"

"He?" Startled, Kali's fingers slipped over the pins
she had been placing in her hair.

"Yes," said her father. "You know. Chief One Bull. The Blackfeet chief."

"Oh, y-yes," Kali stuttered. "Chief One Bull."

"That's right, m'dear. Who else would I be speaking of?"

"No one else, father. No one else," Kali responded, although she couldn't help but wonder, would *he* be there?

At the thought, a warmth stole over her. Had the man she'd seen on the mountaintop been real or illusion?

Oh, to be sure, she had touched the poor fellow's fan, but even now, in the light of day, she nurtured uncertainties about it.

She said, "I would imagine that Chief One Bull will attend the festivities. After all, he is their tribe's leader."

"I hope so, m'dear, that's why I'm thinking you might want to wear the white tonight."

Nonchalantly Kali shrugged. "I hardly think it matters. Truth is, if I am correct in my estimation, I will hardly be noticed."

"You would be if you wore something else. You might even attract the eye of several of the males in this part of the country."

Kali tried to smile, but the effect was little more than a grimace. "Stop that, Father. I have no interest in appearing fetching to some good-for-nothing man, so set your thoughts onto something else. You, my distinguished and handsome father, are my focus, and the author of over twenty books on native studies. It is you who should be in the limelight, not I."

"But m'dear—"

"Hear me on this. The only impression I want to

leave tonight is that of being a businesswoman. I have no desire to be more than that which I am, and if I want to give others a correct opinion of me—and the nature of our work—I had best look professional."

Her father paused and frowned, looking as though he might like to say another word or two. But at last, with a shake of his head, he smiled at her and said, "Yes, Kalifornia," which only caused Kali to wince even more.

Kalifornia. It was her full name. She sighed.

Truth was, Kali had never come to terms with her name. Oh, it was a practical enough name—for someone in her father's position, who had lived with the adventure of travel all his life. She was certain William Wallace had christened his only child much in the way of keeping with his profession, and had probably thought the name, Kalifornia, a rather exotic endearment. But to Kali, who had been raised in the conservative halls of New England—far away from her father's gallivanting ways—the name had been a never ending source of teasing and personal embarrassment.

A battle she'd had to withstand alone. She'd had no brothers or sisters to defend her, her father had never stayed home for any length of time and her mother had never been well. Truth be known, no sooner had Kali turned eleven, than her mother had passed away.

Unfortunately for Kali, she'd been old enough to experience her mother's loss as a genuine tragedy. And though she had tried to tell herself that her mother's passing was probably for the best, that she had gone on to a better place—a world where she suffered no more—it hadn't helped.

Nothing had brought relief. Nothing, that is, except

to lose herself in her schoolwork and the logic of rational thought. Ah, yes. That's when she had realized the value of logic, deduction, reasoning.

It had been a blessing, of sorts. Rather than submit to the rigors of personal trauma, Kali had instead developed her mind. With logic she could weather unwanted emotions; with reasoning she could lock away her grief; with careful deduction of facts, she could avoid pain and a good deal of anguish.

After his wife's passing, William Wallace had tried to settle down. He had returned to New England, and for an entire year had attempted to become a part of the orthodox society he abhorred. He'd done his best; his wanderings perhaps allowing him to garner an ability at pretense. But in the end, any attempt at stability was as fleeting as a moonbeam's embrace.

Instead a new era came into being, not that William Wallace had been given much say in it. It happened as he was making arrangements for yet another excursion into the world of native studies. He was in for a shock.

True, he had done all the right things to ensure Kali's future—hiring a governess and a new housekeeper—only to discover, when he was set to leave, that his daughter had come into a mind of her own: She would not remain at home alone. Not without him.

And when he had tried to steal away, Kali had sneaked right after him. From then on, it hadn't taken much effort on her part to convince him that his best bet was to hire a tutor and take his daughter with him. In sooth, from then on Kali had become his most constant companion and, if one were to be completely honest, his very best business associate.

Kali brought life and imagination to her father's work. For her father had been more author than photographer and his pictures had reflected this, being more afterthought than a means of bringing notice to a people and their plight.

But Kali, with her innate sense of art, her eye for the unusual and her insistence on perfection, changed all that. And eventually her input catapulted her father's work in the field of native studies into notoriety. His ideas and his sense of what was worthwhile to photograph had made her job easier, yes. But it had been Kali's genius with mood, with lighting and with an empathy for the subject of the photograph that had brought the father and daughter team distinction, as well as a fair measure of financial success.

In the mirror, Kali watched as William Wallace plucked his hat up from a nearby table and, placing it neatly on his head, said, "Even though Chief One Bull and a few other chiefs have been invited to the Indian Agent's dinner party—as a favor to us—that does not ensure that they will come."

"I know, Father. We can only hope. Tell me, was it this hard for you and mother to meet the chiefs when you visited here before?"

William Wallace chuckled. "It wasn't so very arduous to meet them, m'dear, but it was rather difficult to find them, there being no reservation at that time, and certainly no train to carry us to them."

Kali frowned. "It's funny, Father, how little you've told me about that time of your life. It was the last time mother accompanied you on one of your excursions, wasn't it?"

"That it was, m'dear. That it was."

Silently, Kali stared at her father in the mirror. Did she dare hope that her father would throw some insight on that period of his life? On the Indians themselves? It seemed to her as though there must have been something more.

Holding her breath, she met her father's reflected gaze, held it. Cautiously she smiled.

But her father turned away and coughed, saying instead, "The Blackfeet agent tells me that the Indians won't allow us to photograph them," he offered, his eyes avoiding hers. "Nor will they allow us to study their ceremonies. Not without invitation. If Chief One Bull likes us, he might invite us to his camp. The agent also tells me that two members of the Medicine Pipe society are looking for a new man to keep the Pipe. He's insinuated that perhaps the Chief might invite us to watch . . . that is, if he likes us. And I dare say, it would be quite a feather in our cap if he did."

Shaking her head, Kali let out her breath. Maybe someday he'd tell her. Maybe. Aloud she said, "It certainly would be a feather in our cap, Father."

She turned her gaze away from him and, picking up a hairpin, finished pinning a lock into place. "I'll do my best not to disappoint you tonight."

"Oh, you could never do that, m'dear," said William Wallace. "Besides, if the agent is correct, I don't think you need to worry about charming these people overly much. Factually, the Indian agent assures me that he has tremendous influence with his Indian charges and tells me that our invitation is practically assured."

Kali turned. "Yet, nothing is ever completely *assured*," she countered. "Still, if this agent has that much sway with these people, it would be a relief, wouldn't it? Now, what was that you said about the Medicine Pipe?"

"There will be a ceremony for the new owner in a few days."

"It sounds exciting, doesn't it? What is a Medicine Pipe, by the way? Do you know the difference between it and what the common Indian man might use as a pipe?"

"No, I'm afraid that I don't. But apparently it's an honor to be chosen to receive it. According to Mr. Black—their agent—the society must select a man who is prominent in the tribe, as well as one who can afford to pay for the Pipe, since he will have to give many feasts in its honor."

"Hmmm."

"And that's not all. There's a ceremony that goes with the passing of the Pipe."

"Oh my," said Kali, as she quickly, yet firmly, affixed a black lace ribbon into the reddish tresses of her coiffure. "It sounds like just the thing, doesn't it? Something that I'm sure would be a source of excellent pictures—if the Indians invite us and if they will let us photograph them."

William Wallace paced forward to pat Kali's hand. "Don't worry about that, Kalifornia. I've tried to fix everything with the agent . . . at least as well as I can."

"I know. I know. Still one can never be certain until the thing is done, can one?"

Her father harrumphed. "Well, if Mr. Black is wrong—and I don't venture to say he is—I have you to count on, don't I? You've never failed me yet."

Kali swung around toward him and grinned. "Be kind when you say that, Father. I promise I'll do my very best. But it's never the thing to count one's chickens first, now is it? Well, here we go, I'm finally ready." She turned to face him, prepared to leave, but stopped as a thought occurred to her. "Father," she said, "do you know if the Blackfeet are a patriarchic society?"

"I believe they are, m'dear, but I'm not certain of it. Why do you ask?"

"Because if they are, and if the agent hasn't quite 'fixed' things for us, it might be harder for me to acquire an invitation to the Indians' ceremonies. You do realize that much of our work in the past has been done with societies that trace their roots through their mothers' side of the family, not their fathers'. In truth, I think this is what has made it a little easier for me to gain admittance in many cases. But what do we know of the Blackfeet, after all, except that it was once a fierce tribe?" She frowned. "Didn't you learn anything else about them when you were here before?"

William Wallace shrugged. "I hadn't come here to study the Indians, if you will remember, Kalifornia. Your mother and I had come here for her health."

"Yes. So you have said in the past. But you did meet with them, didn't you?"

"Yes. In a way."

"In a way?"

Looking elsewhere, William Wallace's reply was silence.

"Surely," continued Kali, "you must have learned something about them."

Still mute on the subject, her father turned away from her, showing Kali his back. After a time, he said, "We barely had anything to do with them. But you pose a good question—about how they trace their lineage—and I'll see to it as soon as we meet with the agent this evening."

"Very well," said Kali, a note of frustration in her voice. "Perhaps," she added, "we should have tried to learn more about this tribe before we came here. After all, how many times have you told me that our work depends on knowing and observing the customs, manners and taboos of these cultures? Remember? 'No matter how strange they may appear,'" she affected her father's accent, "'or how much they might conflict with our own personal desires, we must abide by them'?"

"Hmmmm, yes, m'dear, yes," her father agreed. "Point well taken. I'll do my best."

"Right," said Kali thoughtfully. "Right. Well, we had best leave to go to this party. I must admit that, after snapping those pictures on the top of Chief Mountain, I am anxious to do more work here. I think this very well might be our best project yet."

"Do you really think so, my dearest daughter?"

"Quite," she said, sweeping away her disappointment from earlier as she stepped forward and took hold of her father's arm. Affixing a bright smile to her countenance, she repeated, "Quite."

It was a warm, summer's eve. The agent's dinner party had gone well, although the Indians hadn't been invited to the feast. They were due to arrive upon its completion, however, and Kali was anxious to meet with them.

It was an odd arrangement, Kali thought, to leave the honored guests out of the main festivities. Still, she had witnessed more peculiar things in her travels, and since she was a stranger to the newly formed state of Montana, she would abide by what the Indian agent thought best.

The sound of hoofbeats striking against the hard, dry ground interrupted Kali's thoughts. Stealing a look out the window, Kali espied fifteen to perhaps twenty riders. Indians.

At last. It must be close to nine-thirty, Kali estimated, although the exact time was hard to tell in this locale. She had already noted that, since it was summer, this territory—so far north—didn't show any signs of the evening until well past eleven o'clock. And even then, the sky was rarely in complete blackness.

Touching her father's shirt sleeve, Kali murmured, "The Blackfeet are here, I think. Perhaps we should go out and greet them from the agency's porch."

"Certainly, m'dear." Her father patted her hand.

Kali and her father led the others out to the veranda, where they were greeted by the thrill of crisp, mountain air, and the splendid phenomena of a golden sunset. It couldn't have been more beautiful, Kali thought, since the setting sun bathed the newly arriving guests in visions of tawny red.

Two by two, the Indians proceeded abreast into the agency like some grand military procession. And what a magnificent, colorful spectacle it was to see.

Each chief was sitting proudly astride a prancing, painted steed. Yellow, red, blue and white designs had been hand etched onto each horse, those colors beaming under the burnished rays of the sun. Something on the horses or perhaps the men's regalia tingled with each movement, the sound pleasant against the accompaniment of the animals' hoofs.

The Indians themselves looked as spectacular as any royalty she had ever seen. Each chief was adorned in a war bonnet, the headgear in many cases boasting perhaps a hundred feathers. Here was a red, white and blue one; there was a yellow and blue one, another of red and white. Kali grinned, her eye catching the difference between the Blackfeet headdresses and those of other tribes she had visited. On these Blackfeet chiefs, the feathers of the headdress stood straight up, instead of falling away from the head at an angle. White strips of ermine fur fell down from each of the headdresses, covering the wearer's ears, and granting the chief a look of dignity. Kali caught her breath when one of the chiefs turned away so that his back faced her. A "tail" of feathers had been attached to his headdress, the feathers being so numerous that this "tail" fell down the entirety of his back and over that of his steed's.

Completing the picture, as might have been expected, each chief wore leggings, breechcloth, shirt and moccasins. But there the likeness to one another ended. Here was a gentleman attired in a beautifully beaded vest of blue, with red, white and yellow flowers. Over there was another whose shirt was dyed a light blue and accented with a vest of light red porcupine quills, flaunting designs of blue, yellow and red. This one's shirt was bleached elkskin, with fringes of yellow, blue and silver; that one's was painted in figures of animals.

Kali blinked. The parade's grandness was dazzling, she thought, and quite something to take in all at once. Suddenly her fingers itched to get hold of her tripod and camera. But Kali curbed the impulse, twisting her hands behind her back. She was all too aware of the circumstances; knew that to snap pictures without first obtaining the Indians' permission would be a breach of etiquette that might mar her relationship with the tribes forever.

Still, excitement raced along her nerve endings. She had been right in thinking that this could be the best collection of photographs she and her father had ever captured . . . *if* she could make the Indians like her and *if* they might open their hearts to her, an unfortunately dubious prospect. For indeed, the agent had confirmed that the Blackfeet were a patriarchic society.

Still, she wouldn't think about that now. Somehow, this evening, she would gain their confidence. Somehow . . .

Kali inhaled, and the fresh fragrance of clean air mixed with the sweet scent of prairie grass, as well as the more effusive odor of horseflesh, reached out to her. With a smile of contentment on her lips, Kali stepped forward and slipped her hand through the crook of her father's arm. She whispered, "Father, they're splendid, aren't they? If I ever had any doubts about coming here, they have all disappeared now. We really must do all we can to get permission to photograph them."

William Wallace patted her hand. "Not to worry, m'dear. I have every faith in you."

She sighed. "Do you? I wish I were so confident. You might need to help me."

"Kali," William Wallace looked shocked, and not a little nervous. "You know I abhor that part of our work. Interacting with others is your expertise." He patted her hand. "You'll find a way. I know it."

Kali shook her head, glancing down at the ground. "I'll do my best, Father. I truly will."

"I know it, m'dear. I know it."

Smiling, Kali glanced up at her father, but instead of seeing him, her gaze alit upon one of the younger men in the procession of chiefs. My, but he was a handsome man, at least from this, her angle, of him. Handsome and familiar . . .

All at once, Kali straightened and dropped her hold on her father's arm. The smile faded from her lips, but she didn't look away from the Indian. How could she, when two orbs of midnight black eyes stared back at her, his glance filled with a look akin to . . . hatred . . .

Involuntarily, Kali gasped, bringing up a black-gloved hand to cover her chest. *He had come here, the one from the mountain . . .*

Suddenly his eyes narrowed and he sent a fierce glance up and down her, appraising her, looking for all the world as if she might be some cheap trader's bargain. Under that glance Kali felt exposed, vulnerable. Her knees threatened to buckle and much to her own chagrin, her pulse rate picked up a beat.

Perhaps to hide her reaction more than anything else, Kali raised an eyebrow, sending the Indian back what she felt was as furious a glance as he was bestowing upon her. And with all due regard, she turned her back on him, giving her father her undivided attention.

"Father," she said, "have you ever seen that particular Indian before?"

"Which one, Kali?"

"The one behind me. The one on the black pinto."

"I'm not certain which one you mean, m'dear. Several of the Indians are riding pintos."

Impatient, Kali snorted. "The young one, Father. The one who is riding a horse with red handprints covering the animal's flanks. Do you see it? There's also a white circle painted around one of the pony's eyes."

"Ah, yes, m'dear. I see him, and I must say, he certainly is staring at us. Handsome horse; handsome figure of a man, too, I would venture."

"Yes, perhaps. But have you ever seen him before?"

"No, I'm afraid I have not, Kali. Why do you ask?"

"Oh," she bit her lip. "No real reason. Just curiosity, I guess."

"Kali," her father began, "have you noticed that the man appears to be angry about something . . ."

"Yes, I know. It's why I—"

"Look at that. What an unusual saddle. Quite pretty, actually, don't you think?"

Kali had no choice now but to turn around and look. Thankfully, the man appeared to have lost interest in both her and her father, for he had directed his sights elsewhere. Kali took a moment to gaze at the saddle in question. "It looks to be no more than a pad saddle, Father," she said. "Elaborately decorated with fringes and beadwork to be sure, but really the same kind as we've seen most Indians use." She didn't add that this one seemed to cushion the man's nether regions, as he rode . . . exactly so.

Kali, realizing where her eyes, as well as her thoughts, were taking her, turned away. Unfortunately, in the process of doing so, her glance riveted straight up . . . at him . . . and this time, he was staring back at her.

Had he seen her look at him *there*? Could he tell what she had been thinking?

Kali felt her face fill with color, though she knew that any embarrassment on her part was wasted. The man had upon his countenance such a look of hostility, Kali wondered if she had somehow misplaced a step with him, or perhaps another member of the tribe.

No, she thought at once. She had only just arrived . . . impossible for her to have neglected some custom or forgotten her manners so soon . . . Or had she?

If this were truly the same man she had witnessed on top of Chief Mountain, then perhaps he did have cause for rancor. After all, she knew enough about these tribes to realize that the man might have been seeking a vision. And if that had been the case, she had certainly interrupted it.

She drew in a deep breath and looked away from him. Should she apologize?

Of course not. Why should she? She had been completely within her rights . . . completely. Although, she thought on a more honest note, the mountain did belong to the Blackfeet, and she had been treading where perhaps she ought not.

She frowned. Had she done something already to alienate these people?

Well, fine. She was certainly big enough to admit it, wasn't she? In faith, she realized on a note of some alarm, if she wanted to nurture the goodwill of these people—and she did—she had better apologize.

Fine. That settled it.

Drawing a deep breath, Kali squared her shoulders, picked up her skirts, took a step toward him and grimaced. Darn, if he wasn't watching her, his glance at her as threatening as if he were issuing a challenge. Well, so be it. She'd render him an apology as quickly as possible, show the man her back and get on with the rest of the evening. After all, he wasn't the only Indian chief here.

Securing what she hoped was a pleasant look upon her face, she approached to within a few feet of the man. Stopping as close to him as she dared, she said, "Excuse me, sir, but I would like to apologize for interrupting you the other evening."

He narrowed his eyes, staring at her down his long nose as though she were no more than a mere pesky insect.

Despite herself, Kali fidgeted. "You remember, don't you? The other evening, on top of Chief Mountain?"

But again, he said not a word.

"You . . . you do speak English, don't you?"

For an answer, he pulled on his reins, maneuvering his horse until its hindquarters faced her. Kali gasped. The insult was obvious.

Now, perhaps she should have let it go at that. After all, she had been trying to make amends for any mistake on her part, no matter how slight it might be. Mayhap another, and probably a wiser woman, would have simply walked away from a confrontation. But for good or for bad, Kali had not attained her position as her father's most trusted business associate because of any lack of assertion.

Caution and experience might have urged her to tread carefully, but Kali ignored them. Picking up the hem of her long skirt, she stepped down from the agent's porch, her slippers falling onto the firm, rocky ground, where a few of the sharp rocks bit into the leather of her shoes.

She ignored the discomfort, stomping around the horse's flanks, and without due regard for any audience she might be attracting, she grabbed hold of the Indian's reins and gave them a yank. "Sir," she said, "I am speaking to you."

The man stared down at her and for a moment she thought he might be a little startled at her behavior. *Good, she thought, let him realize what his impertinence has brought him.*

But upon second glance, she realized her mistake. If the man had experienced any surprise at her boldness, he hid the fact well. No, at this moment, he was bending toward her, ever so slowly, with nothing but the gleam of menace in his eye.

At the look, Kali quailed, but she held her ground. Instead of speaking to her, however, or rising to the bait she might so amply be providing, he slid off his mount. And with what might have been a malicious quirk, he threw the reins at her.

Kali caught them and, opening her mouth, she would have said more, but he silenced her with a quick motion of his arm. In sign language, he said, "Brush down my horse."

"Br-br-Brush down your horse? . . ." Kali stammered in English. But if the man heard her, she would never know.

Turning his back on her, he strode away from her so quickly, Kali was left feeling as though the breath had been knocked out of her.

Warily, she glanced around her surroundings. Great. Perfect. Every other chief who remained in the yard was staring at her with more than a little curiosity. And though not a single smile was evident upon their weathered faces, Kali was certain that later tonight, when the party was over and these men were huddled around their own fires, they might share a joke or two at her expense.

She should do something, she realized; something before that man disappeared altogether. Kali opened her mouth to utter a rejoinder. Surely she could think of something witty to say to the man's fast disappearing back.

Unfortunately, nothing came to mind quickly enough. With a huff, she spun around, presenting her back to the yard. In doing so, her shoulder brushed the man's pony, and looking up, she stared into the curious eyes of the animal. Kali raised her chin a notch, and stretching out her hand, petted the pony. "What a fine-looking horse you are," she said. "But I will have to admit that if we ever get to know one another, you will have to tell me how on earth you put up with him."

In answer, the animal snorted.

Chapter 4

*Free grass, no income tax, no county tax, only a
small state tax, no feed bills, small losses, open
range from the reservation north to the state
line . . .*

Will S. Hughes, Rancher
in the early to late 1890s

The evening was not going well. So much for the
Indian agent's influence over these people—an
empty boast. Truth be told, the chiefs seemed to have
little interest in speaking with Kali on any subject, let
alone on the matter of her work. Even her father was
having little to no influence.

It wasn't that the Indians were impolite. Not by word
or manner had any one of them made her feel slighted
or even unwelcome. No, it was more a matter that they
were simply not interested. Alas, these Indians chiefs
were keeping to themselves, so much so that Kali was
beginning to fear the evening might end before she accomplished her purpose. And then what would she
do? She would need some other means, some other reason to visit them, which of course she could invent. But
it would set her schedule back considerably.

Grimly, her gaze skimmed the figures of each of the

chiefs until, with a start, she realized that one of them was returning her scrutiny. *It was he.* Darn! Why did he look at her as though he wished her off the planet?

It was a shame the man was so antagonistic toward her. Particularly since she would have liked to talk with him, if only to reaffirm that he was, indeed, the same person she had seen on the mountain. It would make her feel better somehow—realizing that there was a logical explanation for what she had seen, what she had experienced. Turning her head away from him so that she might appear disinterested, she studied him from out of the corner of her eye.

He was tall, she would have to give him that, for he was probably a good seven or eight inches taller than she was. Broad shouldered, muscular, he was a big-boned man, yet fashionably slender. Unlike the other chiefs, however, this man wore no headdress, though he had affixed a single feather at the back of his head.

Soaring Eagle. This was the name she had overheard the agent use to address him. Briefly she wondered how he had attained the name, having read some-where that Indian names meant something. If he ever spoke to her—which might never happen—she would have to ask him about it.

He wore his hair strangely, she noted. Forming the length of it into three long braids, two at each side of his head and one in back, while his "bangs" were pulled up and away from his face. This style appeared to be a Blackfeet fashion, she thought, for she had not witnessed it in any of the other tribes she and her father had thus far visited.

More curious still was the ornamentation that he wore. On each side of his face fell a single strand of blue and white beads, with a shell placed at the top and bot-

tom of the strand. There were shell earrings hanging
from each lobe of his ears and around his neck was a
beaded blue-and-silver choker, with a lone, large pink
shell placed in the center. The affect of these adorn-
ments was quite fierce.

His shirt and leggings were of white buckskin, and
upon both were intricate patterns of geometric designs.
A single red and white flower had been beaded into a
circle at the center of his shirt, which covered a chest
that was broad and well defined. Hanging from each of
his sleeves were long strips of fringe, repeated at the
bottom of his shirt, alternately hiding, then exposing
the top of the man's breechcloth. On his feet were black
moccasins, though they, too, were beaded in the same
colors and design as the rest.

His cheekbones were high, his nose straight, his lips
full and sensual. Kali gulped. Where had that thought
come from?

Straight, black eyebrows sat above dark eyes that,
when he wasn't appearing hostile, looked out upon
the world with what looked to be a wisdom far beyond
his age, which she guessed to be twenty-seven or
twenty-eight.

"How are you getting along, Miss Wallace?"

Startled, Kali turned toward the feminine voice and,
taking a moment to compose herself, smiled. "Oh, I'm
doing well, Mrs. Black. Simply splendid, really. This is
a wonderful party."

The other woman leaned toward Kali, whispering,
"He's quite handsome, isn't he?"

"Who?"

"The young Indian man you were staring at."

Kali snorted. "I wasn't staring—"

"Weren't you?"

Kali raised an eyebrow, "There is a saying, I think, that is most apt, if one were to discuss that young man"—she gave him a brief, rather antagonistic nod—"And that is, 'Handsome is as handsome does.'"

Mrs. Black cackled loudly. "Oh, but I would have to agree with you," she said. "I will have to remember the way you said that and if I might, I would venture to tell you how glad I am to know that you are *appreciating*," she emphasized the word, "the natives for what they are. So many of your kind come out here with ridiculous ideas of romanticism. Why, I've even met a few artists who insisted on capturing the Indians' likeness in a way that makes them appear proud, even noble . . . as though they weren't mere savages."

"Oh? Really?" Kali frowned.

"Why, yes."

Kali raised an eyebrow. How Mrs. Black managed to look wise, yet stealthy, all at the same time she might never know.

But the woman was continuing, "I'm so glad to find a champion in you, dear girl. And here I was, so wrong about you, for I had truly considered that you and your father, like the others, had come to our post to immortalize them. . . . .But one never knows does one?"

"No, I suppose not."

"Now, mark my words. There is no good to be found in these heathens, even among their very best. I would know, too. None of them can be trusted." The woman opened her fan, brought it up to cover the lower part of her face and said conspiratorially, "I have learned to my detriment that an Indian would sooner give you his word and break it tomorrow. And he'll do this without the least hesitation or conscience."

Kali, taken aback, stared hard at this woman, who was engaged in the height of carping gossip. Pulling a face, she grimaced.

This was the Indian agent's wife? How, she wondered, could a man represent a people to the best of his ability when his wife held such negative opinions?

Perhaps he and Mrs. Black rarely talked? No, that was too fanciful a thought.

Shame, she thought. These people deserved better than this—at the very least, real justice. Mustering up her voice, she said, "You speak about the Indians as though they were alike, one to the other. I was only referring to that one man."

"Ah," said Mrs. Black. "But the characteristics that you see in that one probably apply to them all, don't you see? Savages, the lot of them. And I would know."

This last was said so irresponsibly, Kali found herself staring at the woman as though she had taken leave of her senses. Didn't the woman know that by her chatter, she cast a rather dim reflection on her husband?

Hoping to change the subject, Kali said, "Tell me, do the Indians usually dress as beautifully as this for most gatherings?"

"Oh, yes, my dear," said Mrs. Black. "These are their best clothes. And I suppose the costumes are pretty, in their own way, though horribly unstylish. Mind you, what you see here tonight is very different from what you'll discover on the reservation once we take you there. Why, this is my husband's second post at an Indian reservation. Our first was in South Dakota." The woman cleared her throat. "And do you know, my dear, in all that time, there's one thing that I've learned about the Indians."

"Oh?" Kali ventured cautiously, looking about the room for a possible escape. "If you'll please excuse me—"

"The Indians only dress in their best when forced to do so," Mrs. Black grabbed hold of Kali's wrist and frowned before muttering, "Most of them are beggars or drunks or lazy no-goods who grub around in filth and dirt all day long."

Kali couldn't have been more startled by these words than if Mrs. Black had suddenly stripped off her outer garments and danced about the room. Kali shook off the woman's hold, wondering again how an agent could justly represent his charges when his wife so clearly hated them.

But it wasn't until the woman added, "Heathens," with a such derisive sneer, that Kali couldn't help but reply, "The Indians are hardly heathens, Mrs. Black. As I understand it, they are quite religious in their own way and practice their devotion to their religion daily . . . quite different from some of our own, wouldn't you say, who only deem to remember the holy teachings one day of the week?"

Mrs. Black sent Kali a deriding look. "Oh," she said, "so you *are* one of those sorts, after all, are you?"

"And what sort is that, Mrs. Black?"

But the woman didn't answer the question, stating instead, "And here I was, thinking you were different from the usual idealist who comes here. Indian lovers, the lot of you."

Mrs. Black spit out the word "Indian" so nastily and looked so righteously contorted, that Kali thought the woman might be suffering from a bad case of "ants in the drawers." The thought caused Kali a brief moment of humor, though she was careful to hide it. Problem was, Kali would have liked to laugh outright. As a guest in this house, however, good manners forbade her such an outlet. In the end, Kali observed straight-faced, "I would have thought that, seeing as your husband is the person who is supposed to keep the best interests of these Indians in the forefront, you should qualify yourself as an 'Indian lover' and be proud of it."

"Proud?" Mrs. Black's face turned so red, she looked as though she might burst a blood vessel. "Never, would I advocate them. Leave it to you Easterners—"

"I have traveled extensively."

"Then you should know better." Mrs. Black stiffened her spine, then chortled. "Have you ever seen their ceremonies?"

"No, I haven't," answered Kali, "but I would like to. It's why I'm—"

"Huh! Then you don't know what you're talking about. You Easterners like to idealize—"

"A good quality."

"But then," the woman continued as though Kali hadn't spoken, "you don't *have* to live with the Indians as I do. You'll see soon enough. Like the rest of us, you'll come to know that the Indians are nothing more than the spawn of the devil."

Kali sighed. Always, she thought, there were prejudices. It didn't matter if she were in South America, South Africa or India, always it seemed that there were those who had to control others, who couldn't allow another to have a different viewpoint from their own. Glancing around the room, hoping to discover a reason to leave, she commented, "Really, Mrs. Black, you shouldn't listen to gossip."

"Gossip? You'll see that I speak the truth. I've heard an awful lot of strange tales."

Kali tried to control herself. She shouldn't say anything. She should let it go. After all, she had come to Montana on a mission of peace. *Be diplomatic.*

But in the end, she couldn't help asking, "Have you ever seen the Indians doing something . . . devilish?"

Mrs. Black crossed her arms, her lips thinning. "Don't need to. You romantic visionaries are all the same. Wait until you've been here a month," the woman wagged her finger in front of Kali's face. "Mark my words. You'll see what I mean."

Kali shook her head, bestowing upon the woman a sad smile. "Pity."

"Pity?"

"Yes. I think it's a shame the Indians have, as someone who is supposed to try to understand them, a man whose wife believes as you do. For I'm certain you influence your husband's opinions, which might cause him to make mistakes in his work, don't you think?"

Mrs. Black frowned, opened her mouth to speak, but no words formed on her lips.

"If there's one thing I've learned in all my studies of the native peoples of earth," continued Kali calmly, "it's that there are always two sides to a story. One should hear both sides of a debate before drawing an opinion on it. In any event, a person—especially someone in your position—should perhaps learn to be more tolerant toward those whose interests are, after all, paying your husband's commission, and are probably funding this party. Perhaps I should thank the Indians for you."

As she spoke, Kali noted that Mrs. Black's flushed face was contorted with so much anger, it had turned a deep crimson—which was a shame, for she could have been pretty were it not for the ugliness within her.

"Well," Mrs. Black said, her lips compressed forcefully. "I can clearly see that you are a lost cause."

Kali sighed and looked away. "Perhaps I am, Mrs. Black. But if I am, it's something that I think I'm pleased with."

Mrs. Black drew her fan forward and snapped it open, hiding her face behind it. "Just you wait," she reiterated. "Just wait."

Sighing, Kali turned away.

The evening breeze was cool and soft upon her face, stirring the tiny strands of hair that had escaped her coiffure. Kali drew her black lace shawl around her shoulders and inhaled a deep breath, sniffing at the smoke-scented air. Smoke from the woodburning stove inside, Kali reckoned.

The evening was almost over, she thought. And it had not gone well. Perhaps, if she were a little more honest, she might admit that it had been a disaster. Not only had she alienated the agent's wife, she had failed to make any inroads into the Indians' confidence. And without that confidence, there would be no ceremonies to attend, no pictures to take and certainly no chance to learn a little bit more about these people.

But, she told herself, she wasn't fully to blame. Her father had been there, too, as well as the Indian agent.

Perhaps she and her father shouldn't have pinned so much hope on this one evening. Or maybe if the Indian agent hadn't painted such a glowing account of his ability to influence these people, she and her father might have been more prepared.

Perhaps.

Of course it wasn't over. She would try again tomorrow. But how? She needed to think.

That was why, a few moments ago, she had excused herself, retreating to the veranda, quite alone. Feeling more than a little defeated, Kali slumped her shoulders, glancing down at the dirt, bits of long grass, and rocks that littered the ground.

"You should go back to where you came from," uttered a baritone, strangely accented voice, which came from somewhere behind her.

Startled, Kali spun around. *It was he, the hateful one.* She said, "You. Y-you speak English."

"Aa," he said, "And yes, I speak English."

Kali frowned, turning away from him so that he couldn't witness the defeat which she supposed was easily read in her demeanor. She said, "Why is it that you speak English when none of the others do?"

"Some of us know this language."

"Really, then why the half-breed interpreter tonight?"

"Most of my people do not speak English well and do not always understand all that is said to them. The interpreter is to ensure that no mistakes are made."

"Ah. And you? Why do you speak the language so well?

He shrugged. "I am an exception because I was sent away to a white man's school."

"Oh, I see."

"Do you?"

It was a question not meant to be answered, and Kali held her tongue. Silence fell between them, causing her to adjust her position, to glance over her shoulder. As though in response to the movement, he reiterated,

"You are not wanted here. I mean what I said. You should go home."

"Why?"

A long pause followed her question before he at last met it with one of his own. "Why what? Why do I want you to go home?"

"No, why do you hate me?"

He took a step toward the edge of the porch, leaning a fringe-covered sleeve on the post. "Did I say that?"

"No," replied Kali, turning to the side, to face him. "Not in so many words. But then this is the first time we have spoken . . . th-though we have seen one another before . . ."

"Humph!"

"Why do you hate me?" she repeated the question.

"Why should I not?"

"Because," she said, turning her face so that she could stare out into the night, instead of at him, ". . . because you don't know me."

"I know enough."

"Do you?"

"You are a foreigner, a stranger to our land."

"Oh, I see. I'm unlike you," she said sarcastically. "And that makes all the difference in the world, does it?"

He didn't react to her words by way of facial expression or motion. After a time, however, he did observe, "The Indian has gained little advantage from other races, particularly this one that surrounds him."

Kali spun around on the ball of her foot, facing him. "Is that so?"

He appeared momentarily surprised by the swiftness of her antics, though he was quick to hide it.

"Well," said Kali, hands on hips, leaning forward, "if

you will kindly gaze around you, you might find a few things that you can't do without that were given to you by 'other races.' "

"Humph!" His eyes became guarded.

"Like the horse, for instance. Like the beads on your clothes, like the guns you carry, like the flint you probably store in your pouch."

"Small things."

"But small things that make life a little easier."

"Ah, this is true. This is the first wise thing you have said since we have begun our talk. For the Indian did lose his country for want of flint and tiny beads. Hardly a fair exchange."

"You have not lost your country."

"Think you not?"

Kali didn't know how to respond to that question. And so she didn't do or say anything. Indeed, she turned her back on him, stepping along the railing of the veranda where she proceeded to gaze out into the night.

So much for charming her way into this society's trust.

"If I were to be truthful," came the baritone voice from directly behind her, "I would have to admit that I do not hate you . . . very much . . ."

Still, Kali didn't turn around. "Well, that's fine, just fine, isn't it?" she said in defeat. "I suppose you can go away now, knowing you've done your best to discourage me."

Silence. Then, just as Kali had begun to think he had left, he said, "Why would I want to discourage you?"

Kali glanced over her shoulder. "Why would you not want to, feeling about me as you do?"

"Perhaps," he said, "I am here merely to look at you."

"Look at me?"

"*Aa*," he said. "You are a stunning sight for the eyes."

Kali watched from over her shoulder as a grin split across his face. Amazing, she thought, what a simple smile could do to a person.

But it was her turn to utter, "Humph!" And with a flip of her head, she turned her face away from him. Silence. But something within nagged at her to keep talking, and she found herself asking, "Don't you see many redheads out this way?"

"Very few—and hardly ever on a woman."

"Perhaps," she said, still with her back to him, "if I wanted to get your chiefs' attention, then, I might make myself into a floor show. Is that what you're saying?"

"I do not know what this 'floor show' is."

"Never mind," she said. "It was a nasty thing for me to say."

"Nasty?"

"Yes," she said, "it was and I'm sorry."

Again her words were met with a stony silence, one that seemed to stretch on and on. He must have left, she decided. She hadn't heard him leave, but it must be so.

After several more moments, quietly wondering where he had gone, she spun around, taking a step forward. But as she did so, she slammed into something very solid, very warm and very male . . .

The contact might have caused her to fall, but he caught her by her forearms, steadying her. However, his touch set off a flicker of something akin to an emotional flood, which proceeded to wash through her. That, plus the feeling that her knees might collapse at any time, threatened her composure.

What in heaven was happening to her?

"Oh, ah . . . thank you," she said, at the same time taking a firm mental hold on herself. She shook off his grip and stepped a pace away, aware that, for some reason, the sooner she retreated from all that muscle and brawn, the better. "I'm sorry. I thought you had left."

"I am here."

"Yes," she said. "Yes, I can see that." *And more,* she added to herself as she became aware that there was something wrong with the man. Why, he looked utterly perturbed. And he frowned down at her. *Now what?*

She took another hasty step backward, pulling at her gloves at the same time to straighten them. "What have I done now to earn your disapproval?"

His frown deepened. "You have done nothing."

"Oh, really?" Her tone was sardonic.

"It is only that I have never heard a white person apologize to an Indian."

"Oh, come now."

"Believe what you will. I have never heard it."

"Why, I apologized to you earlier this evening."

"But you were not sincere."

"I was *very* sincere."

He grinned again, causing the heaviness in his expression to lighten. And the good Lord help her, the effect on the man was incredible. Suddenly he looked younger, more vulnerable perhaps. Kali tried to swallow down her reaction, tried to minimize the involuntary action of her heart.

Drat! She was going to get nowhere with these people if she swooned both physically and emotionally every time a handsome Indian man smiled at her.

But he had more to say, and he continued, "You apologized to me tonight so that the other chiefs would talk to you. It was inspired by self-interest, not by sincerity."

"I . . . I . . ." It was on the tip of her tongue to deny it, but she couldn't. Truth was, that exact thought had gone through her mind.

She sighed. "I supposed that's partially true."

"Partially?"

"The other part of it is that when I am in a society that is strange to me, I always try to observe proper manners. It did occur to me that I had perhaps done something I shouldn't."

"But that only occurred to you because I was angry with you."

"Why, I—I . . ." Kali felt like a small child caught in a lie. Praise be, but that was exactly what had happened. She looked down at the ground, a smile pulling at her lips. After a while, she said, "Yes, yes, that's true."

"That is that, then."

She nodded. "It is."

"Perhaps," he said, after a while, "if I am to be honest with you as well, I would tell you that I, too, have done you an injustice."

"No . . . What?" Again, her tone was that of complete sarcasm. But when she glanced up at him, she was met by a look that was pure intensity. He was serious.

"Your action on the mountaintop needs no repentance," he said. "You should know that you did not interrupt me when I was sitting there."

"Then it *was* you that I saw up there."

He nodded. "It was. Why were you there?"

She ever so slightly relaxed and backed up to the veranda's railing before answering, saying, "My father and I are here to take photographs of your people, your homeland. Our guide thought we should see the morning from atop Chief Mountain."

"*Aa*, your guide was right. And did you like what you saw? Was it worth the effort of the climb to get there?"

"It was the most beautiful sight I have ever seen."

He hadn't been looking at her directly as she spoke. He did so now, his glance skimming over the length of her, up and down. But he said nothing.

After a moment, Kali remarked, "You were singing that night."

He nodded. "*Aa*, I was singing."

"The song was beautiful. In truth, I have been uncertain if you were real, or if I had merely dreamed you . . . and the song."

He frowned at her. "That is a strange thing for a *white* woman to say."

"Why?" Kali blinked. His emphasis on the word "white" left no doubt as to his opinion of her race. But she said, nevertheless, "What does being white have to do with it?"

"A great deal, I think."

She gave him a somber look. "How can you look so wise and yet not know that it's a sign of weakness to generalize about an entire race of people?"

He arched a brow. "How can you come here to my country and not know what is going on between my people and those who surround us?"

Touché.

"All right," she said at last. "You made your point. But please, let me ask you again why is it so strange that I was uncertain if you were real or a figment of my imagination?"

He took his time answering, taking a step around her and away from her before answering. "Because," he said at last, "white people don't have dreams."

"I beg your pardon . . ."

"No visions, no spirituality. Only the physical side of life is viewed as real by the whites—as though it weren't made up of little bits of themselves."

"I don't understand."

"I don't expect you to."

She sucked in her breath. "All right. Fine. I am what I am. But I do have dreams, and I do believe that your people have visions." Which are probably a by-product of their own fears, she added silently to herself.

"Empty words."

"Oh," she uttered. "You are impossible. Whether I am white or red or yellow or . . . or even blue means nothing, except to bind us all to certain mores and customs. A race is made up individuals and you, sir, know nothing about me."

"I disagree."

"Is that so? Then you know everything about me, I suppose?"

"I know enough." He sent her a grin that was half sarcastic, half charming. Then he said, "I disagree that race is unimportant. Do you think it means nothing to the Indian agent who tries to control my people, who tries to order every aspect of our lives? Or to the cattle ranchers who surround us and who covet our land?"

"Whoa, you go too fast," she interrupted. "The Indian agent is trying to do the best job he can for you."

"Is he?"

Wasn't he? Of its own will, the conversation with Mrs. Black came clearly to mind. Was there more going on here than what met the eye?

Perhaps she should have asked the question aloud. But Kali, not one to admit defeat in any argument, couldn't help asking instead, "What are you talking about, ranchers who covet your land? You live on a reservation—land given to you by the government—it's yours."

"Is it?"

"Isn't it?"

"Perhaps if you wish to see what is happening to my people, you will look at what is going on here with eyes that are not clouded with prejudice."

"Clouded with prejudice? Me? What about you? You're the one bringing up race and color and distinction."

"And so would you if you could see what is happening here."

"How can I see, when I have only arrived here?"

He remained silent.

"Look," Kali said, her tone capitulative. "It's a well-known fact that these reservations have been put aside for your exclusive use. It was part of treaty arrangements, I believe, wasn't it?"

"You know it so well, then?"

Kali faltered. "Well, it's what I've been told."

"*Aa*. And of course you believe everything that you hear."

"No, but—"

He spun away from her. And Kali instinctively grabbed hold of his sleeve before he could take a single step. It was an ill-mannered thing to do. Still, the action did produce the desired effect: he stopped. However, with an eyebrow slightly cocked, he surveyed her hand as it lay upon him, as though it were as slimy as a serpent's skin. He didn't speak. He didn't need to.

"Please," Kali said. "Don't leave. Please talk to me."

"Why should I?"

"B-because I don't mean you or your people harm.

Because I'm here to do a job—a good job—one that should benefit your people. I am sincere in this. But if no one will talk to me or tell me what is going on here, I won't be able to represent your people in a light that is perhaps truthful."

His glance narrowed slightly, then he settled his gaze on her, the intensity of it boring into her. As hard as it was to do, she met that stare, one on one, him against her, until soon, as softly as possible, almost mouthing the words, she uttered, "Please. I will do most anything if you will only talk to me. . . ."

Chapter 5

These ranges (Indian reservation lands) are needed for our cattle and they are of no use in the world to the Indians.

The Helena Herald in the 1880s

She watched as his survey of her changed, watched as the flames from his eyes became something softer, watched as it appeared as though he might relent. But still he remained impassive. After a moment, however, he seemed to come to some decision, and he sighed. His voice was still a little harsh as he said, "You will not like what I have to say and you will probably call me a liar."

She gulped. "I promise I will try to be as fair-minded as possible, if you will only give me a chance. Please talk to me."

He shrugged off her hold and said, "I cannot."

"Please. Please, won't you?"

He narrowed his eyes at her. "Good manners forbid me from doing that."

"It would be ill-mannered if you didn't. Please. I beg you."

His lips thinned into a line as a frown settled over his features. He said, "All right. If I do this, however, if I tell you true what is happening here, you cannot come back to me and say that I didn't warn you. Do you promise?"

"I do." She smiled at him, hoping it would give him encouragement.

But if he noticed, he ignored it. He said, "You have freedom."

"Yes, yes, I do."

"Because of your white skin, you can come and go on the reservation."

"Yes, that's right."

"Do you think I can? That any Indian can?"

"Can't you?"

He didn't answer. "Am I free to live my life as my people have always lived it, close to the land? Am I free to hunt? To bring in meat for my family?"

"Aren't you?"

"This treaty land that you speak of, did you know that if the Indian does not use this land as the whites see fit, these whites—the ranchers who surround us— claim that we Indians are inept and incapable? Did you know that they scream how ignorant we are until they are heard in the land far away—in Washington?"

"No, I—"

"And who does the white government protect? We Indians, who are 'wards' of the government? Who have rights by treaty?"

"Doesn't it?"

"Or does the government protect the wealthy ranchers who see in Indian land more wealth for themselves?"

Kali didn't answer.

And he continued, "The truth is, the government protects the whites. Oh, yes, we have an Indian agent. But his best friends are ranchers, who want more, always more land, and where do they get that land?"

"Surely not—"

"And so other treaties are made with us, these giving the Indian fewer and fewer rights. More land is taken. But never is it enough for the white man's thirst. No, the more land we give these ranchers, the more land they want."

"But I don't understand. You can't be talking about the reservation land which was ceded to you by treaty."

He didn't say a word.

"Could you show me these new treaties?"

"I do not have these papers. The agent keeps these things for us—to 'protect' us."

"I will have to see it," she said. "I find this rather hard to believe."

He grunted and looked away from her. Casually he shrugged. "That is easy to understand. You are what you are. Certainly you are not Blackfeet."

He made the fact sound like an insult. "And not being Blackfeet makes me . . ."

"Not Blackfeet." He grinned.

"Yes? And . . ."

"Always when outsiders come, they take. So it has been from our first meetings. A very old, wise man of our tribe once said that when the whites come, they will first want your trade, then your women and next your land. Soon, he said, they will want what no man should have to give: the very spirit of your people. The first three are done."

The implication was obvious. Still, Kali hesitated, until finally she mustered up the nerve to ask, "Are you thinking that by my being here, I am trying to take away your spirit?"

"Aren't you?"

"No," Kali said, backing away from him.

He stared at her. "Perhaps these words are too harsh for you, but I think, if you are having a problem instilling trust for your cause amongst my people, this is the reason."

"I see."

"Do you?" His glance was doubtful.

"I think," said Kali, not answering the question, "that if you were to be honest, you might see that this old, wise man could have been a little prejudiced himself."

"And yet," he replied, "those things he predicted have come to pass."

"I am not speaking of that."

He gave her a questioning look.

"My father and I have visited many, many native peoples of the world," she said, "and if there is one thing I have learned, it is that one should never generalize about an entire people. A society is made up first of individuals; some strong, some brilliant, some weak, but individuals—all different. In fact, in all the world, there are no two people alike. Yet, this man, though I do not doubt he was wise, would generalize and tell you that because of the color of my skin, I feel and have viewpoints that, until this moment, I never even realized existed in me?"

He gave her a questioning look. "I'm not sure I understand."

"You say that I should look at this thing with eyes

that can see both ways. Perhaps you should do this yourself, for if you did, you might find it easier to comprehend my words."

He stood back from her, crossing his arms carefully over his chest. "Perhaps you can tell me why you are here, then, so I might understand it better."

"I already have."

He gave her a smile, amazingly laced with tolerance before speaking. "Humor me," he said.

She sighed. "All right. My father and I are here to record your tribe's history. We are not here to judge you, take your land or imprison you on your reservation. We were hoping to be invited to some of your ceremonies so that we could record these for future generations. That's all."

He paused. "Did you know that my people believe that if an image is drawn of them, or if a picture is taken, you are carrying away a part of their spirit?"

"I . . . no, I didn't."

"Do you know that legend has it that those who allowed their pictures to be painted in the past, died within a matter of a few months?"

"No, but I can show you—"

He held up his hand, saying, "It doesn't matter." Again, he spun around as though he might leave, but once more, he was too slow in doing so.

"It does matter," she had scooted around him quickly, coming face-to-face with him. "I can't explain why those people died. I'm sorry, but I can conjecture that perhaps they did so because they believed that they would. Let me assure you that in the white world, hundreds of pictures are taken daily. None of those people died shortly thereafter. Why is that?"

"I do not know, except maybe the white man's medicine is different than the Indian's."

"Perhaps," she agreed, "but if that is true, then your people have nothing to worry about, for I am white and, by the same logic, my 'medicine' would protect my subjects."

"That is not the point."

"Then what is the point? That you wish to stop me simply because of the color of my skin?"

He glowered at her.

"I can't help who I am," she went on to say. "Listen, please, you must see that the white world is here to stay. There is no escaping it, and only by understanding and tolerance, will your people be able to live well in it or next to it. But understanding and tolerance do not come easily. It's something you have to work at. One has to educate, one has to communicate, one has to show what it is that should be understood. That is where my father and I can do you a service."

He didn't speak, although contrarily, he didn't seem in any urgent hurry to leave either.

She continued, "Just as you would like the whites around you to accept and respect your way of life, so too should you be willing to let the white man live as he sees fit."

"Never!"

"Otherwise," she went on, as though he hadn't spoken, "you are as guilty of doing that which you protest against. Personally, I can't see how this makes you any better than what the white man is. In fact, it's like admitting defeat, isn't it? You've become him."

Kali studied Soaring Eagle's expression closely, trying to determine what possible effect these words were having on him, if any. But when he remained silent, she continued, "Understanding can't occur unless both your people and the white people know each other a little better. These pictures I'm hoping to produce will be an attempt to tell your side of the story, to relate your legends, your way of looking at life. Only a person who had something to hide would be unwilling to share this kind of communication. Only a person who didn't want the conflict resolved would push for strife, rather than understanding."

Silence. Deadly, horrible silence followed these words. And it was perhaps a full minute before he said, "You speak well."

"I know my subject well."

"And yet you do not know what the conflict is that is going on here."

"But I would like to learn. I would like to help."

"Would you? That is hard for me to believe."

"Why is that so hard?" asked Kali.

"You do not wish to know."

"I don't? I don't think I would have asked if I didn't, nor would I be here if I didn't want to—"

"Enough! I will not talk to you about this anymore. I should not have spoken to you in the first place."

"Why not?"

"Because we are throwing harsh words at one another, yet we hardly know each other." He paused, as though to catch his breath. "In the past, this sort of talk at a woman would not have been tolerated."

"True, but also in the past a woman like me would not have been easily suffered."

He grinned, and unfortunately for her composure, it was a beautiful thing to behold.

"Perhaps not," he said, "although a woman who has

something to say was always heard in the past, was never interrupted and was never refuted. Plus, her advice was always considered before decisions were made."

"If that be true," she said, "then we should talk about this more, not less. We should speak to one another about this until we understand each other. At least if we talk, we have a chance to settle our differences. But if we don't . . . Please tell me what is really happening in this territory."

Stepping away from her, he came to lean against the veranda's railing, his gaze catching onto hers. He said, "It might be hard for you to grasp."

"Fine," she said. "Try me."

He slanted her a frown, yet for all that, he went on, "Very well." He turned around, presenting her with his back and leaning his elbows against the railing, he began, "It started long ago, more than a hundred years back. At that time, there were few white people who came to our country. As time went on, more and more people came here. They have been religious people, traders, government men, agents. All these people have been white; all have told us they have our own 'good' in mind and that they wish to help. So it was with the first traders, then with the missionaries, and now with the Indian agents. My people have rarely been bettered. Instead, we see our land broken up into pieces, our way of life destroyed, our families scattered, our lives ruined. Many of my people are starving, yet you have seen the grandness by which the Indian agent eats. Several years ago, the government parceled up our land, making my people live on smaller and smaller tracts which are too small to farm or raise cattle, even if the red man wished to walk in the white man's shadow. Yet, even with these small tracts, if the Indian does not use his land as the whites believe is right, this becomes good enough reason to grab it."

"But surely—"

Looking over his shoulder, he held up a hand, silencing her. "You look to the written records before you tell me how this is not true. You see for yourself, then we will talk more about it. If I am wrong, then maybe you can show me the error of my thinking."

Kali inhaled deeply. "All right. I will do this."

He nodded.

"But . . ."

He quirked an eyebrow.

"But is it necessary to hate me in the meantime?"

He shrugged, turning around so that he faced her. "Hate is a strong word. Have I not already said that I don't dislike you too much?"

"Yes, but—"

"I do not give my trust easily. For the Indian of today, it is a matter of survival."

She frowned. "I don't understand."

"Then let me explain. We learned many years ago that when a white man speaks on something that has to do with his own interest, he is usually lying. I admit this is not a good state of affairs, or a good frame of mind to be in. But thus far, for good or for bad, we have only failed when we did not keep this in mind; when we trusted the white man blindly."

Kali paused. What he said held a note of truth. Nevertheless, putting people into particular categories simply by the tint of one's skin seemed hardly fair, either. And so she found herself countering, "Then an Indian never lies, I suppose?"

"No that's not true, although in the past," he said,

"the days of my grandfathers, a man did not lie and live well. If a man was caught in a fib, he was berated by the women and never trusted again, ever. But the old ways are dying. More and more of my people are following the example set by our conquerors. And even those of my people who are still truthful have become careful, saying only what they think should be heard—and of course, in all societies there are those of weak spirit, who deal not in truth but in lies as a matter of course."

"Then you admit there are differences person to person, even in a race of people?"

"*Aa,*" he said. "You spoke true. We are not all alike."

"Which was the only point I was making."

"Was it? I thought you also wished to take pictures of my people."

"I do."

"And if you take these pictures, what will you do with them?"

Kali felt herself relax. On this subject, she was on familiar ground. She said, "My father and I will make them into a book, which will be sold back East."

"Ah," he said. "Then this is how you and your father make your living in the white man's world?"

"Yes."

"Then it is your wish to make money off us Indians."

Kali shrugged. "Yes," she said. "In a way. But in a way, not."

"And how will we Indians profit by your pictures?"

"By bringing more understanding of you and your people's plight to the world. After all, if the native people of America were better understood, you would be able to enlist more aid to your cause."

He raised an eyebrow, his glance at her hard-hitting.

"You are a wise woman," he said, "yet I don't think you are wise enough. You tell me that you wish to take our pictures, tell our stories, relate our adventures, yet you do not offer the Indian anything in compensation, though these adventures are rightfully ours."

"I hadn't thought about it. It's not something that has ever been brought up to us before."

"Always," he said, "the white man has explanations."

Kali shook her head and pulled a face. "That's too bad, really."

"Too bad?"

"You are a very prejudiced man."

"I am a realistic man."

"All right, then. I suppose you are too realistic to take a dare, then, as well?"

"A dare?"

"Yes, I must admit that I have come into this project blind. I should have learned more about the situation and what was confronting the people I wished to contact—before I arrived. However, I didn't. Be that as it may, I am prepared to liaise with you."

"Liaise? In what way?"

"Tonight I was besieged with bigotry not only from you but from the agent's wife, Mrs. Black. It leads me to believe that there is something going on here that needs investigation. Therefore, I am prepared to make a bargain with you."

"Humph."

"Here it is. I will acquaint you with what I do so that you can more fully understand why I am here. You, for your part, will show me what is going on between you and the ranchers—who share this land with you. Then we will examine the facts and make our own judgments. If I am right, and my pictures do not do harm, you will do all you can to help introduce me to your chiefs and your people, perhaps talk them around to meeting me and letting me take their pictures. If, on the other hand, you convince me that I am hurting people by doing this, I will leave."

He opened his mouth to speak, but she held up a hand.

"You will, for your part, show me what is happening on your reservation. If you are right, and the white ranchers are trying to push you out, I will do all I can to help you fight this. If, however, you are wrong and the ranchers have just cause to do as they are, you will do all you can to convince your people to help them."

"I will never help the white ranchers. And I will not put myself into a position where I might ever have to do so. No, I don't think I will bet with you."

"I see," she said, biting down on her lip. "You're afraid."

He frowned at her. "Only at the prospect of being hoodwinked by a small redheaded woman." He softened the words with a grin. Then, after a moment, "Who would decide if the white ranchers have 'just cause?'"

"Why, both you and I, of course."

"And you will listen to me?"

"I will listen to you."

"And if we don't agree?"

"We will examine only the facts and keep examining them until we do agree," she said. "In truth, I would be willing to bet that you have simply misunderstood the actions of those who live around you. If it's not a case of simple misunderstanding then—"

"And if I am right, if you discover that I speak the truth? What then?"

"Then you will win the bet, I would help you and I would have to pay you whatever we decide are the stakes."

He leaned in toward her. "And what are the stakes?"

"Well, for my part, if I win, I would like you to help me get as many pictures as I can. If you win, hadn't we already decided that my father and I would leave?"

He pursed his lips, nodding. "It sounds good, but I'm not sure I like it."

"What about it don't you like?"

"It is not personal enough."

"Personal?"

"*Aa*, it is not a small thing that you ask of me if you should win the bet. I think you should wager with something you do not wish to part with."

"I am." She crossed her arms. "If you win I would have to leave."

"Yes, but is that enough? At least in comparison to what you ask of me."

"I see," she said, then a little sarcastically, "I suppose you have something in mind?"

He appeared to mull this over, although Kali was certain he had something firmly fixed in his thoughts. Several moments passed. At last, however, he spoke up, saying, "If you win, I will do as you say and try to persuade the others to agree to your photos and to try to understand the whites around us. But if I win . . ."

Kali waited. "Yes?"

"If I win, you will do as I say . . . even though the request might be a little intimate."

Kali's stomach dropped; she raised her chin. "Exactly how intimate?"

He grinned. "It is told by our elders that, in the past, young men were willing to use their wives as the stakes in a wager. The women had no say in it, even if she loved her husband. She went to the winner willingly, and in marriage."

Kali stared at this man, who stood before her so handsome and proud, who probably had half the female members of his village running after him. And he was asking her to . . . what? Aloud, she said, "Are you telling me that if you win you might ask me to marry you?"

"Or something like that."

"How much like that?"

He cocked an eyebrow. "Perhaps the physical side of it."

Kali spun away from him, although it did her little good. She could feel the heat of his glance on her back. She said, "If you are asking what I think you are, it is immoral. And I'm certain that your society isn't that much different than mine when it comes to such things."

He didn't speak for some time, and he must have come up close to her, for when he next spoke, she could feel his breath on the back of her neck. He said, "Yet, it is certainly a high enough stake. And you are an attractive woman."

"I'm not."

"You are."

These were thrilling words, wonderful words, even if she didn't believe them, and she clenched her fists to keep herself from reacting to him. She said, "I think you are being impertinent."

She could feel him shrug. "It would, at least, make the wager interesting."

She sniffed. "I'm not that desperate."

His face must have been close to her ear, for when he had whispered *Neither am I*, she heard him distinctly, then he went on to say, "But then, a kiss is perhaps too much to ask of a white woman."

A kiss? She spun around so quickly, she wheeled off balance. He caught her, his hands grabbing hold of her waist to steady her. "That's all you've been speaking of? A kiss?"

He gave her a devilish grin, his lips close to her own, before he said, "Maybe two, if you please."

She took a step backwards, out of his arms, watching as his arms fell to his sides.

"What kind of kiss?"

Darn. There it was again, that dazzling smile. It made his face light up as though mood alone ruled his countenance. Worse, when she looked at him, her insides went all soft and warm, as though she were made of nothing but butter and rum. He said, "Should I show you the kind of kiss that I like?"

"Sir!"

He chuckled, closed one eyelid and winked at her. "It would be a simple kiss, two pairs of lips squeezed against each other." He leaned down to her, but simply pressed his lips against one of his own fingers, which he then placed over her lips.

At the contact, her body reacted as though it were ready for so much more. She shut her eyes, feeling slightly faint.

"But I would reserve the right . . ." He paused, causing her to open her eyes. Drat! His handsome face swam in front of her and at the sight, a smoldering fire fanned to life within her; her stomach somersaulted. He stood close; so close, she could smell the scent of mint on his breath, the musky fragrance of his skin, the fresh odor of buckskin. "The right," he continued, "to hold you in my arms when I kiss you."

"Oh, I see. I . . . I'm not sure."

"Are *you* afraid, then? Afraid you might start to feel something besides a white woman's contempt for an Indian?"

"You know that's not true," she whispered. "You know from speaking to me tonight that I don't hold this opinion."

He drew in a deep, ragged breath. "*Aa*, yes," he said. "You are right, and I apologize for saying that. You are not the kind of person to feel scorn for another, are you? Simply because he is different than you are. So, if not that, what are you afraid of?"

"I . . . I'm afraid that I might . . ." She didn't finish the sentence. She wasn't certain that she, herself, understood what she'd been about to say. Although there was one thing she knew she could count on . . . her mind's ability to reason. She said, "Y-you are correct. The stakes should be something we are unwilling to part with. You, to aid something alien to you. Me, to give up my work, and a kiss."

He nodded. "Seems fair."

"All right, then I . . . I believe we have a venture, Mister, ah . . . Soaring Eagle. Sh-shall we shake on it?" She would have held out her hand, except that he stood too close to her to do so.

"We could," he said, "or perhaps we could do something better."

And before she could stop him, he gathered her hand in his, bringing it, glove and all, to his lips. She gasped. Not because of what he was doing, but because . . .

He glanced up at her and smirked. "When I was at

the white man's school," he said, "I learned an odd custom. At first I thought it was a strange practice, but the more I thought about it, the more and more I appreciated the wit of the white man." And turning her hand palm up, he pressed another kiss against her wrist.

Kali's heartbeat raced out of proportion to the action, and it was all she could do to stand upright at the moment, for her knees threatened to collapse beneath her. And truth to tell, she had little time to hide her reaction from him, for when he raised his head and said, "I believe we have a wager, Little Miss Redhead," his look was so full of mischief, she wondered if she had, perhaps, made a tactical error . . .

Chapter 6

They've been living in heaven for a thousand years, and we took it away from 'em for forty dollars a month.

Charlie Russell, Western artist

Soaring Eagle jumped over the porch railing and strode toward the open pasture to his pony. As he progressed, he could feel the heat of the white woman's gaze on his back, but he chose to ignore it.

Silently, he grinned, congratulating himself. She'd be gone on the morrow, he reasoned. If she were at all like any of the other white folk with whom he'd had dealings, he felt fairly certain that she wouldn't waste a moment's breath waiting around here.

Truth be known, in his experience, it was the women of the white race—perhaps even more so than their men—who showed the most intolerance toward his people, snubbing their noses at a white man who might consider marriage to an Indian maid. At one time, in the not too distant past, it had been a common practice amongst the trappers and traders, even some of the ranchers, to marry into a tribe. The custom had been the cause of some degree of harmony, permitting understandings to arise between his own people and the newcomers.

But with the coming of the white woman to the West, all that had changed. Perhaps, he thought, she was jealous, though why she might be so was hard to understand, since the men outnumbered the women in this country by ten to one. Still, while the white man appeared to have few qualms about marrying an Indian woman, the reverse did not hold true. Maybe, he reckoned, the white woman did not believe the Indian male to be good husband material. But whatever the truth was, he knew very few of them who would risk her reputation on an Indian man . . . not even for a small kiss.

Lost in thought, he didn't at first notice how far he had trekked from the agent's home before he found his mount.

"Discovered a greener pasture, did you, boy?" he said to the pinto, rubbing the animal's neck before bending down to remove the hobble from its front legs. The pony whinnied softly, nipping gently at his master's shoulder. "I know," he said. "I, too, wish for more adventures than those that our agent allows. Oh, what a duo we would have made, if we were allowed to follow the war trail, like our ancestors did." Soaring Eagle glanced up toward the midnight sky. "But those days are gone, my friend, even though you would have been the best war pony a man ever had. We Indians do not go to war . . . not anymore."

At least, he added to himself, not the sort of war his forefathers had known. No, since the reservation days had been forced upon them, his people were engaged in a different kind of battle—one waged with fences, with deception, with guile, with trickery. No one called it a fight, yet Soaring Eagle knew it by its proper name. War.

INDIAN LAND—CHEAP.

So the poster at the general store had read. Was it only last week that Soaring Eagle had obtained permission to go into one of the bordering towns, that he might purchase some trade goods? There, he had seen people gathered round a post. Curious at the attraction, he had looked closer.

That was when he'd seen the words. He recalled again the feeling of disgust within him as he'd read the advertisement, remembered the meaningless talk of those around him, the sting of laughter from townspeople, who had no awareness that Soaring Eagle was more than what he appeared—a man who could read.

Worse, as he'd stood there, he'd felt powerless to prevent what was taking place.

Truth was, this land grabbing was something no Indian mind could readily assimilate. While already owning most of the territory, land-hungry whites were trying to take away reservation territory, bit by bit, piece by piece. Justifying themselves by screaming to Washington that they needed more land in order to survive, the government had eventually capitulated.

It had come down to the Indians in the form of an act of Congress. Called the General Allotment Act of 1887, or better known as the Dawes Act, it had arrived at a time when the red man was trying to come to terms with an alien way of life—and to find his place in it. And while he struggled to understand the unfathomable and to come to terms with the present, the white man had been sitting on the edges of the reservations like hungry coyotes, waiting to wrest away land that was not theirs to take. Always, he thought, these whites wanted more.

The Dawes Act. Most of his people could little comprehend the words of it, let alone understand what was taking place. Each member of the tribe had been allotted a small parcel of land . . . not enough land to farm or to ranch. No, never that. Then when each member of the tribe had been given their portion, the rest of the reservation was divided up and sold on the open market—dirt cheap.

The rest was the making of history. Land-hungry ranchers had bought up the property as though it were a field of diamonds. And perhaps to them it was. It certainly did give them opportunity, while it doomed his own people.

The worst part of it was that the land hadn't been divided up so that the Indian could make a living off it. Fearing, perhaps, that the Indians might own property side-by-side and open up their hearts as well as their lands to one another, the Dawes Act had parceled off the reservations in a checkerboard fashion—Indian property interspersed with white landholdings.

And though Soaring Eagle had heard the Indian agent claim that the parceling was a brilliant plan—one that would teach the Indians to mimic their white "superiors," and show them how to live like a civilized man—Soaring Eagle knew it for what it was: another scheme to subdue the Indian.

But what could he do? One alone against a mob?

Soaring Eagle was tired of it; tired of being an interpreter for his people, tired of reading the legal documents to them, tired of trying to explain what was not understandable, what was really treasonable, as though he were part of that which sought to overrun his people.

It was like trying to fight the wind. One could no more than reach for an opponent, than he was blown off course. Or worse, trying to fight blind, unable to see from where the bunch came, one was blown hither and thither, unable to gain a single foothold.

And now this woman wanted to take their pictures, claiming she wished no more than to reach an understanding between her people and his. Soaring Eagle snorted.

He didn't believe her. He didn't trust her. But then he didn't trust any white person.

Still, she was an awfully pretty little thing, he supposed. She, with her startling color of red hair, which in some lights appeared to shimmer like burnished gold. Her eyes were green, a deep forest green, the first eyes of that color that he'd ever seen; her face intelligent, and a mouth that made a man long to experience its taste. A slender figure completed the pleasing image.

He shook himself, realizing that the direction of his thoughts would do him little good.

Nonetheless, he couldn't help thinking back to the first time he had seen her. Not tonight. It had been there on the top of Chief Mountain only a few days ago. Moonlight had bathed her then in an unearthly light, making him wonder if she were of flesh and blood or a mere mirage. At the time, he thought he'd never seen anyone more beautiful; had believed at first that this woman might be a part of him, a part of his life, his vision. But when he had reached out to her, hoping to unite her to him, she had turned away and run.

It was then that he'd known the truth for what it was: She was no more than a silly white person. Worse, she was a trespasser.

Well, enough. He needn't think about it any further.

She would be gone by morning. He didn't doubt it for a moment.

Scratch, scratch, scratch.

"Are you awake?"

Naked, Soaring Eagle rolled over, kicking off the warm buffalo robe which served as his covering.

Scratch, scratch, came the "sound" on the tepee's entryway. Then again the feminine inquiry, "Soaring Eagle, are you awake?"

The words were English. *English?* Worse, he recognized the pitch and accent of that voice, the owner being a small feminine persona with red hair.

What did she want?

"May I come in?"

"*Saa!* No!"

"Oh," she said, "then you're not ready to go?"

"Go?" He stood up, grabbing for his clothes. "Go where?"

"Well, after last night, I thought it best that we get started as early as possible."

"Started? Doing what?"

"Well, aren't you going to see what I do, and vice versa?"

Soaring Eagle sighed. *Why wasn't the woman gone? Surely he wasn't wrong about her, was he?* He asked, "Is there no train today?"

A pause, as though the little redhead might be puzzled, then she repeated, "Train?"

"*Aa*, the iron horse, the choo-choo. Chugga-chuggachug. You know, the train," he finished, throwing his arms through his shirt and stumbling into his breeches. "Why aren't you on it? Is the Great Northern not running today?"

"I beg your pardon," she said, and he could hear the censor in her voice "I thought we'd come to an agreement last night. A wager I think we called it."

"Ah," he said, taking a few steps to the back of his lodge where he picked up a towel, "so we did." Retracing his steps he came to the east side of the tepee and, bending, stepped out through the flap opening. Straightening up, he came face-to-face with what could only be termed a "vision."

Red hair gathered into a knot at the back of her head, with flyaway tendrils escaping the arrangement, her green eyes flashed with curiosity. Upturned nose, wide cheekbones which tapered to a delicate, yet strongly set chin. She looked poised, fresh and, truth be told, as delightful as a drop of morning dew bedecking a wild rose.

He glanced down at himself, feeling dirty and grimy in comparison. A little overly grumpy, he asked, "You're still happy with the terms that we set?"

"Terms?"

"The stakes."

"Phew!" She raised a brow. "Didn't I say that I was?"

In response, he gave her what he hoped was a leer, saying, "And you're still happy enough with them to abide by them?"

"Of course I am. Did you think I'd feel otherwise?"

"The thought did occur to me." He frowned at her. "How did you find my lodge?"

"My guide, Gilda." She nodded toward another woman. This one, he noticed, was dressed in buckskin breeches and shirt, looking more like a young boy than a girl. He didn't know her; hadn't seen her in these parts. But if the design on her shirt were an indication of her tribe, she was Blackfoot—probably from the reserve in Canada.

Soaring Eagle pulled a face at the girl, saying, "Thanks," as sarcastically as possible.

"Pleasure," came the feminine response.

Perfect. Just what he needed: two females.

Without another word to either of them, he turned and strode away, his path angling toward the lake, beside which were camped about fifty other graceful Blackfeet lodges. He took long purposeful steps, daring to hope that he might leave the two of them far behind him. But in this he failed. Though the Indian guide stayed behind, the white woman simply ran to keep up, her constant chatter doing a great deal to puzzle him.

"I thought we might start here in camp. Gilda is willing for me to take pictures of her—she's not afraid of the mystique about photography. I could set some of them next to a few lodges, or perhaps with some of the children, or maybe have some of the old men in the background. Of course I realize that they would have to agree. And then—"

He stopped without warning. She tripped and fell. He sighed, reaching down to help her up, trying his best not to notice how soft her skin felt at his touch. Grumbling beneath his breath, he set her back on her feet as gruffly as possible and trod away, hoping she might take the hint. But his attempts were unsuccessful. She continued to follow him, even skipping to keep up, acting as though nothing in the least were wrong.

"Then I thought," she prattled, "that we might go

out to the mountains, or maybe to some lake where there are no people and then—"

"Enough! What are you talking about?" He spun around, hoping to catch her off guard.

But she merely halted, gazing up at him, the green in her eyes sparkling as she smiled. "Why," she said, "taking pictures, of course. I thought we'd start with my project and then you could show me what you're talking about—"

"*We?*" He scowled at her. "Let me be very specific. There is no agreement that I made with you that makes us a *we.*"

She merely grinned. "Oh?" She raised one eyebrow. "I beg to differ. How could you possibly learn about what I do without spending any time with me and, of course, the reverse is true, too. So to this end I thought that *we* might—"

Grunting, he threw up his hands, and turning away from her, made his steps fast and long . . . very long. He said, "I'm taking a bath."

"Oh, that's fine. I'll just wait here, then."

"Good enough," he said, not bothering to explain. He threw down the towel, stripped off his shirt, noticing that she was fiddling with her equipment and therefore didn't see what he was doing. Well, what did he care? If she didn't, he surely didn't.

The pants came next. Then, sprinting, he ran toward the lake.

"Oh, Soaring Eagle. I was thinking that—*Oh!*"

The embarrassed silence said it all. It was like music to his ears.

"You could have told me you were taking off your clothes. I would have left you alone."

"I did," he shouted at her.

"No, you didn't. You said you were taking a bath. I didn't know that meant stripping down to take a swim."

"Can you think of a better way to bathe?"

"Well, yes, as a matter of fact. I thought there might be some place here where you could bathe. Like some bathhouse or something."

"A bathhouse?" He couldn't keep the scorn out of his voice. "I thought you said you were used to traveling among the savages of the world."

"I am."

"And do you often find that native peoples build bath houses?"

"Of course not. But I had heard of sweat lodges, or . . . I just wasn't thinking, that's all. I'm so excited to get started on this at last, that I—"

He stood up, not that he revealed anything in particular to her, but it did occur to him that perhaps the view of his chest might send her running back to camp. At least he hoped it might.

"Really!" she said, looking as though the idea of flight were foreign to her. "You might tell me when you're going to do that so I can look away."

He shook his head and said, "You stay here, you take your chances."

"Oh? Don't you want to talk about our plans for today?"

"No." Brief, curt, to the point.

"Oh. Then I suppose I might meet you back at camp after you've had a chance to freshen up."

He rolled his eyes toward the heavens. "After I've had a chance to 'freshen up,' I intend to herd my horses and ride out to the range. I'm afraid I don't have time to learn about picturemaking today."

She had jumped down from the rock where she had been sitting, and paused briefly to send him a smile. "Oh, that's perfect, then," she said. "I'd like to get to know the range and what goes on there. I'll see you back at camp."

"No, you won't," he said at once, but it was useless. She had already begun trotting away.

Sending her a look of utter, complete frustration, Soaring Eagle fell back into the water, the action creating waves that splashed toward the shore.

Chapter 7

> *. . . (the Dawes Act) breaks up their tribal organizations and sandwiches them in among the whites where they must learn by force of example.*
>
> Granville Stuart, a Montana Rancher,
> who helped to divide tribal
> land and erode tradition.
> He eventually received his just reward
> by losing his family, 40,000 head of cattle
> and his land. He died a broken man.
> Peter Iverson, *When Indians Became Cowboys*

Kali set up the tripod a short distance away from the herd of horses she wished to photograph. Looking up, she caught her breath. No matter the beauty of other places, other lands, other vistas, this Montana had to rival them all for being the most beautiful, the most peaceful and probably the most soulful spot on earth.

Before her, stretched out in all directions, was a fragrant mix of prairie grasses and flowers which might have spanned a universe were it not for its intersection with the distant mountains, whose white peaks jutted up to greet a cloudless blue sky. Sweet smells of wildflowers, grass, and clean, untouched earth scented the air, giving Kali the sensation that her lungs expanded with each breath. Why, even the wind at her back felt as though it kept a rhythm, all attuned to the beat of the earth and the chirping songs of the birds.

Shutting her eyes for a moment, Kali paused. Odd, how the luminous beams from the sun, the solidness of the ground at her feet, the scent of the grasses and sagebrush in the air gave her the feeling that time just didn't move very fast, not out here. The land, this place, seemed as though it were as young or as old as it had ever been.

Opening her eyes, she looked out on the world before her with contentment, letting her vision rest upon the horse herd that sat in the middle of all this open space. The animals numbered from about fifty to sixty small horses. No two of the animals were the same either. There were whites, blacks, roans, grays, a few sorrels, and in particular, several spotted pintos. It was a dazzling sight for the eyes, a radiant mixture of sun, earth, sky, the soft, fluid sensation of peace, as well as the feeling of life all around her.

At present Soaring Eagle stood in the middle of the herd, looking as if he belonged to this time, to this place, this land. Gone, however, were the traditional buckskin and beaded clothing from the previous evening. In its place he wore trousers, chaps, shirt and boots, along with a kerchief at his neck. And though shell earrings dangled from his ears and his hair remained braided, a cowboy hat sat at an angle atop his head.

He looked like . . . a cowboy; an Indian cowboy. Ah, to get a picture. Of course, Kali knew she would have to give him warning before she snapped a shot. But hopefully she could talk him into letting her have her way with him. Or could she?

Remembering the sting of his antagonism and his failure to sympathize with her plight, she sighed. It might not be so easy.

Shrugging, she looked out upon the scene with a more professional eye. How was she to capture on film the feeling of all this life? Of course, she realized, this was a problem that faced all great photographers. Anyone could take a picture, but not everyone could make it come alive.

First, as she had learned from hard experience, her equipment had to be in good order. To this end, she checked the legs of the tripod; good, it was steady. Next, she mounted her Eastman Kodak glass-plate camera, complete with a hand clicker and flash stick. Bending, she checked the composition of the picture in the viewfinder.

Too much scrub bush in the way. It would detract from the calm beauty of her subject.

Treading out in front of the camera, she began clearing off the unwanted plants. Gilda came over to help.

"What's wrong with him?" Kali asked Gilda, pointing toward Soaring Eagle. "I thought we'd settled everything last night, but you'd think from the way he's acting that we hadn't even spoken to one another."

Gilda grinned. "Him," she pointed, "probably thought white woman would back down. Him don't think you are serious."

"Why?"

Gilda shrugged. "Maybe it never his intention that you should agree."

"Well," said Kali, "he certainly doesn't know me very well, does he?"

Gilda smirked. "Him going to learn, real quick."

Straightening up from her task, Kali waved her

hands in the air, that Soaring Eagle might see her better, and called, "Soaring Eagle, over here."

He didn't look up.

Darn. "Soaring Eagle, if you'll come over here, I'll show you how a picture is taken."

He didn't respond.

Drat. She bit her lip. He was going to make this as difficult as possible for her, wasn't he?

Fine. Looking over her shoulder to ensure her camera was secure, she trod toward the horse herd.

"Mr. Eagle," she said, "if you'll come with me, we can begin. First, I'll show you how I snap a picture—I'll explain it all to you."

He turned his back on her and stooped over, while she came up to him and stopped, hands on her hips. "Mr. Eagle?"

Arising, he paced away from her; all without looking over his shoulder or uttering a single word. Well, this was great. He wasn't going to listen to her, and there was very little she could do about it. Now what?

Well, she supposed that if the man wouldn't come to the camera, the camera could go to the man. She turned, stepping back toward the tripod.

It might cost her a camera, taking it into the pony herd, but she was willing to chance it. Besides, she would be careful. She had to do something.

Carefully disengaging the camera from its stand, she retraced her steps, only this time she didn't hesitate as she marched right up to him. He was bent over one of his ponies, as if checking its limbs for a broken bone.

Coming down on her haunches, she said, "Hello."

No response.

"Ah, all right. I've brought my camera here to show it to you, so that you can see what it is and how it works. Now, if you'll only turn your head, you'll see that I'm holding a camera."

Again, no response, not even a mutter.

She took a deep breath and plunged. "Light goes in here through this little hole," she pointed toward it, "and gets reflected onto the glass film inside the camera. The film holds the images there until one can develop it—using chemicals and such—and then it is printed onto paper, making what we know as a picture. There's nothing mysterious about it and the only thing inside the camera is glass, which has a silvery solution on it. It's this that holds an image. It's really quite simple."

"I know what a camera is and how it works."

"Oh." More silence, then, "How do you know that?"

He sucked in his breath noisily, as though she tested his very patience, although at last he said, "Do you remember my telling you that I had been sent away to a white man's school?"

"Yes."

"There were many people there who took pictures— I even had some taken of myself."

"But I thought that—"

"It is the old ones and perhaps some of the more superstitious ones who believe that a camera takes away part of a man's spirit. At school, I didn't have a choice and I learned to put up with it."

"Oh, I see. Then you don't mind if I take your picture?"

"No."

"Then why did you make the bet with me?"

"I'm not the one you need to convince. It is the other members of my tribe. Not me."

"Oh," she said. "I see. May I take your picture, then? Here in the herd?"

He shrugged.

"That's fine, then." She touched his shoulder. "Over there." She pointed. "Next to the pinto. I think that will make the best picture."

He glanced up at her. "I will not pose for you."

"Oh, right," she couldn't keep the disappointment out of her voice. "I see. But you have no objections to standing still if I wish to snap a picture of the horse herd."

He grimaced at her.

"Please?"

He clenched his jaw, but said, "I suppose I can stand still for a moment."

"That's fine, then," she acknowledged. "I'll just go back to where I left the tripod. You go ahead. I'll tell you when I need you to be still."

He grunted, not looking up.

And Kali retreated to the side, muttering. "I don't know what he thinks he has to be so crabby about." She said it more to herself than to Gilda. "It's not like I'm asking him for too terribly much."

She didn't see Gilda's grin until she glanced up. "What?" Kali asked. "What did I say that you find humorous?"

"Don't you remember how, on the way here, him had to stop or slow down many times, so that you could catch your wagon up?"

"Is that so much to ask?"

"And him have to come back to horse who was nipping the other. Him have to discover . . . cause."

"Yes, well, the horses would have pulled the buggy eventually."

"But harness also slipped and you stopped, not realizing that leather was worn, which him have to fix."

"It could have happened to anyone."

Kali glanced toward Gilda, and when the other woman's smile didn't fade, Kali found herself chuckling, as well. "I guess I have been a bit of a problem, haven't I?"

"Him not happy about having to do this with you."

"I know, Gilda. I know. But at least I have his cooperation . . . well, his word, at least. And I will keep up my end of the bargain. I intend to go and speak with the agent tonight. I want to see all these treaty papers and the deeds and anything else I can find."

Gilda nodded.

Kali looked out upon the scene before her. "I wonder if I could get him to sit atop one of those ponies."

Gilda laughed. "White woman maybe press her luck."

"Do you think so?" Casting a quick glance at her setup, she said, "Watch this for me, while I go ask."

Gilda nodded and smiled. "I watch."

How Soaring Eagle came to be sitting astride a pony, in the middle of his herd, at a time of day when he should be working, with the only objective being to let Kali Wallace snap a picture, he could never quite understand. One moment he had been talking to her, shaking his head at her, the next he had found himself scrambling up onto the pony.

He sent Kali an annoyed, pointed look. Not that she would see it. She and that darned camera were too far away. What was it about the woman, he wondered, that held sway over him? For try as he may, he could not deny that she affected him.

Was it because she was pretty?

Possibly, although he doubted that. Her beauty was

too foreign for his taste. Different, not only from the comeliness of the Indian maids who surrounded him, but also from a great majority of the white women in this territory.

For instance, there was the way she was dressed. The outfit she was wearing today looked odd, even for a white woman. Made of a bluish green material, it consisted of a blouse and jacket, along with a skirt that flaunted an unnaturally tiny waist. The skirt was short, hitting just below the knee, a style much briefer than any he had seen on either white or Indian females. That the skirt fell over what looked to be wide, puffy pants, which peeked out beneath it, was stranger still. Knee-high boots completed the outfit along with a blue-green hat that sprouted a short brim and a single feather. She looked, he thought, altogether unfamiliar.

Annoyed at the direction his thoughts were taking him, he was frowning at her when he heard her shout, "One, two, three," then came the boom of the flash stick, which she held in one hand while she snapped the picture with the other. Immediately she changed the glass plate, placing the used one into a packet.

The ponies shifted nervously.

"One more for good measure," she hollered as he watched her set up another flash stick before inserting a different plate into the camera. "On the count of three once again; one, two, three." Another boom, followed by an instant snap, then, "That's fine now. Thank you. You can go back to what you were doing."

As though he would take her orders.

He remained where he was, if only in defiance. And perhaps it was a good thing that he had.

The sound of hooves in the distance, hundreds of hooves, alerted him that all was not as it should be. The distant roar had the sound of a stampede—of cattle, since buffalo no longer roamed the range. Looking toward the horizon, he espied the telltale cloud of dust that told the rest of the story. It had to be quite a large herd, he thought, to be kicking up that much dirt, and . . . they were headed this way.

Anger stirred his blood. Although The Flowerree Cattle Company had been discovered to be trespassing on the reservation range for years, nothing had ever been done about it. Complaints were made with the Indian agent, and though Black had promised time and again that the matter would soon be under control, nothing ever happened.

However, a stampede was not in the normal course of events. Usually the ranchers were more covert in their infringement on Indian rights; a few cattle turned loose here, another several there, seemingly harmless until one realized that hundreds, even thousands of their steers were grazing over the lush, Indian tracts.

But this sound, this was different. If the clamor of those hooves told true, this was more than a handful of cattle on the run.

Soaring Eagle darted a barbed look toward the white woman before returning his gaze to the horizon. Was this her doing?

Of course not, he corrected himself at once. The white woman was new to this country and probably had no idea of the problems involved here. Indeed, she would most likely not even connect the noise to danger.

Briefly he wondered if she realized that she should start packing her equipment, get it into the wagon and speed out of the way. Glancing in her direction, what he saw there made the fire in his blood turn cold.

She was doing nothing to avert a disaster; not a single thing. In fact, instead of taking her gear down, she was setting it up for another shot.

Was she deaf? Where did she think she was? On a picnic? Didn't she realize that she was in the middle of the most untamed stretches of this country?

Or childlike, did she expect him to provide her with a safe environment regardless of the circumstances?

He grimaced. Probably the latter. Well, this was no white man's manicured lawn and he was no white man's savior.

Still, he couldn't leave her to her own devices. Regardless of the fact that she was probably the most annoying little creature he had yet to meet, it would be difficult to save himself and ignore her.

Where was Gilda? Surely she would recognize the danger? And if she did, why wasn't she warning the white woman?

He scanned the countryside, his sights finally resting off to the north, on the guide, who was clearing away scrub brush. Probably she was making too much noise herself to hear the danger.

"Damn," he swore to himself. How had he managed to bring this down on himself?

He cursed. He had to do something.

Waving at the white woman, he shouted, "Danger. You must leave at once. Danger."

"What?" she called back, looking up at him.

"Quickly!" he cried. "Pack up your things." He didn't bother to elaborate. Instead, he reluctantly goaded his pony into a trot, spurring the animal toward her.

She watched his progress happily, he noted, even greeted him with a smile, as though the world were a sunny, bright place, with no hint of peril. "Yes?"

"You must go at once," he said, drawing rein and coming directly to the point. "Cattle coming—may be a stampede. Get in wagon and go. Now!"

She glanced around her surroundings. "I don't see a thing."

He drew in a breath, trying hard to keep hold of his temper. "Don't need to see," he said through pinched lips. "Hear the hooves of many cattle. Coming this way."

"This way? But this is reservation land. Now, look at it logically."

"Do not stand there and argue with me," he commanded. "Get camera onto wagon and go while you still can. If you wait much longer, you will lose your equipment. I would stay and help you, but I have to move my ponies to safer ground. Take heed. You must be quick. Do you understand?"

She grinned. "Fully, Mr. Eagle. Fully and completely," she said, her look full of sweet sarcasm. "It's obvious you haven't wanted me here from the start, but honestly . . ."

He shook his head, drowning out the rest of whatever she was saying. Damn! He didn't have time for this. *Haiya.* Let her think what she would; bring the wrath of hell down upon her, for all he cared. He had done what he could.

Giving rein to his mount, he turned back toward his herd. But before setting off, he called over his shoulder, "Do not tell me later that I didn't warn you in time. If you stay, you have only yourself to blame."

"Yes. Yes. I understand that perfectly well," she said, a prim little smile on her face.

Terrific. He glanced at her scout, who had just joined them. "*You,*" he called to Gilda. "You know the danger. Ensure that you get her out of here."

Gilda nodded and Soaring Eagle spun his pony around, heading back toward his own concerns: his pony herd. There, on the right and some distance away, was a stand of trees which graced a section of high ground; it wasn't far. It should serve as protection enough.

"Yah! Yah!" He sent his black pinto into the herd, there grabbing hold of the lead mare. "C'mon, girl," he called to the animal, "let's lead your friends to safety."

Ugh! The task became a much harder chore than he had at first envisioned, mostly because the animals, alerted themselves to danger, were afraid. By the time he had completed the job, costly minutes had ticked away. He glanced back to see how the white woman was faring.

Groaning, he couldn't believe what he saw. She had barely moved. Indeed, at this moment, she and her guide looked to be arguing.

Soaring Eagle rolled his eyes toward the heavens. What was wrong with the woman? Didn't she know that she had lost precious time?

Still, it little mattered. He had already decided that, like it or not, he had a duty toward her. She had come here with him; that made him responsible for her, which meant he had best get down there.

"Damn!" he spit the word out to himself. What a nuisance. He was beginning to look forward to her departure from Indian country with greater and greater delight.

Nonetheless, he urged his pinto forward.

Keeping the women in sight, he saw Gilda point toward the horizon, observed the white woman turn her head, witnessed her eyes go wide; her fear, even from this distance, a tangible thing.

Soka'pii. At last she understood.

Curious, he looked toward the horizon himself, gaining his first sighting of the cattle, recognizing the signs of what he had feared: a stampede. He compressed his lips together as the anger, which was never far from his mind, once more flamed to life within him.

He was tired of the struggle for dominance out here on the range; tired of white ranchers taking advantage of the Indians' insecurity; tired of himself being labeled "stupid," simply because the color of his skin was a few shades darker than that of his neighbors'; tired of being thought of as having no rights, even to his own land, simply because his culture, even his beliefs, were different from theirs.

But at this moment, he was mostly tired of the woman; she, who had followed him; she, who did not recognize danger when it was pointed out to her; she, who might, because of her own ignorance, come to harm.

Bitterness rose up in his throat; bitterness that might have resorted to unreasonable thought had he been a weaker man. But Soaring Eagle was no one's fool.

Glancing back toward the women, he did his best to ignore the fresh wave of fury which raced over him.

It was her own fault, and within him, a nasty little impulse goaded him to leave her to her own devices. Yet, he knew, even as he acknowledged the thought, that he could never stand idly by and watch her come to harm.

Gazing once more toward the horizon, then back at the woman, he felt his stomach tighten as though it were made of a series of twisting knots. But it wasn't fear that he felt. He had been this close to danger too many times to fall victim to simple fright.

No, this was something else. Something more like . . . concern—as though he might actually care for the white woman.

Preposterous.

However, improbable or not, he bent over his pinto, muttering into the animal's ear, "Looks like we're gonna have to go and save her, boy. Do you think you can do it?"

The horse snickered.

"All right, then, let's run like the wind and get this over with." And making a clicking sound, Soaring Eagle gave the pony full rein.

Chapter 8

Sensible people knew it would be wrong to take cattle land like ours and divide it up into little pieces—big enough for grazing rabbits, but not cattle . . .

John Wooden Legs, "Back on the War Ponies,"
Association of Indian Affairs Newsletter

The sound of the hooves was deafening when Soaring Eagle came back into sight. Seeing him, Kali let out a sigh of relief.

He had been right, of course. She should have listened to him. And now? Because of her inattention, was she going to lose her equipment, her precious pictures?

It made her want to cry. She had taken such pains to capture the beauty of the wild horses. Moreover she had been able to convince Soaring Eagle to let her snap his picture. There he'd been, sitting majestically in the middle of the horse herd, looking as though he were a princely lord rather than a cowboy—and what a photograph that would be . . . if she could save it.

She gulped back tears. To lose it all?

Not if she could help it. True, she knew that her situation was less than advantageous. True, the buggy might be too slow to outrun a herd of cattle, possibly even to get her to safety. But what other choice did she have?

And so it was that she was mid-action—tossing gear into the back of the buggy—when Soaring Eagle sprinted to her side, vaulting from his horse as easily as if he were a circus performer. But his visage, as she caught sight of it, was hardly that of an entertainer. He hit the ground at a run, shouting, "Unhitch the horses."

"What?" she called.

"Unhitch the horses," he ordered again, and darted to one of the sorrels in the team, where he began the process of undoing their harnesses.

"Stop that." Kali dropped what she was doing, and stamping up to him, jerked the reins out of his hands.

"Are you crazy?" he asked, little waiting for her response. He hollered, "Look behind you."

She did. "I know. I've seen them."

"You will never get this buggy to safe ground; there isn't time. And there is no need to kill these animals." He continued to work over the harnesses.

"No!" She tried to pull his hands away. "There *is* time; there has to be time, and I will not leave this buggy and my equipment behind. If it goes down, I do, too."

At these words, Soaring Eagle's fingers stilled; he turned toward her, a frown marring his face. "That is a foolish thing to say," he said, catching hold of her hand and pulling her in close to him. He leered at her. "You can always buy another camera."

"Not that easily."

"Yes, you can," he said. As if to convince her with the force of his presence, he leaned down and positioned his face mere inches away from her.

Kali stood her ground, however, meeting his determined glance with one of her own. She came up onto her tiptoes; indeed, their bodies were so close, they stood practically nose to nose.

And then he said, "I will not let you die here."

Time seemed to stop as she felt the heat of his breath on her face, the force of his anger on her being, but she refused to be intimidated, and she said, "It's my choice to make."

"Not today it isn't."

And that's when it happened.

He closed the distance between them, his head coming down to hers. And before Kali could utter a word of protest, he had taken her lips with his own, swept his arms around her waist and pulled her into his embrace. His tongue unerringly found her own, danced with it until a low groan escaped from his throat.

Or was that her own voice?

Lifting his head a little, his breathing was fast and hard when his lips moved against hers in a whisper, "It is easier to replace an object than it is a life. In comparison, your camera and your equipment are cheap."

"But—"

"Why do you risk something so valuable?" he asked. "Why do you do this when . . ."

When what? she wanted to ask.

But he remained silent, an odd look coming over his face.

When we have finally found one another? Was that what he'd been about to say?

The thought was alien to her. Still, she opened her mouth, perhaps to utter the words, herself, but the good Lord help her, she couldn't articulate a thing. Not when his handsome face swam so closely to her own.

· And taking advantage, he kissed her again.

Kali forgot to breathe, forgot to think, even about the impending disaster.

In truth, a lifetime might have passed in that short space of time from the moment when his lips touched hers. Chest to chest they stood, so very close that she could feel the imprint of his rigid muscles beneath her hands. And truth be told, with his lips, his tongue, his very breath, he adored her.

Their breath commingled, the clean scent of him intoxicating to her. In addition, he had brought up his hands to her face, where his fingers caressed her cheeks, making her feel as though she were as rare as a handful of jewels. She breathed in, and the essence of who and what he was filled her being.

What was happening to her? To him? To them? What was happening to the world as she knew it? It was as though she and Soaring Eagle were a part of it, as they had always been, yet not. For in this moment, time ceased to rule their existence. There was no space, no discord, no prejudice, no distance, not even the span between his thoughts and hers. She knew him as easily, as surely and as logically as he must know her. And he was, she thought, beautiful . . .

At last he lifted his head, his dark eyes filled with unrest, with questions. Still, he smiled down at her before saying, "Do you see?" he said, "You cannot give up so easily. Not now."

Now? She opened her mouth to utter a word or two, but he was continuing, murmuring softly, "Believe me when I tell you that you have no choice but to let your horses go, if you wish them to live. Do not choose death, for them, for yourself."

Death? What was he talking about? All she could think of at this moment was life; wonderful, fascinating life . . . with him.

With him?

Suddenly the bubble burst, time once again intruded. It all came back to her. She was in danger. He was in danger. How could she have forgotten? Wasn't the roar of the hooves enough to remind her of the impossibility of their situation? The need for quick action?

And *he* was in the way.

As though she had been jerked unwillingly back into the throb of present time, she awoke, remembering exactly who she was and worse, who he was. She gave him a push. "No," she stated firmly, "you are wrong. I do not have to choose anything. And though I don't intend to die, I will not lose my equipment."

Not giving him a chance to answer, she broke out of his arms and ran as fast as she could back to the wagon, where, rounding it, she heaved the remaining pieces of her tools into the carry-all. Then she sprinted toward the front of the buggy, where she jumped up onto the seat and, taking hold of the reins, gave them a jerk and cried, "Yah!"

But it was pointless, the team was already loose. Soaring Eagle had unhitched them.

"No!" she screamed. "What have you done?"

But Soaring Eagle, still on the ground, ignored her. Instead of speaking, he sent her a glance so full of raw heat, Kali was taken aback. There was no denying it: Whatever he felt for her, it was strong. But what was it? Passion or hate?

She had no time, however, in which to debate the matter philosophically, since he had turned and was racing toward her, his movements so agile and quick, she was barely able to scoot an inch away before he had reached her. And without another minute passing, he had picked her up from the seat as though she weighed no more than a sack of potatoes.

She kicked out at him. "Let me down."

"*Haiya*, what trouble you are. Listen with your ears instead of your white man's pocketbook. Do you know that you could die here?" He tramped quickly toward one of the team horses. "You are to get on this animal, do you understand? You are to ride him to the rise over there where I led my other horses," he pointed. "You will be safe there."

Oh, no she wouldn't.

She kicked out at him again, not that it did her any good. Failing this, she screamed at him, "I will not."

"You will, too."

"Will not!" She gave a jerk of her foot toward that portion of his anatomy she knew might be vulnerable. It was a low blow and she knew it. However . . .

"*Haiya!*" He held her at arm's length. "You do not play fair."

"Neither do you, using your brute strength on me."

"I am trying to save you." As if to give emphasis to the fact, he heaved her up onto the back of the animal, but in doing so, she came free from him, and like a small child, squirmed through his arms, jumping to the ground and shooting back to the wagon as fast as she could go.

He followed her, catching her before she reached it. "What great, terrible trouble you are," he repeated himself, picking her up and holding her under the crook of his arm, her feet at his back, where she could do little damage.

"Then don't bother with me," she hollered, struggling.

"At this moment, I would like nothing better than to see you never again," he agreed, "but because you followed me here, I am responsible for you and I will not let you die."

She looked up to catch a range of emotions—anger, fear, annoyance—warring across the battlefield of his features. But something else was there, too. What? Concern, surely. But also another emotion—anxiety? Anxiety and . . . *passion* . . . for her? She stared hard at him, hoping to capture that look again and commit it to memory. But too quickly, it was gone.

So she reverted to her tongue, spitting out again, "You won't get me on that horse, I promise you."

"*Annisa.* Fine," he acknowledged at last, drawing in a deep breath. With barely a pause, he motioned to Gilda, bringing her to his side, while he took giant steps to his horse. Keeping Kali tucked under his arm, he drew out his rifle. "You take the horses to the rise over there and stay put," he said to Gilda. "Do not return once you get to safety, no matter what this one says." He sent Kali a sharp glare. "Do you understand?"

It was Gilda who nodded.

"*Soka'pii,*" he said to the other woman. "Now go."

"No!" Kali wiggled, kicked, then wiggled some more until she found herself dropping free. She hit the ground with an omph. But this was no deterrent to her. "Soaring Eagle, please," she shouted, coming to her feet, "the wagon's our only escape."

"Are you batty? Look behind you."

She did. In the heat of their escapades, she had failed to notice how close the danger was. Alas, if the dust in the air and the commotion all around them were an indicator, they had only a few moments left before . . .

"Come," he said and he swept Kali once more into his arms.

She glanced up at him, wide-eyed. "We're not leaving?"

"No."

"Then . . . you're going to stay with me?" Awed, she couldn't keep the relief from her tone. She added, "We're going to die together?"

But his response was unusual. He grinned down at her. "Not if I can help it."

This said, he darted forward, leaping up into the buggy seat so easily, he might have flown there. He deposited her in the back, saying, "Stay there, and take out your gun."

She did as told, and as she did so, he raised his own rifle into the sky. "Now, when I give the word, fire a shot into the air and keep shooting until the cattle either stop, or go in another direction. Do you understand?"

She nodded.

The moment of truth had come. She could hear nothing; nothing but the thunder of beating hooves over the dry prairie dirt.

"Get ready," he shouted. "We must allow your guide to get to the rise. She's almost there. All right. On the count of three. One, two . . . three."

They both fired at the same time. Again, another shot, then another.

Heart pumping, Kali held her breath. Were they going to make it? It seemed doubtful.

One moment. Two. Then it happened. A miracle. It had to be a miracle. The steers turned.

Kali sat still, shocked, speechless. She had been saved. Saved. And as she stared at the impossible, she was unable to move, say or do anything. It was odd. Poised for the worst, there was a strange feeling of being let down. But also, within her was a stronger emotion. One of great relief.

Kali licked her lips, and in doing so realized there was more than prairie dust that clung to them. The memory of this man's kiss remained there, too. She sent him a surreptitious glance.

He was breathing hard, the movement emphasizing the width and breadth of his chest, and Kali found it difficult to look away. All the same, she managed it, staring off in the same direction that he was.

It was another few moments before she was able to talk, and even then, all she could do was whisper, "It worked," not thinking that he might hear her over the clamor of the pounding hooves.

But he did hear, and looking back at her, he brought her face around to him, placing a finger under her chin and tilting her face up toward him as he so very slowly bent close to her. And without another word being spoken between them, he kissed her, the touch of his lips over hers as sweet as a lazy midsummer day. "Of course it worked," he murmured against her lips, his breath sweet, fresh and musky all at the same time. "It was not in my mind that we should perish here this day." And then he did the unthinkable one more time; he kissed her as though he had every right to do so.

Perhaps it was because her senses were already so heightened. Or maybe it was because everything about him seemed right. All she knew was that, while her arms crept around him to nuzzle his neck, she wanted more. More of him, more of this, more of . . . something . . . And she uttered, "Please."

"Please what?" he asked, lifting his head only a fraction from hers.

She couldn't say. In truth, she didn't know the answer to that question, herself. Indeed, the extent of her certainty was limited to this moment, restricted to the knowledge that she didn't ever want to leave the comfort of Soaring Eagle's arms. Was it possible that he could hold her like this forever?

Dumbfounded at her thoughts, she gulped, staring up at him. "Soaring Eagle," she said, "I—I . . ."

She what?

Patiently he appeared to wait for her to finish whatever it was that was on her mind, but it was difficult for her to continue when she wasn't sure of her intent herself.

However, she tried again, "Soaring Eagle, I—I seem to have . . ."

Again, she stopped. Still, he didn't speak, though he did watch her with guarded eyes, as though he might like to read her thoughts—while holding his own close to him.

At last she tried again, "Soaring Eagle, I—I seem to have . . ." *some feeling for you,* she finished to herself. *Some strange inclination that feels as though it is as deep, as entrenched and as vital as the very air that I breathe . . .*

Aloud, she uttered, "I seem to have placed my life into the right hands, your very capable hands. I wouldn't be here now if not for you. You've saved my life, as well as my camera, my buggy, my horses. I . . ." she couldn't finish.

And he didn't react; not in the least, not even to utter a word of acknowledgment. But he did reach up a hand to her, trailing the backs of his fingers down over her cheek.

At his touch, shock waves reverberated through her body, and she shut her eyes against the frenzy of raw hunger that washed over her. *Dear Lord,* she prayed, *what was all this excitement? How could a mere graze from a man create such longing?* Not knowing the answer— alas, little caring—she swooned in toward him, her body fitting up snugly against his.

She wouldn't think. She needed this. She needed him, wanted him; his touch, his beingness, his attention. All of him.

Ah, she thought. This was surely love.

No! came the instantaneous rejoinder.

It couldn't be love. Such a thing would be impossible. Why, the very thought of it was forbidden, for her, for him.

Still . . .

Mouth open, she gazed up at him with what probably amounted to shock, though she tried her best to hide any emotion from his watchful eyes.

She looked away, off into the distance. What she required was time; time and distance. Yes, that was it.

She needed to be alone, needed to sort this out analytically. After all, she had her entire life before her, her career, her ambition.

Still . . .

All at once, he seemed too close to her, and she to him. Could he read her thoughts? Would he realize what was happening to her?

Hoping she hadn't presented him with the key to her heart written there on her sleeve, she scooted away from him, sighing when his arms dropped to his side. She said, "Thank you for what you have done, Soaring Eagle, but I'll be fine now." She glanced away from him. "I—I'm sorry if I have clung to you overly much."

He must have sensed what was happening to her, for all he replied was, "No problem, ma'am," as though nothing untoward had happened to them. He added, however, "I enjoyed it."

And out the corner of her eye, she saw his lips turn up in a half grin, a look that was as disturbing to her as his kiss had been a few moments earlier. He continued, saying, "I enjoyed myself very much. Just as I'll be relishing your company all through the night tonight."

That rather suggestive comment earned him a startled glance from her. "Tonight?"

"Unless you want to miss the Medicine Pipe ceremony."

Kali knew her eyes must have popped open. "The Medicine Pipe ceremony? Then you've changed your mind? You'll take me to it?"

She saw him glance skyward, watched him grimace before he said, "I guess so, ma'am. I guess so."

Chapter 9

*. . . comfortable and convenient myths eased
the way.*

Peter Iverson, *When Indians Became Cowboys*

It was a good thing, Kali thought a few minutes later, that she had scooted away from Soaring Eagle when she did, putting some distance between them. The sounds of gunshots, of masculine voices; of hooting, hollering, and loud, blustering yelping came upon them rather quickly.

Four cowpunchers rode into view, looking as unkempt and as greasy as if they hadn't bathed or changed clothes in well over a month. They were obviously on the tail end of the stampeding herd and, Kali thought, none too generously, might have started it. They espied Soaring Eagle at once.

"Why looky at what we've got here, boys, would ya," said one of them. "An Injun. Soaring Eagle, ain't it?"

Soaring Eagle didn't utter a word, though he did stand up in the wagon seat with shotgun in hand, ready to confront these men if need be.

128

"Now, we ain't disturbin' you none, are we?"

Again Soaring Eagle didn't deign to answer. It would have been difficult to do so, perhaps even folly, to say even a single word: All four cowboys had their guns drawn, and they were aimed at him.

A shot was fired at Soaring Eagle's head; missed. Soaring Eagle barely blinked.

But that was enough to spur Kali to her feet. She came up sputtering, mad as the flaming color of her hair, and she hissed, "Well, well, well," she took a step forward. "What's this? Cowboys who don't belong on Indian land running their cattle on it, just the same? Taking potshots at a man? What for?"

All four men looked taken aback, if only for a second.

Kali pressed advantage, saying, "Well, I must admit, boys, that if you didn't disturb him," she pointed to Soaring Eagle, "you certainly did me."

One of the bullies, the one who'd been doing all the talking so far, eased back his Stetson with the barrel of his gun. "Ma'am?" he said, for the moment looking more than a little puzzled. "What're you doing out here with this Injun?"

Kali grinned. "Maybe I'm a government agent who's been sent to spy on you cowboys."

"Ma'am?"

"Perhaps I'm a newspaper reporter, wanting to get the latest scoop on poaching by the surrounding ranchers and cowhands. Or maybe I'm only here to take pictures of the Indians."

"Ma'am?" the cowboy repeated, as though his vocabulary had taken a steep dive for the worst. "Ma'am, you're here with an Injun."

Kali frowned. "Good observation. Do you have any objections?"

"Why I reckon so, ma'am. Plenty of 'em."

Choosing to ignore this, Kali didn't respond. Instead, she climbed over the seat and came to stand next to Soaring Eagle. He tried to place her behind him, but she elbowed her way forward.

And Kali, never one to fear coming directly to the point, asked, "What are you four good-for-nothings doing on this land?"

Each one of the cowboys grinned, as though caught out in a lie, although only one of them answered. "Why, ma'am," he said, "them cows, they plumb got outa hand. I do declare, they did. . . . *What?*" he snapped as Kali sent the man a poisonous stare.

It was in her mind to jump to the ground and give these men the tongue lashing they so richly deserved. Soaring Eagle, however, held her back, reaching out to catch her by the wrist. It was as though he had read her mind. But when she glanced back, Soaring Eagle shook his head.

"Why, ma'am, don't 'ya believe us?" said the cowboy.

"No," she stated plainly. "And I think you know you're trespassing. Now why, may I ask, are you aiming your guns at me and my friend, gentlemen? You're not afraid of a woman and a . . . an Injun, are you? . . . *What?*"—Kali mimicked the cowpoke—"Didn't your mothers teach you better manners?"

All four men scowled at her, however, all four men pocketed their fire arms.

"Now," Kali said, brushing the dust off her skirt, "since no real harm has been done, I won't press charges."

"Ma'am?" Again the talkative cowboy looked baffled, as though she might be speaking to him in Greek rather than plain English.

She ignored him. "But I am going to have to take this up with the Indian agent unless those cows are off this land within the hour."

"Oh, are ya now?" came the sardonic rejoinder. "Well, you do that, ma'am. You jest do that." And he laughed.

"Or," she said, "I might have to press charges with the sheriff."

More laughter.

"Or the governor or the press. Whomever. I'm not particular," she added. "You almost killed me with your runaway cows, gentlemen. And you've certainly brought my work for the day to an end. It's a good thing for you that this Indian was here and was quick thinking enough to avert a disaster."

"Well, now, would ya jes listen to that? An Injun savin' a white girl?"

"That's right," she said. "And he saved your reputations, too, gentlemen. You don't want to become known as murderers, do you?"

More laughter, although what these men found funny about that particular statement escaped Kali.

She said, "So remember that if you're figuring to keep those cattle on this land. There will be trouble. Now get out of my sight." And with no desire for further conversation, she spun around and sat down in the seat with such a huff, the wagon swayed.

So caught up was she in her own thoughts, she didn't notice that Soaring Eagle sent a wicked grin to the cowboys, although she did hear him say, "Well, boys, you heard the lady," before he jumped down from the wagon.

She watched as Soaring Eagle made his way to the front of the wagon where he picked up two harnesses.

She worried for him, since she didn't hear the imminent sounds of the cowboys' departure. Why wasn't Soaring Eagle alarmed? she wondered as she watched him jaunt toward the small rise, the place where Gilda and the rest of the horses still stood.

Out of the corner of her eye, Kali beheld a sight she dreaded: One of the cowboys had raised his gun, his eye trained on the small of Soaring Eagle's back.

Without thinking, Kali jumped up and turned to face the culprit, frowning. "What are you doing?" she asked. "Have you no honor?"

A nervous chuckle was all the answer she received, as all four cowpokes reined in their geldings and without so much as a tip of their hats to her, galloped off.

Good, thought Kali. *Let them go shoot at rocks instead of people.*

In a huff, she resumed her seat.

"How dare they talk to me that way. How dare they talk to you that way." Kali sat fuming, long after the cowmen had made their exit. Both Soaring Eagle and Gilda stood beside the wagon, having brought back the team horses. "I won't have it, I tell you. I simply won't have it. Is this the sort of prejudice you have to endure on a daily basis?" she asked of Soaring Eagle.

"Not every day," he replied. "Only when I go into town."

"It could be worse," said Gilda, "if white woman not be here. Might have killed Soaring Eagle."

"Killed him? Oh, surely not. They were only poking fun, weren't they? I must admit it was hardly what I would call great entertainment, but . . . I mean, Soaring Eagle is, after all, on his own land. They're the interlopers."

Gilda shrugged, while Soaring Eagle remained sto-ically silent.

"Do you think they'll get their cattle and go?" asked Kali.

"Maybe." It was Soaring Eagle who answered. "You might have frightened them into doing it . . . at least for today. But we'll have to see what tomorrow brings."

"Yes, we'll see," said Kali thoughtfully. "We'll just see. I don't intend to let this drop so easily."

"Neither do they." It was Soaring Eagle speaking from over his shoulder. Both he and Gilda were fast at work, hitching up the team. "Neither do they."

Kali jumped down from her seat and came toward them. "Here," she said, "let me help." She grabbed hold of a harness and set to work herself. "I'm sorry," she said to Soaring Eagle. "I was wrong when I said that what was going on here might be a case of simple misunderstanding."

Soaring Eagle nodded.

But Kali went on, "Why, those men were nothing but bullies, keeping their guns trained on me while I was talking . . . Drawing on you when your back was turned."

"*Au*, they are bullies," said Soaring Eagle, "and have no more wit than to think they are big because they carry big guns. Perhaps they try to make up for . . . something else which is too small to men-tion."

And while he and Gilda snickered, Kali, not under-standing, frowned at them. "What do you mean?"

"Never mind," said Soaring Eagle. "They might be hired killers."

"Hired?"

"*Aa*," said Soaring Eagle. "It is a strange practice that

the white man engages in. And it is hard to understand what sort of weakness in a man allows him to pay another to do his killing for him."

Kali frowned. "What makes you think they could be hired?"

"I have heard tales of other whites, those who plow the land or those who raise sheep. These people speak of this thing."

Kali didn't comment. In faith, she was shocked. What sort of hypocrisy was this? Landowners who professed to be law-abiding, God-fearing people, hiring killers? For what? For the price of a bit more land?

Soaring Eagle's look at her was full of scorn. "Does that make you afraid?"

Kali shrugged.

"It is possible," he said, "that those men will leave you alone if you ignore them and what they have done this day."

Kali turned on him. "Ignore them? How could I ignore them after what I've seen?"

"It would be safer for you if you did."

"Perhaps," she said, "but I've never been one to take an easy road simply because it would be safer."

"Still," he said, "it might be more pleasant for you if you did."

"Pleasant? As if I would want that."

"Wouldn't you?"

Kali threw down the buckle she was securing and took a step away. "Do you need to ask?"

He didn't respond.

"This is unbelievable. How can you think that, after what happened here today, I would try to pretend that . . . that . . . Is that all the respect you have for me?"

He arched a bow, giving her a questioning look.

"Didn't we already have this talk? If what you are telling me is true, I will do all I can to help you learn the truth."

He shrugged. "Will you? Is your skin not white?"

Kali reeled under the remark. It was a low blow, pure prejudice, and she knew it. But she kept her opinion to herself. In the past, however, her reaction might have been different; she might have spoken up and argued with him for all it was worth. But not now. It could be entirely possible that he *did* have good reason to speak as he was.

She said, "This whole thing is going to need investigation. I'll start with Mr. Black tomorrow. Whatever is happening here on this range, I swear I'm going to get to the bottom of it."

"That is good," said Soaring Eagle. "Just ensure you don't end up *at* the bottom of it. But I don't think you'll be seeing Mr. Black tomorrow."

"Oh?"

"The Medicine Pipe ceremony is tonight. If you want to attend that ceremony, you will have to come with me."

"Really?"

"*Aa*, really." He pulled in a cinch. "There. Done. Gilda, take my pinto and go on back to the village. But do not tell them what has happened. I'll follow you with my herd and with Miss Wallace here."

Gilda nodded, and without another word to either of them, mounted the pony and left.

From her peripheral vision, Kali marked that Soaring Eagle watched the woman until she was no more than a speck on the horizon. Finally, he turned back to Kali, his eyes suddenly alight with mischief.

What now?

They were alone; utterly, completely alone—and she was not immune to his charms, a fact he probably knew well. But he didn't reach out to touch her as she had thought he might. Instead, cocking his head to the side, he said, "You came to my defense."

She shrugged.

"I did not expect that."

Looking away from him, she noted, "You would have done the same for me, I'm certain."

"True, but that is different, I think."

"Is it? I don't see how."

His eyes narrowed, as though he might dispute her, but in the end he merely commented, "It is possible that I owe you my life. So perhaps we are even. I saved you. You saved me. That way neither one of us is in each other's debt."

She nodded.

But then he grinned, adding, "Pity."

Chapter 10

*Without being romantic or naive, we can argue
that studies of reservation life that see only
poverty and despair do not see the whole picture.*

Peter Iverson, *When Indians Became Cowboys*

Had he been asleep all these years? What was happening to him?

Something was, that was a certainty, for Soaring Eagle's spirits were as buoyant as a feather caught in the up-current of a wind. Indeed, he felt as innocent as a child and as carefree as an adolescent. And why?

Because of a kiss. Because of a woman. Because he had found her at last. The one.

Shifting his weight in the saddle, Soaring Eagle glanced at Kali as she sat upon the wagon seat, her beautiful red hair aglow, shining beneath the radiant rays of a brilliant sun. Her skin was a delicate, pale affair, though, he noted, she was turning slightly pink despite the covering from the brim of her hat. Slim to a fault, Soaring Eagle thought she might surely blow away with the slightest hint of a breeze.

But that delicacy was an illusion, he realized. He had

137

only known her for little more than a day, yet already he had witnessed her spirit and her courage, both more dynamic than many men of his acquaintance.

He'd thought he'd hated her. He'd thought she was like all the rest, and had been ready to send her packing. But with no more than a few hours of being in her presence, he had changed his mind.

This afternoon, everything about her had been right. And he wondered, was it possible for a man to be ensnared by a kiss?

It must be so. Truly, it must be so. Even now, he recalled how her red lips had fit his perfectly, as though made for him. Her breath had been sweet, tasting of honey, mint and pure, intoxicating female. Her fragile scent still clung to him; it alone, a stimulant, making him wish he could do things he dare not do . . . at least not yet.

What would she say if he told her his thoughts? Would she think him crazy? After all, they barely knew one another.

No, that didn't seem right. He felt as though he'd known her a lifetime.

And she? Did she feel the same way? Dare he ask?

Probably not, he decided. After all, she was female . . . and white. And to date, his acquaintance with this breed of person was not full of promise.

Yet, remembering back to the way she had stood up to those cowboys, defying them to do their worst . . .

Aa, there was something different about this one. What that was exactly, however, he didn't know. But this he did realize: Somehow, in some way, that kiss had opened his senses to her. It was as though he'd caught a glimpse; a glimpse of a life they might share together . . . a life filled with love, with passion, with devotion.

He wanted that. *Aa*, he wanted that.

Yes, there would be barriers to cross, but he wouldn't think of that now. After all, what was life if not one barrier after another?

He sighed. Sometimes he wished the world around him would go away and let him live the life he was meant to live, without censure, without interference and without prejudice—if only for a few days.

But, he finished to himself, he was who he was. And Kali was who she was.

And though on the surface, their worlds seemed universes apart, were they really? What was prejudice, after all, but a failure to communicate fully and completely?

Perhaps he should speak to her on the subject. Certainly, she was not repelled by him. She had proved that earlier today, there in his arms.

It would take courage on his part; courage to speak out and tell her the truth, courage to say what was in his heart, for he was treading on unknown ground.

It would be an about face for him, as well, and she might doubt him. She might even laugh at him. Was he willing to chance that?

Still, life without a few risks was no more than mere existence, wasn't it? At this moment, opportunity was his. Would he reach out and take it?

Or should he adhere to the easier, the calmer path? After all, he was not without romantic involvements, and with women he understood much more easily than this one.

And yet he couldn't deny that today, with her, he'd

felt alive, whole, complete, as if he might be able to take on the whole white world alone. And that was something.

Aa, *that was something . . .*

The sun was setting by the time they reached the Indian encampment. Sitting high atop a butte and looking down on the village, Kali wondered if she had ever witnessed a more peaceful sight. In the reddening rays of twilight, the lodges looked picturesque and serene, their images reflected colorfully from their inside fires. Streaks of gray-blue smoke curled up from each of the lodges, and on the air was the appetizing aroma of supper.

She let her gaze meander a short distance from the camp, there espying a pony herd grazing silently in the lush, tall grasses. All about her, above and below, were larks, sparrows, even thrushes serenading the listening ear with sweet, soulful music. Enchanted, Kali inhaled and was set upon not only by the scents of many campfires but by the fragrant meadows, the wildflowers and the clean, solid feel of the earth.

Oh, how she would love to capture this moment on film, and her fingers itched to grab her camera. But she controlled the impulse. She dared not do it. Plus, the camera was loaded on her wagon, which sat at the foot of the butte.

She and Soaring Eagle had left the vehicle a while earlier and climbed to this spot, coming to a halt, here at the butte's crest. Both she and Soaring Eagle were silent, bathing themselves in the beauty that surrounded them. Before them, vast mountains sat off to the west, while the last rays of the sun were sketching the clouds above in kaleidoscopic colors of deep reds, pinks and oranges.

What an artist was nature, Kali thought, as a feeling of well-being swept through her. With only a slight turn of her head, she glanced toward Soaring Eagle. At the sight, she caught her breath. Did he know, she wondered, what a handsome silhouette he made? Standing there against the crimson rays of the glorious sunset?

And the only thing that came to mind as she continued to gaze at him was that of dignity, of majesty, as though he were lord and master over all this domain. Not even his cowboy attire could detract from the image of quiet strength, of fellowship and understanding.

All at once it came to her: This man possessed an unearthly trait; a spirituality that was as rich as this lush prairie. He was different from anyone she had ever encountered; as though he were the embodiment of thousands of years of cultural perfection. And for a moment, she understood. He didn't merely believe in the godly qualities of the world around him, he lived his spiritual nature day to day, as easily as if he were the very soul of this vast, beautiful land.

It was an odd thing for a sensible girl like Kali to realize. Never, on any of her previous expeditions, had she ever been given cause to become even remotely attracted to the beliefs of any of the native peoples that she had photographed. Certainly, though her interest was centered on the aboriginal cultures of the world, she had never considered that a single one of these communities might have something to offer her in the way of personal insight.

She'd been wrong.

But perhaps she'd never really looked at them with unbiased eyes . . . until now.

She studied him. Though outwardly Soaring Eagle was as different from her as a summer day is to winter, there was much about him that was familiar. Like a nobleman, he possessed obvious pride, though in truth, Soaring Eagle exuded more magnetism, more charisma and perhaps more presence of mind than any other man she had ever met.

Staring at him, she knew without doubt that the rumors she had heard about his people—if Soaring Eagle were to be a representative—were false. Dirty heathens, filthy beggars, thieves. So far she had found none of these descriptions to be true. In faith, far the opposite.

And if the rumors were false, she carried the thought one step further, what was the truth? Could she discover it? Could she capture that truth, whatever it was, on film? For coming generations?

"Soaring Eagle," she voiced softly, drawing his attention to her. "It's almost night and it occurs to me that I'm far away from home."

He nodded. "Do not be afraid. No one will hurt you here."

"I'm not afraid."

He grinned at her. "Of course not."

"It's true. I'm only thinking that perhaps, if I'm to stay here, we might send word to my father to join me. Otherwise," she said, "if I'm not home soon, he will worry."

"I will see to it as soon as we enter camp."

"Thank you. Ah, Soaring Eagle?"

He raised an eyebrow.

"Where am I to stay in the meantime?"

"Do not worry. You can stay with me."

With him? Kali gasped. She opened her mouth to speak; however, no words of censor, nor even of wisdom, spilled forth.

Shaking herself, she knew she had to say something. Soaring Eagle was, after all, only a man. And like men everywhere, she supposed, he would test the ground, leaving it to the woman to erect barriers.

"Ah, Soaring Eagle—"

"My grandmother has a lodge," he interrupted, "that is large and will provide you with enough room to sleep comfortably . . . that is, if you sleep this night."

"Oh. Ah . . . and is there a r-reason," she stumbled, "why you are thinking I might not sleep?"

He turned his gaze on her, his look telling her clearly that he was enjoying himself. Worse, that he sensed her discomfort and was amused by it.

All he said, however, was, "Keeping a Medicine Pipe is not without its difficulties."

"Oh?" said Kali.

"*Aa*. He who would have the Pipe must pay well for it with many ceremonials and feasts. It is not a duty for a weak or a poor man."

"I see," said Kali, and she did. Her father had intimated as much. "And this has something to do with why I might not sleep?"

"Perhaps," he agreed, his eyes bright. "When a man is ready to pass on the duties of the Medicine Pipe to another, this is not kept secret from others in the tribe. One of our chiefs, Comes Running Bird, has had the Pipe in his possession for several years and he is getting ready to find a new member who can take it. And so any able-bodied man who does not wish to accept the responsibility for the Pipe, may sleep outside his lodge, that he not be given it. For to be offered the Pipe and not accept it can bring on death or hardship to one's family."

"Oh? Is that so?" She paused. "I'm still a little unclear about what this has to do with my sleep."

Soaring Eagle grinned. "Do you hear the sound of singing from the camp?"

She listened. "Yes."

"That is the Medicine Pipe society singing Owl songs and drumming. They will keep this up all night, sending out people from the society who will accompany Comes Running Bird. He will have the Pipe concealed beneath his robes. If they can catch a man unaware, he being a man of some importance and wealth, there will be a ceremony to transfer the duties and the rites of the Pipe to the other. This singing and going about will take place throughout the night."

"Oh, I see. So, is this what I might be able to photograph?"

Soaring Eagle shrugged. "I have not promised you that. Only that I will speak to the council on your behalf."

"All right. I expect that's good enough."

He nodded, then eased his lips into another of those disarming smiles before he commented, "Did you think there could be another reason you might not sleep?"

She turned away, momentarily embarrassed by the intimacy of the question, unaware that her chin reached for the sky.

As though to put her at ease, however, he said, "I do not share my grandmother's lodge if that is what you are thinking."

"The thought never entered my mind," she lied, still looking away from him.

"Come, let us sit here on the prairie," he gently placed a hand beneath her elbow, "and I will tell you the story of how the Medicine Pipe came to be in our possession. Would you like to hear it?"

"Yes," she admitted, turning toward him, her embarrassment disappearing as easily as that. "Very much."

"*Soka'pii*," he said, bending gracefully into a sitting position, motioning her to do the same. But it wasn't to be an easy task for her. To sit down daintily required a much longer dress than her hunting outfit provided, especially since she couldn't very well sit as he was; her skirt was too short. True, she wore puffy trousers beneath her skirt, but that didn't mean her modesty was more easily shielded. Finally she settled for sitting with her knees and legs to the side.

He began, "It is told to us that it happened long ago . . ." He frowned at her as she tried to straighten her skirt.

She glanced up, catching his eye, which was trained on her. "Yes?" she said, bestowing him with what she trusted would be a sweet smile, perhaps in hopes of encouraging him to keep speaking, thereby drawing attention away from her discomfort.

But this was not to be, and he said, "May I be of any help?"

She laughed self-consciously. "It's this skirt. Though the outfit is good for hunting or for walking through the prairie's grasslands, it doesn't cover my legs adequately. And even though I wear boots and these Turkish trousers, it's not quite the same, is it?" She pulled at the offending article, trying to lengthen it, if only by intention alone.

"I think I can help," he said, coming to his feet, and before she could utter a word of protest, he was clamoring down the butte, in the direction where they had left his pony herd and her wagon. He came back to her presently with a brightly colored red and blue blanket under one arm and an orange and yellow one under the other.

"They were on a few of my ponies," he informed her as he unfolded one of the blankets and set it out over the grassy soil. Then helping her first to her feet, he sat her down on the blanket, finishing by throwing the other of the two over her lap. Standing back, as though observing his handiwork, he said, "Is that better?"

She grinned up at him. "Much. Thank you." And pulling the warmth of the quilt over her legs, she said, "Do continue your story. Please."

Once again, he settled himself gracefully into a sitting position, only this time, he sat on the blanket, quite close to her.

But she didn't pull away. In truth, she wanted him to be close.

As though he were perfectly aware of this, he leaned in even nearer to her, his head mere inches from hers as he began, "It is told by our elders that there was once a Blackfeet man who was struck down by the Thunder. Now as the man lay there on the prairie, barely alive, the Thunder Chief came to him in vision, holding a pipe. The man was instructed to make a pipe like the one the Thunder Chief was holding. He was also told to make a medicine bundle for it, and the medicine bundle was to contain the skins of many animals. In this way, if ever any of our people are sick or are dying, if a vow is made and a ceremony given, the sick will be cured."

Kali nodded. "And has this happened?"

"*Aa*, many times." Soaring Eagle scooted an inch closer to her so that his arm was touching her arm. It was no more than a slight graze, yet Kali felt the effect of it all the way to the tips of her toes. But she didn't pull away. Alas, she leaned in toward him as well. He continued, "But there is more," he said, his voice very, very low. "After the Thunder Chief appeared to this man, a grizzly bear came to him, telling him that he, the grizzly, was giving up his skin so that the man might make a large bundle. Said the grizzly, 'If you ever transfer the Medicine Pipe, you must steal upon the man quietly in the time before dawn, as does the grizzly. Take him by surprise, singing my song and give him the Pipe. He dare not refuse.'"

"Oh, I see," Kali whispered, her head so close to his that her breath fanned the wisps of hair at the side of his face. "Then that's why the men steal about in the middle of the night?"

"*Aa*," said Soaring Eagle softly. "The Owl songs that you hear down there are sung because the owl is an animal of the night, and by singing his song, the members ask the owl for help, that they might catch a man in sleep. This casts a spell over the man, that he may not escape. Before this time, the Blackfeet had never seen a Medicine Pipe, but now the ceremony is continued on and on, as the power of the bundle has cured many of our people."

"Oh," Kali stared at him, her eyes almost on a level with his as he bent in toward her.

He caught her gaze, his eyes mirroring a hushed intensity, as though he were anticipating something. But what?

She looked down and fidgeted with her hands nervously. She was awaiting something from him, too, she realized; needed something from him. However, exactly what that was, remained a mystery to her. She murmured, "That is a wonderful story," and chanced to glance up at him. But he wasn't looking at her directly then.

His attention seemed to be centered on her hands, seemingly engrossed with them. Feeling momentarily reprieved, Kali took a bit of time to watch him, herself mesmerized by the feeling that something imminent was upon them.

Finally he reached out and caught one of her hands in his own. At once, a rush of excitement swept up that arm, there where he touched.

Kali drew in closer to him; he turned her hand over in his own until her palm lay faceup. Then, before she knew it, he brought her hand to his lips, pressing a kiss there, square center.

Her breath caught as though her heart had stopped; then contrarily it picked up its pace, racing along as though it were swept up in a rush of gushing rapids, being drawn toward some unknown deluge. However, he was talking, giving her little opportunity to catch her breath.

"Once we get to camp," he said, "I would ask that you not mention anything about what you have seen today. The steers, the bullies, the stampede."

She nodded, although she sent him a quizzical look. When he didn't elaborate, she said, "All right. Is there any particular reason why I shouldn't?"

"In time I will tell the council what has transpired this day, but not until the ceremony has finished. There is no need to upset anyone until the function, which has already started, is done."

Kali nodded. "Fair enough. It isn't as though anyone

will be asking me questions anyway, is it?"

"*Saa*, no, but it is possible there might be some who are curious about you."

"What do you plan to tell y—your friends about me?"

He grinned, squeezing her hand, and she swallowed what felt like a congealed lump in her throat. "It's simple, I think," he said. "I will tell them that I have at last found a . . . wife."

Chapter 11

[Their songs] ought to be rescued from oblivion and permanently preserved.

Walter McClintock, *The Old North Trail*

"**W**ife?" She drew back at once, trying to pull her hand away from his, but he held on tightly. "Please, Soaring Eagle, be serious."

"I am."

"No, you're not. You're teasing me, though the good Lord only knows why."

"And if I were serious?"

"But you're not."

"But if I were, are you saying that you do not wish to marry me?"

"No, what I'm trying to say is that—"

"Then you *do* wish to marry me?"

She snorted. "Please Soaring Eagle . . ."

"Please what?"

"I—I'm not sure. But truly, tell me what you intend to say to your people about me?"

"Besides the fact that I have found the one; she, who

would be my wife—if I could only convince her of my sincerity, and if she would take me."

"Soaring Eagle . . . I—I know you're playing with me, that you don't mean the things you're saying."

"Of course not," he whispered, his face very close to her own.

She grunted, gazing away from him. "Will you tell them that I'm a photographer? That I wish to take their pictures?"

He paused, causing her to shift, to gaze at him. She caught her breath. He was already close, so near to her that all she had to do was breathe in and his clean scent filled her lungs.

And she thought, *even if he is playing a joke, I will never forget this; him, the land, the beauty, the West.*

He brought her hand to his heart, holding it there as he sighed into her ear. "I will tell my people what they will need to hear in order that they see you in the same light as I do. But it occurs to me that I still know very little about you, and yet, if I could, I would understand everything. So why don't you tell me every aspect about yourself, from your first memory in this life until this very moment. But in doing so, I would ask that you reveal it to me slowly. I would have it take a lifetime in the telling, if you please."

She gasped, her free hand coming up to brush across her chest, as though her heart required the contact in order to keep beating. She said, "Soaring Eagle, please. Y-you—what you're telling me defies good sense. I—I barely know you, and you, sir, are moving too swiftly."

"Am I? And yet you feel it too, don't you?"

"I—I admit there is something. I had thought to ignore whatever it is that is happening between us, for I don't understand it. I—I thought you disliked me."

"And so did I at first." He stared away from her, toward the Blackfeet camp, his grasp still clutching hers, keeping her fingers spread, there above his heart. "It's hard for me to like any white person, and you are white. But if I were to make an exception, you would be it, I think."

"But—"

"When I saw you talking to those men today, and you were defending me against them, I knew that you were . . . different. You are a good person, I think."

"I would like to believe so."

He nodded. "Until that moment, it had not occurred to me that the white race, much like the Indian, has its good and its bad people. Out here on the range, I have only seen the bad that your culture has to offer."

She sniffed. "Surely you exaggerate."

"Think you so?"

"Yes," she said, shaking her head. "Yes, I do."

"Ah," was his only response, though he looked deeply into her eyes. He asked, "And what is your answer?"

"To what?"

With his free hand, he placed a finger under her chin, bringing her face up close to his. He whispered, "I would make you my wife." With these simple words, he kissed her. And Kali, for all her analytical cleverness, forgot to think.

It wasn't a simple kiss, either. His lips spread over hers, opening her mouth to him with the gentle insistence of his tongue. And Kali, barely daring to breathe, found she was a willing recipient for all he had to give. He let go of her fingers to bring both his hands to her face, his thumbs tracing over her chin and cheeks.

It left her own hand free to rest there on his chest. And Kali was quick to note that the texture of his taut muscles, there through the material of his shirt, created a feeling within her that made her ache for that shirt's absence. But she was too shy to initiate the action. Alas, the mere idea of it was scandalous.

In that instant, however, his tongue found hers, frolicking with it. He nipped her lower lip, then kissed her again, making love to her with his lips as another man might use his entire body And when she thought she might at last be able to catch her breath, he kissed her all over again, repeating the entire affair.

Of their own accord, her arms scooted around his neck, bringing him closer. His hand came up to the back of her head, pulling her to him. And Kali surrendered.

"Do you feel it?" he whispered.

How could he talk? She nodded, breaking lip-to-lip contact, needing air, but her movement only gave him access to the sensitive places on her neck. Kali withered in his arms.

And it seemed a most natural act that he draw her onto her back, lying down, while he rested beside her, one of his legs thrown over hers, his arms surrounding her, his body leaning over hers.

He said, "A marriage between us would be almost impossible."

"Yes," she agreed.

"And yet I would not have you without it, and I think that I would very much like to have you."

"Have me?"

He just grinned down at her, the same sort of smile that had the ability to charm her right out of her wits. He said, "Have you in my arms. Keep you by my side. But my people would not understand why I would want you, yours would probably try to kill me if we attempted to do these things."

"Yes," she said. "That's true."

"And yet my heart demands that I risk it. What does yours say?"

"I—I don't know."

He pushed her hair back from her face as he gazed so tenderly down at her. "I think we should marry."

"I think you're crazy. Aren't you the same man who hated me last night?"

"*Aa*, yes, I thought I did," he said, bestowing her with a kiss, first against one eyelid, then the other. "But I have changed my mind. Would you like to know what I was doing that night we first met? The night on top of Chief Mountain?"

She nodded, reaching toward him, that she might touch him as he was touching her, desiring the feel of his skin, the warmth of it. She said, "I would like to hear that very much."

She didn't get very far in her caress of him, however, for he grabbed her hands and stilled them, kissing each of her fingers in turn. He smiled at her. "And now, dear Kali, I think you move too fast."

"Me?" she asked incredulously.

"*Aa*, you." With a grin, he lifted his head and said, "That night on the mountain, I was singing to the Night Light, our Mother, the Moon. I was asking her for guidance with my affections."

"Oh?" asked Kali, withdrawing from him, even if so very slightly. That statement had the sound of a man who was surrounded by maidens, all awaiting their chance at him. "Were you having difficulties with your . . . ah, affections?"

"*Aa*, that I was," he admitted. "I am twenty-eight

winters old, an age when many men have married. And yet I had not met a girl to whom I could give my devotion."

"Had?"

He smiled, nodding. "Had. Now, in the past, this would not have presented a problem to me, as I could have married anyone, knowing that if I found the one that I love with all my heart, I could still take her to my home and make her my wife."

Kali nodded. He was speaking of polygamy, of course. Didn't she already know that Indian men had once engaged in the practice?

"But now," he continued, "with the coming of the white man, and the white man's religion and his laws, I must be more selective. I had begun to fear that I would never meet the one, she to whom I could give everything that is in my heart to give."

"Oh, I see." Kali stared up and away from him, into the ever darkening sky above her. And once more she asked, "Had?"

But he merely gave her that half grin, the one that was becoming familiar to her. And he said, "My life has changed recently."

"Oh?"

He nodded, and taking her hand in his own, he said, *Iihtawaakomimmot. Inihkatsimat. A'painahkimma.* It's what I was singing that night."

> *"Ooooooooooo. Iihtawaakomimmot.*
> *Ooooooooooo. Inihkatsimat*
> *Ooooooooooo. A'painahkimma."*

He sang it again.

His voice was deep, clear, unfettered by the convention of classical training. At the sound of it, chills raced up and down her body.

To say that Kali sat beside him spellbound would not have done the word or Kali, for that matter, justice. Until this moment, no one had ever sung to her, let alone in such a hauntingly beautiful way.

Odd that these things had come from a man whom many of her contemporaries might consider inferior. And she couldn't help wondering, who was really the inferior? He who would chase after matters of material wealth, or he who would live with the balance of nature? Perhaps each was necessary, she conjectured, neither one being superior to the other; merely different.

She smiled at her thoughts.

"Now you sing it to me."

"Me?" She pulled back slightly.

He nodded.

"But I don't sing."

He scoffed. "All people sing. Some more than others, some better than others. But to sing is the breath of life. Now you do it. Here, I will help you."

He began:

"*Oooooooooooooooooooooo . . .*"

He stopped. "You are not singing."

"I . . . I couldn't. Really, I . . . I don't know the words. And I don't know your language."

"Then sing me one of your own."

"I . . . I don't know any."

But he was not to be put off. "Then," he said, "we will make up a song of our own. It will be our song. *Aa*, it is true, there might be trying times ahead of us, and I think we will need a song. Something that will bind us together."

Her throat constricted, and she felt the threat of tears in the back of her eyes. *Their song?*

Oh, how she liked the sound of that. Too much.

Looking toward him, she almost sobbed at the sight of the pure magic of him, at the thought of what he was suggesting. After a moment, she managed to say, "I— I'm no poet. I'm merely a photographer."

"You don't have to be a poet," he said, bringing his lips in close to her cheek. "We could start it this way . . ."

> *"Ooooovooooooooooo. When you hear my voice*
> *   on the wind,*
> *When you see the eagle fly,*
> *Know that these tell of my love for you."*

"That is beautiful, the words, the melody." She shifted her face until her lips were almost on a level with his.

He grinned at her, she felt it, there, against her cheek. He said, "Now you sing it."

"I . . . I couldn't." She backed away slightly, glancing at him. "My, but you are quite a poet."

"Ah," he slanted her a devilish grin. "And do you like me better as a poet or as a cowboy?"

"I . . . I think I like you fine the way you are, both ways."

"Enough to become one with me?"

She turned her face away from him and frowned. She was beginning to believe the man was serious. And this could never be—must never be. Though he touched her heart in a way no one had ever done, there was something within her that demanded she hold back from him. It was as though she distrusted the man, as though she knew instinctively that this one man could cause her great hurt.

Besides, didn't he realize? Didn't he know? Couldn't he see? She had a life of her own—responsibilities, obligations: her father, her work. She was a roamer, a seeker of new heights.

And Soaring Eagle? Didn't he have duties to perform for his people, for his tribe? Hadn't he been sent away to school so that he could become an asset to his community? It didn't take a genius to realize that while he would be tied to the reservation, she would be off, roaming the world, studying some faraway culture.

No, he, like she, had a life ahead that was as disconnected from the other as anything could be.

He might send her to dizzying heights, but, she thought soberly, perhaps there were some dreams that were not meant to be made into realities.

Well, best to take the tiger by the tail.

Inhaling deeply, she began, "You know that a . . . a union between us isn't possible. Though I might find you . . . charming, there are too many differences that mark us, differences that would make such a . . . a marriage . . . an unhappy state of affairs."

"You mean because I am Indian and you are not? Now, who is being prejudiced?"

His words came close to her ear, but she wouldn't turn her head that tiny distance to look at him. She dared not. His charm was too endearing, his pull too magnetic. And so she said, "It's not prejudice. As even you've pointed out, your people would never accept me for who I am. Always, I would be the white woman who stole away one of their own. And my people . . .

well, I don't need to say more. Apparently, you've already seen this for yourself."

"It would be difficult to create a marriage, it is true, but not impossible."

"I disagree," she said. "Besides, the petty intolerances would only be the beginning of our troubles. There are other things that set us apart, I'm afraid."

"Other things?"

"Yes. Contrasting mind-sets, if you will. Both those of a spiritual nature and those that are social. It would require quite a bridge to gap our differences. And I'm afraid I'm not very good at spanning distances."

"And yet," he countered, "no two people are ever alike. What a boring life it would be if no one had contrasting viewpoints about life."

"True. But most couples start with common realities—at least about the way life is lived, about the society in which they exist. But ours . . . No, I'm afraid you'd always be trying to change me, wouldn't you? And me you. I don't think that's a good way to start something as important as marriage."

"And yet some people begin with less than what we have."

She spun around, finding his face very close to her own. It was almost more than she could take. She wanted his arms around her, and yet at this moment she feared that. He was too potent, too desirable. And she had to keep her distance. She *had* to.

Still, she was curious, and she could barely help herself as she asked, "Please, Soaring Eagle, tell me. What things do we share? What do we have in common?"

For answer, he traced his fingers down her cheek, the simple action causing shivers of anticipation to leap about and within her, as though awakening her. And there in his eyes, she saw something she had never thought to witness in another's gaze: admiration, purely sensual and carnal.

She was held in awe by the look until at last he whispered, "Passion, excitement, that's what we have. Passion for life; admiration for one another. Surely you feel it, too."

"I—I . . ."

He placed a finger over her lips. "If you will listen, I will tell you a story that might help. It is about two people who were so different, it seemed that there would never be a happy ending for them. But what neither of them realized was that one alone, without the other, was only half alive. For you see, these things mean much. Would you like to hear the story?"

She nodded. "Yes. Yes, I think I would."

"Very well." He brushed his fingers down her arm, before gently taking her hand in his own. "This is a tale of a poor boy, who once loved a girl of some wealth. She would have nothing to do with him, that is, until he sang her this song."

"*Ooooooooooooooooooooo. Nitawahkahtaahiksi,
Miina'pitsiihtaat.
Ooooooooooooooooooooo. Kitsikakomimmokoo.
Kitsiikakomimmo.*"

As his voice lingered over the words, Kali felt awestruck by the beauty of the moment.

"It means," he said, " 'Sweetheart, do not worry. You are loved. I love you.' "

Kali shut her eyes and inhaled deeply. She hadn't known; hadn't been told, hadn't realized the enchantment of these people's legends. With a hand over her chest, she found it hard to utter a single word.

But she didn't need to speak at all, for Soaring Eagle was continuing,

"He captured her heart with this song, but her parents would not let her marry him, for he was too poor and could not provide for her. To them, their daughter was of a different ilk than he was, and they wanted nothing to do with him."

"But she loved him?"

"Very much," he replied. "Now in order to win the affection of the girl's parents, the young lad went to war to win honors and wealth. For only in this way might her parents look upon him as a potential husband for their daughter. And so, this he did, but he was gone so long that when he returned, he found that his love had fled her home and had not been seen in many, many moons. All assumed she was dead. It used to happen sometimes, although not very often. Parents arrange marriages to the best of their ability, but sometimes, the girl is so saddened by these agreements, that she will go out onto the prairie and kill herself."

"Oh, no, that's so sad. Please don't tell me this has a sad ending."

He grinned at her. "You must wait to decide for yourself. Now, this young man, coming back to camp, felt in his heart that his love was still alive and rather than settle down with another, he spent his life searching for her. He was called the wanderer and wherever he went, he would sing this song, their song, so that she would know him."

"And did he ever find her?"

Soaring Eagle nodded. "That he did, but by the time they finally did come together, they were old people, in the last years of their lives. He was blind, she almost so, but one day he heard her song in the hills behind his village, and when he heard it, his heart gladdened, for he knew her at once. He went to her and gave himself to her, and she to him. For you see, she, too, had never married. Some hearts are like that. They are made for each other, and no one else will do."

Kali sighed, drawing in toward him. "That's a lovely story."

"*Aa,* so it is. It is said that they are still together, in the Sand Hills, where my ancestors have all gone to live. And there, it is said, the two lovers are forever young and are forever in love."

Kali's heart quickened.

"And now, what do you think? Is that a happy ending?"

"Oh, very much so. It would have been tragic if they had never been able to meet in the flesh."

"Yes," he said, squeezing her hand. He was silent for many moments, until at last, he said, "And so, too, should we marry, that we may yet know one another in the flesh."

"I—I—I . . . No. I'm not convinced. Legends are beautiful things, but they're not about real people and they're not the stuff out of which reality is made."

He sighed. "Think you not?"

"That's what I believe."

"Then," he said on a sigh, "we may never marry, for it's true. Our path would be difficult and it would take us both, acting together, to conquer the bigotry that surrounds us. But there is one other thing: Have you considered that our differences could make us stronger? closer? deeper in love?"

Kali paused, for the pull of his attraction was that strong. At last, however, she shook herself, as though to free herself from his appeal. And she said, "No, I fear it would not work out that way. You see, I don't trust matters of the heart."

"Ah, I understand. You are afraid of love."

"No, I'm not. I'm simply being reasonable about it. Few couples are ever happy who start with as much against them as we would have. Don't you see? There are some things one must think through completely, before acting. It's not good to simply presume that all will be well, without any forethought."

"And yet," he said, "there are few couples who ever have the promise of complete, lasting, and devoted love. Kali, I would have you know what is in my heart, and I what is in yours, so that, if the time ever comes, and you wish me by your side, you have merely to open your mouth."

At these words, Kali's heart ached. In faith, she felt close to tears. But why, she couldn't say. She was doing the right thing. She *knew* she was doing the right thing.

"I should tell you what is in my heart," he continued, "but sometimes a man can be reticent. It is not always easy for a man to put his deepest longings into words. Do you see? And so in my culture, there are times when a young man will sing a song . . . especially he will sing one to his sweetheart. It is the only way he can tell her the things he dare not speak."

"He does?" She asked, feeling practically mesmerized by Soaring Eagle's words.

He nodded. Alas, he was little more than a hairsbreadth away, but he leaned in closer still, and began softly:

> *"Ooooooooooooooooooooo.*
> *When you hear the wolf howl.*
> *He brings you my message.*
> *I cry for you.*
> *Ooooooooooooooooooooo.*
> *When the wind calls your name,*
> *Know that I search for you.*
> *And when we find one another,*
> *   the earth will become a happy place.*
> *Ooooooooooooooooooooo. You are my love."*

Shivers ran up and down Kali's spine. She shut her eyes, the feeling within her so rich, so intense, she thought she might perish if she didn't respond in kind.

But he gave her little chance to do so. When the last note trailed away, he kissed her, his lips as gentle a caress as the wind about which he sang.

And then, lifting his head, he said those few words she had been waiting all her life to hear, "I love you, Kali Wallace. I think I have always loved you."

"Oh, Soaring Eagle," she replied in a rush.

"Marry me, Kali. Know that it is not an easy thing for me to ask. But I have never meant anything more in my life."

She drew back from him, her gaze trained on some spot midway between his kerchief and the top buttons of his shirt. "Please, Soaring Eagle, please understand. I—I can't," she said. "Though your legends are beautiful, and your songs touch my heart in a way none other has ever done, you must know that I can't . . . that we can't. For your sake, as much as for mine, I have to think logically, with an eye to the future. Perhaps," she offered, "legends can afford to indulge the desire of the heart. Real people, however, seldom can."

"I disagree," he said. "Real people must follow their hearts, if they are to attain peace with themselves and within the circle of life."

Kali came up onto her knees before standing up entirely. To her horror she was shaking. "I can't marry you, Soaring Eagle. Not with conditions as they are. It's been a day of adventure, it's been fun and I am in your debt. But you move too fast. In truth, I cannot forget that last night, even this morning, you acted as though I were as annoying to you as a thorn in your heel."

"Merely a wish to remain a bachelor for a while longer, I think."

"No, please understand that whatever happened out there on the prairie this afternoon, and perhaps here, also, should never have happened. I'm sorry for my part in it. But please accept my final word on this, and don't ask me to marry you again. I—I don't think I could . . ." *keep saying no*, she finished to herself, gulping.

She knew she was being curt, being firm; perhaps a little too firm. But someone had to be.

Casting him a quick look, she was aware that he had questions, questions he might likely pose. But Kali knew she would never last through them. Even now she was close to tears.

And so, with the hope that she could hide behind the facade of disagreement, she turned away from him, to make her way back down to the pony herd and to her wagon, feeling horribly, utterly alone.

She stumbled. Indeed, she had gone no more than a few paces when she heard him call after her, saying, "Do what you wish. Say what you will. I'll do as you ask and not pose the marriage question to you again. But married or not, separated or not, you will never forget me, as I will not forget you. This I promise you."

Chapter 12

Alas! Alas! why could not this simple life have continued?

James Willard Schultz, *My Life as an Indian*

A council was called. The spirits had been appeased, the four directions extolled. Inside the tepee, a pipe had been passed around the council circle, and back again, but, as was custom, not past the tepee's entryway. It was an old custom, one that no one saw fit to alter simply because the world around them had changed.

An old chief rose. "Warriors, chiefs, wise men," he began, "one of us has come here to say a few words. He has been with the whites. And he has much to tell us. We should all listen to what he has to say."

Several of the assembled chiefs voiced encouragement, and amid their praise, Soaring Eagle rose to his feet.

After a brief pause, he began, "As many of you already know, this council has been held that I might speak with you."

The elders nodded, their eyes politely turned down.

"I have come to talk to you tonight to tell you that I have spoken with the white woman," he said, "the one whom you all met last night, the one that the Indian agent has asked us to accommodate."

Again more nods.

"There have been doubts about how we should deal with her. During my talk with her, I learned why she is here and what she means to do. In her wagon, she waits for me at the outskirts of our village. I have discovered that she is here with her father to record a history of our people—in words and in photographs. She would tell the white people, with these pictures and with their written words, the story of our people.

"I have brought her to our village to witness the Medicine Pipe ceremony in order that you meet her and talk to her and decide for yourself the truth of her words—of my words. Though she is white, I believe her heart is good and that it is in the right place.

"She has also offered to help us discover what we can about the thievery of our land, in exchange for granting her this privilege. I believe her, and I would ask you to open your eyes to her that you might see her as I have."

He sat down. Though it was customary that he add that he hoped the chiefs would take her into their hearts as he had, Soaring Eagle had deliberately omitted this particular announcement, since he could not truthfully say that he wished any other to know her heart as intimately as he. Not that he might ever realize her in this way again.

She had said no, and if he were to do what pride was

urging him to do, he would take her advice, walk away and be done with her.

He grimaced at the thought. It wasn't right. In his heart, he felt it wasn't right. They belonged together.

However, were he to think it through logically, as she had asked him to do, he could understand her reasoning; in fact, he might even agree with her. Perhaps, in keeping her wits about her, she spoke with a wisdom he had yet to grasp. Maybe . . .

No, that couldn't be right. When he had kissed her, with her body pressed up closely to his, he had looked into her heart; had seen her for exactly who she was. And what he had beheld there was exquisite. *Aa*, he had loved her at once.

And she? He had perceived a hunger in her that was more than a match for his own. She must love him—or at least feel something . . .

But if these things were right, then what problem were they really facing? Yes, their cultures were diverse, but if that were the only force at work here, why wouldn't obvious solutions cure it?

Could it be that there was something else? Something else she wasn't admitting? And if that were true, was it simply racial prejudice?

Possibly, although that didn't seem valid, either. She couldn't easily hold a prejudice toward his people and act as she had this afternoon.

Perhaps she was being too sensible. Possibly, too, he had moved too fast, as she had said. Should he try again?

Only to be turned down once more?

Pride and an overwhelming sense of self-preservation urged Soaring Eagle to forget her. It hadn't been easy to speak of his heart's desire. It had taken courage and a certain amount of gall.

Aa, yes. What was done was done. She had declined him; he should accept her answer. What he needed now was a little time to sort through his thoughts; some space away from her. Maybe then he could think clearly.

A chief arose, requiring Soaring Eagle's complete attention. The man said, "What is Soaring Eagle, son of Comes Running Bird, asking of this council?"

Soaring Eagle came up easily to his feet and said, "I would ask the wise men of this council that you talk with her, allow her to photograph this ceremony, those parts of it that are not sacred. In this way, you may come to know her and see for yourself her true nature, for I do not believe she is here to take away our spirit."

Another chief held up a hand, coming himself to his feet. He said, "And if she is? If she turns out to be as treacherous as the white ranchers who surround us?"

"Then we need not invite her to any other function," said Soaring Eagle. "Neither she nor her father can make their book or their history about us, if we do not agree to talk to them. I have seen her heart, and I do not think she speaks with a forked tongue."

The old chief nodded and Soaring Eagle returned to his seat.

"Is there anyone else who would like to say something on this matter?"

Kicking Stone arose.

"Yes, Kicking Stone. Speak."

"For many years we have trusted the whites to their words. For as many years we have thought them to be as truthful as we ourselves are. Yet, in all these years, we have not seen a promise that has not been broken by these people. It seems to me that the whites make promises only to suit themselves and when they have what they want, they quickly forget. I say we should remember this and beware of the white woman and send her away from us."

Soaring Eagle rose up onto his feet, asking for recognition that he might speak. It was given.

"Kicking Stone is a very wise man, and I agree with him. But only today, the white woman defended me against some white bullies who might have killed me . . . and her. She spoke harshly to them and swore that she would have justice. I believe her."

"Thank you, Soaring Eagle," said the old chief. "Is there another who wishes to say a few words about this?"

When no one indicated that he might, the chief continued. "Then we will have a vote."

"Wait," said Comes Running Bird. "I trust my son's judgment, but perhaps not his heart."

Startled by these words, Soaring Eagle reined in his surprise and stared out in front of him. How could his father know what was in his heart? Not by word or by gesture had Soaring Eagle given any indication as to his feelings. Had his father mastered the art of reading his son's mind?

But Comes Running Bird was continuing to speak, and he said, "Perhaps we might allow her some rights, but not all. Maybe we could permit her to witness the ceremony, to take pictures, but to select only those that Soaring Eagle approves."

That only he would approve?

Soaring Eagle clamped down on the urge to spring to his feet in protest. Hadn't he barely determined that

for his own good, he should put some distance between them?

Yet if he had to approve all that she did, he would
have to be with her, *have* to be close to her.

It was too soon. Without sorting through his own
mind on the matter first, it would be nothing short of
torture.

Soaring Eagle raised his hand, that he might speak.

"*Aa*, Soaring Eagle wishes to say something else to
the council?"

He did, and he stood. "In my defense, I think I
should let this council know that I do not know the
Medicine Pipe ceremony well enough to decide what
pictures she should or should not take. I might allow
her too much freedom, and we would come to regret
it. Though my father has kept the Medicine Pipe bundle these past few years, I do not feel I should rightfully take on this responsibility. Perhaps there is
someone else? My sister might be happy to accompany her."

His words were met with absolute quiet.

He sat down, and the spell was broken. Almost at
once there were murmurs around the circle.

The old chief nodded. "Thank you Comes Running
Bird, Soaring Eagle. You have heard what each one of
these fine men has to say. Perhaps we should remember that it is Comes Running Bird who is this night
seeking another to carry on the tradition of the Medicine Pipe. We will vote now."

"I would say one more thing." It was Comes Running Bird speaking.

"*Aa*," said the old chief. "Please speak."

"My son, Soaring Eagle, talks well and with good intent. However, I fear he also speaks as a man who might fear the passion of his heart."

Soaring Eagle didn't react outwardly, though it took every bit of strength he possessed to simply stare at the ground.

"For as you all know," Comes Running Bird continued, "Soaring Eagle's sister would know as much about the ceremony as her brother."

The old chief nodded. "This council thanks you Comes Running Bird. And now I think we will vote."

In the end, it was decided that Comes Running Bird's suggestion would be followed. And Soaring Eagle, more than a little puzzled and anxious of what the night ahead might yet present, arose.

Filing out, he kept his place in the circle, his steps keeping pace with those of the old wise men who had been assembled around the council fire. Bending at the entrance, he stepped through the entrance flap, trying to decide in his own mind the best way to approach the coming evening.

And though he knew he would never go against the council's decision, he did wonder at their wisdom.

Still, even that thought dimmed in comparison to the real problem at hand. *How was he to be with her and keep his hands off her?*

As promised, Kali waited well to the outside of the Blackfeet encampment. She sat in the buggy's seat, nervously twiddling her fingers. Children had crowded around the wagon, some had popped into the back of it, while several others had brought treats to feed to the horses. All the youngsters stared at her as though she might be some stage performer.

At last, she saw him, Soaring Eagle, walking toward her as though with great purpose. Her pulses leapt at the sight, and for more reasons than one. But she wouldn't think of that now. She couldn't. Not and keep her peace of mind.

She smiled at him, hoping the simple grin might hide her nervousness.

"What did the council decide?" she asked as soon as he came within voice range.

He didn't answer, and Kali knew a moment of anxiety. For as he tread toward her, his expression was far from happy.

Oh, dear. What has happened?

He didn't falter in his step, nor did he utter a word until he had reached the wagon and had climbed up onto the seat, the wooden joints creaking under his weight. He sat next to her, arms crossed over his chest, his glance, brooding, staring straight ahead of him.

"It was that bad, was it?" she asked.

"*Saa*, it was not bad at all. Comes Running Bird, the owner of the Pipe, was not opposed to your photographing parts of the ceremony. And so the council decided that you might be allowed to—"

"Really? I have permission to take pictures?" She couldn't help herself. She flung out a hand to touch him. "Thank you, Soaring Eagle."

Quickly he moved away from her. "Do not thank me."

"Why not?"

"There is more."

"More?" she echoed. "Oh." The flatness of the word escaped her lips before she could prevent it. "What else is there?" She scooted away from him.

"The council's decision, since they do not know

you, is to let you photograph the ceremony, as long as I am with you. You may only take those pictures that I approve."

"I see," said Kali. Was this a problem? "Well," she said, "that's fine, isn't it?"

"Fine?" He practically spit out the word. "How is that fine?"

Kali was baffled. "I'm not sure why that isn't to your liking."

"To my liking?" He gave her a glare. "Do you realize that this means we will have to be with one another—constantly—throughout the entire evening?"

"Yes?" What was she missing here? To her, the mere thought of gaining more time with the man was more than a little exciting. "And? . . ."

His glance at her was intent, urgent. And Kali recognized it deeply, there to the tip of her very feminine soul. And she couldn't have stopped herself responding to it had she tried. She shut her eyes.

He said, "Do you think it will be easy for me to be with you in the coming hours of darkness, and having touched you as I already have, to keep away from you?"

"Oh." So that was it. She opened her eyes and stared straight in front of her.

"And I have promised myself that I will not take you to my sleeping robes without becoming first man and wife."

"I see," she gulped. "Well, it is possible th—that I might have a say in the evening as well, don't you think? Perhaps I might be able to avoid your . . . ah . . . charms."

She cast him a surreptitious glance, finding him frowning at her in a most sardonic way. He said, "Do you honestly think I could not convince you to lie with me?"

Her pulses leapt at the very suggestion, but Kali sat stiffly beside him, pretending an immunity to him that she was far from feeling. In faith, mental images of exactly what this might entail flashed in her mind's eye. But she damped such things down.

Instead she said, "Surely, there are other things we could do with the evening. Besides, you might be exaggerating your . . . ah, ability."

Oh, dear, that had escaped her lips before she'd had a chance to think thoroughly about it. Even to her own ears her words sounded like a challenge.

His eyes riveted to hers. "Do you think that I exaggerate?" he asked, bending toward her. A simple move. Hardly anything. But Kali's stomach tied itself in knots because of it. She gasped, and awareness swept through her in a downpour. All at once the need to touch and be touched seemed paramount within her. And she really didn't require him pointing out, "Would you like me to demonstrate how simple it would be to have you melting in my arms?"

As though to substantiate the suggestion, he reached out toward her. Kali, however, scooted as far away from him as their seat would allow, stuttering, "A-ah, that isn't necessary. I—I think I get the message."

He drew back at once, again crossing his arms over his chest and staring out into the night.

"Wh-what are we to do, then? Are you thinking of forgetting the entire thing?"

"*Saa*, we cannot do that. The council has decreed what must be, and it is not my place to disobey them. No, I must do this, you must do it, too, if you wish to write your book. *Aa*, I will stay by you tonight and assume the duty the chiefs have given to me. It's only that it won't be easy for me, perhaps not for you, either."

"*Perhaps* not for me, either? Y-you are uncertain? About me?" Was he really unaware of what she felt? To her own mind, she was more than obvious.

But he nodded in response. "That's right. I am uncertain of you."

"Oh," said Kali. "Oh." She gulped in a breath, but didn't seek to enlighten him. In faith, it would have been a hard thing for her to do, since Kali, herself, was a little confused on that account. Yes, his mere presence might cause her heart to beat faster, her arms to ache for him, but she could not, she would not give herself quarter. She had to hold herself back. After all, it was only reasonable to assume that anything that could bring about so much pleasure could also produce as much pain.

But he was still speaking, saying, "And so, I would ask that you keep your distance from me, and I from you. Perhaps, after setting up your equipment, you could take a short rest, while I stay alert and watch for signs that the ceremony is beginning."

"Yes," she acknowledged, although secretly she doubted she would be able to nap. She was simply too excited, by the prospect of her work, and by . . . other things. Aloud she said, "I—I'm not certain that this is all necessary, is it? . . ."

She tilted her head, glancing at him, watching as his jaw clenched; watching as a muscle in his cheek flicked angrily. ". . . But, perhaps it is," she finished, "Of course, I will agree with you."

He inhaled. "*Soka'pii*, good." He scooted off the seat, hitting the ground with a dull thud. There he stood, gazing up at her with an expression of mild tolerance. "Come, help me unhitch your ponies and together we can lead them into the meadow where they can graze with the rest of our herd. And in the morning you can gather your animals together without difficulty, since they are much larger than our Indian ponies. They will be no worse for their adventure this evening, I think."

Kali nodded, and spurring herself into action, jumped down from the seat, wondering if her horses would have the only adventure yet this night? And with that thought she felt a faint stab of disappointment stir within her . . .

"There are many must and must-nots that accompany ownership of the Medicine Pipe," said Soaring Eagle as he ushered Kali toward Comes Running Bird's lodge. "Perhaps it is lucky that none of these rules prevent a person from photographing the opening moments of the ceremony."

"I see. Yes, that's good."

He gazed down at her, only to find her grinning up at him. And despite himself, he responded to that smile, to her, wanting to take her in his arms, if only to keep her happy. He looked away from her, and picked up his pace instead.

"Tell me," she chatted, as she trotted along beside him. "Where do you live? Do you have a lodge of your own, or being single, do you live with your father and mother?"

"I live with my family," he affirmed, still without looking at her. He didn't tell her that Comes Running Bird was his father. For a reason he couldn't define, he kept that knowledge from her.

"Ah, then single, young men remain with their parents until they are married?"

"Usually they do," he said, "unless they have a sister or an aunt who might be able to help them with the things they need for a household. But my sister is married and has her own family to keep clothed and housed. I would not burden her with my own needs. Now," he began, coming to a stop outside Comes Running Bird's tepee. The drumming from inside the lodge was loud, so much so that it required him to lean toward Kali in order to be heard, coming in so close to her that he could practically taste the fragrance of her skin. In reaction to her, his head reeled, but there was little he could do about it, except to tell her what he had to say with as little commotion as possible. "Now, remember," he began, "it's allowed that you snap pictures of this lodge, as well as the singers and drummers within. But do not do more unless you ask me first."

"I wi-will." She stumbled over the word, then chuckled. "That is, I will not take pictures without asking you first." She grinned at him.

"*Soka'pii.* And remember that you must never come between a person in the circle and the fire. You must always walk behind them and when you enter you must enter to the south, that would be to your left. Do you understand?"

"Yes," she said, "yes I do." She wrinkled her nose at him in a cheeky sort of grin.

In response, however, Soaring Eagle frowned and, opening the tepee flap, stepped inside.

As she followed him, she tripped and tumbled into him, causing her to grab hold of his waist. Accidently, her hand touched him . . . there, privately. In self-defense, he turned and steadied her, keeping his own balance by taking her in his arms.

It was a tense moment. *Haiya*, how could a mere touch set him afire? Yet, he could not deny the surge of longing that swept over him.

He swallowed, realizing with a start the exact spot on his body where the blood rushed. He bent toward her, she did the same. *Haiya*, it was as he feared. He could not be this close to her and not grow ready for her.

"Soaring Eagle," she said, "I—I . . ."

All at once Soaring Eagle became aware that the drumming had stopped; the lodge had grown quiet, as well. Almost fearing to look, Soaring Eagle slowly glanced to the side; Kali did the same.

Every face was turned toward them.

Shutting his eyes, he dropped his arms from around her.

And wide-eyed, she stared back at him, her lips rounding on the words, "I—I'm sorry."

He sighed and said, "It is nothing." And with a quick motion he urged her to the left of the circle.

She stepped left, but was looking at him instead of where she was going. She tripped and fell over another woman.

"Excuse me," he heard her utter as she picked herself up, straightening first her dress, then the other woman's. Looking up, she sent Soaring Eagle a glance, laced with urgency, as though she might beg him to help her.

But he had done all he could, more than enough. He had already rushed to her aid once, a thing no man did for a woman—at least not in front of other men.

Again, with a look and a quick motion of the hand, Soaring Eagle gave her to understand that she could set up her equipment. She nodded, beaming at him from across the circle. Then, turning this way and that, she appeared to be appraising the ground for the best possible location to begin her work.

He watched as she set up the camera, grimaced as it fell over, winced as it hit the side of the tepee. Kali, he noted, coughed anxiously, glanced back at him, then bent to pick up the equipment.

He breathed in and stared upward, as though for guidance. Then letting his breath out in a quick sigh, he stepped to the right and took his place next to his father.

She was nervous. That was all that was wrong with her. It would pass.

At last the drumming began again, a pipe was beginning its way around the circle and Soaring Eagle started to relax. However, Comes Running Bird leaned toward him, saying, "The white woman is very pretty," he made a motion toward her, then murmured softly, "Unusual and clumsy. But pretty."

Soaring Eagle nodded.

But Comes Running Bird was continuing, and he said, "She is persistent, too, is she not?"

"That she is," said Soaring Eagle, his voice low and hushed.

"It is good," said Comes Running Bird. "A good thing, indeed. A fine quality in a woman. For our paths in life are often difficult, but a woman who remains true to her chosen course is a rare and valuable creature."

"*Aa*, my father."

But Comes Running Bird wasn't finished, and he went on to say, "And so it is with most men and women. The winds are often strong, the force of the gales demanding, the whisperings of the wind deceiving, but if a man or a woman has chosen a path that is from the heart, he or she must hold true and stand firm. For the wind is but a gust that will be gone on the morrow."

"*Aa,* father. Yes." However, no sooner had Soaring Eagle spoken those few words than he sent his father a long look. Comes Running Bird didn't often voice an opinion on matters of the heart, but when he did, it was, indeed, a wise person who heeded the advice.

Comes Running Bird continued, "It is one of the reasons why I was in favor of you bringing the white woman here. I recognized that she would persist until she accomplished what she came here to do. Did you wonder at my reasons?"

"*Aa,* that I did, my father. *That* I did."

"*Soka'pii,*" said Comes Running Bird, motioning outward from his chest with his right hand, the sign for "good." Then, reaching out to the side, he accepted the pipe being offered him. He grabbed hold of the object, took a puff and passed it on to Soaring Eagle, observing calmly as he did so, "It is as I thought. And now, my son, I think you understand."

Soaring Eagle nodded, was reaching for the pipe, when his father's words suddenly took on greater meaning.

What was wrong with him? Was he doomed to be continually blind? He was being handed the chance of a lifetime, a chance to spend an entire evening with the one woman, in all the years of his life, who had captured his heart . . . and he was worried about it; in truth, had been troubled by it.

And though Kali had elicited a promise from him that he would not speak to her again on the subject of marriage, that didn't mean that he couldn't woo her, utilizing every means known to man or beast.

Yes. His father was right. It was, indeed, a good thing

to persist on a given course—to see it to the end.

Glancing to his right, toward his father, Soaring Eagle moved his right hand out and away from his chest in the same jerky motion that his father had used, the sign for "good." He said, "*Soka'pii*. And now, my father, I understand."

Chapter 13

Many a time I've thought of that robe couch, the cheerful little fire, the quaint things scattered around. It was a place to rest and to dream.

James Willard Schultz, *My Life as an Indian*

Kali had snapped pictures of the seven drummers; the members of the Medicine Pipe society, as they sat around the circle; the interior of the tepee and the outside pictographs which adorned Comes Running Bird's lodge. All of these pictures, however, were still mere images set on glass plates, which themselves had been stored in their own separate packets and had been placed in her pouch. She had even managed to procure the cooperation of a small boy, who had been lingering outside the Medicine Pipe lodge, before his mother had come and ushered him quickly away.

It had taken her less than an hour to gain what pictures she could. That was all; no more than an hour. Now what was she to do? It would still be several hours, almost the entire night, before a new Pipe owner would be found.

She fretted. For there were still several things that bothered her.

Would her pictures develop well? It was impossible to tell. The lighting here was bad; the moon, the stars and the fires, both inside and out, being her only light source. What if none of the shots turned out to be recognizable?

Still, she tried to soothe herself, perhaps the illumination from her flash stick would be enough to grab hold of an image. She could only hope it would be so.

"There, to your right, do you see those men?" Soaring Eagle interrupted her thoughts to point with his thumb toward a place in the village.

Kali looked in the direction he indicated. She and Soaring Eagle had left the interior of Comes Running Bird's lodge only a little while previous, and had retreated to the edge of the Indian encampment, where the two of them sat beneath a stand of cottonwood trees. A buffalo robe—one that Soaring Eagle had produced—cushioned them, as well as provided a barrier from the coolness of the hard ground and the dew on the grass.

It was an isolated spot, a fragrant one, too. For the cottonwoods, the pine trees and everything that was green emitted a pleasant odor of pure prairie air, grass and dirt. Indeed, the aroma sat well on the senses.

Unbidden, Kali shivered. Despite the warmth of the day, the evenings in this northern climate were cool.

"Are you cold?"

"I . . . yes, I am, a bit."

"Here, wait." He rose, treading off quickly in the direction of the encampment. He was back within a few minutes, holding a blanket in his hand, which he immediately placed around her shoulders. His arms lingered around her, his breath fanning her neck, making her feel warm, cozy, content.

It came as a shock when he raised her hair and kissed the back of her neck. Kali jumped, scooting away from him as fast as she could.

She said, "Wh-whose blanket is this?"

"Mine."

"Is it? It's wonderfully soft and warm," she said, not adding that the woolen article, laced with a hint of smoke, grass and the musky scent of humanity was making her heart throb uncontrollably.

"Humph."

She took a deep breath. "Wh-what was that you were telling me? Something that was off in that direction?" She pointed with a nod.

"Hmmm." Soaring Eagle had retreated to a cottonwood tree and was at present leaning back against it. However, he turned his head to look in the direction indicated. "I don't see them now. Wait, there they are. Do you see the two figures over there to the west, making their way to one of the lodges?"

"Yes, I think so. Do you mean those two shadows? They look as though they're sneaking through the camp. Are they?"

"*Aa*, they are."

Kali strained to get a better look. There they were, two people, men most likely, their faces hidden beneath their robes, which were drawn up over their heads. The two of them were moving slowly toward a lodge, which was lit up from within by a bright fire. She watched as they stopped outside of the lodge. One of the figures crept forward, pausing to peer inside. But no sooner had he done so, than he returned to his partner, the two of them hurrying away.

"Brightly Spotted Elk is not home," explained Soaring Eagle.

"Come again?"

"That is Brightly Spotted Elk's lodge. Those two men are from the Medicine Pipe society. Had Brightly Spotted Elk been home, they would have entered the lodge and surprised him; they would have sung the Owl songs which cast a spell over him, so that when offered the Pipe, he would not be able to refuse it."

"I see," she said. "Although actually I don't. Tell me again, why would they have to cast a spell over him in order to get him to take the Pipe? If it is an honor to be the recipient of it, wouldn't he be proud to have it?"

"It is too great a responsibility for many men."

"So you have said. Why is that?"

"Because," he said, leaning away from the tree, "if ever one of the people are sick, a man may pray to the Medicine Pipe, and a ceremony must be given, that he may take a vow. When this is done, the sickly one will recover. Sometimes even marriages are realized during the Pipe ceremony."

"Really? By 'realized,' do you mean that it is a marriage service of sorts?"

He nodded. "I do. It is always a very sacred vow that is given between two such people, for when a union is made during the Pipe ceremony, it is directed by the spirits."

"Truly? That's fascinating. And are many marriages made this way?"

"Very few," he said, "for these ceremonies are costly, not only for the Pipe holder, but for the ones who make the vows."

"I see. Then the Pipe ceremony is really a way of allowing others to make vows? To . . . ah . . . help a loved one recover, or perhaps to make a marriage."

"*Aa*, it is so."

"Are there any other sorts of vows that can be made?"

He nodded. "A person is free to promise whatever it is that he chooses. But he must give something in exchange to the one who owns the Medicine Pipe, just as the Medicine Pipe holder must prepare the ceremony."

"Ah, now I think I understand. So, if these ceremonies are a costly affair, a person's objection to becoming a Pipe holder is simply a matter of finance?"

"*Saa*, it is not quite that simple. There are many rules that accompany the ownership of the Pipe, and it must be owned for four years. These rules are a burden, not only to the owner of the Pipe, but to his family, for they must be followed to the last detail or else ill fortune could come to the owner and his family."

"And what are some of these rules?"

"There are too many to tell you, but a few of them are: Never bathe in a river without first having sprinkled with water, while singing the Water Bird song. Always take a place at the back of a lodge, never sit near a door. Do not allow anyone to sleep in or upon your sleeping robes. Never say the word 'bear' if the Pipe is near, use the word 'badger' instead. You must burn sweet pine in your lodge upon first rising in the morning; the Medicine Pipe bundle may hang outside the door of your lodge, but must never be left out in bad weather. The Pipe must be taken outside on the right and brought back into the lodge on the left. Never point using a finger, always the thumb. Never curse or blacken the character of another by word or deed. These are a few. There are more; many, many more."

"I see. And the owner must take care of this bundle in this way for four years?"

Soaring Eagle nodded.

"And he must do all these things exactly lest misfortune be his lot?"

"Or his family's."

"Oh, dear. That is a bit of a burden, isn't it?"

"It is. My father and our family have borne it these last four years. It is now time for a new owner."

"Your *father* is the Medicine Pipe owner? The one you call Comes Running Bird?"

"*Aa.*"

"I didn't know that. Was he sitting in the circle tonight?"

"*Aa*, that he was. He was sitting to my right."

"And it was he—your father—who gave permission for me to witness the ceremony?"

"*Saa*, not completely. The council gave the order."

"Oh."

"But my father was in favor of it and helped to convince the council of its decision."

Kali shot a quick glance at Soaring Eagle. *His father had been her champion? Why?* She asked, "Does your father know anything about me?"

Soaring Eagle grunted. "A bit too much, I fear."

"Too much? What do you mean?"

Soaring Eagle darted a frown at her. "It was he who suggested I spend the evening with you."

"It was? Why?"

"He tells me that it is because he believes you will be persistent in your desire to take our pictures."

Kali sat up straighter, a scowl pulling at the corners of her lips. At length, she asked, "Isn't that a bit odd?"

Soaring Eagle shrugged. "Not necessarily. He is a

very wise man. He sees much. He knows much."

He knows much. It was an odd sensation, Kali thought, this feeling that a man she had never met might know something about her. Stranger still was the sensation that she also shared some dim knowledge of him.

But Soaring Eagle was speaking, interrupting her thoughts, and he said, "He also seems to have looked into my heart, for he said that he believed you had captured my affections."

Kali looked away. At first she didn't speak, preferring to absorb this piece of information in silence. That's when it happened. A sensation of déjà vu stole over her, as though she had been here before, lived this before; as though she *belonged here with Soaring Eagle*, and had done so for years too numerous to count.

Worse, there was more.

She said aloud, "Ah . . . does your father wear a yellow and blue headdress?" She asked the question as casually as she could, though secretly she dreaded the answer.

Soaring Eagle spun around toward her, giving her his full attention. And in his look was some amazement. He said, "He does sometimes."

"With a black and yellow beaded circle in the center?"

"*Aa*, he does, but for special things." Soaring Eagle raised an eyebrow.

Kali gulped.

"How do you know this? He was not dressed in those clothes tonight."

"I . . . I'm not sure. It's only that when you told me that your father is a wise man, that he seemed to know me and that he guessed what was in your heart—when you told me all those things, an image of an older man flashed before my eyes."

"Flashed? Before your eyes?" Soaring Eagle was doing more than leaning toward her. He had come up onto his knees before her, staring at her in a most unusual way.

"Y-yes." She tried to laugh, but the sound materialized as a jerky sort of cough.

"You have had a vision about my father?"

"I—I would hardly say that I . . . I mean I did catch sight of him tonight, after all."

"Tell me what it was that he held in his hand."

"In his hand?" Kali asked, barely daring to glance at Soaring Eagle. "I—I don't remember."

"Yes, you do. What did you see?"

"Why I—I didn't see anything that—"

"Tell me the truth."

"I—I . . ." Soaring Eagle grabbed hold of her hand, held it between both of his own as though it were precious. "An animal skin," she said after a pause. "That's what I saw in your father's hand. And don't ask me what kind of animal, because I don't know."

Soaring Eagle dropped her hand and sat back, and truth be told, Kali was relieved. Relieved that there were no more questions, at least not right away; relieved that, at his touch, he hadn't noticed the shiver of anticipation that had swept over her. Quickly, she stole a glance at him, discovering that his attention was riveted to something else, not her. And at this moment, he appeared to be as puzzled as she.

At last, however, he sat up straighter, gazed in her direction and gave her a most perplexing look. He said, "You are a very strange white woman."

"Strange? Why?"

"I have never known a white person to speak of having a vision. I had assumed they had none."

Kali didn't know quite how to respond to that, and so she remained silent.

"You wouldn't have native ancestry, would you? A grandmother, perhaps, whom the family tries to hide?"

"No. Why would you think that?"

"Because all the white people of my acquaintance—at least those who surround our reservation—would certainly not admit to having a vision, even if it happened to them. Indeed, most look upon our Indian ceremonies, our beliefs and traditions, even our knowledge of the spirits, with some disfavor."

"Surely not."

He sneered.

"Look, Soaring Eagle, although I'm not an expert on history, I do know that this country was founded on the principle that all people in it are free to believe as they choose."

He shrugged. "Free, as long as their beliefs are those of the white man."

"Soaring Eagle, I know what I'm talking about."

"Do you?" He scowled at her. "Have you researched my tribe's plight yet, as you said you would?"

"You know that I haven't. There hasn't been time."

"Then don't talk to me about what is and what isn't until you discover for yourself what is happening here."

"But—"

He held up a hand. "Let us speak no more about it. It upsets us both."

"But I—"

He glanced away from her, bringing his arms up to cross over his chest.

Silence descended upon them. As it had once before, Mrs. Black's commentary came back to haunt her, but Kali tried to push those thoughts away. It was pointless to mull the upset over and over with no hope of resolving it. Particularly since Soaring Eagle wasn't going to speak of these things further, and, truth to tell, she really did need to keep her promise and do her research.

Meanwhile, the air between them hung heavy with an unusual quietness. At last, Kali couldn't help asking, "Is your father a medicine man?"

"*Saa*, no."

"But he holds the Medicine Pipe—at least he does presently?"

"He does."

"Then, since he is the Pipe holder, he must be fairly well-to-do?"

"By Indian standards, he is," said Soaring Eagle. "Although few of us have as great a wealth as we did in the days when the buffalo still roamed the plains."

"I see." She sat contemplating that statement for a moment. Then commented, "It must be difficult."

"Difficult?"

"To live so near the same region that was once so abundant with game and buffalo. To look out upon it day after day—and to remember how it used to be. Then seeing it now, so barren. . . ."

He pulled forward, his gaze catching hers. "That was a perceptive thing to say."

"Was it? Perhaps it's only because I'm here now and surrounded by those who feel these things strongly. It's a little like walking into a room where people have been arguing. A person always knows . . . somehow."

He drew ever closer to her, his face so near, she had only to reach out . . .

"It is strange." He practically whispered the words.

"Wh—what is?"

"You."

"Me?"

He blinked, giving her a slight nod. "At first, I thought you were merely something good for the eyes to feast upon. But then I talked to you—at the party last night—and I realized then that there was more to you. There's a fire in you, Kali Wallace."

She gave him a nervous chuckle. "A fire? In me? Pooh!"

"*Aa*, I speak true. Your hair, its color, is witness to it." He swept a strand of it into his fingers, twirling it round and round.

Oh, dear. That touch, soft and faint though it was, felt good. Kali inhaled deeply, but remained silent.

At length, he asked, "Do you see this little tuft of hair?"

She glanced downward to observe him brushing his fingers through a curl that had come loose.

He continued, "With this color, your hair is as alive as you are."

"Is it? I think you are just being poetic."

He smiled. "And yet, Miss Kali Wallace, this is what I see. I only wish I could experience all of the fire that burns within you. Experience it in every way a man possibly can."

Although Kali was certain there was more than a hint of sexual connotation behind these words, the true meaning of it escaped her. Still, that didn't stop her from responding to the warmth of his words, or the sincerity emanating from his tone.

Hardly knowing what she did, she bent in toward him, barely catching herself. Quickly she straightened.

But the die was cast. Somehow, somewhere along the line tonight, she had changed.

Yes, from the beginning, she had responded to this man; yes, it was undeniable that she found him attractive. But previously she'd been able to hold herself separate from him.

And now? Now, all she wanted to do was melt into him. Indeed, so strong was the impulse, she began to wonder how she was to get through this night without demanding his touch.

And she must keep her distance. She must. After all, to allow another into one's heart was to give that person a certain power, to be used for good or for bad, wasn't it?

And truthfully, Kali wasn't prepared to give anyone that sort of advantage.

Trying to break the spell, she gazed away from him. "Ah, Soaring Eagle," she began, her voice breaking through the silence, "ah . . . how much longer do you think it will be before they find a new owner for the Pipe?"

Soaring Eagle didn't answer right away, appearing to be more interested in discovering the tiny nuances in her eyes, her composure; anything that might reflect her thoughts. He stared at her long and hard. However, when she continued to sit before him, as though unmoved, frozen, he at last drew back from her and nodded toward the evening sky, saying, "When the last brother points toward the earth, that is when the society should have a new owner."

"Last brother?"

With his thumb, he indicated the Big Dipper. "The last brother—the last star in the handle of the Dipper—tells time in the night sky. When it is pointing toward the earth, it is certain that dawn is approaching. Judging from where the last brother is now, that time is still many hours away."

She sighed and glanced away from him, avoiding direct eye contact.

She couldn't do it. She couldn't look at this man without realizing the futility of her situation.

And now perhaps she understood why he had been so glum earlier. She was well and truly stuck; stuck with a man whom she desired as readily as if they had already been lovers.

And yet, whispered a hidden voice—one concealed somewhere deep inside her—she must never give in to him. Yes, she might enjoy his kisses; she might even yearn for his embrace, but she must not lose sight of who she was and what she was doing here.

To do so would be to court certain disaster. Wouldn't it? . . .

Chapter 14

*Wide, brown plains, distant, slender, flat-topped
buttes; still more distant giant mountains, blue-
sided, sharp-peaked, snow-capped; odour of sage
and smoke of camp fire; . . . long-drawn melancholy howl of wolves breaking the silence of the
night, how I loved you all!*

James Willard Schultz, *My Life as an Indian*

Kali's tripod sat off to the side, set up as though
awaiting its owner's immediate response. Her
camera rested close beside it; the flash sticks, glass
plates and packets were in order and lay close to hand.
Everything was ready and waiting. There was nothing
else to do, at least not for the moment. She might as
well attempt to rest, especially since it could be several
hours before the members of the Medicine Pipe society
had found a new Pipe owner.

In the meantime Kali and Soaring Eagle, who were
still resting toward the edge of the encampment, had
formed a truce of sorts. They had ceased speaking of
things that upset one or the other. And amazingly, it
made for a much more pleasant evening.

There had been talk at first of Kali spending the evening in the lodge of Sits-in-sun Woman, Soaring Eagle's grandmother. But Kali had pooh-poohed the idea.

As soon as a new Pipe owner had been found, she wanted to be able to jump into the thick of it without the social obligation of thanking her hostess.

Besides, deep within her was the desire to remain with Soaring Eagle. Like it or not, trust him or not, she was attracted to him, and there was very little she could do about it.

And so it had come to pass that Soaring Eagle, and Soaring Eagle alone, remained with her; her constant companion this evening.

He was still reclining against a cottonwood tree, while Kali lay prone on the buffalo robe, pretending as best she could, indifference. It was a beautiful spot they had chosen.

The stars, her ceiling, were twinkling above her through the branches of the cottonwood, the ever-darkening sky appearing as though it had been sprinkled with glitter. The robe beneath her, her floor, not only cushioned her gently, like a babe, but kept out the cold. And underneath her head was Soaring Eagle's blanket, its softness and musky fragrance like a soothing balm.

How wonderful it must have been, she thought, in days of old to lie beneath the stars, to listen to the sounds of the crickets and locust; to the nighthawks, the wind and the gurgling of a running brook. Ah, to live as perhaps nature had intended. How thrilling it must have been to awaken each morning, to greet the open spaces with outstretched arms. For the only boundaries would have been the sky above you and the ground below you.

She sighed and inhaled the crisp night air; air, she recalled, which had become famous for its promotion of good health. No wonder, she thought, the Indians fought to keep their way of life. For to live here, as the Indians had once lived, would have been as to exist with constant aesthetics.

Alas, it was a shame it all had to come to an end; that the new, incoming culture had not embraced the old.

She chanced a quick glance at Soaring Eagle, noting that his gaze was trained, not on her, but on some sight which lay farther out into the night. And he was singing, the melody reminding her of this spacious land, as though the song had captured and put sound to an image of the pure mountain streams, to the sun-kissed mountains. The key was minor, his voice clear and soft, deep and baritone . . .

"Oooooooooooooooooooooo.
When you hear my voice on the wind,
When you see the eagle fly,
Know that these tell of my love for you."

Kali's heart constricted. Her breath caught, and the beauty of the moment pulled a response from her, bringing tears to her eyes. He was singing of passion, of love, of things she had once thought to be no more than silly sentimentality.

But it wasn't so. These things were real. Oh, how she would like to rethink her position with this man, to let go of her reserve and let him into her soul.

Was she being foolish not to? Indeed, what evidence did she have that she couldn't trust him? Were their worlds really so distant, one to the other? What would be the worst thing that would happen were she to succumb to him?

A wasted career?

So what? Was it really that important? Somehow, out

here under the grand canopy of stars, it was hard to imagine that it was so.

He glanced at her, his gaze studiously intent, as though he might have perceived some of what she was thinking. He said, "I am singing the same song that I sang to you earlier tonight."

She didn't know why that statement set off a sweep of emotion within her, but it did. A tear fell over her cheek and there was nothing she could do to prevent it. It was as though the beauty of the moment was too much for her.

She didn't trust herself to speak, and so she turned her head away, and shaking it right and left, she murmured, "I know."

"Won't you sing it with me, for it is our song?"

Our song? That simple reminder set off a fresh surge of longing. Kali bit her lip. How was she supposed to resist him? How was she supposed to do it when everything within her wanted him, his touch, his love . . . right now.

His voice came close to her ear when he whispered, "Please, won't you sing?"

She gulped down the knot in her throat, and said, "I can't, Soaring Eagle. As I told you earlier this evening, I don't have a very pretty voice—not like yours."

"Do not say that. Your voice is beautiful."

"No, not my speaking voice. I mean a singing voice. I—"

"If you can speak, sweet Kali, you can learn to sing. I could teach you."

Sweet Kali? Oh, how she liked that. "No . . . no . . . Some things are best left alone. Besides, I—I think I've forgotten the words."

"So soon?"

She rolled her head around toward him and glanced up, only to catch his look. He had come down onto his knees beside her.

She gasped. Raw passion stared back at her from the depths of his gaze.

But the look was quickly gone. He moved, and settling back once more against the tree, Soaring Eagle treated her to a teasing leer, as though he were a lover sporting a broken heart. And even this, such a small thing—and done in jest—had Kali's insides twisting, as though her body might be in as much turmoil as she was, herself.

However, he was continuing to speak, saving Kali the need for a reply, and he said, "Let me remind you of the words of the song, then, that you might never forget them."

Forget them? How could she ever?

"It starts this way:

"Ooooooooooooooooooooo.
When you hear the wolf howl,
He brings you my message.
I cry for you.
Ooooooooooooooooooooo.
When the wind calls your name,
Know that I search for you.
And when we find one another,
    the earth will be a happy place.
Ooooooooooooooooooooo. You are my love."

Kali listened to the last note. Not only was there beauty in the song, there was sadness; a sadness that made her long to take him in her arms, to cradle him and nurture him until the melancholy abated.

She began to tremble.

"Are you cold?" he asked.

"Ah, . . . no, not really . . . well, maybe a little."

She'd been using his blanket as a pillow. Perhaps she should wrap it around her body instead. But before she could make a move to change it, he was stripping off his shirt. And dropping to his knees, he set it over her.

Kali looked away from him. Not only because there were tears in her eyes, ones that she couldn't easily explain, but because she did not trust herself to look at this man's muscle and brawn. To maintain her composure, the image of a prim, nineties woman, she had to turn away from him.

Soon he was tucking the material around her; his touch, though impersonal, setting off sparks within her. "No, please," she said, scooting a little away from him. "You should leave your shirt on. It's a chilly night and I—I don't want you to catch cold."

"I won't catch cold. You probably need it more than I do."

Did she? Somehow she didn't think her problem was attributable to the briskness in the air.

Still, the shirt lay over her, its heady fragrance of sturdy cotton and the warm, male scent reached out to her, tempting her, prompting a response. It was pure torment.

"Please, Soaring Eagle," she found herself saying, almost pleading. "I don't need it. Really I don't. Won't you take it back?" She seized hold of the shirt, and pulling it from around her, held it out to him.

He sat forward, accepting the article from her, but in doing so, as though it gave him a reason, he drew still closer. Intently, critically, he gazed at her for a moment before saying, "What is wrong?"

"N-nothing."

Coming nearer even yet, he breathed, "I don't believe it's nothing. I see tears in your eyes."

"Do you?"

"*Aa.*"

"I . . . it's . . . yes, I-I've managed to get something in my eye, that's all." She turned her head away from him.

"Are you certain that's all?"

The words came close to her ear, so near, she could feel the movement of his lips.

Fire, raw, urgent and demanding tore through her. But all she said was, "Yes, I—I am . . . sure of it." She shut her eyes. "That was beautiful, by the way."

"What? The song? Or the shirt?"

He was still very close. With barely any effort at all, she could bring her lips to his.

Do it, a voice urged. *Do it.*

But all of this was unreal to her; too new, too untried. She paused, as though uncertain, but in the end all she did was speak, saying, "The song. It—it touched me deeply."

"That's because it is our song, sweet Kali. You should learn the words, that you might always know it."

"Should I?" she asked, hating the pleading quality of her voice.

"*Aa*, yes, you should. The melody, the words, all of it. They are ours. They belong only to us."

A sob tore from her throat. Disconcerted, she froze and closed her eyes, catching her lower lip with her teeth.

And then it happened. He touched her under her chin. It was a simple graze, merely a finger placed gently, urging her face around, toward him. Nothing to cause excitement. Yet Kali's heightened senses exploded. She sighed.

Softly he observed, "You have been crying."

"N-no . . . I . . ."

But he didn't hear her. He kissed each one of her eyelids, gently, softly, his breath, scented with mint and the fragrance of ceremonial smoking tugged at her heartstrings—and a sensation of such raw affection flooded her system quickly and effusively. She felt as though she might faint, were it not for the fact that she was already positioned on her back.

He said, "Do you grieve over your mistakes this evening?"

She didn't answer.

But he continued, as though she had, "Do not anguish over your clumsiness inside my father's lodge this evening," he said. "All those within understood that you were nervous and do not judge you because of it."

He didn't know? He honestly didn't realize his effect on her?

Somehow, it seemed impossible.

"You must remember our song," he was continuing to speak. "For if you ever should sing it, I will know that you want me and I will come to you . . . if I can."

Gazing up at him, at his features, as the night bathed him with mixtures of shadow and light, Kali caught her breath, held it. Never, not ever, had she beheld the visage of a man as handsome as he. Kali swallowed—hard.

Dear Lord, why were the accounts about these people so terrible? Why, when all she could perceive, with her own powers of observation, was beauty? And it was not simply a beauty of the flesh. No, there was about him, about many of the others she had seen here, a radiance of spirit, as though they, as a group, had perfected that ideal balance between the physical and the ethereal.

At her thoughts, a fresh round of tears welled up behind her eyes. It was as though her outward facade, the one she hid behind, was disappearing, leaving her alone, exposed . . . yet completely herself.

Nervously, she squared her chin, trying to hold back the tears. How was she supposed to respond to this situation? For lack of an answer, she turned her face aside once more. Ultimately, the only thing she could think to say was, "I know that you will come to me if you can. You told me that you would earlier tonight."

"So I did." After a moment, he suggested, "You could at least speak the words, couldn't you?"

"Yes," she said softly. "Yes, I could speak them. I will."

Soaring Eagle sighed into her hair, and a shiver of pleasure raced over her skin, for she felt the warmth of his breath, there at the back of her ear. He said, "It is good; very, very good."

"Is it?"

"*Aa*, it is, for your willingness gives me hope."

Gives him hope? At the thought, a warm glow settled over her.

"Now, repeat after me. 'When you hear the wolf howl . . .'"

"When you hear the wolf howl . . . he brings you my message." Kali smiled, and turning back, beamed up at him, "You see. I already know some of it."

"*Aa*, you do." He grinned. "Now, the next line is, 'I cry for you.'"

"I cry for you," she repeated, her gaze catching his.

They stared at one another. "Do you really?" he asked, his voice no more than a whisper. "Are you now?"

"I—I . . . told you that this is nothing more than . . ." She shut her eyes.

"Don't cry," he said, his fingers pushing back her hair from her forehead.

Oh, how good that felt. She shifted position, presenting him with the vulnerability of her neck.

As though unable to help himself, he bent, placing a soft kiss there, saying, "Know that I would have you if I could."

She took a deep breath, and to her horror, she sobbed.

"Please," he said, "tell me what is wrong."

"It . . . it is nothing . . . really. I'll be fine."

"But," he said, his voice near her ear, "will I?"

Kali glanced at him, her face brushing up against his, so near was he to her. "I don't understand."

He merely smiled at her, moving until he lay on his side next to her, and coming up onto an elbow, he cradled his head in his hand. Only then did he speak again, saying, " 'When the wind calls your name . . . ' "

Kali didn't respond. She didn't know what to say.

"That's the next line," he prompted.

"Oh. 'When the wind calls your name . . . ,' " she echoed.

" 'Know that I search for you . . . ' "

He had bent forward, was leaning over her, his lips so close that all she would need do is raise up a slim, narrow quarter-inch and she would kiss him. *Should she do it?*

" 'Know that I search for you . . . ' " she repeated.

His fingers cupped her face. "Have you?

"Soaring Eagle, I—I'm merely repeating what you say."

"I know. But have you? Searched for me?"

"I . . . yes . . . no."

"Yes?"

"Soaring Eagle, in truth, I have been searching for nothing."

"Haven't you?" He asked. "Then why have you been traveling the world through? Studying other cultures?"

"Because I am interested in them, and because my father has taken me there."

He raised an eyebrow. "There is no other reason?"

"I . . . I'm . . ." Kali stopped herself from finishing the statement. Whatever she'd been about to say was a part of her past. In faith, at this present moment, she wasn't certain she hadn't been doing precisely that. There did seem to be a ring of truth to it.

He paused, as though awaiting her comment. After a moment, however, when it appeared she would say no more, he continued, "The next phrase is, 'And when we find one another, the earth will be a happy place.'"

She murmured, "'And when we find one another, the earth will be a happy place.'"

He reached out, taking her hand into his own. Bending, he inhaled deeply before he kissed that hand, as though he might be memorizing her fragrance. He whispered, "'You are my love . . .'"

Kali gulped.

"That is the next line in the song."

Kali let out her breath, at last saying, "'You . . . are . . . my . . . love . . .'"

"I mean it," he said, his look at her somber. "Do you?"

She raised up to meet him. "Soaring Eagle, please, I—I can't think. Please just hold me, for I need—"

"Excuse me," a feminine voice said, the words coming from behind them. "I'm sorry to interrupt, but your father sent me . . . find you."

Startled, both Soaring Eagle and Kali glanced up.

Soaring Eagle appeared briefly puzzled. "My father sent you?"

Gilda Shadow Runner shook her head. "Not you. Her." She inclined her head toward Kali.

"Oh, that's right"—Kali turned over, onto her stomach, feeling foolish somehow—"I had almost forgotten, Soaring Eagle sent you into town, carrying a message to my father. Is he here?"

Gilda once more shook her head. "Him . . . not come until morning—sun up. Him sent me . . . find you. Him concerned about you. Him want me . . . stay with you till he come."

"Oh, I see." Kali gave Soaring Eagle an apologetic glance. And Soaring Eagle, for his part, rolled away from her.

Disappointed, Kali sat up, onto her knees. "Well, I suppose that's . . . all right. Soaring Eagle and I have been ah . . . talking while we await the transfer of the Medicine Pipe. We may still have many hours to go before a new owner is found."

"That true," said Gilda, glancing toward the midnight sky. "Many hours yet before dawn. Much time." Gilda leaned against a tree trunk, her face fading into shadow, hiding her expression. "Heard singing."

"Ah, yes. Soaring Eagle has been singing—and has been trying to give me lessons, all to no avail, I might add."

Kali glanced at Soaring Eagle, who had retreated to the tree and had once more assumed a sitting position against it. Arms folded across his chest, his features were set, impossible to read.

"Soaring Eagle has also been telling me legends of Indian lovers who have special songs that they sing to one another."

"That true. Remember legend I told you?"

"Yes, yes, I do." Kali dropped her voice to a whisper. "I had no idea, you know."

"No idea?" asked Gilda.

"I didn't know that Indian country was filled with music, and that your legends are as hauntingly beautiful as those of Greek mythology. It's interesting how your culture combines the element of a great deal of song, along with the myth."

Gilda said, "There much to learn. Do you want . . . me to . . . sing songs. I . . . know some love songs . . . Indian love songs."

"Do you?"

Kali glanced toward Soaring Eagle. What did he think about all this?

But if she'd hoped to glean anything from his countenance, she was to be disappointed. His features didn't show any emotion, nor did he change his position in the least, nor utter a single word.

At last she said, "Yes, Gilda, I would like it very much if you would sing."

Gilda nodded. "I . . . begin, then . . ."

Chapter 15

*Dreams are actual experiences of their shadows
(souls) while their bodies sleep . . .*

James Willard Schultz, *Blackfeet and Buffalo*

*"Hey, hey, hey, hey-a.
Kitsikakomimmotsspoaawa.
Hey, hey, hey, hey-a.
Kitsikakomimmotsspoaawa.
Aa, aa, aa, sskapiim, hey, hey, hey, hey-a.
Aa, aa, aa, sskapiim, hey, hey, hey, hey-a."*

Gilda possessed a soft, soothing voice, the minor key in which she sang melodic and mysterious. And it wasn't long before Kali began to feel her eyelids droop. Why hadn't she realized before now how tired she was?

Several times she tried to pinch herself to keep awake—she didn't want to miss anything; the Medicine Pipe, the ceremony. But in the end it was useless. She fell into a sleep that was as deep as it was relaxing. That is, except for one thing: She dreamed . . . a strange, wonderful dream. The kind of dream that encourages and allows fantasies to come true . . . if only for a moment . . .

Soaring Eagle was beside her. Hand in hand, they stood in front of the honored guests—who were, quite strangely, all Indian. However, no reservation Indians were these. No, these people were the sort of Native Americans that one might have expected to encounter on the plains sixty, perhaps seventy, years earlier. Each one was attired in savage splendor, their buckskin clothing decorated with porcupine quills, beads and painted designs of blue and white.

There might have been other colors etched onto their clothing as well, but Kali failed to notice. She was distracted. The sun, which should have been stationed permanently in the sky, was becoming brighter and brighter, almost painfully so, as though it might be falling to the earth.

Closer and closer it came, its rays ever more radiant, until Kali had no choice but to turn aside and shield her eyes. And then it stopped. All was darkness again.

Opening her eyes, Kali glanced up to meet the piercing gaze of an elderly man. White hair peeked out from beneath a heavy Indian headdress, and between his eyes sat a lock of hair, which fell to the bridge of his nose. On his head sat a headdress of white fur. Two buffalo horns, decorated with scalp locks on the pointed ends, angled straight up and away from the head in two semicircles. Feathers, too numerous to count, fell to the floor and, like a train, followed the man as he paced slowly forward. A long, painted buckskin tunic reached well below his knees; beaded and quilled leggings stretched to the tops of his moccasins. Scalp locks and fringe dangled from sleeves, from the sides of his leggings, the bottom of his tunic and the back of his moccasins. In his hand he carried a lance decorated with more scalp locks, medicine bags, feathers and an animal skin.

Kali couldn't take her eyes from him, though she tightened her grip on Soaring Eagle's hand. One slow step followed another as the old man came toward them. He didn't relax his stare at her, either, not even when he at last came to stand directly in front of them.

Kali alternately wanted to run, then remain where she was. She leaned toward Soaring Eagle, who threw his arm around her shoulders.

The old man waved his lance in front of them. At once two women came forward, each one carrying a large shell and a braid of sweet-smelling sage, which was smoking at one end.

"Smudge them," said the old man.

At once, the two women went to work. One of them brushed smoke from the sage over the top of Kali's head, down to her face, her shoulders, over her entire body. The other woman was doing the same to Soaring Eagle.

"May your minds be free," said the old man as this was being done. "May your hearts be true."

The entire process was repeated. Then again and once more, four being the sacred number.

At last it was done, and the old man stepped forward. He said to Kali, "So long have we been apart. So long have we suffered. But now go from here as one. For from this day onward, where there was but one heartbeat, now there are two."

Then turning to Soaring Eagle, he said, "Do you promise to love this woman and no other?"

"I will."

Kali smiled, and it eased some aching part of her to hear Soaring Eagle speak these words.

The old man turned to her. "And do you accept this man's promise? Do you believe he will honor you from now, for the rest of your lives?"

"Yes," she said. "I do."

Again Kali smiled.

The old man waved his arms, ordering, "Come forward, my wife, and clothe our children in their ceremonial gowns."

An old woman stepped forward, holding in one arm a dress of the skins of a deer or mountain goat. It was a white three-skinned dress, with row after row of elk teeth on its yoke. At the center of the dress, front and back, was a triangular piece of hide, painted blue and sewn into the dress. At the bottom end of the dress were two square patches, also painted blue. Knee-length moccasins completed the regalia and were sewn with beads and quillwork in geometric patterns that matched the dress.

Men's white buckskin tunic, leggings and moccasins, painted with the same geometric designs as the dress, were held in her other arm. With a clap of the old woman's hands, both Kali and Soaring Eagle were donned in the clothes, which shimmered over their forms as though the material had been sewn with magic instead of stitches.

"Know then that the past lives in you no longer. Go now my children," said the old man. "Go and be merry, aware that from this day and for the rest of your lives, your search is done." He clapped his hands.

Soaring Eagle turned to Kali, took her in his arms and kissed her. And Kali, closing her eyes, forgot to breathe.

"Come, my wife," said Soaring Eagle, raising his head.

Kali, perfectly content, smiled back at him. "Yes, my love," she said, placing her hand in his.

Arms around one another, they turned toward the waiting assemblage, only to face . . . nothing. Where previously had stood the old man, the old woman and all the honored guests, now there was nothing save ground, grass and a slight wind that whistled through the cottonwood tree.

Soaring Eagle leaned back against the cottonwood tree and glared at Gilda.

Damn, he muttered under his breath. There was something wrong with intrusion when one least expected it—it left one with the feeling of having committed some wrong. Indeed, for Soaring Eagle, the interruption might even be physically painful, for Kali had more than a little excited him.

Would he have to start at the beginning again with Kali? he wondered idly. Trying to regain what precious ground he might have won this night?

Grimacing at his thoughts, he listened to Gilda's song. Odd that he'd never heard that particular chant, since he was familiar with most Blackfeet melodies. It was an unusual ditty, too, a soothing song. He shut his eyes—if only for a moment. Strange, he thought, this lethargy that had come over him. Stranger still, how young he felt, as though he were no more than a child, being sung to sleep . . .

She lay beside him, beautiful and pure, here in their wedding bed. She was perfect, lovely, and he wanted her as a man needs the woman he adores.

He had been right about Kali. She was the one, the only one for him. And now she was his.

He let his fingers graze down the length of her cheek, so soft, so flawless. He watched as shivers of anticipation raced over her skin, making her tremble. Repeating the gesture, he observed the same movement within her yet again. In faith, he could feel her need.

All in good time, he thought to himself. All in good time.

For now, he longed to kiss away every shudder, every quiver. And he drew his hands down the length of her neck, as though he might begin the process this moment.

But not quite yet.

Picking up a lock of her mane, he twirled the reddish curl through his fingers. She was startlingly beautiful, his sweet Kali, with her unusual coloring of golden, red hair and deep green eyes. She mesmerized him with her comeliness, he thought, gazing lengthily at her. He was truly ensnared, caught, held captive by the beauty of her.

Ah, that time could cease at this moment. And he thought that perhaps for him, it might have done so. Always would he see her as she was now; his Kali, his love, the perfection of his most exquisite fantasy.

It was then that he resolved that this night, their wedding night, would not be a painful experience for her. No, he would make this, her first time, memorable, wonderful. Yes, with the pleasure and passion of sweet love, he would bind her to him; and he, to her.

Bending, he brushed his lips over the path his fingers had so recently forged. So silky was her cheek where he kissed it, so fragrant her skin, that his senses spun. "You are my love," he whispered. "Know that I will do all I can to make this, our wedding night, good for you."

"Yes," she nodded. "I would make it good for you, too."

"It is already perfect for me. You are here with me."

"But there is more, isn't there?"

"There is more, much more," he said, "but we are in no rush."

"Aren't we?" she asked. "It seems as though there is something urgent awaiting me."

"Not in this, our dream."

"Oh, yes," she said, "not in our dream."

He reached down to gather a soft breast in his hand, kneading it gently. In reaction, she moaned, the sound pure music to his eager ears.

He murmured, "It is good that we are, at last, united in marriage, for it would be a great wrong were we to be apart. Together," he said, "we can be strong; greater than if we stood one, alone."

"Yes," she mumbled, smiling at him, "the two of us together could be our strength . . . Oh, that's nice," she said, as his lips found a vulnerable spot on her neck. She shifted, throwing back her shoulders and presenting him with the full length of her neck and breasts.

He accepted the gift as a child might a present, and he nuzzled against her, tasting the sweetness of her skin.

And with his lips, with his fingers, he paid homage to her, though after a moment, he rose up, coming to look down on her face-to-face. He whispered, "Were I blindfolded, I would always know you. For your skin tastes of honey, its fragrance like nectar, its touch softer than the wild rose."

"Really? You're only saying that so that I'll make

love with you," she said, winding her arms around his neck and pulling him to her.

"No, for that is a given. What I say is true. I am glad that you changed your mind about us."

"As I am, too."

Again, he grinned at her, wishing with all his heart that this were real, not simply an illusion. Still, as he looked at her, he knew pure joy: for she was as naked as the day she was born, and what was going to happen between them was as inevitable as day turning to evening.

He murmured, "You are mine now. Whatever may come, we will face it together, do you agree?"

"Always."

"It will not always be an easy road for us."

"I know."

"There is much prejudice from your people, from mine. But together we can weather it."

"We will," she said. "And I will do what I can to bring the truth to light about your people, your problems."

"That is good, and I know that you will," he said. "But your cooperation in this is not the reason why I wish to love you."

"I know that, too," she said.

"Are you aware of the first time I knew what was in my own heart?"

"You mean as regards me?"

"Yes."

"No, no, I don't," she said, reaching up to run her fingers through the length of his hair. "When was that?"

"There, on top of Chief Mountain, under the beams of a midnight moon. The first thing I thought when I

*first saw you was that I had at last found beauty. I was
drawn to you, and I believed initially that you might
be a part of my fast, my vision. For it is on Chief
Mountain that many of my people experience contact
with the spirits. At that time I thought you were from
their realm, the spiritual world, for your hair seemed to
be on fire. And then you touched my fan and I knew
you were of this world . . . and that we were, perhaps,
tied to each other."*

She nodded. "I felt that way, too."

"Some hearts are like that," he said. "No one else
will do for them. And so it could be with us, I think."

"Do you?"

"Yes, but I must admit that you also confused me
that night."

"I did?"

"Yes, when you left, I did not know what to think.
Were you part of my vision, or just a silly white
woman who had chanced upon me at an inopportune
moment? It occurred to me that you could be a bad
thing to come into my life."

"Oh, no. You did? Is that why you were so angry at
me at first?"

He nodded. "What was I to think? You had run
away."

"But—"

"And then I kissed you, out there on the range, and
you responded. And somehow, at that moment, something powerful took hold of me. For as I looked at you, I
understood who you are. Joy filled me, and I think I lost
a little bit of myself in that kiss, for I have not been the
same since then."

"Truly?"

He nodded. "Though these feelings, too, confused

me. You are, obviously, from a section of humanity that has caused great turmoil to mine. However, had there been any doubt about my feelings, it would have been dispelled when I watched you stand up to those hired cowboys. It was then that I knew that if I wanted the happiness you might present me, I had to reach out and take it."

"I see," she said, her fingers combing through his long hair. "And is that why you asked me to marry you?"

"Yes."

She was silent for so long, he began to wonder if perhaps he had said too much, had been too open with her. And for a moment, he sensed about himself a vulnerability that was almost shocking.

At last, however, she said, "I, too, experienced something that caused me some confusion, as well as joy."

He swallowed. "What was that?"

"I'm not certain. As you did, there, that first night on Chief Mountain, I thought you might be an apparition, or perhaps a dream. Something drew me to you . . . something I can't explain. I kept telling myself that I was imagining things, that you weren't real, and when I reached out and touched your fan, it was as though I awoke. It scared me. You scared me . . . and I am not one easily frightened."

"I see. That is why you left so quickly?"

"Yes."

"And now, are you still frightened of me?"

Her mouth twisted as though she might smile. "A little," she admitted.

"And for the same reason?"

"Oh, no. Not for the same reason at all."

"And yet," he said, "there might be more cause for

fear now, for the spirits have united us, one to the other."

"Soaring Eagle," she sat up slightly, "do you know of many people who have been married in this way?"

He shook his head. "There are some who have been married within the Medicine Pipe ceremony, and when that happens, it is as though they have been united by the spirits. But I know of only one other couple who were brought together by the spirits themselves, and they are now very old."

"Have you met them?"

"Yes. She was once a white woman."

"Was?"

"No one remembers that about her now."

"I see. She has been here so long that she is now Blackfeet?"

He nodded.

"I would like to meet them. Do you think I might?"

"Perhaps it could be arranged. But not now. There are, I think, other pressing needs."

He glanced at her to witness a most radiant smile. She said, "Yes."

He leaned over her, his lips finding hers, tasting hers. "I will never forget the pure joy of your taste. Perhaps I should warn you that before this night is done, I should know every part of you."

She groaned.

And with his lips, he proceeded to make good his word. He forged a path to a sensitive spot on her ear, tasted it, then treated the other to the same.

She melted against him as though her body had suddenly become as soft as wet clay.

He murmured, "How exciting is your response. I will never forget it."

She made another high-pitched whimper, deep in her throat, the sound inviting such excitement from him that he could feel the effects of it to the very tips of his toes.

"I love you very much," he said.

"And I love you," she admitted. "Promise me," she said, "that you will always be true to me, no matter what comes."

"I promise."

She sighed against him, and he hugged her. He moved lower, toward the length of her neck, where he proceeded to make good his word.

She shivered in his arms. "That feels good."

"Yes," he said, "doesn't it?"

He lingered there, his lips, his tongue, showering praise on her, and in response, he felt the stirrings of her hips as she began to twist against him. Ah, yes, he would come to know all of her yet this night.

He moved lower, his lips tasting the tip of one sweet breast. And this time, it was he whose moans whispered on the wind.

He murmured, "It is good between us."

"Yes."

He nibbled on one and then the other breast for some time, being in absolutely no hurry. Aa, slowly, slowly. He would have her experience pleasure even this, her first time.

She shivered beneath his ministrations, and he rejoiced to see it, for it meant the right moment had come for him; he would shift his attentions lower still. Rising up, onto his elbows, he scooted downward, over her feminine curves and valleys, his lips skimming lower, opening her legs to accommodate him.

"Soaring Eagle," she protested at once, shifting her

weight and tightening her thighs, as though she might oust him from her.

Briefly he glanced up at her. His eyes met hers, and without a word being spoken, he let her know that he would have his way in this matter.

Silently, she objected.

And just as silently, he made his wishes known once more. He touched her . . . there.

"Soaring Eagle, I—I . . ."

He didn't speak. Instead he smiled at her and continued his caress.

"Soaring Eagle—"

"Sh-h-h-h. You will like it. I promise."

"I like it already. But—"

"There is not a part of you that I would not know." And with this said, with his lips, he proceeded to adore her.

Shy at first, she at last began to respond. In answer, his excitement rose. Her breathing changed, becoming short and rapid. Ever so gradually she changed position, opening to him, straining against him.

It practically sent him soaring into the heavens.

And then, he felt her rising ardor, pushing upward as though toward a peak. She was almost there, he knew it; there, at the edge of their carefully made precipice, ready to fall. And as she pushed higher and higher, her inhibitions seemed to dissipate. Gladly, she opened to him fully.

Her hips swayed, her breathing caught and tiny beads of perspiration appeared on her skin. It was as though he were witnessing the opening of a blossom. And then it happened. She reached the apex, the accompaniment of tiny high-pitched sounds like pure music.

*His head spun. He groaned, he growled. What rap-
ture, what bliss. Aa, yes, she was his. His alone.*

*And he could not remember being ready for someone
or something more.*

*Rising up onto his forearms over her, he rained
kisses over her belly, her breasts, her throat, slowly
kissing his way back up to the very top of her head.*

*At last, he came to rest over her, on her, and she
whispered, "That was wonderful."*

*"Yes," he said, and nothing more. He wasn't certain
how capable he was of speaking at the moment, for the
desire still burned deeply within him.*

*"But you . . ." she said, "you didn't have the same
release, did you?"*

*He grinned, the effect being lost in her hair, where
his face had come to rest. However, he managed to say,
"Not yet."*

"But you must."

*He couldn't help the small laugh that escaped his
lips. He said, "I assure you, my love, that it is not over
yet."*

"It isn't?"

*He shook his head, a very slight movement. "That
place where I was caressing you . . ."*

"Yes?"

*"That is where our bodies will join, soon, very
soon."*

"Oh," she said, as though she hadn't known.

*He came up onto his elbows and gazed down at her.
Her eyes were wide, and he couldn't help but ask, "You
knew that, didn't you?"*

She shook her head.

*And he sighed. What sort of a people, he wondered,
did not make known to their young girls the pleasure*

to be had between a man and a woman? Did they not care that a woman's reputation hinged on such things? For without complete knowledge of the nature of men, as well as the nature of women, a girl might fall victim to the first boy to give her attention.

Still, he would not mar this moment with further criticism of her society. Hadn't he done that enough?

Brushing his fingers over the soft skin of her neck, then further still to her breast, he said, "A man and a woman are meant to join in this way. There is much pleasure to be had in the act, but it will hurt at first."

"I know," she said. "It is the one thing that I know about it. That it hurts."

"That is all?"

She nodded.

He sighed. He knew of no other way to indoctrinate her in the truth, except perhaps by example. He asked, "Have you never watched animals mate?"

"Well, no, not really."

He grinned. "Then you will have to trust me. I promise that if you will forbear the pain, there is more pleasure to be had."

"Trust you?" She paused as though confused. Then, "Soaring Eagle. Please show me, please."

He didn't need to be asked twice. "I will," he said, "I will."

He kissed her while he moved over her. Slowly at first, so that he didn't overwhelm her, he gradually sought to become one with her in a most physical sense.

He felt her pain as though it were his own. "There is no stopping it this first time," he said. "I am sorry."

She nodded.

But for him, it was pure pleasure, pure beauty. Leaning down, he took her lips with his own, all the while making small movements.

At first she stiffened.

And he stopped . . . but only for a moment. Then another tiny movement. Another stall. Holding back, always holding back. Over and over, he repeated the movement controlling himself until he felt her at last relax.

Coming up onto his forearms, he asked, "Has the pain gone?"

"Not completely," she responded. "But it's getting better."

He nodded. He rested, then engineered another tiny thrust, followed by another and another, until she pulled him down to her and whispered in his ear, "The pain has gone."

Simple words, yet with this knowledge, he was filled with such delight, he could little understand it, and pleasure surged through him so quickly that he almost lost himself at that moment. Control, control, he cautioned himself.

But if he thought to take charge of their lovemaking completely, he was in for a surprise, for she began to move with him.

He sucked in his breath. The sensuality of feeling was exquisite . . . almost too much. Still, he held back. For, he thought, might it not be possible to give her yet more pleasure? Aa, yes, this he would do for her, before he sought his own.

He moved little, suppressing his urge, controlling himself as best he could. And then it happened. So close were they, so attuned, he felt her begin the upward spi-

ral yet again. Luckily, he had been keeping most of his weight away from her, leaning on his elbows, and so he was able to catch her look of surprise. Ah, what a treasure, that glance.

She said, "Soaring Eagle, I feel it again."

"I know. I sense it in you, too."

"But you? I would have you—"

"Don't worry about me."

"But—"

"Your pleasure gives me pleasure."

"Oh," was all she uttered before she began a series of rapid movements. She strained against him, fidgeting with him, over and over, until . . . He drew in a rapid breath. Hold steady, he cautioned himself. Just a little longer.

And then it happened. As though he had become a vital part of her, he felt the tide of frenzy within her begin to peak, and in reaction, his mind went blank. He surged forward and upward, giving her all he had to give.

They peaked together, their urgent moans, their heartfelt groans mixing one with the other until it would have been hard to tell where one stopped and the other began.

At last, he collapsed against her. His body was spent. Yet there was about him an element that rejoiced. It was as though he were part of the body, yet separate from it. In truth, from a distance above, he seemed to look down upon the two of them.

And then the oddest thing happened: Suddenly she was there beside him. She, whom he loved with all his heart; she, whom he had promised his devotion; she shared this moment with him, his very space. And if it were possible, a feeling of intimacy, much greater than that of the physical, swept over him. It was as though he knew her every thought . . . and in doing so, had found her beautiful.

And he knew in that moment that he loved her more than life itself. Ah, what joy. What complete happiness . . .

Chapter 16

And they were of much pride and dignity; that one could see at a glance.

James Willard Schultz, *My Life as an Indian*

"**B**uild your fires, prepare your breakfast," sang out the voice of the camp crier. "We have a new Medicine Pipe owner. Sitting Beaver has smoked the Pipe with Comes Running Bird. All look to your hearts that you might help provide the feast and share in the cost, for this thing that happens is very honorable. Be quick. The ceremony will begin with the rising of the sun. Bring what you can. Everyone come."

The drums began.

Kali awoke, feeling more than a little strange. What was that around her waist? And that over her breasts?

Was it an arm? A leg? *Dear Lord!*

Whose?

Her eyelids flew wide. She peeked over to her right.

Soaring Eagle. It was Soaring Eagle. And he was naked. *Naked.*

She glanced downward, at herself. And so was she.

Worse, the feeling of something sticky at the junction of her legs gave her warning that all was not as it should be. Shock, alarm and more than a little outrage filled her.

She glanced upward, espying a scattering of stars through the opening at the top of the tepee. *Tepee?* Where was she?

"Wake up." Shoving at Soaring Eagle's arm, she sat up, holding a blanket over her chest. Avoiding the fire to her left because the embers were still red-hot, she quickly felt around the ground for her clothes. They had to be here somewhere.

Soaring Eagle came awake in an instant, jumping to his feet and grabbing hold of his weapons, his gun and knife.

"What has happened?" he asked, his voice deep and choked with the aftereffects of sleep. "Is there an enemy?"

"Yes," Kali said, glaring at him. "Me."

"You?"

He looked at her as though she might have suddenly grown horns. But Kali was having none of that.

"How could you take advantage of me, seduce me, when I was sleeping?"

"Me? Take advantage of you?"

"Yes," she said, her ire building. "That's what it's normally called, isn't it? And where are my clothes?"

He gave her another one of those confused looks, as though he had only become aware of their state of dress—or rather their lack of it.

He said, "It was real? . . . I thought I was dreaming . . . I—I did not do this. Not consciously."

"Oh, really? I suppose you're going to try to convince me next that I seduced you?"

"I—I . . ." he stuttered.

And though Kali recognized his frustration and his fluster for exactly what it was, she was not about to give quarter. Throwing back her shoulders, she tossed him what she hoped was her most smug, most condescending look.

"I cannot explain this," he went on to say, "except to tell you that, though I am aware of how bad this appears, I did not seduce you. I would not have taken you to me without your consent, and certainly not without marriage."

"A likely story." She thrust out her chin. "Tell that to my father and the Indian agent and see if they believe you."

It was a threat. Even to her own ears, it sounded like a threat. Not that she would ever act on it, but she wasn't going to take the words back.

Darn him. At this moment, she felt mad enough to roast him alive.

"Where are my clothes?" She stared up at Soaring Eagle, not bothering to disguise her animosity, nor her contempt, as though she expected him to be on his hands and knees, helping her search.

But instead of assistance, he stood ramrod straight, appearing as though he might have become an image in stone. And all at once a deadening silence filled the space around them, while a mask of stoicism descended over his features. It gave Kali cause for some alarm, for she couldn't tell what he was thinking. Couldn't tell if he were as angry as she.

She also noticed that his nakedness seemed not to bother him at all, though it did a great deal to plague Kali. For, despite her indignation, she couldn't help but admire him. What a magnificent specimen of manhood he presented.

"Soaring Eagle, could you please cover yourself? I know it is dark in here, but not that dark." She glanced around the space as though his cooperation were assured, nothing of concern. "Where are we?" she added.

But he stirred not at all, although she noticed that he did take a moment to scan his surroundings. He said, his expression, even his tone of voice, barren of emotion, "We are in a lodge, though I don't know whose tepee this is. I do not recognize it."

"I see." She grimaced. "Let me ensure that I understand this correctly. You just happened to find a deserted tepee to have your way with me?"

Soaring Eagle let his stoicism slip for a moment as he frowned. He said, "I had a dream, but I—"

"A dream? I think this is more than a dream. And you are going to have to do some pretty fancy explaining. Here help me find my clothes. The camp crier has announced that the Medicine Pipe ceremony is about to begin."

But Soaring Eagle didn't budge, not to aid her, not to clothe himself.

"Soaring Eagle, please. If you don't want me to cause trouble, you had better help me."

He crossed his arms over his chest. "Another threat?"

Tears of frustration filled Kali's eyes. This was terrible; a complete disaster. She was missing it; missing the beginning of the Pipe ceremony. Not only that. She was in the process of alienating the one person who had, thus far, offered her assistance.

But what other choice did she have? She couldn't

very well pretend that nothing had happened between them.

"Damn!" she spit out the word.

"Do white women often curse?" he asked, his voice, his manner, still void of emotion.

"No . . . yes, white women often curse if there's reason, and I think I have grounds for plenty more where that came from." Raising the buffalo robe on which she sat, Kali felt beneath it, her fingers coming in contact with some sort of material. She pulled and heaved a sigh of relief . . . it was her dress.

"So do I," he said.

"I beg your pardon? So do you what?" She drew her arms through the dress.

But he didn't elaborate. Instead he said, "Gilda is your friend, is she not?"

"She is my guide. But what has that got to do with—"

"What is the last thing you consciously remember?"

Kali thought for a moment. Consciously? She bit her lip, for she, too, had been dreaming . . . wonderful, pleasant dreams about herself, about Soaring Eagle . . .

Kali shook her head. "I remember that Gilda came and told me that my father couldn't come here until morning."

"Is that all?"

"No," Kali glanced up to send him a glare. "You know very well that she sang songs for us."

"And then?"

Kali frowned. "That's all I remember. I fell asleep."

He nodded. "As did I."

"What are you trying to tell me? That Gilda did this to me? To you?"

He didn't answer.

And Kali frowned. What, after all, did she really know about Gilda?

"I don't have time for this," Kali observed at last. "If I don't hurry, I'm going to miss—"

"I will not leave this spot until this matter is settled between the two of us."

Kali felt as though the air had been forcefully dragged from her. "Y-you," she stuttered, "w-will not leave? But I must. I must go—"

"I will not let this thing, this misunderstanding, come between us."

"It is already between us."

"Then you are willing for me to think the worst of you?"

"The worst of me? What are you talking about? I . . . I am the injured party. I'm the one who woke up to find myself in the most compromising situation a woman can be in. And you . . . you are threatening to think the worst of me? Soaring Eagle, I don't give a . . . what you think of me."

"Yet," he said matter-of-factly, "you should. After all, Gilda is your friend, your guide, not mine."

"What's that got to do with—"

"What else am I to believe?"

Kali shrugged, as though to reiterate her lack of interest.

"You, with your beauty and sweet talk," he said. "You manage to charm your way into my affection, endeavor to enlist my aid in bringing you to my village. And what do you do? You set your guide upon us."

"I set my? . . . Oh, this is too much."

"Is it? Suppose for a moment that I am as innocent as you say you are. You have already told me that I will need to explain myself to your father and the Indian agent as soon as we leave here—why? In order to have me arrested?"

Kali's mouth opened. "I—I—"

"Did you come here only to cause trouble, sweet Kali?"

"You know that can't possibly be true."

He arched a brow, his look disbelieving.

"All right. Suppose, just suppose that I am a trouble-maker, and that's my only intention. Explain to me, then, why I would set this all into motion *before* the Medicine Pipe ceremony? Why would I do that when I still very much need your help?"

"Yes, why, indeed? Unless you are not here to see the ceremony, but to—"

"Oh, really. This is absurd."

He ignored her. "Tell me, what sort of magic did Gilda possess that let you accomplish this?"

"Me accomplish? . . . Magic?"

"*Aa*, magic," he said leaning toward her as though he might either threaten her or kiss her. At the moment, Kali didn't know which was the most dangerous. He continued, "I think we have experienced more than an illusion, Kali."

She snorted. "We?"

"I dreamed we were married. Did you, too?"

"I . . ." Kali clamped down on whatever it was she'd been about to say. Yes, she had dreamed they were married . . . and more. But that wasn't real. That had been a dream, for heaven's sake. Besides, she wasn't about to admit anything to Soaring Eagle right now.

He asked, "Where is Gilda?"

Kali stared around the room as though the woman

might materialize at the mere mention of her name. She shrugged. "I don't know."

"Then let us go and find her and determine from her the truth or not of your vows."

"My vows? What vows have I given you?"

His look at her was patronizing, as though he might be speaking to a child. Nevertheless, he said, "You have told me that you are here to help my people, to record our history in pictures. I believed you and have told this to the council. But now I have reason to doubt you, and I fear that perhaps you only spouted words at me that you believed I needed to hear."

Kali swallowed hard. What sort of a silver-tongued devil was this man? Perhaps she had underestimated exactly how intelligent he was, for he had scarcely said more than a few words, yet he was somehow managing to turn this entire plight around on her.

Well, fine. Good. He was free to believe whatever he might, but he could do his fancy talking elsewhere; she wasn't about to put up with it. And she wasn't going to defend herself, either. She had no need. Instead, she said simply, "How like a man."

He raised an eyebrow.

"Yes, how like a man," she said with a little more gusto, holding the blanket up around her so that she could settle her dress around her hips and over her legs as she spoke. "Only a man," she continued, "could get himself into a compromising situation and then seek to extricate himself by making it appear as if the problem is all the woman's doing. Well, I won't be having it, Mr. Soaring Eagle. I've told you the truth about myself, about my intentions whether you decide to believe me or not. It's not my fault that I awoke to find myself . . .

in trouble." She glanced up, and despite herself, she gulped. What a spectacular image he presented, for he had not bothered to hide any of his assets from her.

She looked away and began searching for her Turkish trousers, the ones that fit beneath her skirt. "Please, Soaring Eagle, if we are to talk, I would ask that you clothe yourself."

Kali had found her trousers and was about to pull them on when she realized she couldn't. They were unbearably soiled and stained from her late night *affaire d'amour*. She blushed. How terribly personal, for the clothing was marked in a way that spoke of her very recent departure from maidenhood.

Was her dress soiled in the same way? Oh, dear. She hadn't taken the time to look.

She frowned. She needed to wash her trousers, possibly her dress, too. In truth, she needed an overall bath. But right now, she'd settle for enough water to repair the damage to her clothing.

Which meant she was going to have to ask this man for his help . . . again. She pulled a face. The mere thought of having to do so was humbling beyond words.

Nevertheless, she knew she couldn't go out in public in such a state.

She took a deep breath. And one more for courage. "Ah, Soaring Eagle," she began, tossing her head back and raising her chin, if only to hide the fact that she knew her face was filling with color. "I—I," she continued, "can't dress completely without some water to wash. Could you . . . get some for me?"

She chanced a quick glance up at him, hating the feeling of being at his mercy. Especially when he glared at her.

"Wash?"

"Ah, yes. I'm afraid that my clothes are . . . stained, and I really need to—"

Without warning, he bent toward her, taking hold of her trousers and holding them up to the light. After a moment, he gave her a sheepish sort of look. "Are they ruined beyond repair?" he asked.

"No," she responded, her voice softening. "I just need some water. That's all."

"And probably a bath, too."

"A bath would be lovely, but right now I would be happy if I could have enough water to wash these— and perhaps some soap if you have any."

She glanced up at that moment to catch him gazing back at her, and was, herself, surprised. Gone was his anger, his indignation.

It seemed incredible, but true. It was as though the unpleasantness between them had never happened. And this, because she had a personal problem?

Yet, instead of resentment, there was about him a look of gentleness. In truth, his expression at this moment reminded her of the tender care she had always assumed a man might give his . . . wife. And even his voice was warm, when he said, "I could bring you water, but would it not be better if you went to the river where you could bathe?"

"I-I can't," she said, glancing away from him. Goodness, how embarrassing this was. "My, ah, trousers are too soiled to wear, and my skirt is too short to be worn in public without them."

"I see," he said as though he only now understood the real problem. "I could carry you to the stream."

"Ah, no. That would draw attention to us, don't you think?"

"*Saa*. All in the village are involved in the Medicine Pipe ceremony."

She inhaled quickly, the sound of it loud to her own ears. It was as though the mere mention of the ceremony pained her. She was missing it; missing her one and perhaps only chance to capture the ceremony on film. And this was the one reason she was even here.

She bit back tears of frustration and straightened her shoulders, making an effort to compose herself. She'd be darned if she'd let this man see her cry.

Collecting herself, at least enough so that her voice didn't shake, she said, "Your offer is generous, Soaring Eagle, but just the water would be fine, I think."

But she had reckoned without taking Soaring Eagle's character into account. "Nonsense," he said as he quickly drew on his own clothes and, stepping toward her, placed his arms around her and picked her up.

"Really, this is unnecessary. Please put me down." She struggled against his hold.

However, with two large steps, he managed to reach the entrance before she could do any damage to him, and pulling open the flap, he stepped out into the darkness of an early morning.

He was right, she thought, as she glanced around the village. No one seemed to pay them any attention.

Briefly, she considered struggling out of Soaring Eagle's arms, but decided against it. She wasn't dressed for this, and modesty would not allow her to take a chance on drawing anyone's notice. And so, like it or not, for the moment, she accepted his embrace.

Quickly, he trod through the village. But before he had taken her very far, he asked, "Does your dress, the one you are wearing, also need washing?"

The question brought to mind too clearly her involvement with this man, her utter dependence on him while in this village, and Kali, completely flustered, clenched her hands into fists, as though she might strike out at him. However, her voice was even when she said, quite honestly, "I—I don't know. I haven't looked at my dress closely. But the colors of the dress, and of my other things, are dark. Perhaps, even if soiled, they won't show stains."

"Maybe," he said. "But I think that I will see that they are washed while you bathe, nonetheless."

"Oh, no. I can do it myself. Besides, these are the only clothes I have with me."

"I will get you some other clothes. That way you can enjoy your bath without worry."

"Oh," she nodded. Was it too good to be true? "That . . . that would be kind of you."

The impulse to relax against him was strong. His arms felt good around her, and she was tired. But Kali fought against the temptation. How could she give in when she now knew that her instincts about him had been correct? She couldn't trust the man.

It did occur to her that he was helping her. It also crossed her mind that perhaps he deserved some thanks for the aid he was giving her. But Kali wasn't completely charmed. No, and she'd be darned if she'd ever say thank you and Soaring Eagle's name in the same sentence again.

"While you bathe," he said, interrupting her thoughts, "I will set up your tripod near my father's lodge, if you like."

Kali slanted him a frown. "You will? You are still going to help me? But I thought you said that you are doubtful of me, of my intentions."

"True, but I did give you my promise to help you. Besides, the council expects me to do this for you."

"Oh, I see. Ah"—she hated to be made into a liar so soon, but before she could stop herself, the words tripped over her tongue and she found herself saying— "Thank you, Soaring Eagle."

"You're welcome," he replied, arriving at their destination and depositing her at the bank of the river. Luckily, there were many trees nearby, providing cover and a place to hide, should she need it. "Here," he said, reaching a hand out to her, "give me your clothes."

Kali gazed up into Soaring Eagle's face. With only the starlight to see by, most of his features were hidden by the darkness. Even still, she yearned to stretch out her hand, to touch him, to comfort him.

What was happening to her? she wondered. Why, only a few moments ago, she'd been ready to feed this man to the lions. And now?

She said, "I'm afraid I won't do that . . ." she coughed. "That is, I can't possibly give you my clothes unless you turn your back."

Dutifully and without a word, he spun around.

"Can I trust you not to peek?" she asked.

"You have no choice," he said, a note of humor in his tone.

But Kali, hearing those words, read more into the phrase than perhaps he intended. Did he mean she should trust him about last night? About other things, too? Not likely. The evidence against him was too overwhelming.

She said, "And might I ask you for your word, that you will return these clothes to me in a timely fashion?"

"I promise that I will bring them back to you as soon as they are washed."

"How do I know you'll keep your word?"

He shrugged. "You will have to decide that yourself. I have already told you what I will do."

Not satisfied, but still not knowing what else she might ask, she said, "Very well. Then, please leave here while I undress."

"Leave?"

"Yes. How can I possibly disrobe when you are still here?"

She heard him chuckle, the sound of it maddening. "Soaring Eagle?"

He shook his head. "How can you undress when I am *not* in your sight?" he countered. "For I will have to return to get your clothing."

"I'm not sure I understand what you're saying."

"While I'm here before you, you can ensure that my back is to you. If I leave, I must still stay close-by to you in order to get your clothing and take it to my grandmother to wash."

"Yes?"

"I could always hide and watch you."

"Oh," she said. "I see."

"Besides, I have already observed you dressing once this morning, and I have beheld you with much less on than your dress."

"Soaring Eagle!"

He chuckled. "Perhaps," he said, "you might simply have to trust me to my word."

Never! Although, even as they talked, Kali was doing as he suggested and was carefully removing her dress. Perhaps she was making too much of this. After all, she was no more than a few steps from the river. She would simply throw her dress over his shoulder and plunge into the water before he would have a chance to turn around.

It took but a moment to remove the garment, while she commented, "I don't think I need trust you, Soaring Eagle. I might have to put up with you at the moment, but trust is something one earns. It is not given freely."

"Is that so? In that case, maybe I'll just turn around."

Kali, who had at that moment released her dress, gasped. Quickly, she drew back the apparel and held it up. And not even the sound of his soft laughter calmed her.

"It is a shame," he said, his backside still toward her.

"Shame?" she asked. "What's a shame?"

"You did not need to resort to magic to have me, my wife. If you will remember back to the early evening—before your guide joined us—I was yours for the taking . . ."

"Oh!" The word was more reaction than speech. How dare he?

And what was that he had called her? *Wife*?

Well, really . . . She was no more his wife than . . .

All at once a feeling of warmth stole over her. And try as she might, Kali couldn't deny that the thought of this man being her very own husband was stimulating . . . quite beyond belief . . .

Soaring Eagle made his way back to camp. He had a few questions that needed answering.

First and foremost, where was Gilda? Second, what magic had she worked on he and Kali, and why? Third, what was Kali's involvement in it? Could he trust her?

Soaring Eagle was no fool. It didn't take genius to realize that what had happened with Kali had been no mere dream. The spirits had married them, had ensured the marriage was consummated.

Why?

As he retraced his steps to the wedding tepee, he frowned. Whose lodge was this? No canvas tepee was this. Pure buffalo hides formed the covering, the skins bleached until they were white. They had also been painted in horizonal designs of blue and red, accented with yellow balls that looked like the sun, the moon or stars.

Odd, that Soaring Eagle did not recognize the painter's motif. Since most of his people adorned their tepees in a manner to honor their dreams, Soaring Eagle prided himself on being able to recognize each and every one of them. But not this one.

He shook his head, still puzzling. He needed answers. He would have them.

He pulled back the lodge's entrance flap and stepped inside. His buffalo robe, his blanket and weapons lay where he had set them. Kali's tripod, her camera, packs, flash sticks and other assorted items lay to the left of the entrance.

Outside of that, the rest of the furnishings were unfamiliar to him. This was no poor man's lodge. Why, the inner tepee lining alone was splendidly spun in a checkered pattern of reds and blues, worth a fortune even by the white man's standards.

There were other items scattered around the lodge that indicated grandness, as well: several willow backrests, many more buffalo robes and more than twenty blankets, as well as beautifully crafted parfleches, which were set up against the lodge poles. Cooking utensils, pots and pans sat to the back of the lodge. And in the center were the dying embers of a fire; more firewood was stacked next to it, ready to be used, ready to serve.

Who had done this? His grandmother? Impossible. His father? His mother? Unlikely. Gilda? Possibly.

But if it had been the guide, where would she have obtained goods like these? With what revenue had she bought them? And perhaps more importantly, what reason did she have for doing all this?

Revenge seemed the most likely answer. Had his family, perhaps long ago, insulted hers? Did he know her?

Yet if she were motivated by revenge alone, why would her actions have brought him happiness? Unless . . . Had Kali or her father, perhaps, offended Gilda?

Thinking back, he recalled Kali mentioning that Gilda had brought her to Chief Mountain on that momentous evening. Also, Gilda had been present during the cattle stampede. And last night she had sung them to sleep; a night that would forever change their lives.

Aa, it seemed likely that Gilda was the source of their problems. The only thing he couldn't understand was why.

Perhaps he should endeavor to learn more about her. Where was she from? How had she become Kali's guide? Who were her family members? But probably most importantly, where was she now?

Was it possible that she'd done her worst—or maybe her best—and then left?

Soaring Eagle sighed. He was afraid he would find no answers here in this lodge—only more questions.

It was too bad that his father was busily engaged with other matters, for Soaring Eagle longed to seek his advice.

In the meanwhile, he had promised Kali that he would set up her equipment. He would do that as quickly as possible, then engage a woman—perhaps his grandmother—to wash Kali's dress, her trousers and other articles of her clothing. Maybe his grandmother might even loan him a dress that Kali could wear, thus ending his obligation to her, and gaining him some moments alone, in which he could further ponder this mystery.

Alas, he had best set about doing these things and then return to the river where he could question Kali more directly. That he would also have to field more of her disparaging remarks was probably a given.

He grinned at the thought. What a spitfire he had married. What a woman.

Chapter 17

*They knew not care, nor hunger, nor want of any
kind.*

James Willard Schultz, *My Life as an Indian*

Victorian-raised Kali Wallace had never gone
skinny-dipping in her life. Perhaps that's why it
felt so good. It was scandalous, to be sure, but oh, so
lovely.

The water was brisk, cold, and at any other time,
might have sent her hurrying back to shelter, shivering.
But not this morning.

This morning it felt soothing and refreshing—just
right.

After Soaring Eagle had delivered his coup de the-
atre, Kali had plunged herself into the river with all
possible speed. The water had been a shock at first, but
then, as she had swum from one side of the river to the
other, and back again, her body had adjusted to the
temperature.

Had he really called her his wife?

Kali wrinkled her brow. Did Soaring Eagle truly believe their dream had been a reality? It seemed an impossible concept, at best.

Their dream? Now he had her doing it, too.

Kali knew that many of her contemporaries would laugh at the mere concept of their conversation were she to disclose it. Spirits performing a marriage ceremony? She would be called foolish, no doubt. And per haps she was.

But out here in Indian country, the idea didn't seem quite as farfetched. It was as though the land itself were cloaked in mystery; a place where anything could happen; a country where the stuff of one's secret longings came true.

Kali trembled, but it wasn't from the temperature of the water. Things she didn't understand were occurring here. Things were changing. She was changing.

And she wondered, was she awakening, as though from a deep sleep? It seemed odd because if Kali were to let herself go—if only for a moment—she felt inclined toward believing the notion herself.

In truth, *the dream had been that real.*

Or was she losing her sanity? Should she try to remember that none of this had happened when they had been awake? That the most likely story was that Soaring Eagle had seduced her, was merely playing a trick on her?

She pulled a face. Why didn't that thought make her feel better?

Well, what did it matter? The truth was, she was no one's fool, and she was no one's wife, no matter what she—and apparently he, too—chose to believe.

Yet, a part of her protested, she couldn't deny that it was an unusual thing to have happen . . . for them both to have shared such similar illusions at the same time . . . and to have awakened naked . . . and together.

But enough. It was time she accomplished what she had set out to do. With a firm, but gentle stroke, as though to shake off her thoughts, she glided back to the camp side of the river, drifting slowly forward until she was able to set her feet on the pebbly bottom. Reaching down and grabbing a handful of sand, she proceeded to scrub her arms, her legs, as well as a few choice places where she hoped to erase the traces of her departure from innocence.

It was then that it occurred to her. Soaring Eagle hadn't returned, and she had no clothes, no towel, nothing with which to cover herself.

Had he done this intentionally? Was this his idea of a joke?

She stood for a moment, silently accusing him of the worst and berating herself, all the while her temper beginning to boil. Oh, what she'd do to him as soon as he returned.

Suddenly she squealed. Something caught her by the heel, plunging her head first into the water. She came up coughing. But whether she was scared or just plain mad, she wasn't sure.

She spun around, ready to dive underwater and face her attacker, only to be confronted by Soaring Eagle, who had surfaced and was grinning at her like a Cheshire cat.

"Oh," she splashed him. He returned the gesture. "Stop that."

"All right," he said, still grinning, still splashing, "if you will."

"Me?" she asked, returning the fight full-fledged. "You started this. Oh, quit it!"

He had submerged to catch her around her legs. He tickled her feet.

And she gasped, suppressing a giggle. "Soaring Eagle," she said, determined that she would not laugh. "This is outrageous. I am without clothing."

He surfaced once more, beaming at her. "As I am, too."

That was a bit more information than she required at the moment.

She gave him a small splash, one that wouldn't do too much damage. She said, "Go away and let me bathe in peace."

"Oh"—he feigned a look of great hurt—"and here I was, hoping to wash your back for you."

"You were? You mean like a back rub?" Goodness, but the suggestion held great appeal . . . much too much appeal. *Courage,* she cautioned herself. She was supposed to be angry with him. She said, "I couldn't, really."

"You are sure?"

She winced. He must have heard the wistfulness in her tone. "Just my back?" she asked. "You won't seduce me again, if I give you permission, will you?"

He smiled. "I will not seduce you, even if you attempt to lure me to do so."

"I did not—"

He held up his hand. "We have already had this argument."

She blew out her breath. "Fine," she said once, then again, more harshly, "fine."

Nevertheless, she turned around, holding her arms over her breasts, even though the water hid them from his view, or at least she hoped so. From over her shoulder, she said, "Very well. You may rub my back."

She knew the words sounded more command than capitulation, but if she were lucky, he wouldn't take offense.

And apparently he hadn't. He had picked up some sand, and was proceeding to rub her with it. It felt marvelous, absolutely wonderful, and she sighed.

After a moment, she asked, "Why are you here? I thought you were going to see if you could get someone to help me with my clothes."

"It is being done," he said, his voice a little too close for her comfort.

"Oh." While staying within arm's reach, she took a couple of steps forward, saying, "Didn't you say you were going to set up my tripod?"

"Also done." He must have moved with her, for again he sounded too close.

She paced forward another few steps. "You left me without a towel and without any clothes, too," she pouted. "What if I had wanted to get out of the water while you were away? I would have been forced to sit on the bank, naked and cold."

"It was unthinking of me," he said, his hands coming up to rub her neck. She closed her eyes in acquiescence. "Please accept my apology. I have brought some cloth that you may use for a towel. It is there on the bank. There is also a change of clothes for you."

"Really?"

"Aa."

This time his voice was right by her ear, so near that she could feel his warm breath upon her, and she tread forward once more, only this time, there was nothing beneath her footfalls. She plopped into the water . . . and came up spluttering.

He was laughing.

"You . . . you knew that was there, didn't you?"

He leaned forward and leered. "I have bathed here often."

"Oh, you!" she uttered, splashing him with a full frontal assault. "You should not be here. It is indecent."

"Is it? And yet in my experience, a man and wife sometimes bathe together."

"They do not. And besides, we are not married and well you know it."

"I know nothing of the kind. I think that we are. And married couples often do."

"They do not. Now listen, Soaring Eagle, it was a dream. An illusion. Nothing more."

"Kali," he said, shaking his head, "my sweet, dear Kali, we were married by the spirits." He trod toward her. "There is no other way for them to unite us easily—often they must use some intermediate force. But this time, they chose to do it themselves. I do not know why. But I swear to you that we are tied together in marriage. Indeed, there is no more binding tie."

"I don't believe you, and I refuse to accept it." She had been treading water, but now she swam away from him. "Was there a church?" she yelled back to him. "Was there a minister? Because if they were present, I surely missed them."

"There is no better church than the earth below your feet and the sky above you," he gestured toward the heavens. "And as for a minister, I think there is none better than the one that we had, for he was the image of Sun."

He swam toward her.

The image of Sun? How had he known that? Unless . . . Was it possible that they had not only dreamed of the same occurrence, but had populated the illusion with the same people?

Impossible. She said, "No, I refuse to believe any of this . . . you," and she swam even further away from him in the fastest breast stroke she could manage. But she called over her shoulder, "I reserve the right to decide upon these things myself. And you, sir, are swimming in the women's quarters of the river."

"Oh, am I? According to whom?"

"According to me." She turned suddenly and added a splash for good measure. And then, heaven help her, she grinned.

And he reacted as though she had invited him to a picnic—she being the main feast. He lunged at her, catching her easily around the waist, while both of them tread water.

Their legs tangled; she struggled to get free until, as if by accident, their bodies touched full-length. At the contact, liquid fire swept through her, making her wonder if the inner workings of her body might be volcanic in origin. Rocking back, she tried to obtain some distance, but only managed to accomplish the exact opposite. He held her to him, and smoldering sensation erupted through her, so much so it came as a surprise not to see the water around them boiling.

She shut her eyes as a realization took hold of her: the tempest that had started with this man's kiss earlier in the day—which should have ended in the dream and a most physical romp—had not abated. Not in the least. In truth, it was worse now than it had been before. At present, whether she admitted it or not, she knew what pleasure this man held for her. For, illusion or not, in her own mind, she had experienced it. And she hungered for it. Again . . .

How was she supposed to cope with this? Nothing in her life had prepared her for any of this.

And so perhaps more in self-defense than anything else, she said the only thing she could think of to say: the truth. "Soaring Eagle," she began, "you confuse me. I don't know whether to hate you for last night, or surrender and make love to you for how you make me feel. What's wrong with me?"

She had stopped treading water to lean against him, letting him do all the work. He didn't object; merely wrapped her legs around his waist, pulling her chest in toward him.

At her words, he nodded, his lips seeking out the pulse at her neck. "I must confess that you confuse me also."

The touch of his lips wreaked havoc within her. But she couldn't very well tell him that, not when she herself was uncertain of what all this meant. And so she said, "It's wrong, to be here with you like this, isn't it? It must be. All my life, it is what I have been led to believe. A godly woman is not supposed to feel such . . . passion . . . for anything. And yet . . ."

"That is silly," he said, still easily treading water.

"What is?"

"A good woman is not supposed to feel passion? Who told you this?"

"My nannies. My governess."

He sneered. "Do you not feel passionate about your work? Have you not been willing to give up most anything to have that work? Is that wrong?"

"It is true that many women who do this are frowned upon."

"How foolish," he jeered. "What sort of society is it that does not educate their women into the ways of men; that does not acknowledge that a woman experiences the same emotions as a man? It is not as though a woman is a different species, separate from man."

She knew that. All her friends and associates knew that. He simply didn't understand the finer points of the Anglo-American culture. That was all. She said, "Aren't you being a little hypocritical? Indeed, it's a little like the pot calling the kettle black, don't you think?"

"What do you mean?"

"Well, it's a well known fact that the Blackfeet are a patriarchal society, in that the male is dominant in the government and the family. And if that be true . . ."

He slanted her a frown. "While it is correct that my people trace their ancestry on their father's side of the family, that doesn't mean that one should get silly about it. I know my mother would be shocked to learn that, simply because she is female, she is not supposed to feel emotion." Gathering Kali into his arms, he set out for the shoreline with a firm stroke, saying, "Come, let's talk about this some more."

She glided along with him, in no particular hurry to disentangle herself. She said, "But your men look down on a woman, don't they? Treating her as though she might be inferior? A mere slave?"

"Who has told you this?"

"Well, I . . ." Kali thought for a moment. Where had she gleaned that particular information? "I guess these are things I have read from people who were here and lived amongst the Indians."

He snorted. "Then what you read is what that person, himself, thought, for it is not true of my people. It is a fact that women have a different physical makeup than a man and that she might emphasize different aspects of camp life because of it. But that doesn't mean she is not the same sort of being as a man, or that her work is less important or less valuable than a man's. It is simply different."

"But I thought—"

"Without woman, our tribe would cease to exist. Without a woman's touch, a man would have little reason to go on living. The Blackfeet have a saying, '*Mat'-ah-kwi tam-ap-i-ni-po-ke-mi-o-sin*. Not found is happiness without woman.'"

"Oh."

"She is the heart of our tribe and she is our voice. Her arguments are always listened to by he who would be wise."

"Oh, I see. I didn't know that. I guess there has been a great deal that I didn't know about you, about your people."

"And now you do. Perhaps you can put this into your books."

"Yes," she said. "Yes, I can. I will."

"Know that I do not tell you these things so that I might convince you to make love with me again, or to influence you to feel passionate with me," he added as they floated together, back toward the bank. "I tell you this because I believe these things are true." Reaching a shallower section of the river, he stood, but kept her legs anchored around his waist. Taking her hand in his, he placed her palm over his chest. "Do you feel the beat of my heart?"

She nodded.

"Know that in my heart, I desire you. Not because you are beautiful; not because you are wise; not because you are my wife. But because you are who you are. Know that a man feels the matters of his heart

deeply. And it is a wise man who follows these longings. For the mind, like the body, can be a weak thing.
But never the heart."

The heart? She bit her bottom lip, as though the action
might hold back a floodgate of emotion. For her own
heart suddenly ached. She drew back from him, if only
slightly, in order to gaze upon his countenance. "Then
you trust your basic urges?"

"I trust my heart, not urges. There is a difference."

She said, "Is there? I have been taught, and I do believe, that one should use one's head, and think
through matters of the heart. After all, what if one's
deepest longing is bad? What if one's passions lead
him to commit crimes against others? There are, after
all, evil things that happen in the world—usually because someone desires something another might
have."

He shook his head. "Then that person has not been
taught the difference between greed and an urge to
succeed. You are confusing the two. They are only similar in that they can both be passionate. But they are not
the same thing."

Not the same thing?

"A man who is ambitious only goes bad when he
does not realize that there is also life around him. Greed
takes without giving, without allowing another to live
also. But a tribe would be nothing if not for men of ambition. It is they who care for others, who ensure there
is food for all, who hunt for all, ensure happiness for all.
And so a woman, too, might be ambitious and might
rise above those around her. But not by taking does she
live well. Only by giving. So my people believe."

Kali paused. It wasn't what he'd said. It wasn't
whether or not the things he spoke of were true or

false. The fact was, what he had related to her, and the way in which he'd spoken, was beautiful.

She uttered, "I didn't know." Raising her hand, she ran her fingertips gently over his cheek, delighting in the smooth texture of his skin beneath her touch. She continued, "I didn't realize there was such compassion in your culture. The West, the Indian tribes, are not at all as I had expected. In truth, I had been led to believe that Indians were fierce and cruel, with little heart or human decency."

"You have thought this?" He sounded incredulous. "You, who once told me that a person should not generalize about an entire people?"

"True. How true."

"Perhaps," he said, "in my own defense I might add that an Indian might show cruelty, as any man might," he said, catching hold of her hand and bringing it to his lips, kissing first her fingers, then her palm. "If you were fighting for your own, your family's and your tribe's way of life, so you, too, might be fierce."

"Yes," she said. "I might be."

"Humph," was all he said, his attention clearly not on their conversation, but upon her, as his lips made a path to the pulse at her wrist.

"Where did you learn these things?" she asked, melting against him. "For you speak like a man who has lived to old age. And yet you are quite young."

"My father is a very wise man."

"Ah, yes, your father." *The man she had seen in vision.* "Still," she continued, "I can't quite abolish the idea that a woman of quality should not be sensual, nor should she experience the more erotic side of life."

"I would agree with you somewhat, for a woman's reputation is easier to blemish than a man's. But her reputation is not in danger when she is with her husband. After all, the pleasure between a man and a woman is not a bad thing."

"Yet I have been led to believe that a marriage bed is not supposed to be a source of pleasure . . . not for a woman of quality."

"Nonsense. Are you telling me that only a man is supposed to have fun?"

She laughed, the reaction one of pure instinct.

"No, sweet Kali. What we are doing is right. From the top of my head to the tip of my feet, I feel it is right. We are meant for each other."

Meant for each other. Ah, she liked the sound of that.

"And this is, after all, our wedding night," he said, bringing her hand to his chest and wrapping his fingers through her hair until he could position her face up close to his. "And my dearest wife, you are my love."

His love. She breathed out deeply.

"Can you say it back to me?"

"What?"

"Do you love me, too?"

A simple question; one that should have a simple answer. Yet it was far from elementary. At the suggestion, a thousand, pulsating explosions swept through her. *Did she love him?*

Oddly, until this moment, the thought had not occurred to her, not in its entirety. Yes, she thought him handsome, wonderful and intriguing. But love?

"I . . . I . . ." She didn't know what to say. "I barely know you."

"And yet you know me well enough to stand here before me like this."

"Yes, I do. I am, although perhaps I shouldn't be," she said, pressing her hands to his chest trying to shove against him. The only thing she accomplished, however, was being pulled in closer. Continuing in the same vein, she said, "But I am only here with you like this because you have tricked me into going swimming with you."

"Is that the only reason, my wife?"

Of course it wasn't the only reason, but he assumed too much, asked too much of her too soon, and her barriers were still firmly in place.

"Stop calling me your wife," she reprimanded softly, even though she had curled herself into his arms. "You know I don't know whether to believe the things you tell me or not. A part of me wants to hold on to everything you've said and keep it dear to my heart. But another more logical part begs me to remember that our dreams were a coincidence. That this was all it was. A mere coincidence."

He shrugged. "Believe what you will. You are my wife." As he held her there, he spread kisses along the length of her neck. "Do you feel it? There is something that binds us together, something spiritual."

"Spiritual? Binding? What do you mean?"

"When we are like this, it is as though your presence adds to mine, gives me more. It is hard for me to tell you in words for it is a feeling of space. It is even a little difficult for me to understand. For my wife, you do not take away from that which I am. I become more."

Kali gulped. She might have said something, too, but she couldn't. Her breath had caught; her throat constricted.

"And, my sweet, sweet Kali, I want you as a husband wants the one he loves. I promise you that I will give you all there is of me to give, if you will only take what I am offering."

"I—I . . ." What did a woman say to a man like this? What did she say and still retain her own sense of identity? For she longed to take him in her arms, hold him, comfort him, unite with him.

She inhaled deeply, shutting her eyes. "I—I . . ."

Again she couldn't voice a single word. It was impossible; the moment was too exquisite, too precious, too rare. And she forgot to think.

She breathed out slowly. What was happening to her? Where were all her well-thought-out plans? Because right now, there was nothing in her world; nothing in the whole scheme of things more important than Soaring Eagle, his love for her, her love for him.

Ah, yes, there it was at last. She loved him. Why had it taken her so long to realize it?

She opened her mouth as though she might voice the idea aloud, but the words never left her lips. Bending, he kissed her.

That was all it took to have Kali responding in kind, and as she collapsed against him, she returned his kiss wholeheartedly. His breath filled her lungs, and his being merged with hers.

Was he right? Were they attuned spiritually? It was true that when he was near, she felt as though she somehow gained space. Not that she became him. She was still very much herself . . . but more so.

She broke off the kiss to gaze up at him. Should she tell him what was in her heart?

His face was so close, so dear, so handsome, and as she stared at him, she knew that she must memorize this instant and keep it with her. Always would she cling to his image, to the tenderness in his eyes, the compassion that was expressed in his every facial feature. Gulping, she whispered, "You are probably the most beautiful man I have ever known."

He grinned. "I am glad that you think so."

"Soaring Eagle," she murmured, her voice low. "I . . . I think that I do lo-love you. It must be love, for I feel that you are part of me. You see, what you were saying . . . about being more yourself? I, too, feel this. It is as though what is happening to you happens to me, also. Does that sound silly?"

"*Saa*, no," he said. "It reminds me of something my father might say . . . very wise."

"Oh, Soaring Eagle, what are we to do?"

"Live our lives together."

She sucked in her breath. "Oh, that I could."

"You can."

"No, no, I can't. Just because I have come to understand my feelings for you doesn't mean that I have changed my mind about us, about marriage. I might know now that I love you, it's true, but it changes very little. Our lives are too different, our goals too individually diverse." *And I'm still not sure you won't hurt me terribly,* she said to herself.

"And yet," he said, "you are my wife. In our dreams you took me easily and gladly."

"Many things come true in dreams." Kali's smile was a melancholy affair as she added, "Tell me, how willing would you be to travel the world with me?"

Looking at him, Kali had her answer without a word being spoken. A sadness had come over Soaring Eagle's features that was so real, so effusive, it was almost tangible. Nonetheless, he said, "It would be a difficult thing for me to do. My people need me here."

Kali looked away. "And I would not want to take

you from here, from your tribe, your people. It would be as to take away a part of you. I couldn't do that."

"Then stay here. You and your father could write more than one book about our people."

Our people? Had he realized what he'd said?

But Kali shook her head, managing to affect a bland smile. "Do you see? Already you try to persuade me."

He didn't respond to this, though his lips thinned perceptively.

"No," she continued, "it's a grand idea, a marriage between us, but that's all that it is, I think. I'm afraid, Soaring Eagle, that it would be best if we kept our wits about us and realized that our time together is simply that—a splendid intrigue—memories for our old age."

"Memories?" He brought his cheek next to hers where he proceeded to nuzzle it against her own. He said, "I am here with you now."

"Yes, and we should capture this moment for what it is. I will always remember you."

"I will have no need of memories, my wife, for always will a part of me be with you."

"What do you mean?

He pulled her to him, and standing chest to chest, his fingers rummaged through her hair, as he said, "When you write your book, there I will be with you. When you read it, when you tell your stories, when you remember this time, there I will be."

Kali sucked in her breath as shivers of delight, exquisite and delicate, raced up and down her spine. This man, the things he said, the way he said them, were entirely beyond her experience. And his words, him, the beauty of the moment seized hold of her, capturing her as surely as if he'd thrown a net over her head. And the odd thing was, she understood exactly what he meant.

He said, "I think, my sweet Kali, that once you have known love, you will be unhappy without it. Think well on this, my love."

"Yes, but—"

"I ask you to consider what kind of person would merely exist, when he could live? While our path, yours and mine, might be full of obstacles, would it not be more difficult to try to live without one another?"

She had no argument for that, at least not now. In truth, at present she was finding it more and more difficult to think clearly, particularly when he was holding her so close.

She sighed, realizing what she must do. She said, "Let's not argue this any further. Though you state your cause well, my mind is set against marriage, and I must remain firm to what I once knew was right. But something must be resolved between us, if only because of the way in which we awakened, the way we are standing here now. I only hope the good Lord will forgive me for what I am about to suggest to you."

"You have a suggestion?"

"I do," she gave him a brief nod. "And it is not easily given, but as I see no other solution, it is all I can offer."

He raised an eyebrow. "Which is?"

She took a deep breath for courage, and jumped in with both feet. "An affair."

"An affair?"

"Yes, let us make a pact that we have had only an affair, and that anything else that might happen between us would be only a short liaison. Love without marriage. Love without the ties that would restrict us in accomplishing our dreams. It would leave us both free. No ties, no bonds, no inhibitions."

He frowned. "I know what an affair is," he said. "But

why? Why would you want this when you could have everything?"

She shrugged.

And he said, "It's not as though either one of us would keep the other from achieving their heart's dream."

Kali shut her eyes and took a deep breath. She wasn't certain why this was important to her, but it was. Yes, it was outrageous. Yes, it was most likely shameful. Yet, deep within her was the need to remain separate from this man . . . for reasons she had no way of grasping. Besides, she was, after all, a nineties woman; a woman who was only beginning to test the strength of her wingspan.

She said, "I'm not certain you speak the truth. A man will usually expect a woman to conform, and you are, after all, from a . . ."

". . . Paternal society," he finished for her. He scowled, drawing his brows together in an expression of utter confoundment. "There is a problem."

"Yes?"

"I don't see how I can agree to that since I have vowed—if only to myself—that I will not take you to my sleeping robes without marriage. You must realize that this thing you suggest could ruin your reputation."

"Perhaps," she said. "Yes, perhaps it could. Yet I know of no other way to settle this. The deed has already been done . . . the seeds sown, and since we seem to be in a rather compromising situation, even at present . . ."

"And you think an affair will pacify our . . . needs?"

"Yes," she said. "Yes, I do."

He stared down into her eyes with a look that appeared as though he might, with intention alone, likely change her mind. But it was simply not to be, and after a few moments, he said, "I think you might be too innocent in your evaluation of our situation. For once a person has known the pleasures of the flesh, it is not so easily forgotten. But come with me," he said, and settling her into the crook of his arm, he plunged back through the water to the shoreline, where he gently deposited her upon its grassy banks.

She shivered. Her body had adjusted to the temperature of the water, and the combination of wind and the cool morning air seemed frigid.

But he was there beside her, rubbing her arms, her legs, coming close, sharing his body heat. And leaning over her, he said, "Though I desire you, I do not think this is a good idea. First, let me say again that we *are* married."

"We are not."

He held up a hand. "Secondly, there is my vow to consider. I cannot easily take that back."

"Fine," she said huffily. "Then you can believe we are married. Will that help ease your mind?"

"*Saa*, it will not, for you do not believe it, too."

She sighed. "Do you think this is easy for me? I'm going against a great deal that I hold sacred by even suggesting this. And perhaps I will have to atone for my sins at a later date. But I think, if you will examine the facts calmly, without any added emotional involvement, you will see that there is no other way for us. Besides, as I said before, the deed has already been done. And if we have only an affair, we can keep it secret. There will be no trouble. You won't have to tell your people, I won't have to tell mine. It's a good solution."

"I disagree."

"Fine." She rolled away from him, onto her side.

"Soaring Eagle, where are those towels? And the change of clothes?"

"What are you doing?" He touched her shoulder, his voice close to her ear. "You would walk away from me?"

"Yes," she said, leaning out of his reach. "I must. My future happiness, my father's and I think yours, too, depends on it."

Soaring Eagle was silent for several minutes until at last he said, "All right, we will have this affair."

She fidgeted. "I don't know. It seemed a good idea at the time I suggested it. I'm not certain now. Besides, I don't want you to go against your principles."

"Ah, yes," he said. "That would be a terrible thing."

She glanced at him obliquely. Had she detected a note of sarcasm?

He continued, "But I assure you, my principles are firmly intact. Are yours?"

Kali moaned as the double edge of that question hit her square in her center. Nonetheless, she responded with a simple, "Perfectly. Why do you ask?"

Chapter 18

Cupid plays havoc with the hearts of red as well as white people. And—dare I say it?—the love of the red, as a rule, is more lasting, more faithful . . .

James Willard Schultz, *My Life as an Indian*

"**M**y wife, the fallen woman." There was more than a little humor in this observation. But Kali chose to ignore it, which, it appeared, only served to urge him on, for he continued, "Perhaps I should boast to my friends that I have managed to elicit an affair with a married woman."

"Oh, stop it," she said. "If you are only going to make fun of me, maybe we should get dressed. After all, there are many things I should be doing."

Yet when she made a move to rise, he pulled her back down to him. "Where are all these promises?"

"Promises?"

"You are the one who suggested the illicit romance. I am but a helpless victim to your charms, awaiting only your touch and all else that accompanies an *affaire d'amour*."

"Soaring Eagle, cease this."

"What?" he asked, while his hands began to massage her back. "What must I cease? This?" he asked, bringing one of his palms around to rub her breast.

She groaned.

"Or this?" He kissed a sensitive spot on her neck.

And Kali, already mesmerized, felt like sculptor's putty. And as she sank back against him, her body molded itself to his.

She groaned. "That feels heavenly."

"Yes," he said, "it does."

The comment made her smile and lazily, she turned over to face him. "Soaring Eagle," she said, "please, I . . . I yearn for more . . . kisses, I think."

"Do you?" He brushed a strand of hair back from her face, his features softening as he gazed at her. "Then it shall be done, but first you must help me with it, for this is my first affair and I am uncertain of what you might like."

She sniffled.

"Tell me, should I kiss you like this?" He placed a small peck on the top of her head. "Or like this?" He rubbed his lips over her ear. "Or perhaps like this?" He brought his face close to her, his stare at her and his demeanor intent, his lips coming close, closer, closer until finally he skimmed over her lips completely and placed a tiny kiss on her cheek.

"Would you stop that?"

"What? No more kisses? Have I not pleased you?"

Kali blew out her breath. "Would you be serious?"

"I am serious."

"No, you're not. You're teasing me. What I want is a real kiss."

"Are you telling me my kisses aren't real?"

She sent a look up to the heavens.

"Or did you mean for me to kiss you something like this?"

His lips captured hers, fully, completely, his tongue tasting first her upper lip, her lower, then sweeping hungrily into her mouth, sending waves of exhilaration surging through her.

"I think I meant something like that," she whispered as she came up for breath.

"Oh," he said, "then let me repeat it." And he proceeded to do it all over again.

Kali was a willing victim, too. But no matter his urgent kisses or his affectionate murmurings, it wasn't enough. Like it or not, she had been awakened to the full face of love. And she wanted it all, again . . . now . . .

And though the ground beneath her was wet and mushy, she barely noticed. Alas, she was hardly aware of anything else save the hammering fervor of her heart as it pumped life-giving fluid through her veins.

Perhaps, she thought, she had made a tactical error in staying here through the morning. Maybe she should have left last night with all possible speed, rushing back to New England, to safety, to her world as she knew it.

But what was life without a little excitement? Without a little love?

Alas, it was true. She might live to regret her actions this day.

But not now. Goodness, no. Not now . . .

She lay on her back, gazing up at him, while Soaring Eagle pressed her hair back from her face. Ah, his love, his sweet beautiful wife.

He knew she struggled with something he could

hardly understand. Indeed, he wondered if she were aware of the exact source of her problem.

She wanted him; he was well aware of that. Yet, she didn't want to want him. She loved him, too. But he was willing to stake his life on the notion that she didn't *want* to love him, either.

It wasn't an insult. No, and it wasn't what she said it was, either. Not culture, not race, not even her career.

There was something else. Something she was probably unaware of. It was as though she harbored a deep-seated distrust of him. Why?

In some ways he felt as though he'd known her forever. In other ways . . .

"Soaring Eagle," she said, "come here."

He scooted back up her body, pressing his lips to her ear. "I am here," he said.

"Tell me," she said. "Why do I ache so bad?"

He raised an eyebrow. "Stomachache?"

"No."

"Headache?" He grinned.

"No, I feel like I'm on fire."

"Ah," he said, "Does your heart race unsteadily?"

"Yes."

"And does your pulse soar?"

She nodded.

"*Aa*, this could be bad, very bad. I know a good Indian remedy."

"Do you?"

He inclined his head.

"Then please do it and hurry."

But Soaring Eagle was in no particular rush, nor was he inclined to take her orders. And so, as he kissed and caressed her, he dawdled.

"Soaring Eagle," she murmured, arching her back, "I think I am ready."

"I know you are, but, my sweet wife," he said, "you might be sore. It was not long ago that we enjoyed this same act and it is a new venture for you. We will take our time, I think."

"Why," she asked. "How can you tell if I'm sore if you don't attempt to find out?"

Despite himself, Soaring Eagle chuckled. He had been told that the white woman was an unresponsive, cold partner when taken to a man's sleeping robes. Surely, he thought, his sweet wife was proving that remark to be no more than ugly gossip.

"All right," he said, "but if I am right and you are bruised, we will slow the pace down until the fire within you is so bright, you will not notice when I become one with you. You will tell me."

She nodded. "I will tell you."

And with no more haggling to be done, at least for the moment, he joined his body with hers.

"Does it hurt?"

"No," she said, "but you're holding back, aren't you?"

"*Aa*, yes, my wife. It is easier for a man to reach attainment than it is his wife. As your lover, I would have you experience all the pleasure that I can give you and more. A man must learn control."

"Oh, really?"

"*Aa*, yes, really."

"Humph. I'm not certain I like that. I don't want you to be ultra-controlled. I want you to ache for me."

"I do, my wife. I do."

But if she heard him, he would never know. Raising

up, she scooted down until she had positioned her lips over his chest. And before he could ask her not to move, she had sought out one of his flat, sensitive nubs, taking it between her lips. Over and over she kissed him.

He groaned.

But she wasn't finished. Moving to the other side of him, she made a banquet of that part of him, too.

He murmured deep in his throat and drew in his breath, mumbling, "You must cease doing that if you want—"

She stared up into his eyes. "I've decided that I definitely don't like you controlling yourself when you are with me," she said.

"But a man must—"

"Not now. I want you to yearn for me."

"But I do," he said, as though the admission pained him. "I have, I will, I do." And taking her in his arms he proceeded to show her exactly what her efforts had wrought . . .

Inside Comes Running Bird's lodge, rattles beat time on a buffalo hide—"To imitate the sound of a beaver's tail hitting water," Soaring Eagle explained.

Drums pounded out a rhythm so loud that she and Soaring Eagle were forced to lean close in order that they be heard over the noise.

"The drums echo the sound of the grouse," said Soaring Eagle. "It is an important part of the Medicine Pipe ceremony, for the grouse gave its power to the Pipe."

"I see. Why are the drums painted?" she asked.

"They represent different dreams which are part of the ceremony."

"Oh. May I take a picture?"

"Yes."

She arose quickly and stepped behind him, to where her camera was set up. Quickly she inserted a glass plate, adjusted the shot in the viewfinder, held the flash stick in her hand, and snap!

Swiftly, with the skill and care of a professional, Kali removed the plate, put it in a packet and inserted another plate, all in the matter of a few seconds. She'd best get another shot, since she couldn't be certain how many of these pictures would develop well. Once more, she wasn't being helped by the lighting arrangements in the lodge. It was poor, at best.

Snap.

Bending, she came to squat down again, positioning herself slightly behind Soaring Eagle, between him and the camera. Oddly enough, Comes Running Bird had placed Kali next to Soaring Eagle, an extremely unusual affair, Soaring Eagle had told her, since it was the custom that men and women would sit separately within a lodge . . . especially during a ceremony.

But hers was an unusual circumstance, because of her work and because of Soaring Eagle's duty to direct her in the matter of the photographs.

As she had feared, she and Soaring Eagle had missed the initial procession that had accompanied the new and old Medicine Pipe owners. However, luckily enough for Kali, the ceremony itself had yet to begin.

True to his word, Soaring Eagle had set up her equipment within the lodge itself. He had even loaded one plate into the camera, which had been a godsend for Kali, since she had lost precious work time to her riverside romp.

Of course, before she and Soaring Eagle had left that area, there had been a few incidents. Soaring Eagle had hid her change of clothes, had even pretended her clothing had been carried off by a deer. But in the end, Kali had prevailed, and she was now clothed in a long cotton gown which had been donated by Soaring Eagle's grandmother.

It was still early morning and the sky was very much in darkness. Moments before they had entered the lodge, Kali, looking up, had beheld the morning star, arising brightly over the prairie, and had estimated the time to be about four o'clock. And if that were correct, it meant that she and Soaring Eagle were about an hour late for the ceremony.

What had she missed?

Very little according to Soaring Eagle. Besides, he had gone on to explain, no one here lived by a time clock. Each person would attend the ceremony when he was able, and if someone came late, no one frowned or commented on it. The only thing missed by tardiness, perhaps, was that of a choice seat.

Soaring Eagle had discreetly pointed out each of the main players in the ceremony: Comes Running Bird, who was relinquishing the Pipe; Sitting Beaver, who was the recipient; the seven Medicine Pipe singers and the wives of both Comes Running Bird and Sitting Beaver.

Leaning toward Soaring Eagle, she whispered, "May I take a picture of Sitting Beaver, since he is the recipient of the Pipe?"

Soaring Eagle glanced at her from over his shoulder. "Perhaps. But I must ask him. Wait here."

And in one fluid movement, he stood. Bending at the waist, he came around the outside of the circle, past the seven Medicine Pipe men, and squatted down next to the man who sat in the place of honor, its position toward the back of the lodge.

Looking around the circle at them, Kali had to admit that the man was, indeed, a magnificent looking individual, with a noble profile, a dignified bearing and a rugged face that, although weather-beaten, was still very handsome. At present he held a woolen blanket over his shoulders, a beautiful covering of orange, blue and black stripes.

Oh, she thought, to capture this moment on film.

Kali watched as Soaring Eagle spoke to Sitting Beaver. Then with a nod Soaring Eagle made his way back to her.

As soon as he came within voice range, he said, "You may take pictures as soon as the Medicine Pipe bundle is opened and Sitting Beaver has donned the regalia that goes with the Medicine Pipe. It will be soon."

Kali bobbed her head in acknowledgement.

She stared off to her right, toward the back of the circle, paying particular attention to the bundle itself, which had been placed in the seat of honor, directly across from the tepee's entrance. Next to the bundle sat Soaring Eagle's father, Comes Running Bird, with Sitting Beaver, the receiver of the Pipe, seated on his right.

The air was heavily scented with sweet-pine, the incense used for the ceremony. At present, a large piece of the herb sat smoking on an open coal, and as the smoke from it grew larger and larger, ever so gradually, the rhythm of the drumming changed. All at once, Comes Running Bird sat forward along with a woman.

"That is my mother, Many Shots Woman," murmured Soaring Eagle to Kali, who was still squatting next to him.

Kali nodded.

"Soon, my father and mother will began to sing, placing their hands, at the same time, into the rising smoke. Gradually the seven singers will join in song with them. When that happens, they will be singing Thunder songs."

"Thunder songs?"

"*Aa*, do you remember that it was Thunder who first gave our people the Medicine Pipe?"

"Oh, yes, that's right."

"Now, do you see my mother and father making the sign for the buffalo?"

"You mean with the curved fingers?"

"*Aa*. It is during this song that Sitting Beaver and his wife may begin to open the Medicine Pipe bundle. Listen, now is being sung the Antelope song. Do you see how the singers' hand motions have changed, now imitating the grace of the antelope? This is because they are opening the bundle wrapped in antelope skin. And now comes the song of the elk."

"Why are your mother and Sitting Beaver's wife shaking their heads?"

"That is in imitation of the male elk when he is preparing to charge. It is being done as if the bundle were to be opened by the antlers of the elk."

"Oh," said Kali. "How fascinating."

"Soon," continued Soaring Eagle, "Sitting Beaver will take off the clothes he now wears beneath his rcbe. Then he will dress himself in the sacred regalia of the Medicine Pipe bundle. When this is done, that is the time when you may take his picture. Only one may be snapped and then no more for the rest of the ceremony. Do you understand?"

Kali nodded.

"You must wait to take this picture until I give you a signal that it may be done."

"All right."

Kali scooted back toward her tripod and camera, and came up onto her knees. If she had only one chance to obtain a picture, she wanted to ensure all was in readiness. To this end she checked the glass-plate film, her flash stick and clicker. Coming around to the back of the camera, she checked her foreground and picture composition in the viewfinder.

And that's when it happened.

Something caught her eye.

Looking up, away from the camera, she blinked, sucking in her breath.

Sitting Beaver had changed clothes. And now, placed high, atop his head was *the* yellow and blue headdress. The same one she had seen when the vision of Comes Running Bird had flashed before her eyes— only hours ago.

Surely it wasn't the same one.

Yet there in the center of the headdress, as she had related to Soaring Eagle, was the black and yellow circle, beaded in small seed beads.

Was she dreaming? Had she imagined this?

Surely these things weren't possible. Or were they?

No wonder Soaring Eagle had looked at her curiously, she thought. Her insight had included not only an image of his father, but the ceremonial headdress as well.

Did it mean anything? And if it did, what?

Cautiously, as though afraid she might discover something else unexplainable, she surveyed the rest of

Sitting Beaver's new Medicine Pipe regalia, from the fringed, painted shirt he now wore, to the leggings, which were beaded in black, blue and yellow. And since Sitting Beaver was reclined not far away from her, she could see that his moccasins were decorated in the same color motif.

Soaring Eagle, glancing over his shoulder, motioned her close once more. And when she had come forward, he said, "In addition to the clothes that you see Sitting Beaver wearing, my father has given him the horse, along with all its possessions, which also belongs to the Pipe."

Kali nodded.

"Notice that Sitting Beaver's wife is also wearing the same colors as that of the Medicine Pipe regalia. This dress she is given must be worn by her only during ceremonies given by the Pipe."

Again Kali acknowledged with the inclination of her head.

Soon, in came the spectators, who were each one announced, along with his gift. Kali's eyes went wide as she recognized the value of many of these gifts. From beautiful buffalo robes, painted and exquisitely sewn, to food, to horses. In fact, one of the Blackfeet societies gave fifty horses, as well as a pile of clothing.

Stranger yet was to see Sitting Beaver in turn give these gifts over to Comes Running Bird.

"It is a fee to my father for the transfer of the Pipe," explained Soaring Eagle.

"I see," she said as silently as possible, although in truth, she didn't. Why would a person give away the best of their presents?

But she had no time to ponder the question. Sitting Beaver had given a slight motion of his head toward

Soaring Eagle. In turn, Soaring Eagle rose slightly and scooted toward Kali.

"You may now take a picture. But be quick about it."

"Right," said Kali, not needing to be told twice. "One, two, three." She said the numbers almost to herself, for to say them aloud, within others' hearing, might be the height of ill-manners. *Snap, flash, click.*

It was done. Kali removed the glass plate, folded it gently into a packet, and laid her camera aside. Still kneeling, she crawled into position, right behind Soaring Eagle, and squatted down.

And as though on cue, the dancing began. By this time, the sun was beginning to make its first appearance in the sky, and as a tepee's entrance always faced east, the first pinkish gold rays of light began streaking into the lodge, painting all it reached in a luminous, soft pink glow.

"Anyone who desires to make a vow," said Soaring Eagle over his shoulder, "will now dance, individual by individual."

"I see," said Kali, hardly daring to breathe.

Odd, how her body began to sway to the beat of the drums. Stranger yet how excited she felt when she accidentally brushed against Soaring Eagle. She wanted more; more touching, more feeling. And the drums seemed to urge her on.

Her hand crept forward as though it might initiate the action, even if she—or he—would not.

She brought her face close to his face, and blood pounded in her ears, madness raced over her nervous system. It was as though she needed to kiss this man—now.

She was playing with fire. She knew it; but heaven help her, she was filled with need. Alas, the rest of the

world, the dancing, the ceremony, was quickly fading
for her.

And then she did it. She touched him. It was barely
anything, her arm simply coming in contact with his
shirt, her hand brushing his . . . And yet, that part of
her hand, next to his, burned with awareness.

He must have felt it, too, for he turned his head
slightly toward her, a few tendrils of his hair coming in
contact with her lips.

At the contact, smoldering fire swept through her.

He whispered, "When the dancing starts, watch
closely. For each person who has made a vow will rise
up and will dance over the skin of the animal—these
represent the shadow, or the spirit of the animal. Then,
when the dance is ended, the dancer will give that skin
to Sitting Beaver. Watch."

Kali did as bid.

There were many dances: ones to the Antelope, one
to the Crane, the Swan, to name a few. There were
more, even a song and a dance to the Muskrat. And in
all that time, Kali sat behind Soaring Eagle, touching,
sometimes arm to arm; sometimes lips to cheek, if he
were leaning back to tell her something.

And then something stranger happened to her. It was
the drums again. Something about them, their steady
rhythm, began to illicit an odd response within Kali. It
was as though she wanted to dance; as though she
needed to dance . . . with Soaring Eagle. Oh, what she
would do if only she had the nerve. She'd dance to him,
dance with him, around him. She'd make him her own.

Swaying slowly she inched forward as though she
had to do it. She had to dance. She reached out, her fingers encircling Soaring Eagle's hand. Maybe no one

would notice her; after all, there were other people standing, dancing.

Keeping time to the rhythm, she came up onto her feet and rocked to-and-fro. All at once Soaring Eagle was there beside her, standing, placing something in her hand and, keeping hold of a part of it himself, he began to dance with her.

Quietly, he said, "This is an antelope skin."

She raised questioning eyes to his.

"A Medicine Pipe performer must dance with the skin of an animal. I am giving you the hide of the antelope because it suits you. An antelope is almost as graceful as you."

Kali pressed her lips together. What a wonderful thing for him to say.

The drums pounded in her ears, the men's voices rang out through the air, filling the tepee with sound. Together she and Soaring Eagle bent forward and back, to the side, back again, making sweeping, majestic motions. It was as though their movements, their steps, along with the drums, were a prayer.

What was it Soaring Eagle had said? A dancer performed for someone, took a vow for someone?

For whom did she dance? For herself? For Soaring Eagle? For them both, or was it for lovers everywhere?

The drumbeat caught hold of her, became part of her, as though she and it were one and the same. It pushed her toward something . . .

Glancing up, she stared hard at Soaring Eagle, and it seemed the right thing to do that she speak what was in her heart, before she lost her nerve. And so it was that she found herself uttering the words, "I love you."

For a moment, Soaring Eagle shut his eyes, as though he might be overcome with emotion. But when he at last opened them and gazed upon her, Kali was left in no doubt as to his feelings for her.

And softly, for her ears alone, he whispered, "*Kitsikakomimmo*.

Someone called a short break even while Kali felt as though the ground below her had disappeared. What had happened to her? What *was* happening to her?

Glancing around at the assembled guests, Kali thought some of the Indians might have eyed her suspiciously, since in a manner of speaking, she was invading their ceremony. However, such was not the case. No one paid her much attention. And those who did catch her eye, nodded at her, as though they approved of her in some way.

Soaring Eagle placed the antelope hide in front of Sitting Beaver and led Kali back to their place in the circle. As one, they sat down.

A pipe, an ordinary pipe, was sent on its way around the circle. Soaring Eagle sat up straight, received the pipe and after smoking it, passed the object down along the line of men, ignoring Kali at first.

However, turning to her, he said, "A woman's pipe will be offered soon. You should smoke then."

She nodded. "Why?"

"It is expected of you. You have now danced in the ceremony."

"But I have never smoked in my life . . . anything. Will that matter?"

"No. You must not refuse."

Kali nodded.

Gradually, the mood of the assembled guests grew

quiet. Kali glanced up to see what, if anything, was happening.

Comes Running Bird had stood and had barely gained his full height when he began to sing. But whatever he was saying might remain a mystery to Kali forever, as the words were in Blackfeet. After a moment, however, he stopped singing and spoke in English, "Come . . . Kalifornia Wallace."

What? Her?

Had she heard that correctly?

Comes Running Bird repeated the request. "Stand up Kalifornia Wallace. Come . . . stand . . . beside me."

How did Comes Running Bird know her full name?

Kali knew instinctively that she should arise, but she was afraid her legs wouldn't hold her. Perhaps she shouldn't have danced. Was she in trouble because of it?

She had little time to consider her plight, however. Comes Running Bird was continuing to speak, saying in English, "Soaring Eagle, my son, come . . . also."

Soaring Eagle stood.

"Come forward, Kalifornia Wallace."

In a daze, Kali struggled to her feet. "Me?" she asked, pointing to herself.

Comes Running Bird nodded.

Although Kali felt slightly disconnected from the ceremony, and in particular from her body, she nonetheless made her way to where Comes Running Bird was awaiting her.

"Stand . . . here." Comes Running Bird pointed.

Kali did as asked, and stood to his left.

"My son, stand . . . this side." He pointed to his other side.

Soaring Eagle complied.

Comes Running Bird then held out the pipe to Soaring Eagle. "You will smoke now."

Soaring Eagle did as asked, handing the pipe back to his father.

Many Shots Woman stepped forward, producing another pipe, which Kali suspected might be the women's pipe that Soaring Eagle had mentioned. Many Shots Woman handed the pipe to Comes Running Bird.

"Now . . . you, Kalifornia. You . . . smoke . . . too."

Kali took hold of the pipe. Her hands were shaking. Looking up at Comes Running Bird, she asked, "Has there been some mistake?"

He shook his head. "There . . . no mistake. Hold pipe . . . this way," he showed her the proper grip, one hand holding the pipe close to the stem, the other further out, toward the pipe's bowl.

Kali swallowed, noisily and hard, certain the racket she made could be heard by the others. Her knees shook.

At last, she brought the pipe to her lips, inhaled . . . and coughed.

"Again," instructed Comes Running Bird.

Nodding, feeling more than a little sick to her stomach, Kali took one more puff.

The drums began again, this time softly.

"Mat'-ah-kwi tam-ap-i-ni-po-ke-mi-o-sin. Waai'tomo . . ."

The old man spoke on and on in soft, hushed tones, but whatever it was that he said remained unknown to Kali.

At last, he ceased speaking and bent to pick out two feathers from the unrolled bundle. They were eagle feathers. One of these he gave to Soaring Eagle. The other he gave to her.

Next came a blessing. Waving a burning piece of sage first over Soaring Eagle and then her, Comes Running Bird honored them, weaving the smoke up and down Soaring Eagle's body, then hers, up over the head again. Down over the shoulders to the feet. Up again.

At last, Comes Running Bird took back the feather and then the other, laying both at the feet of Sitting Beaver.

"*Iniiyi'taki*," he said, then in English. "The spirits are now happy."

And it was done, but what it was exactly that was done Kali couldn't have said.

More than a little curious, she ached with the need to ask a tirade of questions.

Good manners, however, forbid her doing anything more than taking her seat. Nevertheless, the rest of the ceremony blurred for her, and she barely heard or saw anything further.

She sat stiffly. Even the drums ceased to stir her mood, and she no longer touched Soaring Eagle. In truth, she was afraid to.

The drumming went on and on. The singing went on and on. Dancers stood up, danced and were again seated. At last it was sunset, and the ceremony was about to come to an end.

And it couldn't have come fast enough for Kali.

Comes Running Bird arose and led Sitting Beaver and his wife out of the lodge, where they all, in turn, faced the four directions, chanting.

It was the signal to the guests that the ceremony had, at last, come to a conclusion. At long last.

Kali made to rise, her stiff muscles protesting at the movement.

Soaring Eagle, however, held her back. "Not yet," he said. "Remain where you are and keep smiling."

"All right. But why?" she asked.

He shrugged. "You will see soon enough."

One by one the people filed out of the lodge, all that is except for herself and Soaring Eagle. The two of them remained seated.

Kali waited.

One by one the people returned, each person bearing a gift, which they gave either to Kali or to Soaring Eagle.

"Is this for me?" she asked Soaring Eagle after a woman had placed a beautifully beaded dress at her feet.

"*Aa*," he said.

"But I can't—"

"Sh-h-h. Here comes another."

It was a dark-haired elderly woman, and like all the rest, she held a present in her hand: a beautifully beaded pair of moccasins. She squatted beside and a little behind Kali, and leaning forward, began chattering away in Blackfeet, all the while she drew Kali into her arms, hugging her.

Taking Kali's face into her hands, she stared at her for some moments, before again beginning to prattle. And when she smiled, it was a big, wide affair, one that showed a missing tooth. "Wel . . . come . . ." she said in English, tears in her eyes. And with a final hug, she rose to her feet and left.

"My grandmother," supplied Soaring Eagle.

Kali gave him a wide-eyed stare as the pieces suddenly fell into place. She said, "They know, about us." It was no question.

He nodded.

Dumbfounded, Kali's voice mirrored her confusion. "It was a marriage ceremony that your father performed, wasn't it?"

Soaring Eagle once more inclined his head, saying, "He did as the spirits directed him."

"As the spirits directed him . . . And yet, the spirits married us first."

"But you did not believe."

Kali gulped. "Why would they care? And what spirits?"

"The spirits of my ancestors, perhaps yours, too."

"Mine? I have no relatives here."

Soaring Eagle turned toward her, his gaze seeking out hers in what was a long, studious look, as though he might be looking at her for the first time. He said, "Are you certain?"

"Of course I'm certain."

He didn't say a word, and it was some time before he turned his sights away from her, staring out into the dying embers of the lodge fire. And he uttered, almost under his breath, "I, for one, no longer am."

"You are no longer what?"

He sighed. "My sweet wife, I am no longer certain that you are completely white, at least not spiritually . . ."

Chapter 19

*As in civilised society, so among the Blackfeet,
the woman suffered, but the man went free.*

Walter McClintock, *The Old North Trail*

Not white spiritually? The thought made her want
to laugh, except this was no laughing matter.

She sighed. So much for keeping their affair a secret.
It might have been more discreet had she taken out a
notice in the *Helena Herald*.

Well, she had no one to blame but herself. She was
the one who had *needed* to dance.

There was another scratch at the entrance.

"*Piit*, enter," Soaring Eagle called out.

Comes Running Bird ducked his large frame
through the entryway and came to stand at his full
height. He was quickly followed by the appearance of
a man's boot, gaiters and trousers. Finally the whole
man appeared, a medium-sized elderly fellow dressed
in a gentleman's shooting suit, complete with a rifle
strapped over one arm and a large bag over the other.

"Father!" Kali called out.

"Kalifornia," his voice was full of affection. "Forgive me, Kali, but I wasn't able to get here any sooner. It appears, however, that I've missed all the fun. Comes Running Bird tells me that you've managed to obtain some photographs of their Medicine Pipe ceremony."

"Yes."

"Well," said Wallace, coming forward, "you've done well. I'm proud of you." He smiled, and started across the circle.

But Kali caught him before he had taken a step. "Father," she said, "you should scoot around to the back of me. It's bad manners to come between a person and the fire."

"Oh, is that right? Well, fine then." Dutifully, he paced around the circle and came up beside her, squatting down to Kali's left. He said, "Shall I have our man gather up the equipment and start loading it into the wagon?"

"Hmmm. I'm not certain, Father. I'm afraid I have something to tell you."

"Do you? That's fine then, m'dear. We'll talk in a minute," her father replied. Then, "Kalifornia, what are all these clothes piled up in front of you? Are they gifts of some sort?"

"Yes, they are, Father."

He harrumphed, once, then again. "Indeed, you must have made quite an impression. And to think you were concerned that the Indians might not like you. It's as I told you now, isn't it? You haven't failed me yet."

"Haven't I? I'm not so sure of that," she said softly, almost beneath her breath. Then more clearly, "Father, we need to talk."

"Yes, yes, my dear. In a minute."

There was another scratch at the entryway.

"Piit," called out Soaring Eagle, switching his attention from watching Kali and her father to focusing on the entrance.

Meanwhile William Wallace, unaware of any tension, picked up Kali's hand and, placing it in his own, said, "I have some important news for you, Kalifornia."

Gilda entered.

"Ah," said Wallace, glancing up, "there's our guide now."

Kali frowned. "Did you ask her to come here, Father?"

"Yes, yes, of course I did. We'll need her assistance to guide us back to the agent's house." He coughed, then chuckled. "I'm afraid I don't know my way back."

"But I do, Father. And in truth, I don't think we need this guide anymore."

"What? Not need our guide?"

Kali shrugged. "At least not this one."

"Has she done something unpleasant, m'dear?"

"Not exactly unpleasant," said Kali, "but yes, she has definitely done something. Father, I have much to tell you."

Meanwhile, Gilda glided around the outer circle, stopping behind Kali. Bending forward she offered Kali a beautiful, tanned, white buffalo robe, which was meticulously painted and quilled.

Kali accepted the gift with some reluctance even though the robe was warm to the touch, butter-soft and felt wonderfully luxurious.

Gilda said, *"I'taamiksistsikowa.* This is happy day."

But Kali was in no mood for niceties, and she replied, "Thank you, Gilda, but I think you will understand if I tell you that I want to speak to you."

Gilda nodded. "When ceremony . . . done."

"It is nearly done now. I doubt if I'd be missed if we were to step outside for a moment."

Gilda shook her head. "More people . . . come with gifts. You . . . wait."

"No, this is important. The gifts can wait."

"It . . . bad manners if you leave now."

Kali drew in her breath. Manners, social etiquette. She was becoming a little weary of being reminded of the "correct" behavior for this and that. Nonetheless, she said, "Very well, as soon as the ceremony is finished, we will talk. I will come and find you. Where will you be?"

"At your . . . lodge."

"What lodge?"

"One you sleep in . . . last night."

"The lodge? How do you know about that lodge?"

"All in tribe know of lodge."

"All in the tribe know? . . . Oh, very well. I will meet you there."

"I . . . wait." This said, Gilda rose and stepped around toward Soaring Eagle. Bending once more, she placed a polished wooden bow in front of Soaring Eagle. The bow string glittered as if covered with sparkling dust. Ten to fifteen perfectly straight arrows accompanied the lavish gift, the arrowheads shiny and reflecting the light as though they were made of gold.

Once again, Kali heard Gilda say, *"I'taamiksist-sikowa,"* only this time she didn't repeat the English translation.

Soaring Eagle leaned up toward her to reply, but whatever it was that he said to the woman, Kali would never know. He spoke in Blackfeet.

That's when it happened.

Gilda leaned in closer to Soaring Eagle and placed

both her hands on his shoulders, bending down to whisper something in his ear.

Kali felt an odd sensation flash through her.

Strange, it was nothing. The two of them were simply talking. Nothing to be alarmed about.

Still Kali sat up a little straighter.

"*A'wahkahtaan . . .*" said Gilda, while Kali shifted uncomfortably.

"*Nita'wahkahtaaniksi . . .*" replied Soaring Eagle.

Gilda nodded, and then said in English, "Know . . . truth of . . . marriage. Meet . . . tonight . . ."

"Kalifornia." Kali's father interrupted her concentration. "We're on a bit of a time schedule."

"Are we?" Kali replied absentmindedly. "In a minute, Father." She turned her attention back to Soaring Eagle and Gilda. But once again, the two of them were speaking in Blackfeet.

Obliquely, Kali watched Soaring Eagle as he conversed with Gilda. The other woman remained tightly poised, her hands still resting on Soaring Eagle's shoulders.

Briefly, a tinge of anger stirred within Kali. It seemed to her that Soaring Eagle should release himself from Gilda's hold. Why wasn't he? And why was he leaning in toward her, as if the two of them had many things to discuss?

Did they? And if they did, what sort of matters did these two have in common?

Gilda nodded briefly in response to something Soaring Eagle had said, then whispered, loud enough for Kali to hear, "If you want learn . . ."

William Wallace cleared his throat. "I'm not sure I told you, Kalifornia, but—"

"Not now, Father. In a moment, please."

". . . Meet me at edge of camp . . . by river . . . tonight . . ." came Gilda's whispered words, clearly spoken in English.

Kali's stomach plummeted.

Gilda was inviting Soaring Eagle to meet her at the edge of camp? By the river? By the same stream where Soaring Eagle and I have so recently . . . frolicked?

Kali sat still, momentarily stunned. Had she heard that correctly?

She shut her eyes, inhaled deeply, then opened her lashes and stared straight out in front of her. Yes, she had heard it accurately.

Sitting still, head up, shoulders back, Kali tried to retain her dignity, even as a tempest of confusion swept through her. Had these two betrayed her? Had she been deceived? Was Soaring Eagle carrying on an affair with Gilda?

Impossible . . . Or was it?

Weren't men, and Indian men in particular, notorious for their affairs?

Though these thoughts flickered through her mind, Kali attempted to think reasonably. Simply because Gilda and Soaring Eagle were to meet by the river, didn't justify the assumption that they were enjoying an *affaire d'amour*. There was most likely a reasonable explanation behind the invitation. One she would illicit from Soaring Eagle as soon as she could catch him alone.

Still, despite her best efforts, Kali felt herself draw inward, as though every outward element of her attention had suddenly snapped back on her. Even the space around her seemed to contract, making her feel heavier, denser. And involuntarily, a sort of lethargy settled over her.

She groaned silently.

Should she have been more on guard with Soaring Eagle? Should she have tried to second-guess him?

Kali coughed, trying to take herself in hand. She scolded herself.

Nothing ever came from such speculation, and she was most likely working herself up over nothing. In faith, she couldn't even see the two of them well enough to determine how close they really were to each other. It was all conjecture on her part; after all, Soaring Eagle had been most sincere this morning. She'd stake her life on it.

And yet, there he was . . . there Gilda was . . . the two of them together . . . whispering . . . It couldn't be true, and yet . . .

Enough. Her thoughts were making her feel dizzy. She had to do something. What?

That's when it came to her. She had to get away. She had to think. She needed space. Now. Whatever confrontation she had planned for Gilda was going to have to wait.

As though on cue, her father leaned toward Kali and, pulling out his pocket watch, said, "Kali, m'dear, it would be most proper if we took our leave. The governor of the territory is coming to see us. We're to meet his train in East Glacier, haven't had a chance to tell you that, with all this going on, but that's the news that I had for you . . ." His voice trailed off as he made to rise. "Come on, then, Kalifornia." He reached out for her hand and must have turned his gaze on her, for Kali heard him gasp. "M'dear," he said at once, "you're looking a little pale. Are you all right?"

Kali nodded. She couldn't speak.

"Perhaps we should leave at once. You had best thank your host and his son for their hospitality."

But Kali felt incapable of anything at the moment, except maybe the act of escape. And she mumbled, "No, Father, I don't believe any thanks are necessary."

"Now, now, Kalifornia, remember your manners, m'dear."

Kali swallowed. Drat. There it was again. Manners, social polish, culture taboos. Why now? There had to be a few precious times when a person's own needs had to come first.

However, the habits of a lifetime were a hard thing to break, and setting herself to the task, Kali looked up, hoping to gain Comes Running Bird's attention. Receiving it at once, she said, "Thank you for your kindness today."

Comes Running Bird nodded.

"My father and I must be leaving," Kali said.

Comes Running Bird simply nodded again.

Soaring Eagle, however, turned a glance on her. "Leaving? You are going? Now?"

But Kali couldn't answer. Instead she remembered that Comes Running Bird might be expecting payment of sorts for the ceremony he had performed. She would have to give him something. But what?

Leaning forward, she picked up the gifts which had thus far been given her; gifts that included the beautiful white buffalo robe. Scooting around Soaring Eagle and Gilda, giving them full berth, she made her way toward Comes Running Bird, stopping to the left side of him. With a hand signal and a nod, she said, "*Soka'pii*," and placed the offerings before Comes Running Bird.

Comes Running Bird inclined his head, bestowing a

smile on Kali, as though he knew her turmoil and sympathized with her. He said, softly, for her ears alone, "Take heart . . . my daughter. What is to happen . . . must happen."

But Kali did not understand, nor did she care to understand, not when all she could think of at the moment was how good it would feel to get away from here; back to safety, back to town, back to New England, back to a place where the world made sense.

Soaring Eagle smiled at her as she came around the circle, giving her the sign for "good." And he said, smiling as if the world were still a bright, sunny place, "That was a good thing that you did. It did not even require my reminder that my father needed payment."

Kali stared at him as if she had never seen him until this moment. And she wondered, what on earth could she say to this man?

She sighed, glancing to the side; best to avoid him altogether. Thus, she made a move to leave.

But he grabbed hold of her hand. "Where are you and your father going?"

She couldn't speak to him, not civilly. Not now. Perhaps later she might have a word or two with him. But at present, her heart was too numb, her thoughts too jumbled.

At length, squaring back her shoulders, Kali spared him a glance, noticing that Gilda had left. But she couldn't hold his gaze for long, and looking away she let her sights alight onto something familiar and dear: her father.

At last she knew what she had to say, what she had to do, and so she plunged, saying, "I'm going home." She pulled at her hand.

Soaring Eagle held on to her tightly, however.

"Home?" he said. "Do you mean to the tepee that has been set aside for us? Do you know where it is?"

"No," she managed to say, as an odd feeling came over her, as though she were no longer part of her body, although conversely she felt utterly trapped in it. She said, "I'm leaving here with my father. The Governor of the territory is coming to visit and I have told my father that I will accompany him to the train station. Now, if you wouldn't mind letting go of my hand."

Soaring Eagle narrowed his eyes at her. "Are you all right? You are acting strangely."

"I'm fine."

He narrowed his eyes at her. "And will you return here tonight?"

"Ah . . ."—Kali glanced up, toward Comes Running Bird, who sat calmly at the head of the circle, staring back at her, smiling at her as though to give her courage—"Ah, I don't think so."

"Then I will come with you."

"No," she said a little too quickly. "Ah . . . no. You should stay here," she finished more evenly.

Kali could feel the heat of Soaring Eagle's disapproving frown, but she wouldn't turn to look at him, though she did squirm, trying to wrest herself from his grip.

He said, "Something is wrong, my wife."

Her father harrumphed. "Ah, Kalifornia, m'dear, did this young man call you his wife?"

"Yes, Father, he did, but it's not true."

"It is true." This from Soaring Eagle.

Once more her father coughed. "So tell me, Kalifornia, is it true or isn't it?"

Kali sighed. "Father, I'll explain later."

But Soaring Eagle was not to be ignored and he

pulled on her hand with a little pressure, "Are you upset that Gilda and I were talking?"

"Ah . . . ah . . . of course not. Why would that upset me?"

He shrugged. "It is an unusual thing to have happen, I admit, that a man will speak so intently to a woman who is not his wife. But your guide had something important to tell me. That is all. You have nothing to fear, my wife."

"Wives? Marriage? Someone had best explain, quickly."

"Later, Father, please."

"My son." It was Comes Running Bird speaking. "Your mother has sent word to me that she needs you at once."

"*Aa*, my father. I will go to her," said Soaring Eagle. And then, turning back to Kali, he continued, "You must believe me. Trust me. This once. Please come back tonight. I will explain."

"Yes," she said.

"Yes, you will trust me?"

Kali once more pulled on her hand. "Ah, not exactly. In truth, it would be best if I leave now and speak with my father. As you heard, he's going to need an explanation and I'm sure I'll have quite a time answering his questions. And of course, there are some other things I must attend to."

"And when you finish doing these things you must do, you will return?"

"Ah . . . ah . . ."

Comes Running Bird sat forward. "Excuse me, my son, but your mother is asking for you."

"*Aa*, Father, in a moment. Kali?"

However, Kali couldn't promise anything. She had

to think. She had to sort through the events of the evening. And she had to do it away from here . . . far away from here. Now.

Knowing that to get angry with him would only delay her departure, she mustered up the best smile that she could under the circumstances, and turned to him. "Ah . . . thank you Soaring Eagle," she said, "for all you've done for me today. It has been an enlightening experience. And of course we will see one another again, I'm certain of it. But please excuse me now, as my father does need me, and I really must go."

But Soaring Eagle wasn't to be easily convinced, and turning her hand around in his, he brought it to his lips, holding it there as he said, "I will wait for you."

"Oh, please don't," said Kali, attempting another dazzling smile, another facade. She continued, "I could be quite a while. I mean, I have photographs to develop and your agent's books to read, cover to cover, remember?"

"I remember nothing except that we should be together."

Kali drew in her breath, astonished at the slight hissing sound an inhalation could make.

"Kalifornia," said her father from the entryway. "Come along now. We mustn't keep the governor waiting."

"Yes, Father, I'm coming," she muttered, and pulling back her hand, said, "Thank you again, Soaring Eagle, Comes Running Bird. But I really must go now."

And on these words, she trod to the entryway, stumbling out through the entrance and into the gathering darkness of an evening summer storm.

* * *

Soaring Eagle watched her go, knowing in his heart that Kali was plagued by something.

What had happened? She had been all right during the ceremony. She had seemed fine as his people had showered the two of them with gifts.

Was it Gilda? Was Kali jealous?

She might be. She very well might be, although in his heart, Soaring Eagle knew that it wasn't quite that simple. There had been more at work here tonight than mere envy.

The strange thing was that he felt as though he had lived this all before.

Should he follow Kali?

No, not this time, he decided. Kali needed room; room to think, room to go over her thoughts. Make no mistake, they weren't through, he and his wife. But for now, he would let her attend to other things.

Besides, there was something else he must do. Gilda had told him that she would provide him with some answers to his questions; he thought it best that he see her as soon as possible.

"My son," said Comes Running Bird, "your mother needs your assistance, I think."

"*Aa*, Father. Is she with my grandmother?"

"*Aa, aa.*"

Rising, Soaring Eagle stepped to the lodge's entrance, knowing he had better hasten.

After all, it was time he understood what was going on here. And if what he suspected were true . . .

His mother had wanted nothing more than to speak words of encouragement to him, on this, his wedding day. It had taken little enough time to talk with her, but meanwhile, Kali had gone. He had seen her leave camp with her father, both of them on foot, perhaps en route to their wagon.

Soaring Eagle sighed. Something was not as it should be between Kali and himself, but what that something was exactly, remained a mystery to him. Still, he would let Kali go, at least for now. She had things to attend to, as did he.

He needed this meeting with Gilda, for it was his intention to confront the woman with many questions.

It took precious little time to make his way to the river, even considering the fact that his grandmother accompanied him. In truth, not more than a few moments had passed before Soaring Eagle was laying a blanket out over the ground, helping his grandmother to sit upon it. Gazing down at her, he smiled.

"I am glad that you agreed to accompany me here and act as chaperone," he said to her.

"It is nothing," she said. "After all, my grandson is now a married man."

A loud boom followed her words, causing his grandmother to jumped up and throw herself into Soaring Eagle's arms.

"What is it?" she asked in Blackfeet. "Is our camp being attacked?"

Soaring Eagle listened to the laughter that followed the gunshots, and shook his head, his arms coming around his grandmother to comfort her.

"It is no more than a few of our young men having fun, I think. I'm sure a Dog Chief is on his way to them now."

"*Hannia? Annisa,*" said the old woman, and she laughed, placing her head on Soaring Eagle's shoulder. "I thought it might be the white soldiers attacking, like they have done in the past."

Soaring Eagle stroked the old lady's head. "Those days are in our past now, grandmother. Calm yourself."

"*Aa*," said his grandmother. "You are right. I was being silly." And smiling, she returned to her seat on the blanket.

In the distance, Soaring Eagle heard the noise of a wagon pulling away and turning, he espied Kali's buggy meander out of the village, carrying both Kali and her father away. All at once he yearned to run to her. Somehow, it seemed important that he do so. He made a move . . .

"Ah, it is good to see that my friend's husband waits for me, as planned."

Turning, Soaring Eagle beheld she whom he sought, Gilda. He said, "I am glad that you have come. Here," he gestured toward the blanket where his grandmother was seated, "let us sit and talk for a while. I have many questions to ask you. . . ."

Chapter 20

> *Americans prided themselves on being people of laws, of the sanctity of contracts, of the importance of keeping one's word. Somehow, the treaties fell outside of this framework.*

> Peter Iverson, *When Indians Became Cowboys*

Kali held the wooden frame, along with the glass-plate negative, close to the kerosene lamp; timing the process, allowing the light to shine on it for exactly four minutes. Next would come the chemical bath and then finally the last phase of photo development, where she would place the print facedown on a metal plate, one that she used specially for this.

Here the picture would dry for several hours.

She sighed. This was the last glass-plate negative to be developed. She had taken a total of twenty pictures at the ceremony, many of which had not turned out well; a condition she attributed to the poor lighting conditions.

But some were quite good despite that, and would make a welcome addition to her father's written account of the Medicine Pipe ceremony.

Kali placed a gloved hand on her brow. The pictures

had taken her longer to develop than she had hoped, the entire process spanning almost a week. However, it probably wouldn't have taken her so long had she not set herself to doing research as regards the situation of the Blackfeet and their reservation land.

But she'd had no choice; she had given her word to Soaring Eagle, she would keep it. However, it was not turning out as she had at first suspected: Soaring Eagle had not been exaggerating the offenses against his people.

The thought depressed her, but for more than the obvious reasons. She had promised to help him if she discovered that he had spoken the truth. However, that was quite impossible now.

What he didn't know, what no one knew—not even her father—was that as Kali had left the Indian encampment, she had caught sight of Soaring Eagle. He had been standing in a sparsely wooded grove of trees, those that grew up next to the river. And his back had been to her.

True, it had been a mere glimpse, but it had been a very telling one. For as Soaring Eagle had stood there, Kali had espied feminine arms thrown around his neck, a dark head on his shoulders and his arms out in front of him, holding the woman around the waist.

After what Kali had overheard at the ceremony, she'd almost expected it. Nonetheless, it came as a shock.

She had looked hard at the two figures, for there would be no mistake. Once certain, however, she had glanced away. It had sealed her fate. His, too, for as her wagon had pulled away, she had locked up her emotional ties to this man as surely as another might secure their valuables.

She had been right about him from the beginning, she thought. Right to trust her inclination to keep herself separate from Soaring Eagle; right to distrust him; right to discharge Gilda—well, at least she would as soon as she found the other woman.

Truth was, Kali needed to get away from here. Indeed, it didn't take a genius to know that the sooner she left Indian country, the more joy she might find in life.

The only thing she didn't know how to do was, well, how to do it. The more information she gleaned about the actions being taken against the Indians, the more of a toll it took on her emotionally, for she knew she had to act, even if it simply meant finding someone sympathetic to the cause and turning the research over to them.

Still, it kept her here, tied to the area. But what else could she do? She couldn't walk away. Her own sense of fair play wouldn't allow it.

Certainly, the Indians were not being given a chance. Someone was playing a dangerous game of "take advantage while they're weak." And truth be told, it seemed so unsporting that Kali could little understand it. For instance, if two men were to engage themselves in a duel, was it not expected that both parties be equally well armed?

However, this was not the case here. At present, the white ranchers held the aces, the kings, the queens, even the jokers in this game of land grabbing; lobbying Congress, screaming to Washington, buying off Indian agents. Meanwhile the reservation Indians didn't even own a pack of cards.

She sighed. There were some things that were simply the right thing to do. Some things that were one's duty to do. And unfortunately for her, now that she knew what she knew, ensuring that justice be attained for the Indians was one of them.

Her father, on the other hand, didn't appear to understand her position. Not that she had spoken to him about this subject in its entirety—and that included her marriage to Soaring Eagle. In truth, she feared that he might not understand what she'd done. Albeit, how could he, when even she didn't understand?

Nevertheless, she had claimed illness that first evening she'd been alone with her father, avoiding the subject of Soaring Eagle altogether. This had begun the game of "ye seek and hide" between herself and her father, where she was the one in camouflage and her father, the hunter.

But it couldn't go on forever. There would come a day when she would have to disclose everything. Hopefully, she thought, that time was still in the distant future.

She wiped her brow with the back of her arm. At last, the picture was ready for the next phase.

Carefully removing it from the wooden frame, she turned toward the heavy curtain that surrounded her work area and, pulling it back and stepping forward a pace, drew the curtains around her. The drapery was a precaution. She had lost too many prints to the absent-minded accidents of someone (usually her father) opening the darkroom door, exposing her treasures to the light at the most inopportune times.

Quickly, she placed the paper in chemicals, watching the process as though the changes that would come about might be instantaneous. But she knew it would be a matter of an hour or so before the images would appear. And even then another chemical wash would be needed before the print would be ready to dry.

It was an interesting thing to observe, however; one she loved to watch— for, no matter how many times she saw it, it seemed pure magic.

"You did not return."

Kali jumped at the sound of a voice and swung around, parting the curtain. *Soaring Eagle? . . .*

Up came a hand to her throat while she attempted to catch her breath. "Soaring Eagle?" she said.

He nodded, the light from the entryway behind him, bathing him in a halo of light.

"Please, you frightened me. But, hurry," she said, "either come in or go out. But shut the door. Hurry."

How had he come here? Indians weren't allowed off the reservation without permission. And though it was a rather sad commentary on a free society that the First People of America were now imprisoned in it, Kali had felt quite safe here in a large home in Helena—far away from him—feeling certain he would not be able to obtain permission to leave, or if he could, that he would not find her.

He stepped inside her darkroom, bringing the door shut behind him, shrouding them in darkness. And as that door closed, Kali felt as though she were being suffocated. He was too close.

He repeated, "You did not return."

"Ah . . . no," she responded, her hand coming down on her upper chest as she tried to wish her heartbeat to a more normal pace. "Ah . . . you scared me, Soaring Eagle . . ." She stepped around the curtain, closing it quickly to protect her work.

"Did I? I'm sorry."

"Yes, well, as you can see, I've had a lot to do."

Could he see that? It didn't tax her imagination to believe that he was not impressed with the statement. In faith, before he had shut that door, his look at her had been most condemning.

He came directly to the point and said, "A minister came to see me yesterday."

"Did he?" She turned away from Soaring Eagle, presenting him with her back, though she knew that, in the dark, he wouldn't be able to see.

"*Aa,*" he said. "This minister tried to tell me that without his blessing, our marriage did not occur."

"Oh?" Kali looked down.

"He said also that you want to annul our marriage and pretend that it never happened."

"Ah, yes. Yes, that's right. I do."

"But it did happen."

"I disagree. It was a dream, no more."

"And what about the Medicine Pipe ceremony?"

"Yes? What about it?"

"My father married us, as the spirits directed him."

"Did he? I wouldn't know. The ceremony was in Blackfeet and I didn't understand it."

"But you smoked the pipe."

"Only because you told me I had to." She glanced over her shoulder to see if there might be enough light to observe his reaction to these words. There wasn't.

After a moment, however, he said, "And would you have refused to smoke, even when my father offered the pipe to you?"

Kali paused. Of course she wouldn't have done so; it would have been the height of bad manners. But there was little point in telling him so.

It was an odd thing that happened next, because she felt him take a step toward her. It wasn't that she heard him, for he made no noise. No, she could actually feel him, his presence, coming closer and closer to her.

He spoke, a direct reminder that he was much too near for comfort, and he said, "Do you remember our first kiss?"

She took a step forward, away from him. "I . . . I'm not sure."

He ignored her. "It was then," he said, "that I realized who you were, and I loved you. I thought you then the most beautiful, the most perfect human being I have ever seen."

"No one is perfect."

"I'm not sure. You seemed to be to me."

"Well, I'm not."

He took another step toward her. This time she heard it. He said, "But I was wrong."

Did he mean he didn't love her? Or that she wasn't flawless? She said, "Yes, yes, I know. I've already told you that I'm not inviolate in my actions, though I do try to do the right thing."

"No, I am not talking about that. What I meant is that I was wrong about the time. You see, I thought that I had begun to love you then," he said. "But the truth is, I have loved you for a long time."

"Oh? How is that possible? You didn't know me until only a few weeks ago."

"I know. But it is enough."

Kali flinched. His voice was much too close. Taking another step forward, she said, "Well, if that's true, and you do feel some attachment to me, you have an odd way of showing it."

"Do I?" He touched her arm.

She jerked her arm back, out of his reach.

He said, "And yet, here I am. When things have gone wrong between us, I am still here. But you, you ran away."

"Did I?"

"Didn't you?" He lifted the length of her hair away from her neck, his breath fanning her, touching her as though it were a caress.

She said, a little breathless, "If—if I were running away, I would be out of the country by now."

"Would you? I don't think so."

She turned around, effectively putting herself out of his reach. Frowning, she said, "What do you mean?"

"You gave me a promise, and you are not the sort of person to break your word."

"How would you know that?"

He grinned. Even in the darkness Kali was aware of it. It was as though his mood suddenly lightened. After a moment, he said, "You may not be perfect, but one thing I know about you is that you are trustworthy."

"Humph. I don't see how you would know that."

"When you left," he said, as though she hadn't spoken, "you were very upset with me. I knew it but couldn't understand it. Nevertheless, you remained calm, despite your distress."

"So? . . ."

"A lesser soul would have condemned me or someone else outright. But you were the image of perfect manners, even remembering to give gifts to my father. And now, here you are, still here. You did not run very far. And do you know why?"

"Because I'm a fool?"

"*Saa.* Because you care. Because you have pride in yourself and would sooner die than break a pledge. I would be willing to bet that you have been doing a great deal of reading of treaties lately."

She stepped back, away from him. "Soaring Eagle," she said, "why are you here?"

"To let you know that I won't sign any papers. To tell you that you are still my wife. There was much more than a ceremony that happened between you and me, and there is no chance of a simple annulment."

"I think that there is."

"And," he continued, once again as though she hadn't spoken, "to tell you that I still love you very much, you and only you. I would like you to come home with me."

Home? A tremor seized hold of her, but Kali shook it off and stole yet another step back away from him, this time coming up against the wall. Her arms came down, palms flat against the solid surface. She said, "I don't believe you. Now, please, if you will kindly excuse me, you have caught me at a bad time. I have a great deal of work to do." She nodded toward the door, forgetting for the moment that it was too dark for him to see.

"Kali," he breathed, her name on his lips more of an embrace than sound. "Sweet, sweet Kali, what have I done to deserve your contempt?"

"Nothing." She said the word as sarcastically as possible.

"And now I think you lie."

She shrugged. "And what if I do? I suppose you never lie, am I right?"

He paused. "I am like any other man. Most human beings tell fibs at one time or another. Would you have a husband tell his pregnant wife that she is fat? Or a crippled child that he will never walk?"

"Those are not the sort of life-and-death lies that I am speaking of."

"I see," he said. "And so what you are telling me is that you think I have lied to you about something important?"

"Yes," she said. "Yes, I do."

"And what is that?"

"I don't have to tell you."

"No," he said, "you don't. But if you did, I might grant you a wish, and go away from here."

She thrust out her chin.

"And if I tell you about the lie, you promise to leave?"

He didn't answer. "What is it, Kali?"

She let out her breath in a sigh.

"Kali?"

"Well, all right. If you must know, I don't think you love me. I think it's only something you said to me to get your way. I also believe that you were and are using me, though for what possible purpose, escapes me. Truth is, I'm thinking that you must be some kind of Casanova."

"Casanova? What is this Casanova?"

"He was a man who took many lovers."

A long pause, a very long pause followed.

"Other lovers?" Again he hesitated, and the silence that stretched between them seemed threatening. At last, he asked, "Why would I want another lover when I have held the woman of my dreams in my arms?"

Dear Lord above. The man had a golden tongue. If Kali hadn't seen what she had, if she didn't know what she did, she might be inclined to believe him.

But she *had* seen. She *did* know.

And so she sneered at him. "I don't know why you would want another lover. But I'll tell you what, Soaring Eagle. If you figure that out, I would appreciate your telling me, because I've been wondering the same thing."

He cleared his throat. "Has someone said something bad to you about me?"

"There is no need. I have eyes of my own by which to see."

Again there was no answer from him, and another silence fell between them.

In truth, Kali couldn't stand the strain of it, and she found herself asking, "How did you find me?"

"Rather easily," his voice came from across the room. Odd, that she hadn't heard him move there. "Once I determined that you weren't returning to see me, I figured that you would put as much distance between us as you could. But I did not believe you would leave. Tell me, Kali. What have you seen that makes you think this? Was it Gilda? I know that we spoke together in the circle, when perhaps we shouldn't have done so. Are you jealous of her?"

"I am not jealous."

"Aren't you?"

"No, I'm being very reasonable under the circumstances . . ."

"Circumstances? . . ."

She didn't say a word.

And he went on to say, "In case you have wondered, I am not having an affair with your former guide. I never have. And since I met you, there has been no other female in my life, outside of my mother, my grandmothers and my sister."

Liar, she thought to herself. *I know differently.*

"It is true that I met with Gilda. But I was there only to ask her questions. Nothing else happened between us."

But Kali had been there, at least on the outskirts; Kali had seen them together. She knew.

She raised her chin. "Why do you think I would care if there are other women in your life or not?"

"Because," he said, "we once made love together. Because you once admitted that you loved me. And because I love you."

"Yes, well, things change sometimes. I've changed my mind about you."

"Have you?"

She nodded, again forgetting that he couldn't see. She said, "Yes, yes, I have."

"I don't think that you have," he replied, from not more than a foot away.

The darkness, which at first had been her friend, now betrayed her. For suddenly he was beside her, touching her, taking her in his arms, and before she knew what he meant to do, he kissed her.

And despite herself, Kali found herself kissing him back, as though she'd hungered for nothing more than this all week long. Darn it. Why did even her body betray her?

He said, "I think, my wife, that you are simply afraid. Afraid that I have deceived you. But I have not."

She scooted out of his arms. "Soaring Eagle, perhaps I should be forthright with you. Maybe then you will understand why this talk is meaningless."

"I am listening."

"I saw you with someone."

"Me?"

"Yes." She nodded briefly. "So you see, it's useless for us to continue to talk about it."

He didn't say a word. And Kali wondered what he might be thinking, what he might be doing, for the darkness hid his movements, even his thoughts, from her. He said, "Tell me when this was."

"As I was leaving camp last week; that night with my father."

"Ah, good. Then you must have seen Gilda and myself."

"Yes."

"And you must have seen that my grandmother was there also, acting as chaperone?"

His grandmother? A likely story. She said, "I saw no one else there at all."

"And yet, it is the truth."

"I saw no one else."

"And you looked closely?"

No, she hadn't, but she wasn't going to tell him that. She remained silent.

After a while, he asked, "Do you believe me?"

"No. I don't believe you. But that's not the point. Soaring Eagle, I saw you wrapped in an embrace with another."

"But that was not Gilda, it was my—"

"Don't you understand? I *saw* you."

"But—"

"Please, Soaring Eagle. Just go away."

"I see. So what you are telling me is that there is nothing I can do right here, right now, to convince you of my sincerity? My innocence?"

"There is nothing."

"Fine. Then you are coming with me." He grabbed hold of her hand, pulling her toward the darkroom door.

She let out a slight cry. "I'm not going anywhere with you." She kicked him.

But whether or not she made her target, didn't seem

to be the point, nor did it do her any good. He picked her up as easily as if she were no more than a child, and headed toward the door. He said, "You are a little too stubborn for your own good, do you know that?"

"I am not."

"I don't mean that badly, but you are still going to come with me. If you don't believe me, and there's nothing I can do to convince you, here, now, then we're going to go talk to my grandmother and to Gilda, if I can find her. Gilda seems to have disappeared again. But find her I will if that's what I have to do to settle this between us. And you are coming with me."

"No, I won't go."

"You have no choice."

"I'll cry when we get to the street. Someone will see you and take me away from you."

"Then that's a chance I'll have to take."

She shoved at him with all her might, finally saying, "But it's a two-day journey to your home." More struggling followed, but even she knew it was pointless. Hadn't he already proved to her once before that physically, his was the superior strength?

He said, "We can make it in a day."

"Soaring Eagle, put me down."

"No."

He kicked the door to her darkroom open and stepped out; Kali quickly reached around and shut it tightly.

"I can't go with you now," she said. "I am in the middle of developing a picture and I must remain here, or it will be ruined."

"I don't care. What is happening between us is more important than a picture."

"I might disagree, but I won't," she said sighing. "Very well. You win. If you will put me down, I'll promise you that I will come to your village, or at least I'll start out for there as soon as my work is done here, in about a week. It'll take me a few days to get there, so you could expect me in from seven to ten days."

He stopped and looked at her, and Kali's heart trembled as she gazed up at his handsome face. In the darkroom, she'd had only his voice to charm her. Now she had the full man.

He said, "You will give me your word on this?"

"I will. I do."

He frowned at her. "Once again," he said, "promise me."

"I promise I will come to your village in about seven to ten days."

It was as though the words were magic. He set her on her feet, but kept hold of her upper body, pulling her into his embrace. And then he hugged her, his body fully imprinted on hers.

Kali's legs went weak, but she managed to push away from him—at least an inch or two. "Now, please, Soaring Eagle, I'm working. Please go."

"*Aa*, I will. For a kiss," he said, his arms still around her.

"A what?"

"I will leave if you kiss me."

"Why would I want to kiss you? I'm upset with you."

He leered down at her, his hands coming up to her ribs. "So that you can get rid of me and get back to your work."

She gasped. He had tickled her.

"Soaring Eagle, stop that."

More tickles followed, ensued by Kali's involuntary shrieks and giggles. "Please stop it."

"I will for a kiss. One simple kiss. An innocent request."

"Fine." She reached up to give him a peck on the cheek.

"That's hardly what I had in mind." He found a sensitive spot under her arms, beneath her ribs and at the junction of her waist.

And her screeches filled the air. At last, she said, "Okay, all right, fine." She placed her lips on his.

But his mouth opened to her, his arms coming around her and, as he bent her backward, his tongue swept into her mouth, claiming the moist recess there as easily as if he were a savage conqueror.

And Kali, "poor soul," had no choice but to kiss him back, and closing her eyes, she lost herself to him—if only for a moment.

His free hand came up to push back her hair, to make a forage of her cheek and neck, and to sweep downward toward her breast. Kali moaned, trying to remember all the reasons why she didn't want him, didn't need to be married to him, didn't yearn for his embrace.

Alas, she came up with nothing.

And before she knew what he was about, his hands were at her breasts, massaging her through the material of her dress.

"Kali"—he moaned her name more than spoke it—"Kali, I need you."

He did?

"I have not been the same since you left. I have done nothing but yearn for you. Tell me what I need to hear . . ."

"Tell you? What? What is it that you must hear?" she asked, whispering and leaning heavily against him.

"Tell me that you missed me, too."

He was so near, so handsome, so virile, and her response was unthinking as she said, "I have missed you, in my own—"

He groaned, while his hands came down to lift her skirts. "Kali, Kali, I would have you."

She swallowed what seemed to be a knot caught in her throat, then said, "Here? Now?"

Gazing down into her eyes, he nodded. "*Aa*, here, now."

"But—"

He cut her off with a kiss, and Kali caught her breath.

"I have thought of nothing but this for many days and terrible nights. Nights without you." He picked her up and paced to a corner of the basement where he leaned her against the wall.

"Kali, my sweet, sweet Kali." Already, his hands were lifting her dress, pulling at her drawers, touching her, loving her.

"But what if my father should—"

"Sh-h-h. He is gone. I made certain of it before I came here." His fingers were touching her there, at the junction of her legs. He whispered, "You are ready for me."

I know.

And then he was there, his body joined with hers, doing things to her that she was afraid she had only dreamed.

She sighed. In truth, his insistence came as a relief. Oh, she might try to deny it, but she wanted this, needed this, too. And if she were to be honest with herself, she would have admitted that she'd dreamed of this very moment.

What he was doing was scandalous to be sure, and yet it was *oh, so sweet*. She moved her hips against him, if only to gain a little more pleasure, but she could barely budge.

He murmured, "Put your weight on me, and not the wall. I can hold you."

She did as he suggested, and was filled with instant gratification. She shut her eyes and forgot to think. *Just feel, just experience.*

Darn.

Tears gathered in her eyes. There was no escaping the truth. She loved this man. And despite her own misgivings, she wanted to believe him, to believe in his fidelity. But alas, she knew that this last could not be. She was who she was; was convinced that one's secret desires could too easily turn to bitter realities.

However, convincing her heart of his wandering nature was another matter. Blast her very soul. She was afraid that her very spirit was his, now and forever.

And she, returning his passion, surrendered lock, stock and barrel. At that instant, he smiled at her, as though he knew her thoughts. And in his gaze was so much affection, Kali continued over the brink of passion. *What glory. What sensation.* She strained, she pulled, and she lost herself to him, to the moment, to the exquisite pleasure and to love.

Strange, from a point somewhere above them, she became aware that he was not far behind her in meeting his own release. One thrust, another; moaning, almost growling, he at last gave to her all that was in him to give. And Kali welcomed him every bit.

This was wonderful, beautiful. He was beautiful. This was, however, also strange. Strange, because there, for a moment, they were one. And in that time, she became aware of some dim knowledge. A conviction that he was innocent.

She didn't know how she knew; it didn't matter. Somehow, in some way, he was faultless against her accusations. Or at least, she corrected herself, he believed himself to be guiltless.

His body fell in against hers, and he said, "I love you, Kali Wallace. With everything that is in me, I love you."

"I know," was all she said in response. "I know."

She wound her arms around him, wanting their time together to go on and on. Unfortunately, reality intruded. And at length, he set her back on to her feet, then straightened away, helping to put her dress back in order.

He said, "I must go." But before he left, he brushed his fingers over her lips, gently, softly. And he added, "Thank you for that, my wife. *Soka'pii.*" His gaze softened while his fingers branched out to skim down her hair to a ripe, waiting breast. "And now I hope that you know that there can be no annulment between us. You, sweet Kali, are well and truly married. I wouldn't want you to forget."

"No," she said, somewhat in a daze, unsure if she meant no, she needed no reminder; no, she wasn't married; or no, she wouldn't forget.

"You have seven to ten days. If you're not in my village by then, I'm coming to get you, even if I have to cross a country to do it. Understand?"

Kali nodded.

"Don't overlook that I'm trusting you to your word."

"I won't."

He smiled at her, and with nothing more to be said or done for the moment, he strode to the door. Before he went through and vanished, he turned to her and said, "Think what you will, believe what you will, but I did not hold Gilda in my arms that night." And opening the door, he was gone.

Kali stared at that door momentarily. And though she said the words to nothing but empty space, she asked, "Then who was it?"

Chapter 21

I now look back with the deepest pleasure upon the freedom of that life, the delight of living and of working in that exhilarating mountain atmosphere.

Walter McClintock, *The Old North Trail*

Ah, the last photograph.

Kali picked up the tongs, dipping them into the chemical bath and, grabbing hold of the print, pulled it out of the pan, barely giving the picture a glance.

One more bath to go. She had the next pan of chemicals ready and waiting.

Ah, she thought, *this is going to be a good picture.* All the right things are there: The exposure had been exact, the lighting perfect. Why, the images were practically jumping out. Images of people, Indians, dressed in buckskin clothing . . .

Buckskin clothing?

Odd. Kali looked at the picture more closely.

Most of the reservation Indians clothed themselves in dresses, trousers or shirts made of cloth—usually cotton. Of course those of the Medicine Pipe ceremony would have been wearing their regalia, which might have been made of buckskin . . .

Funny that she didn't remember that.

Frowning, Kali stared at the picture as though it were a foreign object. It wasn't yet fully developed, the images weren't completely clear. Yet there was no mistaking the audience—the buckskin-clad audience— seated in a circle. Nor could she pretend she'd never seen the old man who had been caught standing in the middle of the circle. Nor the figures of two people positioned directly in front of him, their profiles caught and held still by the camera.

A shiver ran up and down Kali's spine. She didn't remember taking this picture. In truth, she couldn't have taken it. She was in it.

Her breathing became shallow. It couldn't be. It simply couldn't be. Such things like this didn't happen in everyday life . . . were merely part of legend and superstition.

Yet, there she was; there was Soaring Eagle; there was the old man, the Sun, and beside him, his wife . . .

The dream . . .

It had been real. *Real.*

Kali gasped and sank to her knees, which had suddenly gone weak. Soaring Eagle had been right all along. The spirits had truly joined them.

Why?

A tear rolled down her cheek. She brushed it away, angry at the emotion.

Why were these things happening to her?

As though in answer, something Soaring Eagle had once said stirred at the recesses of her mind: "Your ancestors care . . . I'm not certain you are completely white . . ."

What did that mean? That she might have Indian ancestry? Would her father know?

Somehow Kali doubted her father would be able to shed light on any of this. In a way she couldn't understand, it seemed the problem was between her and . . . this land . . .

Her eyes alit. That was it. The land.

All this had started that night several weeks ago. That night when she and Gilda had camped atop Chief Mountain.

Had the spirits confused her with someone else? Was it that simple? Perhaps she had camped there at a time when the spirits were looking for someone . . . perhaps the Star Bride.

Was that what this was all about?

Soaring Eagle had been there, seeking a dream; she had been there, innocent, trusting. And Gilda had told her of the legend. Remembering back, Kali admitted that at the time, it had all seemed so mystical, so magical. It was no wonder that the spirits were confused. After all, she had awakened to the singing, had arisen in the middle of the night, had sought out Soaring Eagle . . .

"You will know him by his song . . ." a voice whispered in the back of her mind.

It was something Gilda had told her. Odd that the voice, the accent, didn't sound like Gilda.

Kali drew her brows together.

Well, there was only one thing she could do; that is, it's what she had to do if she wanted to solve this mystery: She was going to have to go back to the Indian encampment, find Gilda and ask some hard questions. And she was going to have to talk to her father, perhaps bring him along with her. Did he know anything about this?

Possibly, although again Kali doubted it.

Head bent, thinking, Kali set her mind on her next course of action. And as she sat there, trying to recall other events that might help her to weave together the mystery, a peace settled over her, one she hadn't felt in a very long time. . . .

"Father, I know you and mother once came West."

"Hmmm."

"And I know that it wasn't a research trip, that you were here for mother's health, right?"

William Wallace made a few clicking sounds to urge the team horses into a quicker pace. Without looking at her, he answered, "Right. Why do you ask?"

"Oh, mere curiosity."

Kali looked out toward the road ahead of her. As she had speculated, she had been able to talk her father into making another trip to the Blackfeet reservation, and at present they were both seated on their wagon, en route.

Hoping to put a good deal of the journey behind them by noon, they had left early in the morning, before the sun had yet made an appearance in the sky. The day was fresh, cool and exciting—seeming to match Kali's spirits.

Kali had helped to hitch up the horses, had set aside provisions for the trip and, since the trip would take a few days, had remembered to pack a tent, sleeping bags and of course the ever-present camera and tripod—just in case.

She asked, "Did you and mother enjoy your trip?"

"We did," William said. "But if I remember correctly there was a little girl with us who might have enjoyed it more."

"A little girl?"

"Yes, Kalifornia. You."

"Me? I've been here before?"

"Yes, m'dear. Of course you were only a little thing at the time, about two years old, I believe. Must have been in 1874 or 1875. I forget which."

"I—I see," said Kali. "Why haven't you ever told me this before now?"

Her father looked, if anything, a little embarrassed. He said, "I guess I forgot."

"Forgot? After we made detailed plans to come here? After we arrived here?"

But if Kali had hoped to elicit any sort of response from her father, she was to be disappointed. He merely shrugged.

Well, this was certainly news. "Father, I can't believe that you—"

He looked away.

And Kali, seeing the reaction, sighed. On a more gentle note, she said, "And what did you . . . we do when we were here?"

"Mostly we visited with the agent, m'dear."

"Ah, the agent for the Blackfeet? It wasn't Mr. Black, was it?"

"No, not at that time. Mr. Black and his wife are newcomers to the territory. Won't be here long either, I would venture. Not unless his wife's attitude changes."

"Yes, I hope you're right." Kali scowled, wondering if now was the right time to ask her father the questions she felt must be asked. Casting a glance heavenward and deciding it was now or never, she said, "Father, did you and mother ever go into the mountains?"

He squinted, staring straight ahead of him, and he

said, "Why, yes, we did, dear. Quite often, actually. Of course, we rarely brought you with us at that time; you stayed at the house with a nanny, an Indian nanny. Although, come to think of it, once we did bring you with us."

"Oh?" She paused. Then, "Father, why didn't you ever write about this trip? Even though it wasn't one of your usual research trips, I would have imagined you would have been curious about the Indians."

William Wallace sighed. "There wasn't the time, Kali. I spent every minute of every day with your mother . . . there, in the mountains."

"I see," said Kali. "And you went to the mountains as often as possible?"

"We did. It was good for her health. Seems there's something about the air here. Fresh, invigorating."

"Yes, yes, I've noticed that myself. Tell me," Kali continued. "Did anything strange ever happen to you while you were in the mountains?"

"Strange? What do you mean?"

Kali fidgeted uneasily. "Unusual, out of the ordinary, I guess."

William Wallace appeared to think about this for a moment, although Kali noted that a sweat had broken out on his brow—and this, on a mild, cool day. In due time, he said, "Nothing too terribly odd, m'dear. Although your mother did recover here. Truth was, she'd never felt better than when she was here. Had I known—" He stopped.

"Known what, Father?"

William Wallace cast Kali a quick glance, then looked away, his features, already hardened by the toil of his unusual life, becoming even more severe. Taking out a handkerchief, he rubbed at his forehead, then said,

"Sometimes," he said, "it's only in looking back that a man can see his mistakes more clearly. I'm sorry to say that I made one here."

"You? Make a mistake?"

William cleared his throat, coughed several times, and said, "I should have told you before now. I knew it was a mistake not to, but . . ."

"Told me?"

Once more William cleared his throat. "This is rather difficult for me, Kalifornia."

Kali laid her hand on his arm, and said, "I'm sorry, Father, but please go on. Believe me, I wouldn't ask if I didn't think this is important somehow."

"I see." He harrumphed nervously, then began, "Your mother made friends easily," he said. "Of course, I never thought anything of it until one day she told me that she had befriended an unusual man."

"A man?" Kali gulped. Did she really want to hear this? Were there some things best left uncovered?

But it was too late to go back, the die was cast—her father was continuing as though, now that the subject had been broached, he couldn't stop.

He said, "The man was a holy man. A medicine man. He gave your mother many things and asked that she stay in his camp."

"He gave my mother things?"

"Yes, dear. It was what upset me the most, I think. At least in the beginning."

"What sort of things did he give her?"

William sat still for a moment, lost in thought. At last he said, "He furnished her with a lodge of her own. One with the sun, moon and stars drawn on it."

Sun, moon and stars? Hadn't the lodge she and Soaring Eagle shared that night been painted thusly?

"That's quite a lavish gift, isn't it, Father. It's easy to understand why you might have been upset."

"Is it? I have often wondered. Because, you see, she didn't want to leave here. I forced her to go away from here, and we never came back, though she wanted to return many, many times." There were tears in her father's eyes. But stubbornly, he held them back, and continued, "Her illness returned to haunt her shortly after we arrived back in the New England area, I'm sorry to say, and had I been more of a man, we would have returned. It might have saved her health. But . . ."

Kali reached out and placed her hand on her father's leg. "You didn't know, Father. How could you have known? You did what you thought was right."

"Yet," he said, his gaze caught on something, or perhaps nothing, off in the distance, "she never got better. Never."

Her father's implication was clear.

In reaction, Kali said, "It wasn't your fault."

"Wasn't it? I'm not so certain."

Kali paused, then said, "Father, sometimes these things happen. And I'm sorry that we both lost her. Truly I am, but you're not any more to blame than I am."

"Am I not? Sometimes I wonder if maybe this isn't why I've never been able to stay put in one place for any length of time. Perhaps the guilt is too much for me." He didn't look at Kali.

"But, Father," she grabbed his hand, "I'm sure you—"

"No, m'dear. It's been many years now since I confronted my demons. I had a chance to make your mother's life better, but instead of grasping at it, I chose to leave. Leave, because of my own jealousy. I know now that there was never anything between them, your mother and the man. It was simply a friendship. But it took time and persistence on her part to help me to understand that. By the time I accepted it, it was too late."

Kali bit her lip. Was there a lesson here for her to learn? And what, she wondered, did a daughter say to such a thing? How did she react?

With no answer immediately imminent, Kali nodded, saying simply, "I'm sorry."

William nodded. "I am, too."

Silence descended over them, then, Kali asked, "Ah, Father, do you know if this man, this medicine man, is still alive?"

William shrugged. "I don't know. I didn't see him at the party that night at the agent's house, or the other night when we were in the Indians' camp, and I have been looking. He was an unusual looking fellow, I'll give him that. Long white hair, tall, straight posture. Your mother gave me an odd story of how she first met him. Said that the man first appeared to her as the sun."

"*The sun?*" Kali sat up straight in her seat, her eyes wide.

"He gave her another present, too," William continued, "but I begged and pleaded with her until she gave it back."

"Oh?"

"Yes, m'dear. It was a white buffalo robe; a beautiful robe, sewn with beadwork and colored porcupine quills."

A white buffalo robe? Gilda had given Kali a white buffalo robe as a wedding present, and she, in turn, had presented the robe to Comes Running Bird.

"Your mother said the robe was special, for the white buffalo belongs to Sun, the Blackfeet God. She beseeched me to understand, told me there was no reason for my jealousy, but I wouldn't listen." He frowned. "No, I wouldn't listen. Not only did I force her to return all the presents, but I took her away from here— here where she was healthy . . . and alive."

"Please, Father, it does no good to berate yourself. You did what you thought best at the time."

"Yes," he said. "But best for whom?"

Kali gulped, having no answer to that. However, question after question filled her mind, and she found herself querying further, "The robe belongs to Sun?

"Yes, dear. That's what your mother told me. But there's more."

"There is?"

"You're right, Kali. I should have told you this long ago, but somehow the right time never seemed to come to me. And I . . . I'm sorry."

Kali nodded. "There's more?"

William inclined his head, and said, "Now, the man also wanted her to bring you to the village, that he might see you."

"Me? He did? And did she bring me?"

"Yes, once, against my wishes. I'm sad to say, Kali, that this was the final straw. I thought your mother was too enamored with the man, you see, and I feared for you. But mostly I was afraid of losing her, and maybe eventually, even you, too. We left shortly after that."

Kali sat stunned. To think all this had occurred, and

she had no recollection of it, nor had either her father or mother ever mentioned it to her. Not even once. She said, "Father, you're right. I think you should have told me this before we came here."

"I'm sorry, Kali. I—I didn't know how to approach the subject."

Kali acknowledged with the bob of her head. Of course he hadn't known what to say, or how to say it. Would she, if their places were reversed?

He had loved her mother with all his heart. It must have torn him apart to think that the woman of his dreams might have shared her affections with another. And then to realize that his actions might have stolen away her health, her life.

William was continuing. "Your mother told me that the medicine man said that you were special. I think it's time you knew that, too."

"He did? She did? Me?"

"And he begged her to leave you here."

Begged? How odd. "He didn't say 'special' in what way, did he?"

"No, my dear. He didn't."

"And mother had never seen him before you came out West?"

"No."

"And I was around two years old?"

"Yes. You are definitely my daughter, m'dear, in case you were wondering."

Kali nodded. The thought had crossed her mind. At last she said, "And so our coming back here—"

"Has been my way of making it up to you, to her, I suppose. I should have done it a long time ago."

Kali patted her father's arm, and smiled. "I understand, Father. I'm only sorry that you and my mother had to suffer because of this. Still, I think it's good that you've told me. It makes some of the things that have been happening since I arrived here a little clearer."

"Clearer? How's that?"

"It's hard to explain."

He gave her a sharp look. "This doesn't have anything to do with that young man you were with the other day, does it?"

Kali grimaced. "It has everything to do with him, Father. Here"—bending, Kali pulled out a photograph from one of her bags—"this was taken the night of the Medicine Pipe ceremony, but it wasn't taken by me."

Her father took hold of the picture, looking at it hard. Suddenly he gasped.

But Kali didn't see his face, and she asked, "Do you remember Soaring Eagle calling me his wife?"

"Yes."

"This is the reason for it," she said, pointing to the picture. "Do you remember I told you that we—you and I—would talk? Perhaps we should have had this conversation then. But Father, Soaring Eagle and I both had a dream, and in it we both imagined that we were married. Now, to Soaring Eagle the deed was done. He told me that we had been married by the spirits. But I wouldn't believe it; I refused to believe it. That is, until I saw this picture."

If William heard her, he didn't indicate it by manner or by word. His attention seemed caught on something else, and after a time, he said, "Kali, where did you get this picture?"

"I developed it yesterday."

William pointed to it. "This man in the picture," he

indicated the old man. "This man is the same medicine man that your mother knew."

The same medicine man?

Kali froze, not knowing what to say, or even how to react. Numbly she took the picture back from her father, and stared at it as though it, all by itself, could speak to her; could take away her confusion.

"I'm sorry, Father. It wasn't my intention to stir up old memories." Gingerly, she replaced the photograph in her pouch.

"Don't be sorry," said William. "Actually, I'm glad it happened. Perhaps, in a way, we were destined to come back here."

"Perhaps," said Kali, but she would keep her own counsel on that matter. At this moment, she had questions, many questions to put to their former guide, Gilda, if she could ever find her.

Somehow Gilda was involved in this. Hadn't it been Gilda who had detailed the legend to her? Gilda who had first led her to the Indian encampment? Gilda who had sung Kali and Soaring Eagle to sleep? Gilda who had openly flirted with Soaring Eagle?

Maybe it had been a mistake to leave Soaring Eagle's village last week without speaking with the woman first. At the time, Kali had thought she'd had good reason to leave. But now?

Where would she find her? In the Blackfeet village? Not likely. Even Soaring Eagle had admitted that she had disappeared.

Then where?

Look to the land, to the mountains, a voice whispered in her mind. *For the spirits reside in the mountains. They will help you.*

On top of Chief Mountain. That was where she would find her. Maybe it was only fitting. After all, the trouble had started there; perhaps it would end there. . . .

Chapter 22

At one time animals and men were able to understand each other. We can still talk to the animals, just as we do to people, but they now seldom reply, excepting in dreams.

Walter McClintock, *The Old North Trail*

It was late afternoon by the time the message was brought to Soaring Eagle, as he worked out on the range. His wife and father-in-law were in the Blackfect encampment, asking for him.

He would go to them at once, although even at a steady pace, it might take him a day or so to get there.

Leaving his cattle herd in the hands of his cousin, Soaring Eagle set out for the village, his pace as fast as he could make it. He only hoped the two of them wouldn't turn around and leave before they had all been given a chance to talk to one another.

At the thought, Soaring Eagle gave his pony full rein.

She was gone. She'd left in the middle of the night, leaving her father still in camp, alone; and Soaring Eagle was more than a little desperate for her welfare.

Why had she left? Where had she gone? Was she up-set, or did she seek something or someone?

These were the things he meant to discover as soon as he could speak with his father-in-law. Luckily for him, William Wallace was seeking Soaring Eagle's counsel as well.

It was early evening; time enough to arrange a talk and determine what had happened and what was needed to be done.

At present, his father-in-law was staying in Comes Running Bird's lodge. And it was perhaps a fortuitous event that neither Soaring Eagle's father nor mother were home. Nor were either one of them due to arrive back home before dark, having gone visiting.

Soaring Eagle paced to the east end of the lodge, and bending, stepped through the entry. A fire burned slowly inside the tepee, making the atmosphere appear as cozy as a midsummer day.

His father-in-law sat to his right, and nodding, Soar-ing Eagle came around the circle, taking his place di-rectly across from the lodge's entrance.

He reached for a pipe, filled it and began smoking without a word yet being spoken between the two of them. As was customary, Soaring Eagle said a prayer, then passed the pipe to William.

His father-in-law accepted the pipe readily and smoked it. Soaring Eagle nodded approval. Reaching out, Soaring Eagle next placed a bunch of sweet pine on a rock and lit it, the smoke from the herb curling up toward the top of the tepee poles. Gradually the clean, fresh fragrance of the pine filled the inside of the tepee. Leaning forward, Soaring Eagle smudged himself with the smoke, then bending from the waist, he did the same thing for his father-in-law, waving the smoke over his head, shoulders, down his body and back up to his head.

He said, "I am saying a prayer for you, for your daughter and her safety. You may pray, too, if you desire."

William nodded.

At last Soaring Eagle was ready to talk, and he said, "I learned only a few days ago that my wife and her father came to my village to visit. I did not expect them so soon, and I was out on the range, herding my cattle. Had I known you were coming, I would have been here. I am disappointed to learn that my wife is no longer in the encampment. I have heard that she snuck out of camp in the middle of the night. Perhaps you can tell me some things about your visit, and together we can determine what happened. Was she upset?"

"Yes and no."

Soaring Eagle nodded. "Perhaps you had better tell me why you both came here. I was expecting her . . . alone."

"She left a message for you."

"She did? What is it?"

"My daughter left a note saying that something else has come to her attention and that she might not be able to meet you here as promised. She will make every effort, but other circumstances have arisen that she must attend to."

Soaring Eagle nodded. "What other circumstances?"

"I believe she has gone off to do more research."

"Then she has returned to Helena?"

"No, no, I don't think so, although anything is possible. I only know that the previous day—before she left—she was speaking of needing to find Gilda, our former guide."

"*Aa*, yes. And where does she expect to find Gilda?"

"I'm not certain, young fellow, but I did hear her talk about needing to get back to a mountaintop. She thinks she may find something there—Gilda or maybe something else. I didn't understand all she said."

"I see," said Soaring Eagle. "Did she take anyone with her on this journey?"

"Just a couple of horses. One to ride, one to carry supplies. Outside of that, I don't believe anyone is with her. I think this is why she crept away in the middle of the night. She didn't want me to go with her. I do remember her telling me that she had questions to ask, said she wouldn't be able to ask them with me in the way."

Soaring Eagle frowned at that. "Which mountain?"

"What was that, dear boy?"

"What mountain has she has decided to climb?"

William shrugged. "That I wouldn't be knowing. She didn't say anything else."

"Humph," said Soaring Eagle, pulling his brows together as he sat deep in thought. "Do you know why she has picked a mountain? Do you know why she might think her guide will be there?"

"I'm afraid I really don't know that, young man. Only thing I can tell you is that she said there were spirits there, wherever it is that she's going."

"Spirits?" asked Soaring Eagle, his frown deepening. "Has your daughter changed her mind about the existence of spirits?"

"I believe so, son."

"Humph. Do you know what happened?"

"A picture happened."

"A picture?"

"Yes. She showed it to me. A very unusual picture. One that was taken at your wedding."

"There were no pictures taken at our marriage ceremony."

"Actually, there were. It was from the wedding in your dreams." William nodded. "I saw it."

To another man, this news might have been startling. But perhaps not to an Indian. After all, the world was filled with magical moments, magical beings and great mystery.

Soaring Eagle simply nodded. At some length, he looked over to his father-in-law and said, "If she has gone looking for the spirits, then she will most likely seek out the summit of Chief Mountain. She might become lost."

"Lost? My Kalifornia?" William laughed. "Why Kalifornia can read a map, scale a mountain or ride a horse better than most men I know. She'll be fine . . . I hope."

"I pray that she will be also," said Soaring Eagle. "But this is the time of year when grizzlies are out in numbers on the mountains. They look for food in order that they fatten themselves before going into their winter sleep. It is not a good time to be trekking through the mountains. Tell me, did she take a gun?"

"Yes, she did. Wouldn't go anywhere without it."

Soaring Eagle nodded. "Still, I had better go and find her."

"Yes," said William. "That would be best. But before you leave, I have some questions for you."

Soaring Eagle nodded. "I am listening."

"Although Kalifornia asked me to accompany her here, I have also come to you as Kalifornia's father.

And I feel compelled to ask you a few things that are important."

Again Soaring Eagle said, "I am listening."

"Young man, do you love my daughter?"

"*Aa, aa,*" said Soaring Eagle. "Yes, I do."

"And what are your intentions toward my daughter?"

"My intentions?"

"That's right. What do you intend to do with her now that you have married her? That is, if Kali will remain married."

Soaring Eagle ignored this last, though he looked away from his father-in-law, his sights coming to rest on the place in the lodge where his mother and father had always slept. He said, "That is an easy question to answer, my father. I will tell you true that I intend to love her every day of my life. I would honor her, help her and do all I can to make her life a happy one. For, do not be deceived, my love for your daughter is great. She is my light. And I am afraid that without her, my life would become a dim, unhappy affair . . . a mere existence."

Wallace cleared his throat. "Yes, yes, that's all very well and fine. However, you must be aware, my good man, that sometimes love is not enough."

"Not enough?"

"That's right. See here, what will you live on? Here, on a reservation where there is almost no opportunity?"

It was a hard question; hard because there were still so many things that Soaring Eagle didn't understand. As though trying to answer the question first to himself, he gazed out upon those things that he loved that surrounded him: the comfortable interior of the lodge, the willow backrest, the brightly colored tepee lining and soft furs and blankets scattered around the floor. At length, however, he began to speak. And he said, "Times are changing and you are right to ask these questions. This is my answer: While there are still those of us who live off the land, I have seen that this thing that we have done for hundreds of years is becoming harder and harder to do. I, myself, have been searching for a means to earn a living in this, the white world. Though I do not like to think about it, I also see that it is our future. Toward this end, I have already amassed a herd of horses and cattle. Perhaps I might become a rancher like my white brothers who surround us. But I have also been educated in the white man's school, and so perhaps I might be able to become a voice for my people, speaking up for our rights, letting others know of the wrongs against us. Your daughter has already said that she would help me do this. It is possible, also, that I could do both."

William coughed nervously. "I see," he said. "Yes, I see. Very well, then. There is, however, one more thing."

"I am listening."

William narrowed his eyes, and Soaring Eagle, seeing it, stiffened his spine. "Now young fellow, times are hard and sometimes young people need a little help. Would you be willing to accept my help, if need be, so that you and Kalifornia might start your lives with as few problems as possible?"

Soaring Eagle met his father-in-law's gaze unflinchingly. He said, "I would be honored to do so. I would only hope that any help would be given without the expectation of dominating either myself or my wife."

William smiled. "I have no desire to rule your life, young fellow. None at all."

Soaring Eagle nodded. "I would be proud to accept your help."

"Ah, well, that's good. Very good. I give you all my blessings, son. I had begun to think that Kali would never marry."

Soaring Eagle smiled. It was the first cheerful gesture he had made so far this afternoon. And he said, "Thank you, my father. This is more than I expected."

"I guess that puts our talk at an end," said William, starting to rise. But a thought seemed to take hold of him, for he sat back down at once, and said, "Welcome to the family, young man. But there is one more thing I might inquire of you, if you would be so kind."

"*Aa, aa.*"

"That picture that my daughter developed?"

"Yes?"

Wallace coughed. "The man who married you. The one in the dream. Who is he?"

"You don't know?"

"No, my good man, I don't, though he and I have crossed one another's path before."

Soaring Eagle frowned, drew his brows together and fixed a hard stare at Wallace. At last, he inquired, "You have met this man before?"

"Why, yes, yes, I have."

Surprised, Soaring Eagle became guarded in his speech, though at some length, he said, "That one in the picture is Sun, or sometimes known as Old Man. And we, the Blackfeet, are His children."

Wallace cleared his throat loudly, adding a few har-rumphs and coughs to the noise. He looked as though he might like to say more, but when he at last spoke, all he said was, "Well, that's fine, then, isn't it?"

Soaring Eagle stepped out from the tepee, having settled his father-in-law in the lodge of the painted sun, moon and stars; the lodge that had been given to Kali and himself. It would be here that Kali's father would be welcome to stay for as long as he wished. It only remained for Soaring Eagle to ask his grandmother to see to his father-in-law's needs.

But Soaring Eagle himself could not stay here. Not now. Not with Kali roaming the plains alone.

Coming around to the back of the tepee, Soaring Eagle stared out into the west, gazing at the craggy mountains and the reddish-gold sunset. The last vestiges of the sun's rays were even now shooting straight up to the clouds, painting the otherwise white, fluffy masses in colors of pink and purple and red. In truth, the entire western sky was awash in deep hues of color, its effect mirrored over the land, covering the prairie in those very same shades as though it were a mirror.

At the sight, a strange feeling of loneliness took hold of him. In some way, the land's beauty of dark shadows and intense color deepened his sense of solitude.

Odd, he thought, how he missed Kali. For though she had been in his life but a short while, it seemed to him as though he had been with her for a lifetime.

He wanted, he needed her in his life. If anything were to happen to her . . .

He had not exaggerated his concern for her. This was the time of year when grizzlies were out by day and night, seeking to fatten themselves for the coming winter. Of course a bear would seldom attack a human unless given reason. But sometimes bears had "reasons" that escaped human understanding. Besides, there could be other dangers; a flooded river, uncertain footing on a ledge, a fall from a horse.

It was never wise to venture out upon the prairie alone, unless a man were seeking a vision. But even then family and friends kept watch over one.

No, Soaring Eagle must find her trail at once, without delay, before Kali had a chance to get too far ahead of him. To this end, he had shouldered his rifle, grabbed his saddle, bridle and a few provisions, and was heading out toward his pony herd.

Curious, he thought as he trudged toward the horses, how Kali had come to the realization that she should seek counsel with Gilda. Hadn't Soaring Eagle become aware of the same thing himself, only a few days earlier?

There was something peculiar about Gilda. Something he couldn't quite grasp.

It was almost as though the woman had orchestrated Kali's anger with him. As though it had been planned . . .

He stilled, and a frown crossed his face as he singled out his black pinto from the other ponies in the herd.

"*Oki*," he said to the animal, moving toward it, petting it, rubbing it from head to foot completely before he threw his saddle over its back.

"Are you ready to have an adventure, my friend?" he said. "We go to seek my wife, who is endeavoring to climb to the top of *Nina Istukwi*, Chief Mountain. It could be a hard ride, for I must hurry."

The pony snorted, throwing its head back as though to nuzzle its owner.

"Don't worry, my friend," said Soaring Eagle, leaning down to breathe into its nostrils. "I will not wear you out, for I'll take along another pony, so that I can change mounts often. Now, come, you are the best war pony a man ever had. I know that together we will find her, but we had best leave while there is still a trace of light. Come."

And with this, he led the pinto and another, an Appaloosa, into the gathering shadows of evening.

Her first night out, Kali had camped by a lake which the Blackfeet called Many Chiefs Gathered River, but which was more appropriately named Duck Lake. There was good reason for the title, thought Kali, since there were flocks of the birds, both redheads and canvasbacks. In truth, she had dined the previous night on fire-roasted duck.

Having taken an early morning start, the sun was barely rising when she had come upon a tract of land so beautiful, she had stopped, dismounted and stared at the scene in front of her, unaware of the passage of time. Before her and straight down was one of the Chief Mountain lakes, its water pure and blue, reflecting the sky, the mountains and a few of the stars still visible in the sky. Close to it and a little above it was the other of the two Chief Mountain lakes. Looking more fairyland than rock and boulder, it was hard to believe that it was real.

It was from these lakes that Chief Mountain rose, its eastern side almost sheer upward rock. Magnificent, inspiring, it was no wonder the Indians looked upon this spot as sacred, a place where the spirits lived and played.

At last she had moved on, winding her way to the western side of Chief Mountain where the ascent to its summit was worn and easy to climb. She passed several mountain goats on her way up, getting a good look at them, for one passed close-by to her.

As Kali wound through a narrow pass, an eagle flew overhead and, glancing up, she smiled. The eagle soared, then circled overhead, its flight graceful, proud. Watching it, she realized that it shared these traits in common with her husband. Perhaps, she thought, her husband was well named.

The day was still new, and at this lower elevation, the dew hung to the mountain grasses, sparkling at her feet as though nature had given each drop a radiant jewel. In the east, the sun was finally beginning its climb, painting the sky and all it touched in shades of silver and pink.

A feeling of well-being came over her. Funny, how it felt as though she belonged here. Here, with this land. Here, on this mountain. Here, with her husband.

She felt her face fill with color. Odd, how she had come so easily to think of him as hers. Well, if that photograph were to be believed, he was hers. The thought gave her peace and, oddly, a sense of security.

It was most curious, for Kali was becoming more and more certain that there was nothing between Gilda and Soaring Eagle. His explanation, that day in her darkroom, had come from his heart. Moreover, that same day, as they were making love, she had seen into his heart, and had found him innocent. Besides, he loved her, and more—his was not the sort of love that hurt.

No, his was the kind of heart that gave, that allowed another the right to be, to grow. And it came as a surprise that she realized she didn't need either Gilda or Soaring Eagle's grandmother to "prove" his innocence. She trusted him . . . trusted him . . .

Strange . . . She wasn't sure when it had happened. Perhaps when he'd sought her out in Helena. Or had it been before then? That night when they'd married, the morning after. He had been kind, considerate, gentle.

Perhaps she'd "known" it then. She just hadn't realized it yet.

Someday, she thought, she would discover the truth of who had been in his arms. But she felt fairly certain that this someone wouldn't be Gilda. Perhaps it had been his grandmother. . . .

Glancing up toward the mountain summit, Kali realized she needed to move quickly. Now that she understood the workings of her heart, she couldn't wait to see Soaring Eagle again. But first there were questions that needed answering. Questions that perhaps only Gilda or the spirits could address.

Urging her horse forward, she reached into one of her packs for a breakfast snack. But instead of food, her fingers came in contact with the picture. She was struck with a sense of intense possessiveness. Now that she had the picture, she doubted she would ever part with it. However, curious to see it once again, she drew it out and stared at it, as though by doing so she could make sense of its mystery.

But it simply was not to be.

No images jumped out at her; no explanations came to mind. She did wonder at a symbol at the top of the photograph, however. It had been the last image to develop in the picture; a dark circle, surrounded by a lighter circle with beams or rays coming out of it, as though it were the sun.

Curious, very curious. Kali had seen the symbol before, knew it was that of an eclipse. But an eclipse? It would have been impossible to capture the symbol on film, for there had been no eclipse the evening it was taken. And yet, there it was.

What could it possibly have to do with her? With Soaring Eagle? Or, for that matter, with her marriage?

Her eyes clouded with confusion, and she shook her head. There was no point, she thought, none at all in dwelling on it, for the more she thought about it, the more flustered she became.

Besides, that was why she was making this journey, what she hoped to discover. Somehow she felt certain that Gilda would be here, perhaps at the very top of the mountain. But if not, her trip would still not be without value. For it was here that she meant to try to speak to the spirits; here that she might determine, if she could, what it was they wanted from her. And maybe, if she were lucky, it was here that she might be able to disclose the secrets of her heart.

She sighed, returning the picture to the bag. She would find no answers in it. Best to put the photograph aside and think of other things.

She inhaled deeply, looking out upon her path.

She remembered this section of the trail. Ah, the thought was a pleasant one. Perhaps, she thought, she wouldn't get lost after all.

The sun had climbed to its greatest height by the time she approached the mountain's crest. She had left her two mounts in a meadow only a few hours ago, while she had gone on, to climb the rest of the way to the top.

One last foothold on a piece of rock and she, at last, pulled herself up to the camping spot where she, her father and Gilda had spent that first night. It seemed so long ago.

Unfortunately, Gilda wasn't here, but the place held other treasures . . . other memories. Over there, she had slept; over there, they had pitched a fire; and over there, up another steep climb, was the place where she had left camp that night.

She made her way there now, down a gully and up again, noticing how, in the light of day, the shadows that had seemed so dark that night and had loomed over her so terrifyingly were no more than rock and boulder, as she had thought they were. She trudged onward, upward, her objective the small level ledge where she had first seen Soaring Eagle.

Ah, there directly in front of her, was the spot. She approached it now, noticing that her pulse was picking up speed. A pleasant sensation washed through her.

This was it. This was where it had all started, where she had first seen him, where she had first heard his song. As she stepped onto the ledge, a gentle wind blew toward her, pushing her hair back from her face. She gazed forward into the breeze, a brief smile crossing her lips.

What had he been looking at that night? At the time, she had not come back to investigate.

Gingerly, she peeked over the edge of the ledge, and caught her breath. The view from here was spectacular . . . beautiful! For from this spot, one could see for miles and miles, practically in all directions. No wonder Soaring Eagle had chosen this location for his vision quest. Even now, as she gazed around her, Kali felt her heart become light. Ah, it felt good. In truth, her thoughts, particularly those that were the most disturbing, seemed to recede from her, as though here in this spot, they had no power to thwart her.

She sighed, content. She really had no further plans, since she hadn't found Gilda, and she wasn't entirely certain how to go about talking to a spirit.

At last, however, she decided to start, and with arms outstretched, she said, "Hear me, O spirit. I think there has been a mistake. I don't know why you have taken an interest in me, for I am only Kali Wallace, a simple American girl. Please tell me what is it you want from me?"

There came no answer.

But Kali wasn't giving up so easily. Again with outstretched arms, she said, "I fear that you have confused me with someone else. Tell me, do you wish me to find this person you seek, perhaps the Star Bride?"

And when there was still no answer, she asked, "Or do you wish me to simply write a book that exposes the crimes which are being committed against your people?"

The wind whistled around a corner, and it seemed to Kali as if it spoke, but what was being said was beyond her. She admitted, "I didn't understand."

She waited.

An eagle flew overhead, joined by another midflight. Kali watched the birds' aerial ballet for a moment before attempting another communication. At last, however, she said, "I'm sorry that I doubted the marriage ceremony. But these matters are out of my experience. Please understand."

Again, she waited.

"I will be staying here for a while. I thought you'd like to know that. What Soaring Eagle has told me is true. And I'm thinking that if I help him, we can expose the crimes being committed here. It's a big job and one filled with danger perhaps, but it's what I want to do."

The eagles dipped down to her, coming within feet of her, as though in grand acknowledgement, and Kali was so caught up in the beauty of them, that she didn't immediately sense the danger. Not until she heard a growl behind her did she think to remember that she had come here with nothing more than a simple revolver.

What was behind her? Calmly, making as little movement as she could, she looked over her shoulder.

Her stomach dropped.

There stood a bear. A big, brown, grizzly bear.

Her heart stopped, then began beating as though to make up for the lapse. Could she kill the animal?

Suddenly, she felt foolish. How could she have come here so ill-prepared? Little good a revolver was going to do her against a bear, especially a grizzly. Yes, she might be able to get in a shot or two, but she knew enough about bears to know that one, two, even three or more shots wouldn't stop a bear.

Was it a mother? And if it were a mother, did she have cubs? Please, Lord, Kali prayed, don't let it be female.

She watched as the bear took a clumsy step forward, and Kali swallowed the scream that rose up in her throat.

Bears don't see well, she told herself. Pretend you are no more than a rock.

But suddenly she remembered that their sense of smell was acute.

Kali gulped.

The bear paced another step forward, and Kali did the only thing she could think to do, the only thing that for one reason or another made sense. She began to sing . . .

Chapter 23

I call the Sun to treat you as you do her.

Spoken by a mother to her daughter's
abductor/husband, as he stole
the young lady from her home,
James Willard Schultz, *My Life as an Indian*

Soaring Eagle found Kali's horses in the meadow.
He left his own two mounts there, but atypically
he didn't hobble them. It was a precaution. Bears lived
in these mountains and the horses might be an irre-
sistible treat to some hungry grizzly. At least if the
ponies weren't tied, they had a chance.

Looking for Kali's trail, he found it easily enough,
and as he had suspected, discovered that it led to the
mountain crown. He knew where he would find her,
and he hurried. For whatever reason there might be, he
felt a sense of urgency.

Bounding over the rocks and boulders as though he
were part mountain goat, he came to the place where
those on foot often camped. But he would not find her
here. He knew he wouldn't.

That's when he heard it. And the sound stopped him
completely still.

Someone was singing. *Kali?*

He stepped forward softly, moving as quickly as he dared, yet holding back, for he feared there was danger.

"Oooooooooooooooooooooo.
When you hear my voice on the wind,
That is my gentle touch, reaching out to your heart.
Oooooooooooooooooooooo.
When you see the eagle fly,
Know that he brings my love to you."

It was his song. *Haiya,* she had listened. Even then she must have cared.

Glancing up, he saw two eagles overhead, caught in the upwind of a current. At any other time, their graceful antics would have brought a pleasant smile to his face. But not now. Now he sensed the birds' agitation, as though there were danger.

Slowly Soaring Eagle crept forward.

That's when he saw her . . . and the bear.

Carefully, noiselessly, he raised his rifle, took aim . . .

"Oooooooooooooooooooooo.
Come to me on the wind, gently, gently . . .
Come to me in my dreams, softly, softly . . .
Come to me, my love, for I love only you."

The bear had stopped. And setting down its great paws, it rested, as though it were listening and captivated by her song.

And perhaps it was, for alas, Soaring Eagle was held spellbound by her voice, her words, the very beauty of her. Until this moment he had never heard her sing, and alas, he had never seen her so beautiful. And it wasn't simply her physical charm, though that was in evidence, from the top of her reddish-gold hair to the tips of her brown boots.

No, it was something else . . . something . . . as though he knew her, as though . . .

The truth struck him like a thunderbolt. That was it. Immediately exhilaration filled his being, and he smiled as though he might never again frown.

He'd thought he'd known her; he'd thought he'd recognized her. But never like this. This was a remembrance that happens perhaps once in a lifetime, if a person is lucky. This was a recognition, soul to soul.

Ah, yes, to be sure, she was his counterpart; she was his very breath. But she was much more than that. And he now understood why Gilda had acted as she did, why she had come into his country. But most of all he realized why Kali was here. And if he'd thought he'd loved her before, it was nothing compared to what he felt now.

But he realized, as though coming out of a daze, something was wrong. The bear had risen to its feet, had emitted a growl, was starting forward, toward Kali.

What had happened? Surely, he hadn't been in a stupor for that long. What was wrong?

Kali had stopped singing. Soaring Eagle glanced at her, noting the way she held herself so tightly. Either she was too afraid to continue the song; she had run out of words or she simply didn't realize what her singing was doing.

Once more he raised his gun, but immediately lowered it. It would do no good, even if he could shoot the animal. It was too close to Kali, and if he didn't kill it in one shot, it would simply swipe out at her with its deadly claws, or run to her and either crush her or push her to her death.

Kali, perhaps hearing the movement of the bear, glanced over her shoulder, and gasped.

And that's when Soaring Eagle took up her lead. He, too, began to sing:

"Ooooooooooooooooooooooooo.
When you hear the wolf howl,
He brings you my message.
I cry for you.
Ooooooooooooooooooooooooo.
When the wind calls your name,
Know that I search for you.
And when we find one another,
    the earth will become a happy place.
You are my love."

He paced forward. One step, another.

Kali swung around toward him. "Soaring Eagle," she called, "I know you said you'd come to me if I ever called. But, please, go back!"

"Never," he called out. "Either we live together, or we die together."

"No."

But he wasn't listening. Instead, he began another song:

"Oooooooooooooooooooooooooooo. Sweetheart,
Do not worry.
You are loved.
I love you."

He took another step toward her, placing one foot slowly after the other. She did the same. "Kali," he called out to her, "keep singing."

"Yes, yes. I will."

The bear snuffed as though disturbed that the two of them were talking instead of doing what it wanted them to do: sing. It came up onto its feet and growled.

"Sing Kali. Sing with me."

"Oooooooooooooooooooooooooooooo.
When you hear the wolf howl,"

Their voices joined in unison.

"He brings you my message,
I cry for you."

Then it happened. Slowly, barely noticeable at first, the sun began to darken at one of its corners. Looking up, Soaring Eagle saw a sight he had only heard about once, a long time ago.

He said, "We must keep singing, Kali, my sweet. Do you see that the moon is traveling across the sun?"

"It's an eclipse, Soaring Eagle. Oh, dear Lord, the symbol on my picture."

"Picture?"

"Yes. There is a picture of our wedding."

"I know, my love. Your father told me."

He watched as Kali took a deep breath. "On the picture—I didn't see it until today—is the symbol of an eclipse. I don't know what it means."

Soaring Eagle pulled his lips into a thin line, frowning, thinking. At last he said, "I don't think it is a bad thing, Kali. But one thing I know we must do. We must keep singing."

And he continued:

"Ooooooooooooooooooooooooooooooo. When the wind calls your name," she joined him, their voices lifted in unison, the two of them singing as though they had practiced for this all their lives. And slowly, step by step, they shortened the distance between themselves.

"Know that I search for you.
And when we find one another,
   the earth will become a happy place.
You are my love."

He came to stand by her. And reaching out for her hand, he pulled her to him and said, "Kali, my sweet. You are the love of my life, my very existence."

"Am I?" She smiled up at him, her look adoring, so devoted, he knew he would never forget this moment, not in all eternity. And she said, "You are my love, Soaring Eagle, now and forever. Know that you were right. I have been looking for you all my life. I'm sorry it took me so long to realize it. Please forgive me."

The bear roared.

"There is nothing to forgive. It merely took you longer to know who I am. But then, perhaps you had more cause."

The bear growled again.

"I think we should keep singing," he said. "The animal hears our song; Sun and Night Light, our mother, the moon, hear our song. These are good things ... very good things."

And they sang.

The bear was no longer a threat. Perhaps it never had been.

Forgetting it for the moment, Kali and Soaring Eagle turned, wrapped in one another's arms and faced out toward the sun and the moon. They sang, over and over, one song after another. And occasionally, if one were to listen closely, one could hear their voices being joined by a bear's fierce roar.

"Ooooooooooooooooooooooo.
A love that's true will never die.
Years may come, years may go,
But the heart remembers.
The heart remembers, it is always so."

Soaring Eagle made up the lyrics, while Kali followed his lead. She watched as slowly the moon enclosed the sun in her darkened embrace, and the sky became shadowy, yet sweetly so.

They were together. At last they were all together. Sun, the moon, she and Soaring Eagle.

And as a feeling of utter joy filled Kali, it happened. Ah, yes, she had been here before. She knew it with quiet certainty, knew exactly who she was. Not only that, she realized who he was, too.

Make no mistake, this was, indeed, her home. This land, this mountain, these people. And Soaring Eagle was her love, a love so true, that neither time nor space could kill it. And so it would be, she thought, now and forever.

A tear spilled over her cheek, but it was not from grief. No, not sorrow. All her life she had been searching for this, searching for Soaring Eagle, searching for home, little knowing it.

It had merely taken a miracle to make her realize it.

Soaring Eagle, however, never stopped singing, and she joined him again, humming when she didn't know the words.

And as they sang, the rays of the sun shone out in all directions, bathing them, the land and all else in its shadowed, tender, golden glow. Behind them came a growl, as the bear stood up, pawing the air as though it, too, would chant its praise.

Soaring Eagle kissed her, lengthily, lovingly. He said, "Welcome home, my wife."

Kali smiled. "My husband. My wonderful, handsome husband. At last we are together."

"*Aa, aa,*" he said. "*Aa, aa.*"

And as they kissed, for a moment the world stood still.

Epilogue

There is no place to be saved except in the sky.

A song sung by Okinai in the legend
*"The Seven Brothers (Great Bear)" or the Big Dipper,
The Old North Trail,* Walter McClintock

The two lovers slowly made their way back down the mountain, having circled around the bear without fear, as though the creature were now a long, lost friend.

They had gone back to their home, back to their reservation, back to start their lives together. But another one still remained. And gradually, as slowly as the world spins on its axis, the bear was changing its form, too, becoming Gilda.

Tears streamed down her face as she gazed up into the sky. "Hear me, my mother, my father. I have accomplished it at last," she spoke in Blackfeet and watched as the two heavenly bodies began to separate. "That which I began in adversity, I have finished in love. My work here is done. Please, Mother, Father, may I come home?"

For answer, the sun bathed her in golden, ethereal

beams. And as a large eagle drifted slowly to the earth, coming to land beside her, Gilda laughed, climbing slowly onto its back. Powerfully, with a vigorous kick-off, it lifted up, soaring into the air, carrying Gilda up high, high, higher, until finally it reached the home of Sun.

It is said that it was on this day that a new star was born. And as the legend goes, if you look very closely at night, you can see Gilda, there in the sky, looking down upon the earth, shining brightly and lighting the way for her sister, the Star Bride, and her sister's dearest, truest love . . .

Ah, at last. They had all come home . . .

Glossary

There are some words and concepts in this book that may need further explanation. Hopefully this glossary will help in this regard.

Aa—Blackfeet word for "yes."

Dreams/visions—this is the way in which one communicated with Sun or other spirits. It was also used by some to try to foresee the future.

Medicine bundle—a bundle of things (usually having to do with one's vision) kept near or on the person. This bundle has powers to protect and often, to heal the person who owns it.

Night Light / Old Woman—both terms refer to the Moon. She is also sometimes called "Mother" by the Blackfeet. She is the wife of Sun.

Saa—Blackfeet word for "no."

Smudge—to use the smoke from herbs which have been set on fire (usually lit in a large shell) to purify or cleanse oneself; to pray. The person doing this usually bathes his face and body with the smoke.

Soka'pii (pronounced *sa-kaa-pe*)—Blackfeet word for "good."

A romance from Avon Books is always a welcome addition at the
❈   beach, the park, the barbecue . . .   ❈

Look for these enchanting love stories in August.

TO LOVE A SCOTTISH LORD by Karen Ranney
An Avon Romantic Treasure

The proud and brooding Hamish MacRae has returned to his
beloved Scotland wanting nothing more than to be left alone.
But Mary Gilly has invaded his lonely castle, and while it's true
that this pretty healer is beyond compare, it will take more than
her miraculous potions to awaken his heart.

TALK OF THE TOWN by Suzanne Macpherson
An Avon Contemporary Romance

Nothing puts a damper on a wedding day quite like discovering your Mr. Right is *Mr. Totally Beyond Wrong*, which is why
Kelly Atwood knocks him flat and boards a bus to tiny
Paradise, Washington. One look at the gorgeous outsider and
attorney Sam Grayson gets hot around his too-tight collar,
because this runaway bride is definitely disturbing his peace.

ONCE A SCOUNDREL by Candice Hern
An Avon Romance

It was bad enough when Anthony Morehouse thought he had
won a piece of furniture in a card game, but when he discovers
that *The Ladies' Fashionable Cabinet* is actually a women's
magazine, he can't wait to get rid of it. Then he sees beautiful
Edwina Parrish behind the editor's desk, and Tony is about to
make the biggest gamble of all.

ALL MEN ARE ROGUES, by Sari Robins
An Avon Romance

When Evelyn Amherst agrees to her father's dying request, she
can scarcely imagine the world of danger she is about to enter —
or that it will bring her tantalizingly close to Lord Justin
Barclay. Here is a man to turn a young lady's head, but Evelyn
refuses to be diverted from her mission, especially not by this
passionate yearning for Justin's embrace.

REL 0703

Avon Romantic Treasures

*Unforgettable, enthralling love stories,
sparkling with passion and adventure
from Romance's bestselling authors*

Discover Contemporary Romances at Their Sizzling Hot Best from Avon Books

Avon Romances—
the best in exceptional authors
and unforgettable novels!

Have you ever dreamed of writing a romance?

*And have you ever wanted
to get a romance published?*

Perhaps you have always wondered how to
become an Avon romance writer?
We are now seeking the best and brightest undiscovered
voices. We invite you to send us your query letter to
avonromance@harpercollins.com

What do you need to do?

Please send no more than two pages telling us
about your book. We'd like to know its setting—is it
contemporary or historical—and a bit about the hero,
heroine, and what happens to them.

Then, if it is right for Avon we'll ask to see part of the
manuscript. Remember, it's important that you have
material to send, in case we want to see your story quickly.

Of course, there are no guarantees of publication,
but you never know unless you try!

*We know there is new talent just waiting
to be found! Don't hesitate . . . send us
your query letter today.*

*The Editors
Avon Romance*